THE SNOW LION'S TURQUOISE MANE

WISDOM TALES FROM TIBET

SURYA DAS

HarperSanFrancisco
A Division of HarperCollins*Publishers*

HarperSanFrancisco and the author, in association with the Rainforest Action Network and Seva Foundation, will facilitate the planting of two trees for every one tree used in the manufacture of this book.

A TREE CLAUSE BOOK

HarperCollins books may be purchased for educational, business, or sales promotional use. For information please write: Special Markets Department, HarperCollins Publishers, Inc., 10 East 53rd Street, New York, NY 10022.

HarperCollins Web Site: http://www.harpercollins.com
HarperCollins®, ■®, HarperSanFrancisco™ and A TREE CLAUSE BOOK® are trademarks of HarperCollins Publishers, Inc.

FIRST HARPERCOLLINS PAPERBACK EDITION PUBLISHED IN 1992

Illustrated by Charles Hastings

Library of Congress Cataloging-in-Publication Data

Das, Surya.
    The snow lion's turquoise mane : wisdom tales from Tibet /
Surya Das. — 1st ed.
      p. cm.
   ISBN 0–06–250183–6 (cloth)
   ISBN 0–06–250849–0 (pbk.)
   1. Tales—China—Tibet. I. Title.
GR337.D37   1992
398.2'09515—dc20   90–55787

02 RRD(H) 10 9 8 7 6

THE
SNOW LION'S
TURQUOISE
MANE

CONTENTS

ACKNOWLEDGMENTS

I wish to acknowledge gratefully the generous assistance and encouragement of Nyoshul Khenpo Rinpoche, as well as the Padmakara International Translation Group in France and Daniel Goleman of the *New York Times*.

Many of these teaching tales were told to me by Nyoshul Khenpo Rinpoche, a Tibetan lama and an inexhaustible mine of Buddhist wisdom and lore. Others were recounted by contemporary Buddhist scholars and masters, including His Holiness Dudjom Rinpoche, His Holiness Dilgo Khyentse Rinpoche, Mahapandita Dezhung Rinpoche, and the Venerable Tulku Pema Wangyal, each of whom contributed several. Still others were passed on by the Very Venerable Kalu Rinpoche, Drukpa Thugsay Rinpoche, His Holiness Gyalwang Drukchen, Khenpo Thrangu Rinpoche, His Eminence Shamar Rinpoche, Khenpo Tsultrim Gyamtso, Khenpo Karthar, Orgyen Tobgyal Rinpoche, Chökyi Nema Rinpoche, Shenphen Dawa Rinpoche, Khetsun Zangpo Rinpoche, Tulku Thondup, Lama Norlha, Lama Sonam Tobgyal, Lama Thubten Yeshé, and Gelong Konchok Tenzin. Charles Hastings, Janis Jolcuvar, Jakob Leschley, Anandi Friend, Chaitanya Samways, and Tara Bennett-Goleman also contributed helpful editorial assistance. My gratitude and respects are offered to one and all.

Any and all merits accumulated through this work I dedicate to the longevity of these compassionate lamas, yogis, and spiritual friends and to the continuance of their teachings.

INSCRIPTION

Sleeping Buddhas, Awaken!

"So, Rinpoche," she asked, "if these grand old living Buddha-lamas are as perfectly enlightened, awakened, omniscient, skillful, powerful, and compassionate as we think they are, why don't they just wake us up from the sleep of delusion?"

"Who's asleep?" the master replied.

BENEDICTION

Ven. Dilgo
Khyentse Rinpoche

ཨ་ལ་ཐོ་ལ་བརྗོད་པ་འདི༔

April 10, 1991

Hearing or reading the biographies of illumined spiritual masters teaches us their wisdom and enlightened way of life. Through such inspiration, heart and mind inevitably turn toward the sublime Dharma, ultimately to become transformed; thus one's life becomes meaningful.

Under the guidance of Nyoshul Khenpo Rinpoche and Venerable Tulku Pema Wangyal, my disciple Surya Das has gathered these oral tales from many of his spiritual teachers, including the great living Tibetan lamas of all four schools of Tibetan Buddhism. Many of these stories concern the compassionate teachings of the remarkable nineteenth-century Dzogchen master Patrul Rinpoche, whose songs, pith-instructions (whispered oral guidance from master to disciple), commentaries, and life-style remain a constant source of inspiration today, as well as other realized sages and yogis of the non-sectarian practice lineage. Others concern simple folk, whose experience exemplifies how anyone can benefit from the spiritual path.

Simply to hear of the lives of such living Buddhas can bring one onto the path of liberation. May this work be a source of spiritual blessings and inspiration to all.

Dilgo Khyentse Rinpoche

INTRODUCTION

THE FOURTEENTH DALAI LAMA

Spiritual teachers have universally used stories to illustrate their teachings, and the lamas of Tibet are no exception. Tibetans have tremendous respect for all things religious, especially the literary tradition and those who embody it. We set great store by the written word, particularly the scriptures translated from Indian sources, as well as those later composed by Tibetan masters themselves in the Land of Snow.

However, Tibetans' sense of respect has a healthy balance to it. Colored by a direct earthy humor, it does not often sink into mere sanctimoniousness. Figures like the saintly poet Milarepa, the Kadampa Geshé Ben, and more recently the great Dzogchen master Patrul Rinpoche, are much loved for the stories of their antics. Yet because these people were incomparable spiritual practitioners, these accounts invariably provide a vivid example for others to follow.

Many such stories have never been written down, being simply passed on from teacher to disciple down the years in a living oral tradition. Surya Das has gathered a selection he has heard from lamas he has met and has retold them here in English. I am grateful to him for recording this delightful aspect of our tradition and trust that readers will enjoy them as much as generations of Tibetans have done.

The Dalai Lama
June 2, 1992

FOREWORD

by Daniel Goleman

The south of France seems an unlikely setting for the transmission of the ancient wisdom of Tibet. But it is there, in the region of the Dordogne not far from the prehistoric caves that hold humanity's earliest known art, that masters of Tibetan Buddhism have built a forest hermitage where students from all over the world gather for traditional meditation retreats that last three years, three months, and three days.

And it is there that Surya Das, a wandering Jew from New York by way of Tibet, Nepal, and India, has found himself dedicating long years of his life to learning the spiritual practices of Tibet. At this writing, Surya was in the middle of his third three-year retreat.

As is true of so many good things, Surya Das's role as the recorder of these Tibetan tales came about unintentionally. In the fifth year of two back-to-back three-year retreats, one of Surya's teachers, Nyoshul Khenpo Rinpoche, asked him to write down stories about the early upholders of their lineage of teachings. The teacher wanted these tales of enlightenment collected and rendered in English so that they might be presented and inspire students in the West. Many of these stories have ended up in this collection.

As Surya recorded the tales, he realized that for over twenty years he had heard many, many stories but that only a few still remained clearly in mind. So he started to collect Tibetan teaching tales, the oral stories that Tibetan masters have always told as part of their bountiful transmission of wisdom and compassion. Many of the tales in this collection, as part of this centuries-old oral tradition, have never been written down before.

The tales captured here for us are glimpses of a living spiritual flame that is passed on from teacher to student in the tantric tradition. In this tradition, it is important that the student hear the tantras directly from the master in order for the living essence of the teaching, the "lhung," to be genuinely transmitted. This oral transmission forms a chain that leads back through the centuries.

While reading these tales is not the same as hearing them told aloud, we can still receive from them a deep richness. Even on paper, the point of a tale is still the point; moreover, it is taught that simply to contact them sows the seeds of liberation.

They come to us at a particularly ripe time in our own cultural evolution. As the very earth and skies reel from the effect of a shallow, materialistic ethic that venerates the short term and unleashes technology without regard for consequence, more and more people in the West are searching for a larger perspective, a timeless wisdom. This perspective is to be found here in abundance.

These tales are timely, too, in that there is currently a growing appreciation of the power of stories to reach the heart. One of the special characteristics of the story is that it is able to bypass the defenses of the logical mind in order to make its point. This is why wisdom, throughout history, has been transmitted through anecdotes and stories.

Stories are artful ways to deliver truth. They disarm us because, even as the mind draws parallels to our own lives, they seem to be about someone else. And it is always easier to hear about someone else's quirks and foibles than to examine our own.

Beyond that, stories set free our intuitive powers. They speak directly to the unconscious in the language of metaphor and the imagination. They can nudge us, waken us a bit, point the way.

But there is something even more immediate here, more earthy than mere spiritual teaching in these tales, for complete naturalness and high-spiritedness is the Tibetan style. These charming stories are great fun. They are at their best when told, when read aloud. Enjoy them. Read them to your children and friends. Keep the tradition alive.

PREFACE

Since time immemorial, spiritual truths have been woven into stories, whether as folktale, fable, legend, parable, historical anecdote, or yarn. With wit and candor, insight and delight, picturesque tales that captivate the imagination have brought a bountiful harvest to countless generations of young and old.

The piquant cornucopia of tales that follows draws on stories still being told today by the living lamas of Tibet in the course of their spiritual teachings. Transmitted through the ancient oral tradition of Tibetan Mahayana Buddhism, which is an inexhaustible repository of sacred lore as well as of Buddhist law, most have never before been committed to writing. Some of these tales date from the time of the historical Buddha himself, twenty-five hundred years ago; others retell interesting incidents from more recent times.

All these tantalizing stories share one thing in common: they are teaching tales, meant to edify, instruct, admonish—and entertain. They are for scholars and sages as well as neophytes, nomads, shepherds, and farmers. As charming as fairy tales yet as pointed as biblical parables, these stories are replete with Himalayan folklore, magic, ribaldry, and the exotic marvels of Oriental culture, while they are also full of uncommon spiritual wisdom and common sense, providing myths to live by. Recorded, translated, gathered, and retold in the same generous spirit in which they have traditionally been received—as spoken instructions from teacher to student, at the feet of contemporary Tibetan masters—these small gifts of love are like ferries to that far shore of genuine inner experience, truth itself. Tales are clues in the search for truth, the universal panacea, as fabulous as the philosophers' stone. Yet truth must be genuinely and intuitively experienced, not merely heard.

As everyone knows, truth is often stranger than fiction, and certainly it is more entertaining. It was a legitimate function of the venerable Tibetan lama to transform ordinary phenomena and perceptions through magical means, thus transforming his listeners' vision. These fantabulous tales, imbued with spiritual significance, evoke the atmosphere of peace, carefree ease, and whimsy that bespeaks the freedom and transcendence of the high Himalayas. They record lessons learned and blessings earned, deeds done and realizations won, as well as things that could, and *should,* have happened. Intent on restoring faith in the fact that authentic enlightenment, spiritual transformation, visionary experiences, and miracles of all kinds can and do still happen, the inspired

Tibetan storyteller unfolds a luminous vision of a universe where basic goodness, universal responsibility, inner fulfillment, love and harmony, humor and hope, perfection, freedom and redemption, greatness of heart, and spiritual illumination still prevail. An enchanted world is revealed—not only in the world of remote Tibet but in the presence of the extraordinary within the ordinary routines of daily existence—right here and now—the miracle of the present moment.

Life is full of contradictions. These tales are not merely descriptions of how certain events unfolded but of how things should and can be. Full of illusions and insights, the magical and the mysterious, with profound echoes of timeless questions, eternal verities, and mythic archetypes, these stories offer models of humane behavior—the kind of behavior that lends value, meaning, and significance to life—at the same time that they irreverently expose the spectacle that is human nature. Such teaching tales are calculated to inculcate specific values, unveil preconceived notions and underlying assumptions, and cut through self-deception. They provoke a wry smile, an inner chuckle, helping us to laugh at ourselves and fly free of the so-called burdens of being; moreover, they intentionally inspire particular states of mind.

Here are trenchant perspectives laid bare before our eyes: the pared-down core of reality in all its immediacy, penetrating insights into fundamental issues of existence, daring flights of fancy, as well as sudden awakenings, ethical lessons, and quaint Himalayan homilies.

The Tibetan raconteur invites his or her listeners into a lighthearted, illumined world—at times plausible, at times astounding. Through truth delightfully disguised, embellished by both fact and fancy, one is transported to a realm in which delights are legion. How long the listener or reader chooses to inhabit such an alluring realm depends for the most part on the artist's magic. To the poet, everything is luminous; to the dull, nothing is remarkable.

More than two dozen categories of stories appear in this collection of ancient and modern tales. Here you will find Himalayan folktales, fairy tales, yarns about fabulous creatures, myths to live by, and legends; records of the historical Buddha and his immediate disciples; doctrinal teaching tales, moral homilies, paradise and rebirth stories; tales of goddesses and muses, of Brahmins, scholars, and lepers; justice stories unveiling karmic concatenation, the law of cause and effect; monastery stories, children's stories, nomad tales, prison tales, devil stories, spirit stories; tales of pilgrims and sacred power places, of saints, relics and talismans, psychic powers, curses, cures, and resurrections; historical anecdotes; records of interaction between masters and disciples in the lineage transmission (the passing of spiritual teachings from one generation to the next); tales of monks and nuns as well as of layfolk, animals, and dreams; trickster tales and humorous stories; tales of treasures lost and found; stories of sudden awakenings and other enlightenment experiences; poems, songs of enlightenment, unadulterated wisdom tales, descriptions of spiritual events, and meditation instructions for followers and practitioners; tales of enlightened men and women; philosophical musings, psychological insights and inquiries; ribald tales, legends, visions of gods and demigods, deities, hungry ghosts, and titans; tales of poets and yogis, sages and sinners, of Dalai Lamas, Abominable Snowmen, blue Himalayan sheep, yaks, faithful animals, and others. . . . All tumble forth like the endless courses at a sumptuous feast.

Shrouded in myth and protected by the snow-capped Himalayas, Tibet has long been known as Shangri-la, a lost world, the forbidden kingdom, the "roof of the world," the Land of Snow. Its one and a half million square miles, an area roughly equivalent to Western Europe, contain many of the world's highest peaks (including Mount Everest, on the Nepalese border). The three-mile-high Tibetan plateau is also the source of several of the great rivers of Asia, including the Indus, Sutlej, Karnalai, Brahmaputra, Yangtze, Yellow, and Mekong. Tibet's Mount Kailash—for Hindu, Buddhist, Jain, and Bonpo alike the legendary throne of the gods (not unlike the Greeks' Olympus) as well as the spiritual epicenter of the universe, the axis mundi—remains even today one of the major pilgrimage places in Asia. Tibet was once a powerful Asian kingdom; the seventh-century Tibetan King Srongtsen Gonpo and his cavalry conquered lands from Kashmir in the west to the Chinese capital at Chang'an in the east and to the Ganges River in India in the south. Today, however, Tibetans are an endangered species, and their culture is all but lost.

Tibet is the only great culture centered on a wisdom tradition to survive intact into modern times. There is a Tibetan saying, oft quoted:

"The sole goal is to accomplish the sublime Dharma,
give one's entire life to it.
Don't harbor long-term plans and expectations.
For spiritual practice, live simply, content with everything.
Die alone, undisturbed and unattended."

Tibet has always been renowned as a repository of arcane knowledge and occult wisdom. Its many monasteries, now ravaged, were the largest in the modern world; some housed over six thousand monks. One-third of Tibet's entire male population inhabited them, in a country where the priesthood was the most prominent profession. Numerous nunneries, as well as female anchorites and mendicants, also flourished.

News of Tibet first reached Europe in the fourteenth century via a wandering Franciscan named Friar Odoric, who may have visited there. Even earlier, Ptolemy and Herodotus had heard rumors of a legendary spiritual kingdom in the high Himalayas. The forbidden city of Lhasa, Tibet's ancient capital (the Vatican City of the Tibetan Buddhist world, over two miles high), remained closed to outsiders until the British Younghusband expedition finally breached its invisible walls in 1904. Few foreigners have sojourned in fabled Tibet until recent times. Fifty years ago, television journalist and traveler Lowell Thomas managed to trek there with movie cameras and crew. Currently, widespread interest in theocratic Tibet and its rich traditional culture and religion has reached new heights, despite Communist China's efforts to suppress and destroy Tibetan traditions while exploiting Tibet's undeveloped natural resources and colonizing its native population.

Since 1959, Tibetan lamas exiled from their conquered homeland have taken up residence in virtually every Western country. His Holiness the Dalai Lama, known as the "divine incarnation of Great Compassion" as well as Tibet's spiritual and temporal leader, has led a tireless crusade on behalf of non-violence, human dignity, universal responsibility, world peace, and civil rights and, at the same time, has worked toward Tibetan independence. His actions demonstrate the Tibetan's resilient faith and inner strength, qualities that lend dignity to life in that isolated country where the living spirit of Buddhism, against all odds, remains unquenchable. One must have an inner life to be genuinely alive. The resourceful Tibetans long ago learned, out of necessity, how to cope cheerfully with a wintry lunar landscape, both in the outer world and within themselves, in order to transcend despair and extract what is delectable from life.

Before the Chinese conquest, Tibet was a sparsely populated country of farmers, traders, and nomads—a vibrant, wholesome people. Heartily grounded in Buddhist ethics and practice, they were also known along the trans-Himalayan caravan routes as shrewd traders. A simple, hardy, and devout folk, Tibetans unilaterally affirm that they were far happier with their traditional society and its preindustrial theocratic values than with whatever progress has forcibly imposed upon them from outside during Mao's reign over the last several decades.

Tibet's national tragedy—the Communist conquest—has paradoxically proved a boon to the rest of the world. The historian Arnold Toynbee predicted that the coming of Buddhism to the West would afterward be perceived as one of the most significant events of the twentieth century. Many of Tibet's most eminent monks have now made direct contact with the rest of humanity for the first time, after being forced to flee their homeland. And what seemed all but lost in Tibet—the celebrated Middle Way (Madhyamika philosophy), the compassionate Buddha's message of all beings' inherent enlightened potential—has found another home in the modern world.

Until recently, the only wheels in general use in Tibet were prayer wheels, which were—along with rosaries—constantly in hand, transforming all activities and one's entire life into an ongoing prayer. At the same time, encounters with deities, with fabulous beasts, as well as invisible inhabitants of other realms of existence and with the supernatural in all its forms, are never far from the average Tibetan's consciousness; even today, whether Tibetans remain in the East or have journeyed to the West, such incidents continue to occur. Therefore, it is only natural that Tibetan religion, history, and oral and written literature abound with incidents that reflect an underlying assumption of a higher order of being, the sacredness upon which all life rests.

Today, the accumulated Buddhist wisdom of Tibet has come down to us under the aegis of the country's recently exiled lamas and monks, many of whom fled with only the clothes on their backs. Many of their teachings have been passed on in the form of tales and stories for the explicit purpose of reigniting the living flame of the listener's or reader's innate goodness and spiritual wisdom. Just as one candle is lit from another, the unborn and undying flame of authentic enlightenment experience is transmitted through these stories from antiquity to today for the benefit of one and all.

From the traditional Buddhist land of Ladakh in northern India near the Tibetan border, the contemporary British poet Andrew Harvey reports, "Once I asked an old lama in Ladakh—a wilderness fragrant with sacredness—what I could do as a writer to stave off the destruction of ancient Buddhist culture in our turbulent, materialistic times.

"He smiled and said, 'Everything passes. Bear witness to what we were like. Pass on what we gave you.'

"'That is not enough,' I said.

"'No,' said he. 'But it's something.'"

Surya Das
Dordogne, France
1991

THE
SNOW LION'S
TURQUOISE
MANE

The Mani Man

A prayer wheel, or mani wheel, is a wheel filled with innumerable mantras and inscriptions wrapped clockwise around a central axis. Some prayer wheels are tiny, like tops; others are huge, filling an entire room, and one turns the wheel by holding its handles and walking clockwise around it. Others are attached to running streams or waterfalls so that they can harness the natural energy and spread benedictions throughout the land. The faithful believe that spinning these prayer wheels or hanging prayer flags in the wind actualizes the inscribed prayers.

The Tibetan province of Kham is akin to America's Wild West. The people of Kham are great equestrians, and like all who ride regularly, they love their horses. Until about a century ago, Kham was carved into dozens of smaller kingdoms, each of which had its own army, raised by forcible conscription.

THERE WAS ONCE AN OLD man in far eastern Kham known as the Mani Man because, day and night, he could always be found devotedly spinning his small homemade prayer wheel. The wheel was filled with the mantra of Great Compassion, *Om Mani Padmé Hung.* The Mani Man lived with his son and their one fine horse. The son was the joy of the man's life; the boy's pride and joy was the horse.

The man's wife, after a long life of virtue and service, had long since departed for more fortunate rebirths. Father and son lived, free from excessive wants or needs, in one of several rough stone houses near a river on the edge of the flat plains.

One day their steed disappeared. The neighbors bewailed the loss of the old man's sole material asset, but the stoic old man just kept turning his prayer wheel, reciting "*Om Mani Padmé Hung,*" Tibet's national mantra. To whoever inquired or expressed condolences, he simply said, "Give thanks for everything. Who can say what is good or bad? We'll see. . . ."

After several days the splendid creature returned, followed by a pair of wild mustangs. These the old man and his son swiftly trained. Then everyone sang songs of celebration and congratulated the old man on his unexpected good fortune. The man simply smiled over his prayer wheel and said, "I am grateful . . . but who knows? We shall see."

Then, while racing one of the mustangs, the boy fell and shattered his leg. Some neighbors carried him home, cursing the wild horse and bemoaning the boy's fate. But the old man, sitting at his beloved son's bedside, just kept turning his prayer wheel around and around while softly muttering gentle Lord Chenrayzig's mantra of Great Compassion. He neither complained nor answered their protestations to fate, but simply nodded his head affably, reiterating what he had said before. "The Buddha is beneficent; I am grateful for my son's life. We shall see."

The next week military officers appeared, seeking young conscripts for an ongoing border war. All the local boys were immediately taken away, except for the bedridden son of the Mani Man. Then the neighbors congratulated the old man on his great good fortune, attributing such luck to the good karma accumulated by the old man's incessantly spinning prayer wheel and the constant mantras on his cracked lips. He smiled and said nothing.

One day when the boy and his father were watching their fine horses graze on the prairie grass, the taciturn old man suddenly began to sing:

"Life just goes around and around, up and down
  like a waterwheel;
  Our lives are like its buckets, being emptied and refilled
  again and again.
  Like the potter's clay, our physical existences
  are fashioned into one form after another:

  the shapes are broken and reformed again and again,
  The low will be high, and the high fall down;
  the dark will grow light, and the rich lose all.

  If you, my son, were an extraordinary child,
  off to a monastery as an incarnation they would carry you.
  If you were too bright, my son,
  shackled to other people's disputes at an official's desk you would be.

  One horse is one horse's worth of trouble.
  Wealth is good,
  But too soon loses its savor,
  and can be a burden, a source of quarrel, in the end.

No one knows what karma awaits us,
but what we sow now will be reaped
in lives to come; that is certain.
So be kind to one and all
and don't be biased,
based upon illusions regarding gain and loss.

Have neither hope nor fear, expectation nor anxiety;
Give thanks for everything, whatever your lot may be.
Accept everything; accept everyone; and follow
the Buddha's infallible Law.
Be simple and carefree, remaining naturally at ease
and in peace.

You can shoot arrows at the sky if you like,
My son, but they'll inevitably fall back to earth."

As he sang, the prayer flags fluttered overhead, and the ancient mani wheel,
filled with hundreds of thousands of handwritten mantras, just kept turning.
Then the old man was silent.

Milarepa's Last Word

*Jetsun Milarepa is Tibet's best-known yogi-sage as well as her most beloved
bard. His* The Hundred Thousand Songs of Milarepa, *extemporaneously sung
nine hundred years ago to disciples and followers in the snowy Himalayan
wilderness, has been translated into many languages. Milarepa's skin displayed
a greenish hue, because he subsisted for many years on wild nettle soup.*

*Milarepa is famous for having attained perfect awakened Buddhahood in a
single lifetime through decades of solitary meditation in mountain caves,
dressed only in white cotton robes. His example as a spiritual practitioner has
been the inspiration for countless generations of lamas, from the eleventh century until today.*

*Milarepa's guru was Marpa the Translator, who spent seventeen years
studying and meditating in India and brought the Mahamudra (Great Symbol)
teachings to Tibet; Milarepa's own disciple was Gampopa. Gampopa sought*

out Milarepa after being blessed by a vision of a green yogi who flicked spit in his face.

Tibetan beer, called chang, *is distilled from fermented barley. In tantric initiations, a consecrated skullcup (a chalice fashioned from a skull) full of alcoholic spirits is often used symbolically to transmit the elixir of gnosis.*

ON THE VERY FIRST OCCASION when the physician-monk Gampopa met Milarepa, his predestined master, Milarepa offered him a skullcup full of chang. Gampopa protested that to drink alcohol was against his vows.

Milarepa, the Laughing Vajra (Diamond), smilingly assured him that the highest spiritual precept is to obey the master's command. At that, Gampopa unhesitatingly drained the vessel; then Milarepa knew the monk would be his spiritual heir.

After years of solitary meditation in a cave, interspersed with visits to Milarepa, Gampopa finally completed his training and was ready to leave his master. Milarepa placed both bare feet upon Gampopa's head as a benediction.

Gampopa asked the singing yogi for final instructions. Milarepa, however, simply said, "What is needed is more *effort,* not more teachings." And he would say no more.

Gampopa set off and had already crossed a narrow stream when Milarepa shouted to attract his attention one last time. The guru knew that he would not see Gampopa again during this lifetime.

"I have one very profound secret instruction," Milarepa said. "It is far too precious to give away to just anyone."

Gampopa looked back. Milarepa suddenly turned around, bent over, and pulled up his ragged robe, displaying buttocks as calloused and pockmarked as a horse's hoof, hardened from so many long years of seated meditation on bare rock.

"That's my final instruction, heart-son!" he shouted. "Do it!"

Better Seek Yourself

ONCE THE BUDDHA WAS SITTING in meditation in a dense forest near Uruvela when a band of villagers chanced upon him. The company was composed of thirty married couples, plus one well-to-do young bachelor.

The night before, while the young man slept, his favored courtesan had found the money hidden beneath his bed and had made off with it. When the theft was discovered, all his friends and neighbors had set off in pursuit, finally stumbling upon the Enlightened One deep in the jungle.

After they had recounted their sad tale to the sage, the Buddha asked, "Instead of roaming around in this dangerous jungle seeking a woman and money, wouldn't it be far better to seek your true self?"

Buddha's peaceful, shining countenance and simple allegorical insight made such an impact on the young householders that they forgot their chase and became his followers. The young bachelor later became a monk and a sage.

Crossing to the Other Shore

Dakinis are enlightened female energies, which are personified as deities. Appearing in any number of forms, they are sometimes called "sky dancers" because they represent the uninhibited dance of awakened awareness within the radiant, skylike expanse of emptiness. Vajra Yogini is the queen of the dakinis.

ONE DAY TWO TIBETAN MONKS who were on a pilgrimage came to a rushing river. There on the bank sat an ugly old leper, begging for alms.

When the monks approached, she asked the priestly pair to assist her in crossing the river. One monk felt an instinctive revulsion. Haughtily, he gathered his flowing monastic robes about himself and waded into the water on his own. Once on the other side, he wondered if he should even wait for his tardy friend. Would the latter abandon the leper or bring her along?

The second monk felt sorry for the helpless hag; compassion blossomed spontaneously in his heart. He picked up the leprous creature and gently hoisted her onto his back. Then he struggled down the riverbank into the swirling current.

It was then that an amazing thing happened. Midstream, where the going seemed to be most difficult, with muddy water boiling about his thighs and his

water-logged woolen robes billowing out like a tent, the kindly monk suddenly and miraculously felt his burden being lifted off his back. Looking up, he beheld the wisdom deity Vajra Yogini soaring gracefully overhead, reaching down to draw him up to the dakini paradise where she reigned.

The first monk, greatly chastened—having been directly instructed in the nature of both compassion and illusory form—had to continue on his pedestrian pilgrimage alone.

The Miraculous Tooth

Faith is like a ring, a grommet; the Buddha's compassion is like a hook, or shepherd's crook. The two can connect and Buddha's blessings can enter wherever there is openness to such grace.

This is illustrated by the tale of the old woman who attained spiritual awakening with the help of a dog's tooth. The faithful have always venerated the teeth and bones of saints as sacred relics; these remains are thought to have become imbued with spiritual presence.

ONCE THERE WAS AN OLD woman whose son was a trader. Often he joined a caravan and went to distant India on business. One day his mother said, "Bodh Gaya in India is the place where the perfect Buddha was enlightened. Please bring me a blessed relic from there, a talisman I can use as a focus for my devotions. I shall place it on the altar, pray and bow to it as a material representation of the Buddha's blessed body."

Many times she repeated her request. However, each time her son returned from a business trip to the holy land of India, he realized that he had forgotten his mother's fervent plea. For several years he failed to bring what she had asked for.

One day, as he was getting ready to depart yet again for India, his mother said to him, "Son, remember my words on your journey. This time, if you do not bring me a relic from Bodh Gaya to use for my prostrations, I shall kill myself in front of you!"

He was shocked by her unexpected intensity. Vowing to fulfill his mother's wish, he left.

At last, after many months, his business affairs were completed and he approached his homeland. Again he had forgotten to acquire for his dear old

mother a genuine relic of the Buddha. It was only when he approached his mother's house that he remembered her words.

"What am I going to do?" he thought. "I haven't brought anything for Mother's altar. If I arrive home empty-handed, she'll kill herself!"

Looking around in dismay, he spotted the desiccated skull of a dog lying by the roadside. Hastily he tore a tooth from the jaw and proceeded to wrap it in silk.

Reaching home, he reverently presented this package to his mother. "Here is one of the Buddha's canine teeth," he said. "I acquired it in Lord Buddha's native land, India. You can use it as a support for your prayers."

The old woman believed him. She had faith in the tooth, believing it to be from Lord Buddha himself. She constantly offered prostrations and prayers to it as the veritable embodiment of all the Buddhas. Through such practices she found the unshakable peace of mind she had long sought.

Miraculously, from the dog's tooth emanated countless tiny translucent pearls and swirls of rainbow light. All the neighbors were delighted to find such blessings free for the taking at the old woman's altar, where they gathered daily. When the old woman finally met death, a canopy of rainbow light surrounded her, and everyone recognized in the beatific smile on her wizened face that she had attained spiritual exaltation.

Although a dog's tooth in itself contains few blessings, the power of the woman's unswerving faith ensured that the blessings of the Buddha would enter that tooth. Thus a mere dog's tooth became no different from an authentic relic of the Buddha, and many were uplifted.

A Statue Speaks

Kongpo, the home of the central figure in this story, is a southern Tibetan province whose people are renowned for piety rather than intellect.

The Jokhang in Lhasa is the holiest temple in Tibet. Inside is the renowned ancient statue of the Buddha cast in the form of a prince, called Jowo Rinpoche (Precious Lord); it was brought from China more than a millennium ago as part of the dowry of a Chinese princess betrothed to the king of Tibet. In the Tibetan tradition, it is customary to bow to the floor three times before entering a temple, shrine, or grand lama's presence.

BEN FROM KONGPO HAD LONG aspired to visit the Jokhang and Tibet's most holy statue. At last the day arrived when the intrepid pilgrim put on his traveling boots and set off on foot for distant Lhasa.

When Ben arrived, he walked the streets in wonder, for there, right before his eyes, was the glorious City of the Gods. . . . What a delight! There was the towering Potala Palace, where dwelt Lord Chenrayzig in the form of the Dalai Lama, surrounded by an endless queue of pilgrims circumambulating the palace on the ring road. There was the divine sovereign's summer palace, Norbu Lingka—what a sight for Ben's devout eyes! There, right before him, were the Sera Monastery and mighty, awe-inspiring Drepung—the two largest monasteries in Tibet—where piety and learning had for centuries reigned unrivaled. How lucky to be alive! thought the overwhelmed wayfarer.

He entered the Jokhang, the central temple situated in the heart of Lhasa like a diamond embedded in the center of a jeweled diadem. And there! There at last was the great smiling Jowo Rinpoche, the fabled Buddha statue, towering above him in sublime splendor.

Prostrating himself before the statue with renewed energy, the weary pilgrim doffed his dusty cap and removed his worn-out boots, placing them in the Jowo's lap for safekeeping. "Keep an eye on these," Kongpo Ben said, before performing his ritual obligations.

As Ben circumambulated the great gold icon, he found rows of brightly glowing golden butter lamps arranged upon the altar, along with long lines of the cone-shaped barley offering cakes called *tormas*. Thanking the omniscient Buddha for his hospitality and warmed by the benevolent Jowo's intimate presence, Ben proceeded to eat the consecrated cakes, neatly dunking them in the melted butter of the votive lamps illumining the shrine.

In return for this unexpected reception, Ben decided to invite the Jowo to dinner at his own humble home in Kongpo, imagining that his wife would gladly slaughter the fattest pig in their pen—what did he know of the compassionate Buddha's non-violent doctrine?—and would prepare an opulent feast for their honored guest. The innocent peasant had no doubt that Jowo Rinpoche would accept his invitation.

Suddenly, in the midst of Kongpo Ben's fervor, bright sunlight flooded the dimly lit shrine: the hunchbacked old temple caretaker had arrived. The door flew open, as if by its own power. . . . Had the caretaker been magically summoned to the scene of the crime by some self-righteous invisible force?

For one long moment the venerable elder stared at the once neatly arranged oblations, now in total disarray, and at the ragged hat and boots ensconced in the Buddha's golden lap. Imagine his dismay!

The outraged monk reached up to snatch the pilgrim's dirty boots from their perch, but as he did so, a deep imperious voice boomed from the smiling Jowo, saying, "Hands off! Those belong to my disciple from Kongpo."

The old monk staggered in astonishment. What could he say? Orders are orders, and those who serve also know how to obey.

He prostrated himself three times on the stone floor before the statue and begged forgiveness. Reflecting piously about this miracle in the holy of holies, he left. Ben simply continued his wholehearted devotions, his faith vindicated, his boots out of harm's way.

Eventually, Ben returned to Kongpo. The news of the miracle had preceded his return; rumors had spread throughout central and southern Tibet that the Jowo statue in the central temple had spoken. But no connection between this marvelous event and Ben himself had yet been made.

Regarding the rumor of the speaking statue, Ben merely said to whoever happened to inquire, "One never knows what to believe these days."

It is said that the Buddha did, in fact, accept Ben's naive invitation to dinner. One day Ben beheld the Jowo's golden face among some rocks at the bottom of a clear spring near his humble abode. He reached into the water and tried to carry the statue home, but its great weight proved too much for him. When Ben dropped the smiling Jowo, it became embedded in the earth in the form of a huge rock.

To this day, the faithful folks of remote Kongpo—many of whom have never been to far-off Lhasa—still circumambulate and prostrate themselves at that blessed rock. Lhasa's central temple may be far away, but they know that the glorious Jowo resides nearby.

Glue Stew

In fertile southern Tibet, simple folk love to ridicule the polite city dwellers of Lhasa. They say that Lhasans use stringy yak hides as stewing beef, while fortunate southern Tibetans can afford to boil tender sheep's hide just for glue.

ONE DAY A TAILOR FROM Lhasa who was visiting southern Tibet was called upon to do some fine stitchery. His needle flying, he sat cross-legged all day on a handwoven woolen carpet. He could not fail to notice, however, the enticing odor of mutton stew emanating from a nearby room. The family was preparing a succulent stew to reward him for his labors!

All day long, a teenage girl carried sheepskins in and out, whetting the greedy tailor's appetite. Dusk fell finally—but there was no delicious stew!

He held his tongue, slyly observing where the young girl stored the remains of the huge stew pot, which had been simmering throughout the day.

Having been graciously invited by the owner of the house to spend the night (in Tibet, hospitality to a traveler is mandatory), the tailor said that he would set out in the morning, and quietly retired for the night. He waited until midnight, when the entire household was asleep and the small herd of sheep sequestered beneath the upraised house had also settled down. . . .

Silently, he stole into the dark storeroom, uncovered the stew pot, and stuffed his sturdy yak-skin shoulder bag with warm, gooey stew. Shouldering his load, he crept out into the night.

A few miles down the road, however, when the dishonest tailor greedily plunged a hand into the bag, seeking meat, he withdrew only great gobs of thickening glue.

Liberating Creatures

AN OLD LAMA LIKED TO sit in meditation on a large flat rock overlooking a placid pool. Yet every time he began his prayers and devotions in earnest, just as soon as he had crossed his legs and settled down, he would spot an insect struggling helplessly in the water. Time after time, he would lift up his creaky old body and deliver the tiny creature to safety, before settling down again on his rocky seat. So his contemplations went, day after day. . . .

His brother monks, dedicated meditators who also went off daily to sit alone in the rocky ravines and caves of that desolate region, eventually became

aware that the old lama hardly ever managed to sit still but actually spent most of his meditation sessions plucking insects out of the tiny pool. Although it certainly seemed fitting to save the life of a helpless sentient being of any kind, large or small, some of them occasionally wondered if the old monk's meditations might not be greatly furthered if he sat undisturbed elsewhere, away from such distractions. One day they finally mentioned their concern to him.

"Wouldn't it be more beneficial to sit elsewhere and meditate deeply, undisturbed all day? That way you would more swiftly gain perfect enlightenment, and then you could free all living beings from the ocean of conditioned existence?" one asked the old man.

"Perhaps you could just meditate by the pool with your eyes closed," another brother suggested.

"How can you develop perfect tranquillity and deep, diamondlike concentration if you keep getting up and sitting down a hundred times in each meditation session?" a young scholarly monk demanded, emboldened by the more tactful queries of his senior brethren. . . . And thus it went.

The venerable old lama listened attentively, saying nothing. When all had had their say, he bowed gratefully and said, "I'm sure my meditations would be deeper and more fruitful if I sat unmoved all day, brothers, as you say. But how can an old worthless one like myself, who has vowed again and again to give this lifetime (and all his lives) to serving and liberating others, just sit with closed eyes and hardened heart, praying and intoning the altruistic mantra of Great Compassion, while right before my very eyes helpless creatures are drowning?"

To that simple, humble question, none of the assembled monks could find a reply.

Prostrations to an Enlightened Vagabond

Dza Patrul Rinpoche was the greatest turn-of-the-century Dzogchen (Great Perfection) master. A popular teacher, poet, and author, he traveled anonymously throughout eastern Tibet, dressed in a nomad's full-length, handmade sheepskin coat. Few recognized this revered lama whom all were eager to meet.

Once Patrul Rinpoche came upon a band of lamas who were on their way to a great gathering, and he joined their party. He was so raggedly outfitted, so self-effacing, that he was treated as an ordinary mendicant practitioner. He had to help make the tea, gather firewood, and serve the monks of the party while they traveled through a remote region of Kham in eastern Tibet.

One day, the group heard that an important lama was nearby giving a major transmission, a Vajrayana (Diamond Vehicle) empowerment and teaching, and the party hastened to attend. When they arrived, all the lamas and important ecclesiasts and monks were decked out in full monastic regalia, with hats, crowns, and pendants; ornamental saddles and festoons decorated their gaily caparisoned mounts. Long horns, conch shells, and brass trumpets offered a veritable symphony of celestial sounds. Each revered lama was seated on a throne, its height set according to the lama's official rank. . . . Then the rituals and initiations commenced.

At the end of the initiation, all went forward to present offerings to the presiding master and receive the blessing of his hand upon their heads. Patrul, who had been sitting quietly at the back of the throng the entire time, stood at the end of the long line waiting for a blessing. As the queue slowly proceeded, person by person prostrated before the grand master's throne, offering a white silk scarf and receiving a benediction.

At first the lama touched each on the head with his hand. Then, as the throng was so great, he began simply to touch each one with a long peacock feather. So it went, until at last the ragged vagabond stood before him. The presiding master's eyes widened with astonishment: this bedraggled figure was none other than the living Buddha, the supreme Dzogchen master Dza Patrul!

Stepping down from his throne, the grand lama bowed low to the ground. While the assembled masses gaped, he offered Patrul the peacock feather and prostrated himself again and again before the gently smiling sage.

Perfecting Patience

Not all dedicated Buddhist practitioners are monks in monasteries. There is a great tradition of Tibetan yogis who live as hermits, meditating and praying alone. Others wander free and unattached, anchorites without possessions or social status, looking like mere beggars or vagabonds but actually being more akin to the divine mad mystics of yore, the siddhas of India.

Patrul Rinpoche was renowned for his earthy life-style, iconoclastic behavior, and unpretentious appearance as well as for his immense erudition and spiritual accomplishments. Deeply concerned with keeping practitioners focused on the essence of spirituality rather than on formal observances, he never hesitated to deflate pomposity or pretense.

ONE CENTURY AGO, THE ENLIGHTENED vagabond Patrul Rinpoche was wandering as an anonymous mendicant when he heard of a renowned hermit who had long lived in seclusion. Patrul went to visit him, entering the monk's dim cave unannounced and peering about with a wry grin on his weathered face.

"Who are you?" asked the hermit. "Where have you come from, and where are you going?"

"I come from behind my back and am going in the direction I am facing," replied Patrul.

The hermit was nonplussed. "Where were you born?"

"On earth," was the reply.

Now the hermit became slightly agitated. "What is your name?" he demanded.

"Yogi Beyond Action," replied the unexpected guest.

Then Patrul Rinpoche innocently inquired why the hermit lived in such a remote place. This was a question that the hermit, with some pride, was prepared to answer.

"I have been here for twenty years. I am meditating on the transcendental Perfection of Patience."

"That's a good one!" said the anonymous visitor. Then, leaning forward as if to confide something to him, Patrul whispered, "A couple of old frauds like us could never manage anything like that!"

The angry hermit rose abruptly from his seat. "Who do you think you are, disturbing my retreat like this? What made you come here? Why couldn't you leave a humble practitioner like me to meditate in peace?" he exploded.

"And now, dear friend," said Patrul calmly, "where is your perfect patience?"

Clairvoyant Compassion

ONE YEAR, PATRUL RINPOCHE DECIDED to offer a hundred thousand prostrations to his teacher Mingyur Namkhai Dorje. But the latter, who was the grand lama of the Dzogchen Monastery, was totally unpredictable.

As soon as Patrul made one prostration, the grand master stood up and prostrated himself to Patrul. This occurred each time Patrul began to bow before the great lama. Finally Patrul hid in the temple, behind Namkhai Dorje's throne, where, unseen, he discreetly offered his prostrations.

Namkhai Dorje was also known for his unimpeded clairvoyance. Once Patrul Rinpoche seemed to be looking for something as he took leave of his teacher; while he was putting on his shoes at the threshold of the room, Namkhai Dorje said, "Did you lose your bootstrap? It is in that meadow near the river." The disciple found what he was seeking just where the master had said it was.

Another time, thieves broke into the Dzogchen Monastery's temple and stole jewels from the neck of a towering statue. Everyone was puzzled, since the temple was locked and the jewels were seemingly unreachable, high on the statue.

When Namkhai Dorje was apprised of the theft, he said calmly, "I know the thief. He entered on the first floor, walked along the parapet inside the temple, reached over and dislodged the ornaments with a long stick."

When the monks went to check, they found the marks of the thief's passage and the stick, which had been left on the parapet. However, Namkhai Dorje refused to reveal the identity of the thief, for the man would be punished severely if caught.

"He needs our prayers, not our punishment," said the benevolent old lama. "May the Buddha's jewels bring him the treasure of everlasting fulfillment and inner peace."

"Old Dog"

Dza Patrul Rinpoche was known for his straightforward manner of speaking and his contempt for pomp and hypocrisy. Patrul Rinpoche was the principal disciple of Jigmé Gyalway Nyugu, Jigmé Lingpa's successor.

Patrul also studied and practiced under the personal guidance of the enlightened crazy yogi Doe Khyentse Yeshé Dorje. Under the aegis of these masters, Patrul became heir to all the profound, secret oral teachings of the Dzogchen Nyingthig (Quintessence of the Great Perfection) school.

DOE KHYENTSE RINPOCHE LIVED IN the wilderness, carrying a hunting rifle that he reputedly used to awaken others. He was a mercurial master whom Jamyang Khyentse Wangpo, the great first Khyentse, called his alter ego. When Doe Khyentse passed away, the clairvoyant first Khyentse sensed what had transpired far away. With reverence, he said, "Now that old vagabond has dissolved into me."

Patrul Rinpoche had already been introduced to the nature of innate Buddha-mind by Gyalway Nyugu when one day Doe Khyentse accosted him with certain provocative statements about how things actually *are*. First Doe Khyentse taunted Patrul, "Hey, Dharma hero, why keep a respectful distance? If you have any courage, come here, you!"

When Patrul approached, Doe Khyentse deftly grabbed him by his long, braided hair and threw him to the ground, kicking dirt all over him.

Smelling beer on the lama's breath, Patrul concluded that the master was drunk and forgave the rough treatment. Doe Khyentse read his thoughts and berated him loudly.

"You intellectuals!" he shouted. "How can such mundane thoughts enter your little mind? Everything is pure and perfect, you old dog!" Giving Patrul the finger—in Tibetan fashion, using his pinkie—he spat at him and stomped off in disgust.

Instantly, everything became as clear as crystal to Patrul. He experienced the utter inseparability of one's own mind and non-dual Buddha-mind, the infinite luminosity of intrinsic awareness. Meanwhile, the sun overhead shone in a perfectly clear blue sky.

Experiencing an ineffable peace, Patrul instinctively sat down to meditate on that very spot, precisely where his irascible master had unveiled the absolute nature of mind.

Later, Patrul Rinpoche would say, "Thanks to Lord Khyentse's unique kindness, now my Dzogchen name is Old Dog. Wanting and needing nothing, I just wander freely 'round and 'round."

The Oral Teachings of the Primordial Buddha

The siddha (enlightened tantric adept) Gyalwa Jangchub predicted that Patrul Rinpoche, the actual incarnation of Avalokitesvara (Chenrayzig, the Buddha of Compassion), would come to Dergé in eastern Tibet and that those with ordinary, deluded perception would not recognize him, perceiving only a ragged mendicant, a vagrant collecting alms in their midst. . . . And thus it came to pass.

The Oral Teachings of the Primordial Buddha (Kunzang Lamai Shalung in Tibetan) is one of Patrul's most renowned writings, a popular and original book of several hundred folios.

ONCE PATRUL RINPOCHE WAS WANDERING in the mountains near Katok, in the Dergé province, where there are several great stupas (these are large bell-shaped monuments enshrining relics of the Buddhist patriarchs). Patrul found hospitality there from an old lama of Gyarong.

Patrul and the lama talked. The Gyarong lama told the anonymous Patrul, who appeared to him to be a sincere religious mendicant, "You seem to be interested in the Buddhist teachings. Do you know much about its actual practice?"

The incomparably erudite and accomplished Patrul replied, "A little bit, just a few odds and ends that I have been fortunate to hear over the years. Indeed, the sublime Dharma is unfathomably deep and vast."

The monk told Patrul, "Listen, there is a marvelous text that explains in full the fundamentals of the Buddhist doctrine; it is full of interesting anecdotes and pithy insights. It was recently written by the enlightened teacher Patrul Rinpoche. The book is called *The Oral Teachings of the Primordial Buddha*. I will explain it to you, if you wish."

Patrul Rinpoche seemed agreeable. The aged lama taught him about the four contemplations that turn the mind away from samsara (worldliness), and about other important topics from the opening chapters of that book containing the essential instructions of the oral lineage, which Patrul *himself* had collected. The lama was pleased to see that he had an attentive student, and he explained everything at length, much to their mutual delight.

A few days later, everyone heard that the illustrious Patrul Rinpoche was going to teach at the nearby Katok Monastery. Patrul himself spent a great deal of time circumambulating the stupas, which, through his sacred outlook, he perceived to be the locus of all the enlightened ones past, present, and future. Some monks from Dzachuka who were also circling the stupas saw him there; recognizing him immediately, they prostrated themselves in the dust. Everyone rejoiced: the glorious Dza Patrul had arrived!

That night the Gyarong lama returned from the marketplace. He told the entire household how wonderful it was that Patrul Rinpoche himself was in the Katok area and would soon teach at the monastery. Turning to the anonymous medicant in their midst, the lama said, "Isn't it splendid that the enlightened author of this very book we are studying is so close?"

Patrul seemed unimpressed. "Perhaps it is him, but on the other hand maybe not. . . . Who can say? What is so special about Dza Patrul, anyway? He is probably just another village lama. 'It is better to revere the teachings than the teacher,' as the Buddha said."

The old lama hit him, shouting, "How dare you talk back like that to your superiors? I ought to order you out of this righteous household! You should have more respect for our gracious teacher, the living Buddha Patrul Rinpoche."

Two days later, Patrul ascended the regal teaching throne at the Katok Monastery, before an assembly of thousands. When the Gyarong lama saw his erstwhile student sitting majestically on the throne, he instantly realized what had happened. Embarrassed, he left in shame, never to be seen in Katok again.

Later, this story came to Patrul's attention. He smiled and said, "That is really too bad. Perhaps he *did* get angry with me; still, he gave me excellent instruction from *The Oral Teachings of the Primordial Buddha* about the four contemplations that turn the mind from samsara, which I never tire of reflecting upon. I truly hope and pray that my kind teacher, the Gyarong lama, finds sublime peace, and that all beings connected with me become enlightened together."

Three Men in a Tree

EIGHT HUNDRED YEARS AGO, DAMPA Deshek, the renowned spiritual teacher who founded the Katok Monastery in eastern Tibet, was conferring an important Vajrayana initiation and tantric teaching. Each and every inch of the huge temple courtyard and even the rooftops of the surrounding monastery buildings and other adjoining structures were crammed with the faithful. High lamas, youthful incarnations, and other notables were seated according to rank on a carpeted dais on both sides of the master's throne.

Three mendicant yogis from Gyarong in the desolate mountains of Amdo had arrived too late to gain entrance to the courtyard of the monastery itself. They unhesitatingly climbed a distant tree from which, perched in the highest branches, they commanded an unobstructed view. Some local peasants spotted the tattered trio up in the branches, intently watching the esoteric proceedings taking place across the furrowed fields, and laughed among themselves. "How futile the naive efforts of those faithful fools in the top of that tree; they came so far to receive so little!" they told each other knowingly.

Although the three ragged yogis could not, at that distance, understand all the words of the empowerment, they could hear and see the tantric initiation ritual in its entirety, and this allowed actual transmission of the esoteric teachings to take place. Such were their faith and devotion—and so thinly veiled their eye of wisdom—that these three alone, among the entire gathering, right then and there spontaneously experienced the profound meaning of the initiation. They instantly attained unshakable spiritual realization.

At the end of the initiation, the omniscient Dampa Deshek, beaming with joy, sang a lighthearted song to the entire assembly:

"Emaho!
The karmas and appearances of beings are infinitely various,
But today—among all the venerables gathered here—
How wondrous it is
That three itinerant beggars found true illumination
Outside these walls
In a treetop!"

Geshé Ben Steals

Geshé Ben was an erudite and accomplished monk of the Kadampa (Oral Precept) school who lived in the eleventh century. He was noted for his rigorous ethical training and conscientiousness in adhering to the altruism of the bodhisattva, the awakening Mahayana practitioner.

WANDERING IN SEARCH OF ALMS one day, the young monk Ben was invited into the home of a devout couple. While the faithful householders went out of the room to prepare some food for the poor young mendicant, youthful Ben suddenly awoke—as if from a reverie—to find himself with his hand in the cookie jar, as it were, pinching some delectable tea for himself from a sack in one corner. There he was, caught red-handed—if only by his own meticulous conscience.

Shouting, "Thief, thief!" Ben created such an uproar that the entire family came running, makeshift weapons in hand. To their amazement and relief, they beheld the novice accusing himself of pilfering and threatening to cut off his offending hand at once if it ever acted so disgracefully again.

Thus the novice met his inner guru, the innate integrity of wisdom itself, from whom he was never thereafter parted.

Tibet's Best Offering

GESHÉ BEN ONCE LIVED IN retreat in a mountain cave. Generations of hermit yogis had furnished it with a crude wooden door, a rocky altar, and a fireplace. Still, it remained a simple cave in which the monk practiced meditation in perfect solitude.

At the end of a lengthy period of total isolation, Geshé Ben received word that his patrons would arrive on the following day to bring supplies, make offerings, and receive his blessings. He cleaned, dusted, and polished everything in the cave and arranged beautiful offerings on the altar in preparation for receiving his visitors. Then he stepped back and surveyed his domain with satisfaction.

"Ah-yii!" Ben suddenly exclaimed in alarm, observing his own handiwork. "What demonic force has entered into this hypocrite's haven?" Reaching into a dark corner, he picked up a handful of dust and dirt and cast it upon the immaculate altar.

"Let them see this hermitage and its occupant as they are!" he exulted. "Better no offerings at all than offerings to the mere facade of virtue."

In that moment, Geshé Ben had realized that all the offerings he had so artfully arranged in the freshly scrubbed hermitage were not offerings to the enlightened Buddha but to his own ego, made in order to impress his benefactors.

"Let them come and visit now," he thought with satisfaction.

Years later, when Padampa Sangyay, the Buddha of Tingri, came from India and heard the tale, he exclaimed, "That handful of dirt was the best offering ever made in Tibet."

Geshé Ben's Conscience

ONCE IN GESHÉ BEN'S LATER years, many learned abbots and scholars were invited to pray and receive offerings at the home of a wealthy patron in Penyul in southern Tibet. Geshé Ben was seated in the middle of the long row of monastic sages, all ranked according to seniority.

In those days, it was the custom for tea, food, and other offerings to be handed individually to each of the seated lamas. Attendants proceeded along the line, starting from the oldest at the head and continuing to the youngest at the end. Geshé Ben noticed that the yogurt being doled out was of excellent quality, and he feared it might be gone by the time it reached him.

Then he caught himself having such a grasping, unseemly thought. Exclaiming, "Glutton! Foodaholic!" Ben immediately reached out and turned his wooden bowl upside down on the table before him.

When the attendant-monk carrying the clay yogurt pot reached Ben and asked him to right his overturned bowl, Ben refused. "My greedy mind has already enjoyed its share," Ben explained.

In this way, practitioners like Geshé Ben vigilantly guard every thought, word, and deed, incorporating all activities into the spiritual path.

The Best Spiritual Practice

There are many forms of spiritual practice—physical and mental, outer and inner—and there are as many opinions about them as there are forms.

ONCE A MONK WAS CIRCUMAMBULATING the Peltring Monastery. Geshé Tenpa, a distinguished old teacher, came upon him and said, "It is nice to circle holy places, but it is much better to practice the sublime Dharma."

Humbly, the monk began to study, memorize, and recite the Buddhist sutras. One day Geshé Tenpa came across him in the middle of his studies and devotions. The old abbot told him, "It's worthwhile to study scriptures and accomplish virtuous acts, but far better to practice the noble Dharma."

After serious thought, the monk decided that intensive meditation was the best thing for him to do, and he began to meditate in earnest. Inevitably, Geshé Tenpa found him sitting in a corner with a fixed, concentrated stare. "Meditation is fine," commented the erudite abbot, "but genuine Dharma practice would be even better."

By now, the monk was totally confused. There was nothing he had not tried. Still the venerable teacher disapproved of his efforts. "Most venerable sir, what should I do?" he pleaded.

"Simply give up all clinging to this life," Geshé Tenpa replied. Then he quietly continued on his way.

The Dalai Lama and the Sheep-Dung Offering

In every culture, those who live in the big cities usually consider people from the hinterlands to be naive, ignorant of the intricacies of city life. City dwellers in Tibet are no exception.

SOME THREE CENTURIES AGO, THE reclusive seventh Dalai Lama, Kelsang Gyatso, wished to know intimately how the people of his country actually lived and thought. It was difficult to determine their true wishes and needs simply by gazing down upon Lhasa from the remote roof of his ivory tower, the Potala Palace.

Dressed as a pilgrim, with a long-billed cap shading his face, His Holiness—the God-King of Tibet—went forth alone and on foot. He journeyed in easily achieved anonymity, his countenance unknown to most Tibetans.

In the southern part of central Tibet, near the salt lake of Yamdrok Tso, the Dalai Lama happened upon a nomadic herdsman. The Yamdrok-pa (person from Yamdrok) generously offered the solitary traveler overnight hospitality. The next morning, the guest told the illiterate herder that if he were to visit the holy city of Lhasa, he should seek out the house of Kelsang Gyatso, where his needs would be provided for. Kelsang Gyatso moreover assured his host that he would have little trouble in finding the house, as his name was not unknown in that town. Then, with great amicability, the pair parted.

Some years later the herdsman did happen to pilgrimage to Lhasa. It was a trek of several months' duration, since he prayed and prostrated all along the way. Upon arriving at Lhasa, the pilgrim found himself in a large square near the Potala Palace. In his native dialect, he shouted, "Where is the house of Kelsang Gyatso?"

Two fierce police officers instantly descended upon the man and took him into custody. No one suspected that the bumpkin had an open invitation to the royal abode of their exalted lord and master.

News travels fast in a small metropolis. The Dalai Lama himself soon heard of the peasant's plight and sent for him.

The shepherd was led from his dungeon. Quietly, he trudged up myriad stone stairways into the labyrinthine inner precincts of the towering palace. Head bowed, he finally reached the threshold of the imperial chamber where the Dalai Lama patiently awaited him.

Kelsang Gyatso was seated on a resplendent throne; an ornate carpeted couch awaited his honored guest.

The Yamdrok-pa was speechless. Tactfully refraining from inquiring about his host's remarkable new status, he entered the private audience chamber. Without much ado, he offered the three prostrations customary in approaching any lama. Then he presented a white silk scarf, the traditional symbolic offering, and seated himself on the cold stone floor before His Holiness.

Kelsang Gyatso welcomed his old friend warmly, beckoning him to be seated on the regal, carpet-covered couch. The Yamdrok-pa misunderstood, mistaking the magnificently arrayed seat for a three-dimensional mandala, representing the symbolic palace of the primordial deity. Never had he beheld such fine silk carpets and gorgeous, multicolored brocades!

Humbly, he declined. "It would be inauspicious for a mere shepherd to sit on the deity's throne," he explained to the amused lama. Then the innocent

Yamdrok-pa observed, "Friend Kelsang Gyatso—seated upon your high pile of brocade cushions, you remind me of one of my own blue sheep perched upon the highest crags. Do you need help to climb down from there?"

Next the irrepressible peasant expressed concern about his friend's chilly floor. "Your mansion is grand but cold. But don't worry," he assured his host. "As soon as I return to Yamdrok Lake—where even the poor have floors insulated with dried sheep patties—I will immediately dispatch a yak loaded with dung to cover your floor."

The Dalai Lama smiled beneficently. In the presence of his solemn chamberlains and erudite old tutors, he graciously accepted the herdsman's offer. Politely, he inquired after the Yamdrok-pa's home and family, his health, occupation, and travels.

After sharing many fascinating anecdotes and homespun tales, the Yamdrok-pa finally arose. For if he wanted to visit the many pilgrimage sites of Lhasa, he must be on his way. He was anxious, too, to return to Lhasa's central marketplace, renowned throughout Tibet for exotic treasures. Moreover, his friend's palatial suite made him uneasy: it was a bit too rarefied for his simple tastes; and as for peace and comfort—he could have stayed home with his flock!

The Dalai Lama inquired if there was some small thing he might offer the Yamdrok-pa as a token of their mutual esteem. The latter cast never a glance upon the ancient statues, gilded ritual vessels, ornate scroll paintings, embroidered silk wall hangings, jewels, ivory, silver, or jade.

Could a knot be tied on top of his head with a red ribbon? he murmured. It was his desire to be impeccably coiffed, just like his friend Kelsang Gyatso.

The God-King immediately granted this simple request. Beckoning the peasant close, His Holiness with his own immaculate hands braided and twisted the nomad's unwashed, lice-ridden hair into a topknot and tied it with a red ribbon drawn from his own jet black, well-oiled hair.

According to the dictates of Tibetan protocol, the Dalai Lama wore two topknots, delicately threaded with red silk each morning by a devoted servant. However, he placed only one topknot on the rough herdsman's matted head, for the Yamdrok-pa could hardly be expected to be able to tie two topknots properly on his own.

Gratefully, the delighted Yamdrok-pa—still completely innocent regarding the true identity of his host—begged his leave and departed. Over the years, His Holiness Kelsang Gyatso was wont to recount numerous hilarious tales he had heard from his "Yamdrok-pa comrade"—as he ever after called him.

To this day, it is said that this fortuitous meeting was the origin of the single topknot worn by the proud and devout herders of Yamdrok.

Horseface and the Copper-Colored Mountain

To take upon oneself the sufferings of others is a principal practice of the bodhisattva, and is called Tonglen.

The Copper-Colored Mountain (Zangdok Palri) is the southwestern Buddhafield, or paradise, presided over by the Lotus-Born Guru Padma Sambhava. It is often said that awakened ones emanate from that enlightened dimension in order to deliver other beings from various unsatisfactory realms of existence.

CLOSE BY A MONASTERY IN eastern Tibet lived an old beggar-lama nicknamed Horseface. He was not particularly attractive; even money could not coerce women into his hut for a night. His main occupation seemed to be gently picking lice, fleas, and ticks from scabrous dogs and itinerant beggars.

An outcast from the monastic community, he seemed incapable of study and learning. In the solitude and simplicity of noble poverty, he pursued his spiritual practices and chanted his daily prayers seated cross-legged in front of an open fire.

One year a great epidemic, apparently connected to a sudden onslaught of black bugs, swept the region. None of the monastic hierarchs or miracle workers could do anything about it. When Horseface was reported ill after practicing Tonglen and performing elaborate rites and rituals to drive the evil forces away, rumor had it that he had magically assumed the area's collective bad karma, for the insect population rapidly declined, and the disease receded.

When Horseface died, alone in an abandoned hovel, a fine cremation ceremony rewarded his selfless efforts. Simultaneously, Horseface arrived at the splendid Copper-Colored Mountain, where Guru Rinpoche Padma Sambhava himself awaited him with open arms.

The Lotus-Born Master asked, "How many followers have you led to liberation since I sent you to Tibet?"

Horseface opened both hands, revealing countless thousands of live insects. Delighted, all the compassionate Buddhas and bodhisattvas rejoiced with him.

Flagpole Sitting

Drukpa Kunley was an outrageous yogi of the Drukpa Kagyu school. This divine madman is affectionately remembered as an uncompromising unmasker of fraud and hypocrisy, especially in the monastic establishment. He is also venerated as a liberating lover and bard.

ONCE DRUKPA KUNLEY HAD NOTHING to do, so he meandered into the midst of a great monastic gathering. It was an auspicious occasion; the monks were congregated in the temple courtyard to recite the Diamond Sutra, which explains the ultimate wisdom of emptiness.

Although Drukpa Kunley looked like a mere tramp, his gleeful demeanor and authentic spiritual presence set him apart. Today many seek the sublime inner peace and fulfillment that he had made his own.

In the very midst of the solemn, sonorous chanting of the Mahayana wisdom scripture, Drukpa Kunley shinned up the flagpole in the center of the courtyard, in plain sight of everyone. Then he perched on top of the pole, flapped his arms, and cawed like a crow—creating, as usual, not a little disturbance. He began to mimic the monks' recitation.

Outraged, the venerable monks in unison invoked a traditional formula to quell the disturbance. "By the power of this sutra, may that mischievous beggar come down," they intoned.

The Drukpa obligingly began a rather theatrical descent.

The monks continued their chant, "By the power of our concentration on the recitation of this sutra, may the malicious beggar come down."

Instantly, the irrepressible divine madman reascended the flagpole.

"Parrots cannot concentrate, parrots cannot comprehend," the crazy yogi cackled.

An Enlightened Cook

Machen *means cook in Tibetan.*
Anonymous saints, known as hidden yogis, are occasionally discovered among us—although the discovery often comes too late.

IN A LARGE MONASTERY IN old Tibet, there was a cook-monk called Machen-la who slept in the kitchen and owned nothing other than pots and pans. Through selfless service, he had found the supreme peace still sought by the monks whom he nourished with broth each day. Brother Machen-la had long ago given up austerities, philosophical studies, and elaborate rites and rituals. Relinquishing all self-centered efforts, personal preoccupations, and willful striving, he was content simply to offer service to the Buddhist brotherhood, and express his gratitude through service to the Lord Buddha.

Whatever Machen-la did, it seemed as if the Enlightened One, the deity in person, was always with him and within him, actually accomplishing his activities for him. Free from anxiety about spiritual progress, the cook felt no need for formal prayer or meditation and always acted without doubts or misgivings. Perfectly surrendered, with impartial acceptance of all, this simple monk experienced everything as if it was all of a single savor; he was prey to neither attachment nor aversion. He did not mind criticism, never cultivated favor, and accomplished whatever had to be done as if it was the single most important thing in the world.

The entire monastery subsisted on the simple, wholesome fare brewed in the gigantic cast-iron cauldrons that simmered continuously in the kitchen. There strips of drying yak meat hung from smoke-blackened rafters, and hot buttered tea and good company were always available. The learned lamas never guessed who was present among them in the guise of their unassuming cook, though their practice, health, and demeanor flourished like those of no other Buddhist congregation in the land. However, this fact was generally attributed to their splendid monastic rites and rituals and the sterling purity of the monks' daily conduct.

After decades, when the wizened old cook finally passed on, several worthy successors remained in his kitchen, all of whom claimed him and him alone—the Simple One—as their root guru. The monastery gave Machen-la a lama's funeral and a fine cremation, although he would have been equally satisfied to be abandoned in the charnel ground as food for jackals and vultures. Cascades of rainbow light swirled above Brother Machen-la's funeral pyre; holy relics and mantric seed-syllables (mantras inscribed on his bones) appeared in the ashes. Now everyone understood that an anonymous saint had dwelt, unrecognized, in their very midst.

Machen-la demonstrated that the way of awakening is more profound than merely following ritual observances. Yet later tales from that monastery asserted that the names of Chenrayzig, Lord of Great Compassion, and of the savioress Tara were constantly on the humble cook's lips. Others presume that, with his mind's eye, Machen-la constantly kept the blessed image of his meditational deity above his head and in his heart as he toiled tirelessly over his pots.

Others affirm that once he realized perfect inseparability from his master and all that is, he never of his own volition made any effort to cultivate, develop, or transform anything. Straightforwardly answering the immediate demands of everyday situations as they presented themselves, he enjoyed the other shore, enlightenment, in this very world, having transcended all vehicles for traversing the path.

Today he is remembered simply as Brother Machen-la: he who nourished multitudes.

A Thief Is Converted

WHEN PATRUL RINPOCHE TAUGHT THE *Bodhicharya-avatara* in Zamthang, an old man offered him a piece of silver cast in the shape of a horse's hoof. The man had few possessions, but feeling great faith in Patrul, he knew it would be meritorious to make an offering.

After one week of teaching, Patrul left the vicinity. A thief, who had seen Patrul receive the ingot, followed him with the intention of stealing it.

Patrul walked alone, with no other goal than to spend his nights at peace beneath the stars. That first night, the thief stole up under the cover of darkness while Patrul was asleep. Next to Patrul lay a small cloth shoulder bag and a clay teapot. Cautiously the thief started to explore Patrul's bedclothes.

His probing hands awoke the lama, who exclaimed, "Ka-ho! What are you doing, rummaging inside my clothes?"

The thief replied with alacrity, "Someone gave you a large piece of silver. Give it to me!"

"Ka-ho!" cried the master. "Look what a mess you make of life, running around like a madman! You came so far, just for that silver—poor fool! Listen:

go right now, and by dawn you will reach the mound of grass where I sat. . . . The silver is nearby. I used it as a stone to support my teapot. Look in the ashes of the campfire."

The thief was skeptical, but he saw that the silver was no longer in Patrul's possession. It seemed most unlikely to him that the ingot lay abandoned in the campfire; nevertheless, he went back to see. When he arrived where the master had taught, he searched and found the silver, amidst the stones of the fire ring.

The thief was totally astounded and lamented, "Ah-zi! This Patrul is a true lama, without worldly attachments, while I have gained only bad karma by intending to steal from him. Now I shall surely go to hell!"

Haunted by remorse, he set off to find Patrul again. When he finally caught up with him, the master accosted him, "Here you are again, driving yourself crazy! I told you where to find what you wanted. What now?"

Greatly agitated, the thief explained, sobbing, "It's not that—I found the silver. But I have sinned by conniving against a spiritual being like yourself! I was ready to beat you and take everything you have! I offer you my confession and beg your forgiveness."

Patrul appeased him. "There is no need to offer a confession or request forgiveness. Just have a good heart and pray to the Three Jewels (Buddha, Dharma, and Sangha); that will do."

Later, when others heard what had happened, they caught the thief and beat him. Patrul Rinpoche loudly berated them, "If you harm my disciple, it is as if you are harming me. Leave him alone!"

Rabjyor and the Old Woman

It has long been a custom in Buddhist countries for pious householders to invite learned monks to read the scriptures aloud in their homes for a period of days, weeks, or more. This virtuous practice helps the hosts to accumulate good karma and merit, preserves the doctrine, and spreads the teachings leading to enlightenment. A group of monks might dwell in a patron's home for a fortnight or more, turning it into a spiritual sanctuary.

ONCE A MONK OF THE Nyingma (Ancient Translation) school was sitting in a family shrine room, reading aloud the Mahayana sutras and Dzogchen tantras for several days at his host's request. Because he couldn't read very well, he stumbled over quite a few of the words in the esoteric texts. Since it was the custom to recite quite quickly (the members of the household rarely listened, anyway), the monk did not worry about his shortcoming. If anything, he only muttered the scriptures even more swiftly.

After a couple of days, the ancient, illiterate grandmother of the family entered the room where the monk was performing his recitation. With painstaking difficulty, she reverently prostrated herself full length on the floor three times. Then she offered tea to the lama, sat down on the floor, and listened to the reading.

After some time, the monk stopped reciting in order to sip his steaming buttered tea. He lifted the lidded wooden tea bowl from the low carved table that stood in front of the thick carpets on which he sat.

Grandma chose this moment to speak. "This family has been fortunate to hear the sutras and tantras recited in this room every year since I was a baby," she said. "Every year venerable lamas come and read that very collection that is before you. From wherever I am in the house, I hear the same name, 'Rabjyor, Rabjyor,' coming up again and again, but you, esteemed monk, never seem to say the name of the venerable Rabjyor. Is it possible, perhaps, that you cannot read very well? Or is it that this old grandma is losing her hearing?"

The monk, not the finest of the breed, answered smoothly, "Not at all, not at all, dear old lady. No problem at all. In fact, we are just now coming to the sutra about Rabjyor!" And sagaciously turning over the page, he simply resumed his recitation, intoning the name of Rabjyor every fourth word precisely for the old lady's benefit.

Grandma smiled. Nodding her head in approval, she continued to tell her prayer beads, satisfied that merits were being accumulated and that all was well in the world.

A Henpecked Husband's Three Wishes

ONCE THERE WAS A HENPECKED peasant named Dorje, a man of meager means who worked the soil for his daily bread. He lived with his nagging wife in the southern part of central Tibet. Often he longed for the day when the gods would put an end to his wife's incessant nagging; such was the extent of his heavenly aspirations.

One morning he was tilling his stony barley field when, lo and behold, he suddenly saw a goddess standing behind a boulder. What sort of celestial being she might be Dorje did not know, yet he instinctively sought her blessing, beseeching her for protection and longevity.

She deigned to grant him the fulfillment of three wishes. Then, in a twinkle, she disappeared.

Dorje was nonplussed. Laying down his hoe, he headed homeward.

It was still early; he knew that a verbal drubbing lay in store for him at the hands of Pema-la, his beloved wife. But he wanted to tell her about the gorgeous goddess and his three wishes. He was certainly going to think carefully about the entire matter and consider in what way to make the most of this unexpected boon!

As Dorje came within sight of his stone cottage, Pema-la appeared in the doorway. She immediately began berating him as a lazy good-for-nothing who couldn't even feed two mouths, let alone an entire family. Why was he returning so early, she demanded, calling him—in the Tibetan idiom, of course—a layabout, a rice bag, a giant potato-nose (for his nose was indeed remarkable).

Suddenly, Dorje's temper, contained until then, flared up. "I wish my ugly giant nose filled your whole kitchen!" he shouted. And lo and behold, his famous nose actually grew and grew, pinning both man and woman to the rough walls.

Pema-la shouted for help. Dorje spontaneously exclaimed, "I wish I had no nose at all!" which was instantaneously the case. On his face was a great hiatus: where before his sole claim to fame had resided, suddenly there were only two empty holes where a pair of great flaring nostrils had been.

Pema-la gaped at her husband in amazement, speechless for once. Dorje, grasping his predicament with alacrity, exclaimed vehemently, "I wish I'd never met that damned field goddess at all!"

That was that. The three fabulous wishes were exhausted, and poor benighted Dorje was right back where he started.

Moreover, to add insult to injury, his wife lambasted him bitterly for days afterward about squandering their three precious wishes. "They could have been eternal boons for us!" she lamented. "We could have been rich!"

Yet no matter how fervently they prayed, no matter how diligently they searched beneath countless boulders surrounding their paltry little field, one hardly need mention the fact that divine intercession was never again forthcoming, and the hapless pair lived unhappily ever after.

Fine-Tune Yourself

ONCE THE INDIAN MONK SRONA was struggling to master meditation. Striving diligently, day after day, he seemed to make little progress.

Agitated, Srona imagined that his efforts to relax only served to increase his tension. And the more he tried to concentrate and control his distracted thoughts, the more thoughts he seemed to have. He brought his problem to Lord Buddha, the meditation master par excellence, and confessed his frustration.

"Do you remember how you used to tune the sitar strings as a young layperson?" the Buddha asked. Like any great leader, he was intimately familiar with the case history of each of his disciples, and the monk before him was, indeed, from the musician caste.

"Was the music sweetest when the strings were taut or slack?" the Buddha quietly inquired.

"Neither too tight nor too loose, Lord; the middle way of moderation and balance always proved best," said Srona.

"Thus it is with meditation, young monk," spoke the Buddha. "In the same way you must moderate the tightness and looseness of your mind and gradually discover what naturally suits you best. Don't worry too much about progress. Continuity is the secret of success. Practice, practice, practice!"

Regarding meditation practice, the Tibetan matriarch of the Chöd (Cutting Ego) school, Machig Labdron, sang:

"Simply relax in the natural state
   of being;
why try to tie knots
   in the sky?

"First tighten loosely,
  then loosen loosely—
  hold onto nothing.

"Let it go
  as it goes,
  and rest at ease
  as you are."

A God Is Punished

ONCE THERE WAS A MOUNTAIN god highly venerated by the inhabitants of a certain region. Many precious metals, foods, brocades, and farm products were always piled upon the offering table before his altar. These accoutrements and oblations were especially splendid because his shrine was in the village at the head of the valley that led in and out of the region, so travelers often dallied there.

One day a layperson came into the shrine, offered the customary prostrations in that dimly lit chamber, and approached the altar with a slightly mincing gait, which attracted the attention of the young novice who was serving as altar boy. Or perhaps it was the fact that the man neglected to remove his hat that attracted the young monk's attention. Be that as it may, the monk felt compelled to eavesdrop on the ensuing conversation.

The man brought a hefty hunk of fresh mutton out from beneath his robe, plunked it down on the altar, and told the deity that he had a deal to propose: he would offer a splendid feast to the god's image once a week without fail for the next year if the deity would protect him while he rustled a herd of horses from a neighboring district. Having spoken, the man slowly retreated, backing his way toward the dim outline of the shrine door, and then went on his way.

The novice thought this transaction a bit odd. But the resident god did not disagree or seem in any way disinclined toward his supplicant's somewhat sinister proposal—in fact, he seemed to smile even more benignly than usual. . . . Or was that just the susceptible imagination of a young novice? The boy soon forgot all about the incident.

Exactly one week later, the rustler returned. Neither prostrating nor removing his hat, this time he boldly approached the altar. The novice monk's ears pricked up, as he sat hidden in gloom behind the shrine. He heard the rustler shamelessly congratulate the god on his share in the profits and thank him for his complicity. Then, plunking down a huge quarter of mutton on the altar, directly beneath the large image's eyes, the bandit beat a hasty retreat, his boot heels sharply striking the old temple's cold stone floor. The boy was astounded.

The novice decided to write to his venerable abbot about all this. But when the elderly abbot read the letter, he thought to himself, "What nonsense is this? That boy must be cracked! Whoever heard of a deity acting as an accomplice in crime and making a deal with a criminal? Even if I believed such things were possible, whoever heard of a statue smiling upon the completion of a deal?" Then the white-haired lama burned the letter in his censer.

The black smoke from the boy's letter wafted up to the King of the Sky, the chief of deities, who read the message as if it was still inscribed in black and white on paper. He was not pleased—not with the skeptical abbot, the deal-making criminal, or the worldly mountain god himself. . . . For he knew very well that statues can smile, even deities can err, and a taste for freshly slaughtered meat bespeaks a less-than-divine lack of compassion.

Therefore, the King of the Sky caused an epidemic to break out in the region. Then he appeared in the trance of the local oracle, prophesying that the sole cure for the disease could be extracted only from the smelted-down statues of the graven images of the offending mountain god. Thus every image of that deity was dismantled and used as medicine. Both the epidemic and the worship of that god came to an abrupt end.

And what of the rustler and his purloined horses? Perhaps he died in the epidemic. . . . Unfortunately, that is not part of the story.

A Debate About Rebirth

One millennium after the historical Buddha's time, there was a great Mahayana (Great Vehicle) philosopher and epistemologist named Chandragomi, a contemporary of the peerless logician Chandrakirti. Through teaching, writing, and debate, together they raised the Middle Way doctrine to preeminence among the various schools of philosophy in India.

In his previous lifetime, Chandragomi had been a learned pandit who was blessed by a vision of Avalokitesvara, the Great Compassionate One, and developed selfless loving-kindness and unconditional compassion.

ONCE THIS ERUDITE MASTER, WHO would later be reborn as Chandragomi, entered into a debate with a non-Buddhist teacher and emerged triumphant. His vanquished opponent respectfully made the point—a cogent one, indeed—that the Buddhist pandit's superior logical arguments depended almost entirely on his intellectual acumen, and therefore whoever was more proficient in the art of debate could inevitably carry the day.

"How does merely winning a debate decisively prove the superiority of the Buddhist viewpoint? It only demonstrates who is the superior debater," he objected.

The non-Buddhist then stated that he did not believe there was firm evidence to support the rebirth doctrine, which therefore brought into question the entire teaching regarding karmic cause and effect. "If there is no proof of former lifetimes, how can we believe in future incarnations?" he said. "Prove conclusively that reincarnation actually exists, and I and all my students will convert to the Buddha's way."

The compassionate Buddhist pandit enjoyed a moment's thought. Then he said, "I will die and intentionally be reborn in a manner that demonstrates that transmigration is possible, taking the king as my witness. Then you shall have your proof."

His opponent was both surprised and impressed by the Buddhist teacher's selfless dedication to his cherished religious beliefs. He acquiesced, although he did not believe that the Buddhist would actually follow the melodrama to its logical conclusion, his own untimely death.

The Buddhist master asked the king and his advisers to keep his corpse in a sealed copper coffin. Then the pandit marked his own forehead with vermilion, placed a pearl in his mouth, and lay down to die. Instantaneously, he left this world.

Having totally mastered the illusion of birth and death, the Buddhist teacher was immediately reborn, as he intended, as the son of a pandit of that region. Many auspicious signs and omens attended the infant's birth; among them were a vermilion mark on the baby's brow and a pearl in his mouth.

These marvels were brought to the attention of the royal advisers, who in turn informed the king.

Then the king summoned the non-Buddhist teacher and other witnesses and ordered the sealed casket opened in their presence. The pearl was gone from the dead pandit's mouth; the vermilion mark was also no longer to be seen, except on the forehead of his undisputed reincarnation.

The non-Buddhist teacher was convinced and led his followers into the Buddhist path. He often inspired his followers by relating how the Buddhist pandit gave up his own life so that others could find the true way.

The little boy subsequently grew up and became the famous master Chandragomi. He became renowned for holding his own for seven whole years in a great public debate at Nalanda with Chandrakirti, Nagarjuna's successor. It was finally decided that the debate was a draw once the pair laughingly realized that while Chandragomi was nightly receiving from his tutelary deity Avalokitesvara his inspired answers to Chandrakirti's incisive and challenging questions, his opponent Chandrakirti was being likewise inspired by his own deity, Manjusri.

Clinging Binds Us

The tenth-century Indian master Naropa was an erudite abbot at Nalanda University in Bihar. After Vajra Yogini admonished him for being more familiar with the letter than with the spirit of Buddhist Law, Naropa became disillusioned with the joys of intellectual life and gave up his prestigious position and monastic life-style. Instead, he sought out his karmically predestined guru, Tilopa, an uninhibited siddha (yogic adept) who lived in Bengal.

Tilopa made Naropa undergo twelve arduous trials before smacking Naropa in the face with his sandal, thus awakening him to Mahamudra—that is, immanent absolute reality. Naropa later became the guru of Marpa the Translator, who was Milarepa's guru.

TILOPA LIVED NEAR A RIVER, surviving on offal as well as on the live fish he caught with his hands. Naropa encountered him for the first time on a riverbank. It was morning; Tilopa was wrapped in cotton rags, his eyes bloodshot.

Naropa prostrated himself, then circumambulated the carefree crazy yogi and reverently begged him for teachings.

"What do you seek, Naropa?" Tilopa asked.

"I seek the freedom of enlightenment," the pandit replied.

"From what do you wish to be freed, Naropa?" the crazy yogi inquired.

"From everything, Lord," answered the disciple.

"It is not outer objects that bind and entangle you, Naropa," Tilopa asserted. "It is clinging that binds you. Simply relinquish clinging, and be free!"

With those simple words, Naropa experienced a great awakening.

Then Tilopa sang:

"Where there is attachment,
  there is suffering.
Where there is bias,
  there is limitation.
Where there are concepts,
  duality reigns;
  duality implies ignorance.

Do not think, scheme,
or seek to understand;
with objects be not concerned.
Radiant and stainless,
leave awareness in its own sphere
and cure your fatigue.

Rest in the unmoved, uncreated,
and spontaneous."

Greatness of Heart Is What Counts

CHUNDAKA, THE BROOM MASTER, WAS born into a Brahmin family in Shravasti. He was so slow that his father could not teach him the hereditary priestly customs; Chunda could not retain even one line of the sacred Hindu scriptures, the Vedas. He learned neither to read nor write.

Chundaka's older brother, however, was intelligent. He greatly pleased all the Brahmins by becoming educated and well-mannered. When their aged father died, the two boys met some of the Buddha's followers; soon afterward, the older brother was ordained as a monk. Chunda, considered too stupid to enter the monastic order, contented himself by living in squalor nearby.

One day Chunda's brother encouraged him to ask Ananda, the Buddha's attendant, for ordination. Chunda replied, "How can one as feebleminded as myself aspire to enter the exalted community of Buddha's monks? I cannot even memorize a single verse. Everyone knows I am a dimwit."

In sympathy, his brother said, "Brother Chundaka, in the compassionate Buddha's doctrine caste, social status and learning mean nothing. Greatness of heart is what counts. You, too, can certainly enter the way. Ask the Lord Buddha yourself."

Reverently, Chunda approached Lord Buddha and his disciple Ananda. The omniscient Buddha perceived Chunda's humility and purity of heart. There in the Jeta Grove, Ananda ordained Chundaka as a monk.

Ananda instructed Chunda with this verse:

"Give up negative actions; free yourself from negative thoughts;
Perform virtuous deeds and selfless service.
Be not attached to the elements of personality.
Mindful and alert, living in purity,
No harm or suffering can befall you.
This is the teaching of the Enlightened One."

After three months, however, poor Chunda was still unable to memorize this single verse, although all the other neophytes had in the same time committed entire scriptures to memory—and even the local shepherds knew this simple verse, as well as several others, by heart.

Discouraged, Chunda went to the venerable Ananda for further teachings and guidance; yet Ananda himself found it impossible to instruct him. "What is the point of taking ordination if one cannot learn and remember anything?"

Ananda thought. Bestowing a benediction, he sent him away. Chunda sat down alone outside the Jeta Grove, disconsolate, until the Buddha himself found him there on the following day.

The Compassionate One intuitively understood all that had transpired. Chunda said to him, "Lord and master, I am not a real practitioner nor a good monk. What's wrong with me? What sort of bad karma have I?"

Buddha told him that because of overweaning pride as a learned Brahmin in a previous life—during which he had mercilessly reviled the doctrines of other scholars, been miserly in sharing his own advantages, and also falsely claimed to have spiritual powers—Chunda suffered from a lack of intelligence in his present incarnation.

Chunda said, "Since I was a boy, my teachers have constantly been scolding me for my stupidity. How can such a dummy ever become wise?"

The Buddha replied in verse:

"It is far better to be belittled by the wise
than praised by children.
The child who knows he is a child
is a wise man;
He who boasts of his wisdom
is a childish fool."

Since even his own learned and wise attendant Ananda could not teach the feebleminded monk, Lord Buddha himself instructed him. He told Chunda to purify his karmic obscurations by attentively sweeping the temple while memorizing and reflecting upon two lines of teaching: "Remove the dust, remove the dirt." Chunda was also given the daily task of cleaning the monks' shoes.

"Can you clean shoes, Chunda?" the Buddha inquired. "Can you sweep the temple?"

Chunda replied, "Master, I can learn to sweep and clean, but I cannot learn to memorize teachings."

Lord Buddha had Chunda repeat after him the simple couplet, "Remove the dust, remove the dirt." Repeating it together again and again, Chunda eventually seemed to have it inscribed in his heart. Then the Buddha gave his benediction and departed.

But when Chunda began sweeping the temple, he could not remember the simple lines the Enlightened One himself had taught him. Fortunately, Ananda was in the courtyard; Chunda asked him now and again to remind him of what he was supposed to be repeating, while he painstakingly went about his work.

Finally he became familiar with the simple phrase and mindfully reflected on it as he worked.

Cleaning the monks' shoes provided a further obstacle to the ignorant monk. While engaged in this new chore, Chunda found it impossible to recall the words he had memorized during his previous work. But patient Ananda again tutored him. Chunda was truly the most feebleminded of the entire Buddhist sangha (congregation).

The compassionate Buddha, through his miraculous powers, blessed the temple dust so that it should prove inexhaustible and keep Chunda continuously busy. He likewise blessed the mud on the monks' shoes. In this way the Wise One facilitated diligent and devoted Chunda's practice. As long as there was work to do, Chunda kept cleaning, conscientiously trying to keep in mind his teacher's instructions. The words "Remove the dust, remove the dirt" became his mantra.

Many laughed at the ignorant fellow but grudgingly admired his faith and industry. The wise ones recognized him as a monk who—whatever his limitations—was actually intent upon purifying his karma and attaining the great goal.

Chunda worked hard, sweeping and cleaning with respect and devotion, as he had been instructed. Moreover, by turning over in his mind the few words the Buddha had made him memorize, he began to delve deeper into their meaning and significance. Although the temple dust seemed limitless, insight began to blossom within the depths of his being.

"Did the Teacher mean outer dust and dirt or inner dust and dirt?" he mused. "What *is* outer dirt and what are inner defilements? Where are my karmic obscurations?" In this way the ignorant temple cleaner, the dunce among Buddha's followers, meditated while engaged in his daily chores.

One day Chunda was in the midst of self-inquiry, quietly sweeping the temple, when a verse of Buddha's teachings spontaneously arose in his mind—lines that he could not remember even having heard, much less having memorized:

"Dust is attachment, not earthly dust;
  the wise abandon such stains.
  Dirt is anger, not earthly mud;
  the wise abandon such stains.
  Dust and dirt are ignorance, nothing else;
  the wise remove such stains and obscurations
  and are free."

With this spontaneously arisen verse in mind, Chundaka understood that the three poisons of attachment, anger, and delusion are the basis of conditioned existence, and he broke through the illusion of self, the ground of all delusion.

Suddenly dumb Chunda exclaimed, "It is seen, it is seen clearly. Homage to the Enlightened One!" For he had seen through the veil of illusion and attained awakening, then and there, with broom in hand.

Meditating diligently for years afterward, Chundaka became one of the sixteen enlightened arhats, or saints, who vastly promulgated the Buddha's teachings. Everyone was amazed that the most ignorant monk in the entire community could have achieved such lofty spiritual heights. Once when the arhat Chundaka was teaching twelve skeptical nuns and an immense throng of householders, twelve thousand members of the audience immediately attained various stages of enlightenment.

On another occasion, Lord Buddha was invited for lunch by a doctor; all the monks except the temple sweeper Chunda were included. The Buddha, however, made a seat near his own for Chundaka and would not accept food until the unlettered arhat had been brought and given his proper place.

Lord Buddha himself said that, of all his numerous disciples, the one most skilled at transforming the minds of others was the good arhat Chundaka, the Broom Master. To this day it is said that those who cannot memorize, or even understand, the Buddha's words will greatly develop their mental faculties through praying wholeheartedly to Chundaka. He exemplifies the fact that sincere spiritual practice is more important for inner development than mere intellectual knowledge.

Nyoshul's Introduction to Things as They Are

Nyoshul Lungtok was Patrul Rinpoche's principal disciple. He received personal instructions on Dzogchen theory and practice from his master for twenty-five years, while meditating in the wilderness.

Dharmakaya refers to the formless body of the Buddha, to ultimate truth itself, reality, or the innate nature of all things. Vajra Sattva (Adamantine Being) is the white purification Buddha.

The awareness-void is the brilliant, centerless openness that is the empty and luminous nature of the awakened heart and mind. Milarepa sang, "Buddhahood cannot be found by searching outside, so contemplate the nature of your own mind." Buddha-mind refers to the innate perfection and transcendence of one's own true nature.

AT ONE TIME, PATRUL RINPOCHE lived with a few disciples in an open field near the Nagchung Hermitage. It was his habit to lie down on his back each evening at dusk, gazing upward. He was practicing Dzogchen Sky-Gazing Yoga, a profound meditation in which one mingles mind with the infinity of open space.

One day, while thus meditating, Patrul called out to Nyoshul Lungtok, who happened to be nearby, asking if he had not yet realized the essential nature of awakened mind. The disciple confirmed that he had not.

Then Patrul said, "Don't worry. There is actually nothing you cannot know! Don't think about it." The master chuckled; then they continued to meditate.

Nyoshul Lungtok had a recurring dream in which Patrul Rinpoche would unravel a mountainous ball of black thread, revealing at its center a golden statue of Vajra Sattva. One evening Patrul summoned Lungtok to lie down next to him. "Now we'll unravel everything," he promised. "Stay awake!"

Together they gazed up into the vast, empty firmament. In the distance they heard the barking of dogs at the Dzogchen Monastery.

Dza Patrul said to Nyoshul Lungtok, "Dear friend, do you hear the dogs barking?"

"Yes," Lungtok answered.

"That's it!" the master exclaimed. He then asked, "Do you see the stars in the sky?"

Lungtok again answered affirmatively.

Patrul exclaimed, "That's exactly it! It's all intrinsic enlightened awareness, Buddha-mind. Don't look elsewhere!"

Just then, in the gloaming, Lungtok's non-dual wisdom eye opened. At that very moment his own mind and the Dharmakaya were absolutely inseparable; there was nothing to know or attain that had not been present all along. Then he wept for joy.

In this way, Nyoshul Lungtok was freed from the net of dualistic clinging. He recognized and directly experienced the non-dual awareness-void. From then on, Buddha-mind and his own awareness were one and inseparable. He intuitively understood all experiences as the functioning of Buddha-mind and soared free from partiality and limitation.

As the tantra called "The King of Deities" proclaims:

In the causal vehicle of the sutra path,
all sentient beings are said to be endowed
with the potential
to achieve Buddhahood.
In the fruition vehicle, the tantric path,
it is recognized that the essential nature
of intrinsic awareness
is Buddhahood.

Years later, Nyoshul Lungtok himself recounted this tale, ending with a quote from Longchenpa:

Everything is in the state of primordial Buddhahood;
recognition of that is spiritual awakening.

The six senses left in their natural state
compose the outlook of the natural Great Perfection.

Enjoying everything, simply
leave it as it is
and rest your weary mind.

Anonymous Lamas

The Dodrup Chen Monastery is in the sparsely inhabited Golok region of Kham. It was one of the principal centers for the practice of omniscient Jigmé Lingpa's Dzogchen teachings, the Longchen Nyingthig (Essence of the Great Perfection). Jigmé Gyalway Nyugu and the first Dodrup Chen Rinpoche were Jigmé Lingpa's foremost disciples; their disciple, in turn, was Patrul Rinpoche.

Powerful masters, accomplished in the transference-of-consciousness yoga called Phowa, can direct the essence of a departed human being through the crown aperture atop the head, allowing the deceased to be reborn in the Buddhafields, which are paradises, or Pure Lands. At the moment of transference, certain outward as well as inner manifestations often occur; these are signs of the success of the endeavor.

ONE DAY AN OLD LADY lay dead in her bed. Her bereaved relatives saw three vagabonds passing by—one old, one middle-aged, and one young. Since the tattered trio wore colors reminiscent of the maroon robes of the Buddhist order, they were invited in. Perhaps these were wandering yogis who, for a fee, could perform the appropriate rites for the deceased.

The head of the household, a herdsman, respectfully inquired, "Can you help our dead mother? There are no monks here. We will give you offerings."

The oldest mendicant replied, "We do not need offerings, only food. We shall do whatever is necessary to deliver your old mother to the Buddhafields." The three began to fashion the ceremonial barley cakes called tormas in preparation for the Nyingthig rituals they would perform.

The members of the household noticed that the three ragged men seemed to know exactly what they were doing. The mendicants spoke of the blessed Buddhafields as if intimately familiar with those sublime spheres. Surprised, the family kept quiet and gathered barley flour, water, butter, grains, incense, and whatever else the men required. Their late mother would have a proper funeral!

"Who could have imagined such poor wanderers would come to our aid in such a way?" the family exclaimed, pleased with their unexpected good fortune. "At least they know how to make a good show of it!"

The youngest of the yogis squatted near the fireplace, molding the offertory tormas with skilled hands. The daughter of the house, in performing her kitchen tasks, found him underfoot. She told him roughly to get out of her way, treating him with disrespect as she would any common beggar.

"If any real lamas were available," the young woman thought to herself, "I wouldn't have to put up with these three tramps. Anyway, at least they can make a show of performing funeral rites."

The young lama understood exactly what was passing through her mind. Smiling benignly and remaining silent, he completed his humble task. Soon all preparations were finished.

When the three yogis began their rite, an awesome silence seemed to fill the room. A rainbow appeared above the house, and at the same time some hairs fell from the head of the corpse. A bump appeared at her crown aperture, out of which the consciousness principle had been ejected and transferred to the Buddhafields. The entire household was astonished. Never had they expected such remarkable results!

"You have performed a miracle!" the herdsman exclaimed. "Out of gratitude, we will offer you three horses and a yak for your journey."

The youngest of the three lamas spoke bluntly, "We have nothing to do with horses and yaks or other beasts of burden. Three horses are just three horses' worth of bother! Nor do we need any other offerings for providing this service for the deceased. Even if you offered us all of your possessions, what would we want with them?"

The owner of the house politely invited them to stay and pray there for three months, three weeks, or at least for three days. Then he respectfully inquired of the young lama who his companions actually were, for it had become obvious that these were not three ordinary itinerants.

The young lama replied, "Have you ever heard of Jigmé Lingpa's illustrious successor, Dodrup Chen Rinpoche?" The herdsman was overawed. Hesitantly, he ventured to ask the name of the other venerable lama as well. "That is the renowned Dzogchen master Jigmé Gyalway Nyugu himself," the young lama said, neglecting to mention his own name.

Instantly, the family prostrated themselves on the earthen floor, begging forgiveness for their ignorance. Loath to part with such saintly company, they accompanied the lamas for one day's walk along their way.

The young lama was none other than the enlightened vagabond Patrul Rinpoche, whose original writings and unimpeachable integrity inspire us today.

Why Didn't I See It Before?

Swayambu is a hilltop pilgrimage place in the Kathmandu Valley of Nepal, a power place that is the site of a stupa that miraculously arose from the ground. Until recently, the late Sabchu Rinpoche was the head lama there.

A vajra (or dorje in Tibetan) is a small, scepter-like ritual instrument. Shaped like a miniature thunderbolt, it is symbolic of the Buddha-mind, ultimate truth. Mahamudra is the highest reality.

OLD LAMA THONDÖ WAS SABCHU Rinpoche's attendant. Over the years his teacher imparted many pith-instructions (oral guidance passed from master to disciple) to him, while Thondö sought enlightenment. He spent his days serving his teacher in prayer, meditation, and circumambulating the holy Swayambu stupa.

One night Thondö dreamt that he was riding a magnificent white elephant and holding a colorful bouquet of flowers. When he related the dream to his master, Sabchu Rinpoche said, "This means that purification is actually taking place within you; the seeds of illumination are ripening."

Several nights later Thondö had another vivid dream, which reminded him of his master. A monk standing high above the temple roof handed him a golden vajra that was connected to the gleaming spire of the stupa atop Swayambu hill by a long, rainbow-colored string. When he told Sabchu Rinpoche, the teacher explained, "Now what I have taught you is blossoming; wisdom has been transmitted into your hands. You will realize the ultimate truth of Mahamudra when I am no longer here."

Lama Thondö wondered what his master meant. Not too long afterward, Sabchu passed away. And his aged disciple began to understand.

During the year following Sabchu Rinpoche's demise, the local people held a great prayer festival at Sabchu's monastery in order to pray and to recite millions of mantras. Deep in prayer one morning, Lama Thondö suddenly realized innate Buddha-mind, and was free. "Why didn't I see it before?" he exclaimed. "It is right before my eyes!"

Everything seemed different. While the sun rose over the snow peaks, he drank tea. Since then, no matter what activity he is engaged in, nothing affects his inner state of illumination.

Lama Thondö never again sought truth. Enlightenment is his.

A Rude Awakening

Sudden awakening is an enlightenment phenomenon not unknown in the tantric teachings of the swift path, the Vajrayana, as well as in Zen Buddhism. An authentic enlightened master can strike a ripe disciple's essential nature just as an expert diamond cutter can tap with a chisel on the precise flaw of a multi-faceted gem, allowing everything to be suddenly, almost inexplicably, revealed. Often masters act in amazing ways to shock disciples beyond their everyday thoughts and awaken them to a deeper inner reality. Treasure finders (tertons) are mystics whose spiritual visions are revelations of tantric teachings hidden centuries earlier.

RECOGNIZED AS THE INCARNATION OF the nineteenth-century treasure finder Chögyur Lingpa, Neten Chöling Rinpoche escaped from Tibet in 1959. He lived his last years in Himachal Pradesh in northern India, where he passed away after founding the Chöling Monastery in Bir.

When he was young, Neten Chöling was a precocious student, like many young incarnate lamas (*tulkus*). He became exceedingly proud of his learning and intelligence. At that time he was studying and practicing under the direct guidance of one of the greatest lamas in eastern Tibet, Jamyang Khyentse Rinpoche, also called Chökyi Lodro.

Full of youthful pride, Neten Chöling decided to go to the capital city of Lhasa, many days' journey by horse, in order to debate with the learned Gelugpa geshés (doctors of divinity of the one of the four main sects of Tibetan Buddhism) and dialecticians. He would show them a thing or two!

He began making preparations for his departure on the long journey. His master, Jamyang Khyentse, when formally asked for the permission and blessing his disciple needed in order to depart, told the young Chöling, "It is fine to go, but just wait a little while."

A few days later, Jamyang Khyentse bestowed an important Vajrayana empowerment. Chöling Tulku happened to be suffering from severe stomach cramps that day. When the distinguished, white-haired, Khyentse Rinpoche came walking with his customary dignity along the row of important lamas and incarnates, he placed the sacred golden initiation vase directly upon the young Chöling's head in blessing. . . . Then, to everyone's amazement, he kicked Neten Chöling in the guts.

Chöling had so much gas in his terribly upset stomach that he suddenly gave forth a magnificent, loud fart—hardly the thing to do in a temple, much less in such spiritual company. How overcome by shame and embarrassment young Chöling was!

Khyentse Rinpoche pointed his right forefinger at the red-faced young tulku and shouted, "That's it!"

Because the boy's mind was, for that instant, totally stripped of conceptual fabrications, Neten Chöling suddenly awoke from a deluded, dreamlike, dualistic existence and recognized the fundamental nature of being.

Chöling Rinpoche himself later recounted this tale, remarking that from then on he never lost that profound realization. Nor did he ever make the trip to the public debates in Lhasa; he no longer needed to prove anything to anyone.

Patrul Rinpoche's Woman

ONCE PATRUL RINPOCHE WAS MEANDERING on the vast plateau of Golok in eastern Tibet north of Dzachuka. He met a miserable woman accompanied by her three children, whose father had recently been killed by a gargantuan red bear. The poor widow was wailing and tearing her hair.

Patrul asked where she was going. To the shabby mendicant before her, she poured forth the woeful tale, concluding, "I must reach Dzachuka and beg for food for my children. There will be a great Dharma gathering there. Alms will certainly be plentiful."

"Ka-ho! That's quite a long way," said Patrul kindly. "Don't go on your own; I am also going there. I shall help you; let's travel together."

For many days, they walked. At night they slept under the blazing, star-filled sky. Patrul would take one or two of the children in the folds of his old sheepskin coat, while the woman similarly sheltered the others. During the day, Patrul carried one child on his back, while the woman carried the smallest; the oldest walked alongside. Each day at dawn and dusk they would prepare tea over their campfire.

Fellow travelers along the way thought they were merely beggars. Nobody—least of all the bereaved widow—could have guessed who the nomad toting a child on his back actually was. When the widow begged in hamlets along the way, Patrul would do the same, gathering enough roasted barley flour, butter, yogurt, and yak cheese to survive.

Eventually they reached Dzachuka. The widow went off alone to beg; Patrul did the same.

Later, Patrul seemed disgruntled. The widow inquired the reason for his uncharacteristic demeanor. "It's nothing. I had something to do, but gossip here makes it difficult."

"What sort of work could you have here?" the surprised woman asked.

Patrul replied simply, "Never mind. Let's go."

The little family soon reached the outskirts of a monastery on the side of a hill. Patrul suddenly halted, turned toward the woman, and told her, "I must go in; you may come, too, after a few days. I shall make a little pilgrimage to the monastery and wait for you there."

This was not at all what the widow had in mind. By this time she had become quite attached to the air of gentle force and carefree ease that habitually surrounded her newfound companion and to the inexplicable peace and sense of well-being that had replaced her grief since picking up Patrul along the road.

She complained, "Don't speak such nonsense! Let's stick together. Until now you've been so kind—don't just abandon us. We could get married, or at least I could stay with you, to benefit from your protection. I don't know why, but I feel very good with you."

The master, however, had already arrived at a decision. "This won't do. Until now I helped you as well as I could, but people here are gossips. We can't continue on together. Come in a few days, and you'll find me in this monastery." Then Patrul walked with a determined stride up the hill. The woman and children stayed below, begging for food.

The next day the entire valley was full of the glad tidings: "The enlightened master Patrul Rinpoche has arrived—he will be teaching on the *Bodhicharya-avatara!*" All the faithful folk hurried up to the monastery, leading yaks loaded with tents and provisions for a lengthy stay, in order to receive the sublime teachings.

Hearing this news and observing the general commotion, the widow felt joyful. She thought, "Such a famous lama has come; this is a truly fortunate opportunity to make an auspicious offering in the name of my late husband." Immediately she hurried up to the monastery with her three young children in tow and offerings in hand from her begging.

When he arrived, Patrul Rinpoche had instructed the monks and lamas, "Keep aside all the foodstuffs offered to me; I have a guest coming soon and will need them." Patrul was renowned for never accepting offerings or accumulating possessions and wealth of any kind, so the monks were surprised, but they had no choice other than to comply with his command.

The widow arrived and found a seat at the edge of the large crowd, far from the grand lama's throne. She listened, not recognizing the eloquent Patrul from such a distance. Finally, when the day's discourse was complete and the final prayers of blessing and dedicating the merit had been intoned, the woman approached the throne in order to receive the lama's personal blessing. There she was overwhelmed to discover her erstwhile traveling companion smiling benevolently down upon her.

The amazed widow reverently requested the master's forgiveness. "Please deign to forgive me for not having recognized you, for making you carry my children, proposing marriage, and the rest!" she cried.

Patrul Rinpoche laughed and told her not to worry. Then he turned to his attendants and said, "Here is my guest. She helped me get here. Give her all the butter, cheese, and other provisions that we set aside. See that she has whatever her family requires."

An Indian Pandit in Tibet

Smriti Jnana was a tenth-century Indian teacher and translator. In his later years he sojourned in Tibet, greatly facilitating the spread of the Buddhist teachings in that wild land.

THE ENLIGHTENED PANDIT SMRITI JNANA knew through his prescient powers that his late mother had been reborn as a frog imprisoned in a stone in the hearth of a household in Tibet. Therefore, at an advanced age and accompanied by an interpreter, he set off on the arduous route across the mountains from India to Tibet in order to liberate and guide her on to higher rebirths and the perfect freedom of enlightenment.

As soon as he crossed the border between the two Buddhist countries, however, his interpreter died. Unfortunately for the people of Tibet, the sagacious scholar could not instruct them without an interpreter. Nevertheless, he picked up a few words of Tibetan along the way, while guided by divine knowledge in his search for his mother's wretched rebirth.

When he eventually found the house, which was owned by an old woman, the anonymous Indian took work in the household as a servant. No one knew that he was one of the most erudite masters of holy India. The lady saddled him with the most strenuous chores. She even sat on him, in lieu of a cushion, when milking the cows.

Meanwhile, the saintly master was praying for his mother, burning offertory lamps and placing flowers near the hearth and on the household altar, and engaging himself in virtue in order to help further his mother and all beings similarly entrapped in the net of karma. He found that innumerable tiny insects were also living in the stones of that hearth, and he resolved—with all the altruistic power of his bodhisattva vow—to emancipate them. Eventually he succeeded in transferring their consciousnesses, along with that of his mother, to the celestial realms.

One day the clairvoyant Indian pandit, in faltering broken Tibetan, told his aged mistress, "Tomorrow we must leave this house; the mountainside above us is going to collapse." He also informed the neighbors.

The old lady had already sensed that her strange servant was no ordinary mendicant. Taking her cow in tow, she left the house along with Smriti Jnana. The other people thought, "How could that great mountain collapse? That illiterate stranger is talking nonsense! He's probably crazy, anyway; he can't even talk Tibetan, the mother tongue of Buddhism. . . . What does he know?"

On the following day, as predicted, the entire mountainside crashed down, burying the whole village. The breach in that mountain can still be seen clearly near Denkok in Kham.

Smriti Jnana, having completed his mission on behalf of his late mother, later visited the famous Tara temple called Drolma Lhakang in Denkok. As he was standing at the door, he heard a Tibetan translator, who had been to India, teaching Buddhist psychology from the Abhidharma. Because the translator was not learned, his teachings were not entirely accurate, either in style or in substance.

In response, the anonymous pandit wrote in immaculate Sanskrit characters on the door of the temple:

Instead of looking at the moon,
fools stare at its reflection in the water;
not finding the true sage,
fools follow the ignorant.

Rather than following the teacher,
follow the teachings.
Do not rely on the letter of the law,
but on its meaning.

Do not rely on the expedient meaning,
but the definite meaning.

Then he departed.

When he had completed his teaching, the translator circumambulated the
temple. Coming around to the door, he noticed the inscription written by the
pandit and instantly realized that these meaningful words had been written by
a learned scholar. He asked all present if they knew who was responsible for
writing them on the door. Someone said they had seen a beggar loitering there,
only minutes before.

In pursuit, the Tibetan teacher eventually caught up with Smriti Jnana on
a small pass above Denkok, where the pandit was leaning on a rock in order to
rest. The translator, suddenly realizing who the famous scholar before him
actually was, offered homage and obeisance. Prostrating himself again and
again in the dust at the Indian's feet, he begged forgiveness for not having
recognized him sooner and offered his humble services as an interpreter. Thus
it came to pass that the great Indian pandit taught for several years in Kham,
benefiting multitudes, before passing away near Denkok.

Smriti Jnana told his disciples not to enshrine his remains in a reliquary
stupa but to bury him underground, facing downward—an unprecedented request—in order to control the *nagas,* the serpentlike creatures who are believed
to be responsible for leprosy. "If you do as I ask," he said, "such afflictions will
never affect this area."

The faithful disciples considered it unseemly and extremely disrespectful to
bury their beloved teacher facing downward; instead, they laid his body on its
side and erected above his grave a large stupa.

Because they disregarded his explicit instructions, Denkok was not immune
when leprosy later afflicted the region.

The ancient stupa was destroyed recently, but the remains of Smriti Jnana's
body were overlooked by the vandals and are still present in that place.

Make Your Own Offerings

Patrul Rinpoche's teacher was the illustrious yogi, the outrageous Dzogchen master Doe Khyentse.

Tormas are cone-shaped cakes made of roasted barley flour and used in various offertory rites. These red and white cakes symbolize the inseparable unity of skillful means and wisdom, bliss and emptiness. To offer and then scatter tormas signifies the dispersion of the illusion of ego.

ONE DAY DZA PATRUL, WANDERING anonymously disguised as a beggar, came to visit his master Doe Khyentse. He happened upon a lama making tormas in the kitchen of the master's camp.

When Patrul Rinpoche asked the lama if he could see Doe Khyentse, the lama, looking askance at the ragged vagabond before him, said, "Oh, sure, I will make an appointment for you, don't worry. In the meantime, would you mind helping me with these tormas?" Then the lama went off, chuckling to himself, while Patrul crafted the cakes for him.

Finding no butter for painting the white torma but sufficient red root dye for red ones, the immensely erudite Patrul painted one torma red that—by its shape—anyone could tell should have been painted white. Even its name, *kartor*, meaning white torma, demanded that it be white. . . . But now it was red.

When the lama eventually returned, he was pleased to see that the beggar had done all his work for him . . . until he noticed that one kartor was painted red instead of white.

"What kind of stupidity is this?" shouted the lama.

Patrul Rinpoche gently replied, "Could you tell me, kind sir, the ritual reason it cannot be red and must unfailingly be white?"

"What!" exploded the lama, rolling his bloodshot eyes skyward in exasperation. "Not only does this filthy tramp make such stupid mistakes but he has the temerity to question me!" Then he proceeded to hit the humble mendicant standing before him and throw him out.

"You can forget about meeting Doe Khyentse as long as I'm around!" shouted the lama at the retreating figure of Patrul Rinpoche, who disappeared into the forest.

That night Doe Khyentse Rinpoche inquired as to whether anyone had come to visit him during the day, since—due to a premonition he had received in a dream—he had been expecting to see his unique protégé, his spiritual son

Patrul Rinpoche. His followers informed him that no one had come all day long.

However, when the clairvoyant master insisted that someone *must* have come, the lama who had been making tormas in the kitchen finally spoke up, telling Doe Khyentse that one beggar had in fact come to the kitchen seeking alms in return for work but that he had been turned out when he made the mistake of painting a white torma red.

"That was Dza Patrul, you fool!" thundered Doe Khyentse, who was known for his wrath as well as for his wisdom and compassion. "Go and get him immediately. I don't want to see any of you until I see him!"

The servants had to find the beggar and persuade him to return, at Doe Khyentse's explicit invitation.

When Patrul finally came into his master's presence on the following morning, Doe Khyentse made him sit on the teaching throne and reverently requested him to elucidate the classic text called "The Bodhisattva's Way of Life" (Bodhicharya-avatara) by Shantideva, for which he was renowned as a commentator.

Before a large assembly, Patrul Rinpoche expounded the classic, explaining the unique Bodhichitta (the altruistic aspiration of enlightenment) along with all its ways and means. Then he said, while his embarrassed torma painting companion hid his scarlet face beneath his red monastic robe, "And although everyone today mouths splendid platitudes about the altruistic enlightenment mind, there are still some among us who don't even know the meaning of the ritual tormas they are so proudly painting, yet they *do* know how to beat those who humbly question them."

Doe Khyentse laughed; through his clairvoyance, he knew perfectly well what had transpired in the kitchen the previous day. He said aloud, "Wonderful! That's a bit of Shantideva I never heard before."

A Basket Weaver

Buddhist monks, or bhikkhus, *often take ordination vows for life. To give up one's monastic vocation can sometimes be problematic, although a certain latitude in the interpretation of the vows exists within the various Buddhist traditions.*

Amitabha, the Buddha of Infinite Light, resides in the western Buddhafield called Dewachen (Great Bliss). Into this paradise the faithful are reborn in order to progress more swiftly on the path to perfect enlightenment.

IN ANCIENT INDIA, A FEW hundred years after the lifetime of the historical Buddha, there was an honest and upstanding monk who daily begged for alms in a village not far from his thatched hut in the forest. It so happened that a young local woman was struck by his good looks, upright bearing, and the peace that seemed to emanate from him, and she unwittingly fell in love.

Gradually this became clear to the monk, who was compelled to gently rebuff her tentative advances. As time passed, however, the situation did not improve, and the girl became increasingly passionate, to the point where she could scarcely control her emotions. The more unreachable the object of her longing seemed to be, the more desire she felt; whatever advice was offered by her friends, relatives, or the village elders, and no matter how kindly and sympathetically the monk and his brethren discussed the entire matter with her, no one could help her to mitigate the intensity of her desperate, unrequited passion.

Crying constantly, the poor young woman eventually became totally distraught and decided to commit suicide.

The humble bhikkhu was apprised of the situation. Faced with such an impasse, he found it impossible simply to move elsewhere and abandon the woman to her unhappy fate. In order to fulfill his altruistic bodhisattva vow, the righteous monk finally consented to the formal betrothal proposed by her despairing parents. Thus the marriage was arranged and eventually came to pass.

"If something is worth doing, it is worth doing impeccably," the bhikkhu thought to himself.

He became a model husband, attentive in every way, and his wife loved him dearly. The couple took up the basket-making craft of their ancestors, and eventually their children labored alongside them. The former monk's lips seemed constantly to be moving in silent prayer as he went about his daily tasks, although there was otherwise little or no outward sign of his previous vocation. His integrity, however, did not go long unnoticed.

Soon the humble business prospered, as it became widely recognized in the region that inordinate good luck and prosperity seemed to descend upon the possessor of the former bhikkhu's handwoven baskets.

Thus decades passed, as they will; the family grew; the community flourished in virtue and well-being, both material and spiritual. The righteous basket weaver, now bent with years, was often sought for advice and benediction. And his children followed in his footsteps, as would their children, and theirs as well. . . .

Time ultimately took its toll, and the loving old couple finally followed one another into the other world, as we all must. When they were each miraculously reborn in the heart of a lotus flower in the delightful western paradise of Dewachen, the sovereign Amitabha predicted their eventual enlightenment.

Moreover, Amitabha Buddha said, "Basket Master, through your selfless relinquishment of your own chosen monastic life-style in order to save a life, you truly demonstrated the meaning of renunciation, altruism, and spirituality—thus infinitely shortening the journey to Nirvana for yourself and for all those fortunate enough to be karmically connected with you."

Beyond Poison

A NON-BUDDHIST TEACHER NAMED KHENPO was jealous of Lord Buddha's increasing popularity. Many of Khenpo's former students and disciples were inexplicably joining the Buddhist order. One day he decided to take revenge.

Khenpo had a follower named Pelbay whose wife had already become a firm believer in Gautama Buddha; now Pelbay also seemed in danger of converting. Pelbay's wife wished to invite the Buddha and his monks to her house for lunch and other offerings. Khenpo pointed out the foolishness of her ignorant ways, but to no avail. The pure-minded woman's resolve remained firm.

In the face of such recalcitrance, the wily Khenpo was undaunted. He stated that if she continued to persist in her folly, Pelbay would satisfy her wishes. Khenpo remarked that if the new teacher, the Buddha Sakyamuni, actually possessed the great powers of omniscience, wisdom, and compassion with which he was credited, he ought to be able to foresee any misfortune that might befall himself and his followers. However, if he could not live up to his reputation, wouldn't it be unwise for Pelbay's wife merely to follow the herd in adopting new doctrines and customs? . . . And this is what Khenpo suggested.

Pelbay would have a large pit, like a tiger trap, dug out from the floor just past the threshold of his house, which would be filled with glowing coals and cleverly covered over just before the Buddha and his followers came for the midday meal. If, in fact, Buddha's omniscience was authentic, he would naturally be forewarned and would not dare to cross the threshold. But if the new teacher was an impostor, he would step on the false floor, plunge into the fire pit, and be consumed.

Moreover, the ignominious Khenpo instructed Pelbay to poison the food prepared for the feast offering, as yet another test in case the Buddha happened to enter the house without mishap. If the Buddha was actually omniscient, would he not decline to partake of the poisoned repast and instruct his followers to do likewise?

Foolish Pelbay, for his part, agreed to the plan. What did he know of ecclesiastical matters? Who was he to question such an exalted personage as his own mentor, the Khenpo?

Pelbay's wife was aghast when presented with the idea, although she had confidence in the Buddha's oft-attested omniscience. But what if one of the other, lesser monks preceded their lord and master and fell prey to such an ignoble fate? And besides, what was the point of such turpitude? . . . Thus she reasoned, amazed at the perfidy of the Khenpo and the extent of his influence over her husband.

However, when she objected to the plot—being a woman, whose opinions unfortunately were worth little in that time and place—her husband Pelbay locked her in a storeroom so she could not interfere with the proceedings. He sent a message offering lunch to Lord Buddha and his saffron-robed followers.

The Buddha accepted the invitation, foreseeing all that would occur. Meanwhile, the Khenpo remained discreetly behind the scenes in a fine room in Pelbay's large house.

Two mornings later, Lord Buddha informed his monks that they were all invited to the layman Pelbay's house for lunch and that under absolutely no circumstances whatsoever was any of them to cross the threshold and enter before he himself did. Soon afterward, the group set out.

When the ordained assembly arrived at Pelbay's house, the gently smiling Buddha entered, unperturbed. Rather than the flimsy false floor collapsing as planned, the entire floor of the spacious front room seemed to become, as if by magic, a lovely fresh lake, full of immaculate lotus blossoms, water lilies, swans, geese, and ducks. Moreover, with each step the Buddha took, a radiant white lotus flower seemed to spring up instantaneously beneath his feet.

All present were totally amazed at this marvelous sight, the dumbfounded Pelbay most of all. He stood awestruck while Lord Buddha smiled benignly upon him.

The humiliated householder understood for the first time how foolish he had been. Then he exposed his ignominy.

The Omniscient One patiently listened to Pelbay's heartbroken confession and then replied:

"The Enlightened One is beyond duality;
How can he be subject to benefit and harm?
The Awakened One is beyond the raging fires
of the three poisons (greed, hatred, and delusion);
How can ordinary flames affect him?"

Poor, benighted Pelbay now knew with certainty that the Buddha was both compassionate and generous as well as omniscient, and that he was not just a mere wonder worker like so many wandering holy men and yogi adepts. He confessed that the food offerings were poisoned as well, as a further trial. Then he offered to have an entirely new meal cooked on the spot for Lord Buddha and his brotherhood.

Buddha again spoke in verse:

"The Enlightened One is totally free,
liberated from good and bad;
He is not subject to benefit and harm.
The Awakened One has totally transcended the noxious
influence of the three poisons,
greed, hatred, and delusion;
How can mere ordinary poison affect him?"

Still, Pelbay was filled with trepidation when Lord Buddha and his monks sat down to receive the feast offering, but the sumptuous poisoned food was imbibed like divine nectar by the entire assembly. Meanwhile, having witnessed this unexpected chain of events, the vanquished and humiliated Khenpo escaped through a rear door, never to be seen in that household or its precincts again.

Thus the faith of the devoted wife was vindicated, truth was triumphant, evil was subdued, the faithful converted, and Pelbay joined his neighbors in becoming faithful lay followers of the tolerant, non-violent creed of the Enlightened One.

A Thief Takes Refuge Under a Bridge

A LAMA IN EASTERN TIBET lived beside the Dzachu River. He received many offerings from the faithful, but having renounced all worldly concerns, he just left them scattered wherever he happened to be.

One day a thief came to steal the ritual objects from his altar, but the lama intuitively sensed evil forces. Vigilant, he caught the thief red-handed. Aware of the thief's negative karma, he decided to dispel the darkness gripping him.

Holding the thief by the neck, the lama hit him on the head with a prayer book, repeating the refuge prayer, "I take refuge in the Buddha, the Dharma, and the Sangha; I take refuge in the Triple Gem." Without another word, he let the thief go. "I have relinquished all possessions; may you relinquish unwholesome activities," the lama chanted after the retreating figure.

The thief huddled under a bridge that night, nursing his wounded pride. Waking after midnight from a troubled sleep, he saw the fearsome forms of evil forces all about him.

He was terrified. Suddenly into his head leapt the refuge prayer that the lama had beaten into him earlier that day, and the thief unconsciously repeated to himself, "I take refuge in the Buddha, Dharma, and Sangha; I take refuge in the Triple Gem," again and again. While doing so, he could actually see the ghosts and demons fleeing before the power of the prayer. As a result, the thief said the refuge prayer constantly and became a disciple of that lama by the Dzachu River.

As everyone knows, taking refuge is the door to the Dharma, the gateway to the path. The refuge prayer, coupled with confidence in the Triple Gem, inevitably pacifies negative influences, purifies unwholesomeness, and brings purity of heart and mind. Turning away from illusion, seeking the ineffable peace of Nirvana, the thief eventually became a teacher himself and led others to freedom and enlightenment.

Cow Karma

IN KASHMIR LONG AGO LIVED a monk named Mirathi, an exemplary up-holder of the Buddhist precepts. Through the power of meditative concentra-tion he had developed miraculous powers. His numerous disciples made firsthand reports of their teacher flying in the air, reading their minds, describ-ing past lives, and accurately foretelling future events.

The great monk Mirathi was a vegetarian. Moreover, in strict adherence to Buddhist tradition, he did not eat after midday. One day he happened to be in his forest abode, dyeing his old ocher monk's robe in a large pot set over an outdoor fire pit, when a band of angry men came upon him looking for a baby cow that had recently been lost. Opening the pot and finding it full of motley bits and pieces of blood-colored hue, they shouted accusations at the silent monk, accusing him of stealing and slaughtering their cow. Then they led him away.

A kangaroo court that was convened in the nearby village immediately sentenced the silent monk to be placed in chains in a dungeonlike hole in the ground, where he remained for several days. He said nothing to disprove the claims made against him and made no attempt to secure his release. His disci-ples beseeched him to rectify the matter, but Mirathi himself said nothing.

After several days, the villagers found the missing cow. Realizing their mis-take, they petitioned the local chief to free the monk, but the chieftain was distracted by other important affairs and neglected the case for months and months. Meanwhile, Mirathi lingered in his earthen pit.

Finally, several of the foremost disciples of the imprisoned monk sought a personal audience with the local king. He was astonished at their tale, fearing that a grave injustice had been done and that immense bad karma would ensue for the entire kingdom as well as for the irresponsible villagers. Therefore, he quickly ordered the monk freed and had him brought forth in order to make amends. It was not every day that a distinguished cleric was condemned under false charges to spend six months in a filthy hole!

When the dignified old monk appeared before the king, the king begged his forgiveness and asked what could be done to right the terrible wrong that had befallen Mirathi through his oversight, promising to punish the parties directly responsible for Mirathi's unjust incarceration. Mirathi replied, "Esteemed king, please punish no one. It was my turn to suffer, and I endured it willingly. No one suffers anything except at the hands of the karma that his or her own actions have ineluctably produced."

The king was astonished. "Why, venerable sir, what have you done?"

Mirathi explained that in a remote past life he had been a thief who had stolen a baby cow from some villagers. While escaping from hot pursuit, he had abandoned his stolen cow near an arhat (liberated sage) who was meditating in the forest, and it came about that the enlightened monk was punished for the crime by being chained for six days in a hole.

Mirathi continued, with downcast eyes, "O gracious and just king, as a result of that negative karmic action, I have endured lifetime after lifetime of misery in the lower realms of existence. Now, at last, my karma has been fully exhausted, and my sin expiated. Therefore I have only gratitude and respect for you and your subjects."

Bowing low, Mirathi went quietly back to the forest to pursue his spiritual practices in peace.

Two Evil Spirits

TWO EVIL BRAHMINS NAMED PANA and Nava lived in Magadha a few centuries after Lord Buddha's parinirvana (final enlightenment). The pair killed animals for pleasure and meat, waylaid travelers, robbed houses, and terrorized the populace. Eventually the odious duo were captured by the police of King Ajatasatru, brought to trial, and sentenced to imprisonment.

Pana and Nava were unrepentant. From prison, using their ill-gotten wealth, they arranged to have many midday meals anonymously offered to the noble sangha members and assembled arhats of Ajatasatru's kingdom, for the purpose of accumulating merit and good fortune. They requested that the monks make this prayer for them: "By virtue of this act of piety, may all the wishes of the generous anonymous donors be fulfilled."

Meanwhile, they themselves prayed, "By virtue of these offerings, in conjunction with the powerful prayers of the holy sangha, may we be reborn as *yakshas* (evil spirits) in order to wreak vengeance by plundering the kingdom of Magadha in the future."

The prayers were fulfilled, as prayers often are. The misguided brigands soon died in prison during an epidemic and were subsequently reborn as yakshas, in accordance with their misguided aspirations. They spread a dreadful epidemic throughout Magadha, causing many people and cattle to die and bringing despair throughout the kingdom. Meanwhile, the two evil spirits flitted about under the cover of darkness, feasting on flesh and blood.

A wise old astrologer, through skillful calculations, ascertained the cause of the plague. He invited the third Buddhist patriarch, the enlightened Sanavasika, to come to the city of Sravasti to remedy the situation by subjugating (through spiritual means) the two yakshas.

Arhat Sanavasika soon appeared. He took as his abode the very cave that the yakshas themselves inhabited. When the two devilish spirits returned from pillaging the countryside, they sensed the impeccable arhat's presence before entering the cave. They stormed the cave with their supernatural powers, bringing the stone ceiling crashing down upon the elderly arhat's silver-gray head. Sanavasika, however, sat unperturbed while the great boulders seemed to arrange themselves magically around him, forming a small crypt in the midst of which he sat untouched.

Three times the yakshas unleashed their fury; thrice the immaculate arhat remained unmoved, as if comfortably ensconced in his niche.

Then the demons brought firewood from the surrounding jungle and set the cave ablaze. Sanavasika, however, magically filled the entire expanse of the sky with flames, until the maleficent spirits were terrified and overawed. Engulfed by flames, they surrendered, confessing their misdeeds before the Buddhist elder.

As the pair did penance, the flames surrounding them gradually dissolved. Sanavasika taught the pair the sublime Dharma, and they were shamed into perfect repentance. Filled with remorse, faith, and devotion for their newfound master, they vowed to give up their evil ways and embrace the compassionate Buddha's teachings. Eventually the two purified their evil, flourished in virtue, and were reborn in the higher realms.

Nagarjuna's Goddess

The immortal philosopher, author, and sage Nagarjuna lived in the centuries immediately after the birth and death of Jesus of Nazareth. He developed and spread the Middle Way philosophy, called Madhyamika, the sovereign teaching of emptiness.

Nagarjuna mystically retrieved the wisdom scriptures called the Prajna Paramita Sutra from the semidivine, half-bestial, serpent-shaped nagas under whose care the Buddha himself had placed them, beneath the ocean, long before. Through his prodigious psychic powers and alchemical exploits, Nagarjuna maintained five hundred Buddhist pandits at Nalanda University in northern India. Once, for example, the Serpent Master Nagarjuna painted an image of a cow that then miraculously provided milk products for the entire community.

ONCE NAGARJUNA BROUGHT UNDER HIS power the goddess Chandika. She offered to convey him to heavenly bliss in a celestial palace beyond the azure sky, but sagacious Nagarjuna remained above temptation. He simply told the goddess that he had invoked her for the sole purpose of supporting the Buddhist sangha, or community, for as long as the Dharma would exist in this world. Moreover, he added, he had absolutely no use for illusory delights, having realized perfect fulfillment through understanding the profound meaning of emptiness through the Middle Path.

The goddess took up her abode in the western sector of Nalanda, in the guise of a noblewoman. The peerless pandit Nagarjuna nailed an immense, daggershaped wooden peg atop the towering stone wall surrounding the nearby Manjusri temple, thus mystically binding Chandika to his service and the service of wisdom. He ordered her to provide for the upkeep and livelihood of the ordained community "as long as this magic dagger is not reduced to dust."

Chandika did as she was told for twelve years, and the erudite community of holy ones flourished. Then an impure monk, who was working as a steward, began to make unwholesome propositions to the attractive lady, although Chandika gave no response or encouragement of any kind. As a goddess in human form, the fleeting pleasures of the senses left her unmoved, for she had enjoyed her share of divine transports.

The importunate monk continued to pursue her with lewd suggestions. Finally Chandika replied, "We shall be united when that huge peg atop the wall around Manju's temple is reduced to dust."

After much consideration, the foolish steward one day contrived, with the help of mustard oil from the larder, to set the great wooden peg ablaze. When that symbolic rivet—on which she was as if impaled—was reduced to ashes, the goddess Chandika instantly disappeared, along with much of the sangha's subsistence.

The steward was held responsible for the absent stores and had to beg daily in order to provide the monks with their meals. Only the Serpent Master Nagarjuna knew exactly what had transpired. He compounded tiny, elixirlike pills from mineral substances, which he and his followers used for purifying fasts and transformational rites. These helped them transcend the need for mortal food.

Through the arcane means of spiritual alchemy, the enlightened teacher Nagarjuna lived for almost as many years as Methuselah. Indomitable in epistemological debate, Madhyamika masters have continued to teach and edify the world until now.

Crocodile Treasure

ONCE AT THE FULL MOON, Chögyur Lingpa arrived in the village of Gawa, where he had been invited to stay for five days. Entering the temple there, he was ceremoniously served tea.

Suddenly the Treasure Master leapt off the teacher's throne and raced out, followed by his disciple Garmé Khenpo.

The lamas' horses had been tied near the door and were still saddled. Chögyur Lingpa jumped on his horse. Startled, the creature began to run, even though it was still tied by a long lead. Garmé Khenpo quickly cut the rope with the knife that all Khampas (people from eastern Tibet, Kham) carry in their belts. Who was he to question a siddha like Chögyur Lingpa?

The horse and rider raced off, as if pursued. They quickly arrived at the banks of a river in spate. All of Chögyur Lingpa's attendants followed; the villagers also went to see what the master was up to. Chögyur Lingpa rode straight into the river and disappeared. After five minutes he emerged on the other side, much to everyone's relief.

In the temple, drinking tea, Chögyur Lingpa had experienced a vision of the Tibetan queen Yeshé Tsogyal. She said that an enormous monster in the river was guarding a Dharma treasure, a terma, that she herself had hidden, at Padma Sambhava's bidding, long ago.

According to the Lotus-Born Guru's prophecy, the great crocodile would close its mouth at noon on that very full-moon day; if he did, no one would be able to recover that important terma for another sixty years. The terma contained teachings on wrathful deity practices suitable for the turbulent times in which Chögyur Lingpa lived; he was the one teacher who could practice and propagate those teachings.

When Chögyur Lingpa emerged from the raging river, he had a yellow parchment scroll in his hand, covered with the shimmering mystic script of the dakinis. He had plucked it from between the crocodile's teeth just before midday.

That river monster was an embodiment of the Dharma protector who had sworn to guard Padma Sambhava's terma centuries ago. The Treasure Master deciphered the terma and taught it widely, liberating and freeing multitudes.

A Monk's Dream

VAJRIPUTRA WAS THE SON OF King Udayi and Queen Vajra Devi of the kingdom of Kosambi in northern India. As a youth he became disillusioned with worldly affairs and was fortunate to meet the august arhat Katyayana.

This erudite and enlightened monk educated and ultimately ordained the world-weary prince who, with his parents' consent, had come under his care. Then the pair left Kosambi—for it is said, "To leave one's family and homeland is to accomplish half the Dharma."

One bright morning the teenage prince-turned-monk was making his daily round for alms when he chanced to enter the courtyard of King Prachanda's palace. There several young queens—smitten by the young bhikkhu's good looks and erect, noble bearing—invited him to take a seat in their midst. Thereupon they proceeded to feed and entertain him in a royal manner, until Vajriputra finally began to talk with them about the compassionate Buddha's path to spiritual fulfillment and peace.

When the king heard what was going on, he immediately came to observe the spectacle. None of his queens noticed him standing under the great stone archway leading into the courtyard where they sat, which made him furious. "Now even a young upstart like this yellow-robed skinhead can replace me in their fickle affections!" he exclaimed to the trusted old minister who was ever at his side.

"A monk who surrounds himself with women is impure!" shouted the king. "Bind and seize him," he ordered, "and give him twenty lashes." His orders were duly accomplished.

After being soundly thrashed and bodily thrown out of the palace, Vajriputra was filled with self-righteous rage. He resolved to return to his native land, raise an army, and come back to destroy King Prachanda.

Then he returned to his master, the arhat Katyayana, recounted his sad tale, and tried to give back his vows of ordination along with his yellow monastic robes. Katyayana, however, suggested that he apply patience and forbearance to the one who wronged him instead of forsaking his altruistic vows and retaliating in kind.

"Did not Lord Buddha say again and again, 'Pleasure and pain, loss and gain, happiness and suffering, fame and shame: accept all equally, without attachment or aversion. . . . This is the path beyond delusion'?"

The hot-blooded youth would not listen. He insisted upon relinquishing his vows of non-violence and loving-kindness and remained intent upon his revenge. Therefore Katyayana pointed out to the boy that darkness was descending, and since the way through the jungle was dangerous he had better rest for the night before setting out for his homeland; then he could leave in the morning, with his benediction. Vajriputra agreed.

Soon after, as the exhausted, black-and-blue boy—still wrapped in his bloodstained yellow robes—slept, the kindly old arhat used his mental powers to send an instructive dream to him. In his sleep, Vajriputra saw himself return home, become king after his father's demise, raise an army, and then set out to destroy King Prachanda and raze his palace to dust.

However, much to Vajriputra's dismay, it was his enemy's army that emerged victorious, while he himself was captured, beaten, treated ignominiously in public, and led to a high black platform atop the towering palace walls to be decapitated. Just as the executioner, carrying a huge two-handed sword, was approaching the chopping block where he knelt, Vajriputra saw the arhat Katyayana humbly collecting alms in the city below and cried out, with all his heart, "O master, help me! Spare my life!"

Then Vajriputra woke up. There was his master standing in the dark bedchamber before him. Katyayana reassured the boy, saying, "Fear not, my son. It is just a dream. You are safe, alone here with me."

Vajriputra suddenly understood that all that had happened to him the previous day was equally dreamlike and unreal, and he found neither anger nor thoughts of revenge poisoning his mind. Then he gratefully bowed down to his compassionate teacher Katyayana, who had saved him from disastrous folly.

Katyayana instructed Vajriputra regarding the insubstantial, ephemeral nature of all things, and Vajriputra gained realization. He later became one of the sixteen arhats who widely disseminated the Buddhist teachings.

To this day it is said that whenever someone is plagued by vengeful and competitive thoughts, lacks a spiritual guide, and is in need of the cooling waters of forgiveness, that person should pray to the arhat Vajriputra.

Upagupta Meets the Evil One

Upagupta, the fourth patriarch (spiritual hierarch and lineage holder) of the Buddhist order, was the son of a devout and faithful Hindu incense seller. Upagupta is acclaimed for finally doing away with Mara, the incarnation of evil, whom the Buddha himself had subdued under the Bodhi Tree while attaining enlightenment. Mara, being the personification of evil, is endowed with magical powers.

Upagupta was converted by the third patriarch, Sanavasika, during a debate in the middle of the Ganges River, when both sages were crossing in opposite directions—a symbolic happenstance indeed. Upagupta took ordination after losing the debate; one week later, through intensive meditation practice, he attained arhatship, or sainthood. He became the foremost teacher in Mathura, northern India, where the Taj Mahal was built.

ONE DAY UPAGUPTA WAS TEACHING a great multitude in Mathura when Mara, the Evil One, showered rice upon the entire populace as a malediction. Many people hurriedly left the assembly in alarm; others ran to see what was happening.

The following day, Mara magically showered clothes down upon the city, and many more people abandoned the Dharma gathering in order to grab their share. And on subsequent days there were downpours of silver, gold, and the seven kinds of jewels, until at last there was almost no one left to attend Upagupta's preaching.

On the sixth day of the patriarch's discourse, Mara, along with his wife and daughters, assumed the gorgeous forms of celestial singers and dancers and formed a troupe of thirty-six heavenly musicians singing marvelous melodies as they paraded through the streets of the city. Now no one was left attending the Buddhist convocation except a few ordained elders of the order. Finally the arhat Upagupta took himself into town to see what had transpired.

The patriarch instantly understood what was occurring. The bemused multitudes swooned over the Evil One's deception, infatuated with the fabulous delights before their eyes.

Upagupta himself praised the divine troupe and hung garlands of flowers around their necks. Immediately the Evil One and his retinue were transformed into decrepit old beggars adorned in reeking rags and with mangy canine carcasses hanging from their necks. People could not bear the stench of putrefaction and turned away in disgust. Try as he might, Mara could do nothing to reestablish his command over appearances; he felt completely and utterly dejected.

Then the patriarch Upagupta accosted Mara, the Evil One, saying, "O horrific incarnation of darkness, why did you deceive my followers? Would you like to make them become like you?"

The subjugated Mara was penitent. Groveling before the powerful Buddhist master, he begged that the compassionate arhat would liberate both his family and himself from their fetters and set them once and for all on the path of righteousness and freedom.

Kindly old Upagupta smiled charitably. He agreed to liberate them on the single condition that they promise never again to harm the Buddha's followers, including all those who in future would have the good fortune to practice the Buddhist teachings. Mara and his family took that solemn oath on pain of death.

Then Mara and all his retinue were restored to their original semidivine forms. The Evil One said, "In days of yore I attacked the Compassionate One with all my magic while he meditated beneath the Bodhi Tree, yet he remained unperturbed. You, however, have violently bound us as soon as we played a tiny joke upon these people—what sort of Buddhist are you?" Thus Mara remonstrated with the patriarch Upagupta.

Implacably, Upagupta replied that he himself had only perceived the Dharmakaya, or formless absolute nature, of the Buddha but had never had the good fortune to perceive the physical form of the Buddha, the Rupakaya, as even evil Mara had been blessed to do.

Therefore, he continued, if Mara would, through his prodigious supernatural powers, show Upagupta the Buddha's own corporeal form, the Buddhist patriarch would bless and liberate Mara and all his followers from the bleak wind of negative karma that had been blowing them like dry leaves through the infernal realms of existence.

Mara instantly transformed his physical appearance into that of the Buddha Sakyamuni himself, effulgent with a rainbow radiance. Arhat Upagupta, full of reverence, bowed three times while intoning the threefold refuge prayer, "I take refuge in the Buddha, the Dharma, and the Sangha."

In the face of such profound veneration for absolute truth and the path to it, Mara was unable to maintain his own delusions and therefore lost the power of illusion. Falling unconscious, he disappeared, and his minions likewise vanished.

All the people of Mathura were filled with awe and devotion. When Upagupta preached the sublime Dharma that night, he was aglow with his recent experience of immanence, and on that very eve of the sixth day of Mara's machinations, tens of thousands of people realized the true nature of ultimate reality and were liberated from the fetters of conditioned existence.

In this way, Upagupta subdued Mara through meeting the form of Lord Buddha himself, and the Evil One was no longer able to obstruct the unerring path to freedom and omniscience trod by the Buddhist fold.

Dhitika Ends a Sacrifice

Brahmins are the priestly caste in the Hindu society of traditional India. Sakyamuni Buddha himself was born a Hindu; he studied and practiced that ancient religious system before discovering enlightenment through his meditations under the Bodhi Tree in Bodh Gaya. Later he reformed Hindu customs by instituting a caste-free Buddhist sangha.

An arhat is a highly realized sage who has purified all defilements and exhausted all accumulated karma; therefore, he or she is free from rebirth in the vicious cycle of samsara (conditioned existence). The emancipated state of the arhat has been described in this way: "Having shattered the eggshell of ignorance, full of peace and equanimity, impartial regarding great and small, desireless, passions exhausted, senses stilled, thought tamed, mind cool and fragrant as a shady sandalwood grove in the summer sun, free from birth and death, he for whom gold and donkey dung are of equal worth, never to be again ensnared by the fetters of this world."

Animal sacrifice plays a part in the traditional offerings to the gods that are prevalent in certain Hindu sects even now. White cows, sometimes called "Brahmin bulls," have been sacred in India since Vedic times, long before recorded history. The Vedas are the oldest religious scriptures known to humanity, originating from the oral tradition of the Vedic seers of ancient India, predating all extant religions.

THERE WAS A WEALTHY AND powerful Brahmin named Adarpa who slaughtered one thousand goats each day as a sacrificial offering. On one special occasion he was inspired to offer ten thousand white cows to the gods.

As the sacrifice was being prepared, the fifth Buddhist patriarch, the arhat Dhitika, suddenly appeared as if by magic before the sacrificial altar. Then no matter what the Brahmin ritualists did, they could neither kindle the sacrificial fire nor slaughter the milling cows; even their recitation of the sacred Vedas became perfectly soundless.

A wise Brahmin saw that it was Dhitika's magical powers that were preventing the priests from performing their duty. He and his colleagues stoned the arhat, but all the rocks turned into flowers that cascaded harmlessly around him.

This caused the Brahmins, who were not fools, to gain faith in the old sage who had come among them. Dhitika said to them, "O cruel sons of religion, why are you performing such evil sacrifices? What do you hope to attain? Far better would it be to make charitable offerings and perform other virtuous acts. How can offerings of warm flesh and blood please a benevolent deity? Would it delight a loving parent to receive feast offerings of his own children's flesh?

"Aren't cows considered deities in your Brahminic faith? Then how can you slaughter them, your own avowed objects of reverence and devotion? Your ancestral creed declares it impure to eat cow meat or even to touch it. Isn't it therefore a sin and an insult to offer it to your gods? Through this path, one only harms and debases oneself and others. If you wish to develop spiritually, give up such perverse and contradictory practices!"

Then the intelligent Brahmins comprehended the folly of their ways. Renouncing animal sacrifice, they became interested in investigating and adopting the non-violent creed of the compassionate Buddha, led by Adarpa himself and the head priests. Becoming students and followers of the arhat Dhitika, they led their entire community into virtue and reverence for all that lives.

Milarepa Sleeps Late

ONCE MILAREPA WAS COLLECTING ALMS in a village. He spent the night in the local monastery, sleeping on the doorstep of a monk's cell.

The monk was the monastery's bursar. As it happened, he spent the entire night lying awake in bed, thinking about how much the brethren were going to profit from his selling of the various parts of a cow that was to be slaughtered on the following day. All night long he took inventory, calculating the respective prices that each part of the beast's anatomy would bring.

By dawn, the monk had completed his calculations, except for the price of the tail. It was only then that he realized that he had gone entirely sleepless.

Jumping from his narrow bed, he said some perfunctory prayers and made offerings of lamps, incense, and water on his altar and then stepped outside. There he found the ragged, cotton-clad yogi asleep on his threshold.

The monk was indignant. "How can you call yourself a spiritual practitioner, when—without offering a single prayer or prostration—here you are, still asleep, when the horse-drawn chariot of the sun has already ascended the sky?" he said, disdainfully nudging Milarepa with one foot. "Have you no sense of responsibility to those who support you so that you may devote yourself to meditation on their behalf?"

"I don't usually sleep like this," Milarepa, the Song Master, replied. "But last night I didn't sleep at all, because I was busy thinking about selling a poor cow of mine that is about to be killed."

The nonplussed monk could barely contain his shame. He recognized that an anonymous emanation of the Buddha had come to teach him a lesson, and bowed low before the smiling Song Master.

A Lake of Gold Coins

A TIBETAN TEENAGER NAMED TASHI heard about a lake full of treasure—and possibly magical powers for the taking—upon the summit of a mountain not too far from his home. What could he do but investigate? He was moreover told that the guardian deity of the lake was intractable, more given to playing with intruders to his domain than to obsequity; but youth will have its way. Off went Tashi, with a sack on his back.

Usually the lakes in Tibet were an astonishing cerulean hue, but when Tashi approached, he saw from a distance that this particular lake seemed to shimmer yellow-gold in the distance. Needless to say, this mirage did little to allay his greed.

When the intrepid teenager reached the shore, near a high windswept mountain pass where the runoff waters from icy peaks gathered, a gargantuan woman cloaked in robes of coarse wool suddenly appeared.

Tashi may not have known much, but his tingling skin instantly informed him that this was none other than the supernatural guardian of the lake who towered over him, assuming human shape.

"What treasures do you have for me?" the intrepid boy boldly demanded.

"More for those who need and don't ask than for those who need not yet demand!" answered the chimerical, mist-girded mountain spirit.

"I have come for my share only," replied Tashi.

"Then take and be gone!" exclaimed the spectral figure, and vanished.

Tashi reached into the sparkling, icy waters, fished about beneath the surface, and brought up three glittering gold coins in his fist. "Aha!" he exulted. "The treasure is mine!" Standing suddenly, he threw his old goatskin sack into the water, along with the three coins, and went off to get his father's assistance—for two sacks are far better than one!

All the way down the mountain he went. Finding his old father, he recounted his adventure. Gathering two huge homemade carryalls, they set off for the mountain pass.

This took hours to accomplish, but finally man and boy reached their destination. Sure enough, there was the spectral woman challenging them at the invisible portal of her domain.

"What now?" she demanded. "I gave you three coins of pure gold; was that not enough?"

"My father insisted on seeing for himself where I'd found those coins," Tashi fibbed. "He feared they were stolen, so I had to bring him back. Please let him have a share, too—then we shall bother you no more."

The gigantic guardian deity swiftly drew her cloak around her with a motion like that of swirling clouds and seemed to give assent. Then she disappeared.

The boy and his father winked slyly at each other, fished around on the lake floor for a moment, and then each brought up three gold coins in his hand. Now greed glinted in their eyes.

"Aha!" exclaimed Tashi Senior.

"He-he-hee!" echoed his son. "Let's go get the rest of my brothers and sisters, a pack yak, and do this right. Then we will never have to break our backs plowing the stony earth again." Tossing their old sacks into the lake with a dismissive gesture, along with their meager haul of six coins, off they went.

By the time the two adventurers had descended the mountain and rounded up their kin, embellishing their account with each retelling—especially emphasizing their bravado in facing down the terrible mountain spirit—night had fallen on their tiny hamlet. "Why not return tomorrow?" they thought to themselves. "Tonight we can relax and celebrate our windfall!"

That is what they did, inviting the entire village to share their stock of homemade barley beer and listen to them recount their courageous coup. Everyone was given to understand that the mountain god's plunder was already tucked safely away in the family's stone storeroom.

The affair lasted far into the night. The next morning, before the village was awake, a hungover Tashi Senior and Tashi Junior quietly led a small party of close relatives up the mountain trail, leading pack animals and carrying the largest sacks they could muster. Intent upon treasure, they all had the gleam of gold glittering in their beady, bloodshot eyes. No one questioned the veracity of the tale told by the two Tashis.

Was there any terrific mountain spirit to behold at the gate to that fabled lake domain? The icy, windswept lake was completely enveloped in black fog and roiling mist. Was there any gold for the greedy adventurers?

It may have been that the moon above the fabled lake displayed a golden yellow face, like a golden coin resting upon smooth black silk—due, no doubt, to the wealth beneath the lake's surface—but "those who need not yet demand" did not find even a single bit of gold in the cold waters in which they waded, back and forth, all day long. They were so exhausted, they could hardly reach their humble home at nightfall.

Did Tashi Senior have any beer left to warm his cold bones when he trudged into his empty house late that night? The answers to these questions only the wise and the childlike can understand.

Visualizations

Tibetan Buddhists utilize various kinds of visualizations in the practice of meditation. Superior practitioners manifest what they visualize as realistically as we perceive everyday reality.

Regarding offerings, it is often said that one gets only as much as one gives; the more one can give, the more one can receive.

ONE DAY, AS A GRAND lama bestowed an initiation upon a large gathering, an old lady entered the temple. In Tibet it is customary at the end of an empowerment to present a goodwill offering as a token of gratitude; the offering is often accompanied by a white silk scarf, symbolic of inner purity.

The old woman had a kilo of fresh yak butter to offer. It was hidden beneath her cloak. She intended to offer it to the master after receiving his blessing.

Ordinarily the presiding lama would touch each disciple on the head with a sacred, nectar-filled vessel. However, because there were so many gathered before him, he simply instructed them to *visualize* the vase he was holding and imagine him placing it atop their individual heads in order to transmit the initiation.

The faithful old lady did exactly as instructed and received the initiation in its entirety. When the lengthy rite was completed, and it was time to offer her precious butter to the venerable master, she merely rose and uttered, in a stentorian voice reminiscent of the lama's, "Now simply visualize, venerable lama, that you are receiving as offering this kilo of fine butter that you see in my hand!"

Chuckling to herself, she made her way homeward, a wiser and wealthier woman, with her butter tucked safely away beneath her cloak.

Young Dodrup Chen Reads and Recites

When he was young, the present Dodrup Chen Rinpoche was famous for performing miracles, remembering his previous lives, making accurate predictions and prophecies, and reading minds. As he grew older, however, he displayed such powers less and less.

ON THE AUSPICIOUS OCCASION OF a great feast-offering day, the tiny, recently enthroned incarnate lama of the Dodrup Chen Monastery in Golok was sitting on the high throne at the head of a large monastic assembly. The four-year-old astonished everyone present by standing up on his throne and singing in a delightful, childish voice the entire seven-line prayer of invocation to Guru Rinpoche, which no one had taught him—a clear indication of his authenticity as a tulku, a realized reincarnate lama. He danced a few spontaneous steps in the majestic manner of the deities, before sitting down and smiling shyly at his followers.

All the sage old abbots and other lamas of the monastery smiled, nodding to themselves with satisfaction. There could be no doubt that their erstwhile master had returned once again to grace their fraternity with his enlightened presence. Then each filed forward, reverently prostrated before him three times in succession, and offered ivory-white silk scarves, bundles of incense, and other gifts. Finally the ceremonies came to their conclusion.

The old lamas led the diminutive fourth Dodrup Chen down from his high seat and took him on his first tour of the monastery. Three of his illustrious predecessors had directed it during the past century; now it was his.

When they came to the shadowy, forbidding, secret temple of the Dharma protectors (the ferocious guardians of the teachings), the abbots hesitated. The young boy, however, walked right in, and they had no choice but to follow.

Until this time, the recently discovered tulku had had little or no formal education. He did not read, write, or perform any of the elaborate daily rites and rituals. Nor had the boy ever been introduced to the esoteric practices that continuously took place, day and night, all year round, in the wrathful protectors' temple.

The boy, however, immediately went and sat down next to the monk who was chanting from the worn, unbound leaves of an ancient prayer book. While the old monk continued to intone his prayers of propitiation with deep, resonant rhythms, banging a drum in time with his powerful hymns and incantations, Dodrup Chen leafed through the old prayer book until he seemed to find what he wanted.

Suddenly all present were amazed to hear the tiny boy reading aloud one of the sublime Dharmapala (Guardian) prayers, leaving out only one line from the entire liturgy and thus clearly demonstrating his uncanny powers. Those present knew that the particular prayer had been written by the first Dodrup Chen. Evidently, it remained imprinted upon the mind stream of the youthful incarnate lama one century later.

And what about the missing line? The most erudite, senior abbot of those assembled reminded his colleagues that the author of the original prayer, Dodrup Chen I, had himself mentioned that the particular line in question was purely optional ... exactly as the four-year-old had so cleverly reminded them—much to their delight.

Drukpa Kunley Blesses an Image

It is customary to ask a high lama to consecrate new religious icons, whether these are statues or paintings. Lamas generally toss blessed rice over the images, thus empowering them as deities.

ONE DAY A FAITHFUL OLD woman hurried toward the hilltop monastery where Drukpa Kunley's brother resided as head lama. In her hands she cradled a new *thangka*, or scroll painting, of the deity Sri Heruka. Surely the venerable abbot would bless it!

Suddenly, she stopped in her tracks. Right in her path stood the legendary divine madman, Drukpa Kunley himself.

The Drukpa inquired politely why anyone would want to visit the monastery. "Nothing much happens up there," he added. "My brother lives there like a lord."

The faithful patron reluctantly revealed her purpose. No one in Tibet could be ignorant of Kunley's opinion of monasteries!

Drukpa Kunley asked the lady to unroll the painted scroll so that he could see the deity. Reverently, she did so.

Swiftly he lifted his robe and squatted and defecated on the scroll. "That's how *I* bless images!" said he.

Horrified, the woman rolled up her precious scroll and fled up the holy hill. Breathless, she rushed into the abbot's quarters.

Hearing her heartrending tale, he laughed aloud. How well he knew his outrageous enlightened brother, Kunley, his alter ego.

"Open the scroll at once," the august abbot ordered. Meekly, the distraught woman obeyed.

Lo and behold! Inside the scroll was a handful of tiny gold nuggets.

"Sri Heruka himself blessed your painting," said the abbot. "You don't need me."

That is how Drukpa Kunley gave blessings.

The Evil Eye

Much, if not all, of what we experience depends upon our underlying assumptions. What we perceive is often a projection. Numerous unconventional tantric practices, such as Chöd *(cutting), help us overcome deluded perceptions by undermining the power that such misperceptions have over us.*

ONCE A CHÖD PRACTITIONER ON a solitary retreat in eastern Tibet was striving to recognize the true nature of reality, the emptiness of all things. Through practicing Chöd he was gradually subjugating imaginary projections, figuratively known as demons.

One dark evening he had left his hut for a moment when his sister appeared with a clay jug of homemade yogurt. She awaited his return. When he failed to materialize, she placed the jug on a stool and left.

At last the hermit returned. It was very dark in the room. The faint glow of a sputtering butter lamp on the altar provided scant illumination, and the round mouth of the yogurt pot appeared to the hermit to be a huge demonic eye.

Being an intrepid yogi, he refused to give in to fear. "Phet!" he shouted. "Demons are devoid of reality!" Then he took off his outer robe and thrashed the demon.

The stool crashed over and the yogurt went flying, spattering the dark walls. Winking white in the flickering lamplight, demonic eyes suddenly stared at him from every corner of the room!

Undaunted, he kept slapping his shawl at them. But the more he hit, the more he produced—they seemed to be everywhere!

Cutting through everything, in a moment of piercing clarity the yogi felt yogurt on his hands. Suddenly he realized how deluded he had been, and laughed aloud.

There were no demons to destroy. Through too much philosophy and too little common-sense investigation with his own eyes, he had made a fool of himself.

A Horse Race for Sages Only

ONE HUNDRED THIRTY YEARS AGO, the three great non-sectarian lamas of Kham—Grand Khyentse, the first Jamgon Kongtrul, and Chögyur Lingpa—had a horse race. People from all the neighboring regions gathered at the spacious riverside fairgrounds in Dergé for the event, for they knew that whenever these three enlightened luminaries got together, some sort of spiritual occurrence was bound to happen. Each master was a treasure trove of initiations and teachings, mystic songs, visions, revelations, cures, and blessings.

None among the faithful yet curious followers knew why the three masters were holding the race—an uncommon event, to say the least, for three august ecclesiasts. Nor was any authoritative information forthcoming to satisfy the curiosity of the crowd.

When the unusual race took place, Jamgon Kongtrul's horse finished last. The entire assembly was united in utter astonishment to see the great lama, the eldest among the extraordinary trio, weeping openly. But before anyone could elicit an explanation of the day's mystifying events, the three grand lamas disappeared; they were simply nowhere to be found.

"How could such an emancipated senior lama cry like a child over losing a mere horse race?" everyone wondered. "What spiritual significance might this have?"

Jamgon Kongtrul went into seclusion to meditate and pray. The entire region continued to wonder about the mysterious race and its equally mysterious outcome.

Days later, Kongtrul Rinpoche, the Gentle Master, emerged. He explained that he had cried because his meditational deity had opened his eyes regarding the symbolic significance of the outcome of that race; it clearly augured that he, Kongtrul, would be the last among the three great visionaries to reach Zangdok Palri, Padma Sambhava's Buddhafield of the glorious Copper-Colored Mountain.

Jamgon Kongtrul elaborated, "It saddens me that I will outlive the others, whose selfless lives I value so highly."

Thus it actually came to pass. Kongtrul Rinpoche passed away in 1899, at a ripe old age, well after his esteemed younger colleagues, whom he then rejoined in blissful Zangdok Palri.

Embracing Tara

IN ANCIENT TIMES, THERE LIVED a monk in Bodh Gaya who often reviled the Mahayana community and its doctrine. Being a follower of the Hinayana, the Lesser Vehicle, he considered the Mahayana, or Great Vehicle, teachings—with its vast pantheon of deities and countless mantras—unorthodox. He was not afraid to say so to whoever would listen.

One day this monk was swept away by the rising current of the flooding Niranjana River. Suddenly, as he struggled to avoid drowning, an unexpected thought entered his head—that the Mahayanists have a goddess called Tara in their pantheon, reputed to save creatures from drowning. In desperation, he cried out her name again and again as the wild current swept him along like a stick of driftwood.

He was struggling in midstream like a trapped insect, his monastic robes offering little assistance to his efforts to stay afloat, when suddenly a huge wooden image of Tara, carved from a sandalwood log, floated up alongside him. Often had he beheld this very statue in the outer vestibule of the courtyard at Bodh Gaya's main temple; often had he publicly reviled it.

The sandalwood Tara spoke to him: "O monk, you never think of me without casting aspersions on my humble name. You slander my fellow deities. Yet now you cry my name again and again, like a mantra. Is this how a follower of our good Lord Buddha behaves?" Then the statue, mute again, began floating away from the drowning monk.

Slipping from the awkward, soggy robes he was so proud of, he swam in pursuit of the savioress Tara. When many hours later he finally washed ashore, the monk was found, naked but breathing, lying exhausted amid the mud and debris—and hugging the sandalwood Tara in his arms.

Needless to say, he became her most ardent follower. He vowed to protect and preserve the precious Mahayana teachings and to deliver all beings from the flood of suffering and delusion.

Don't Take Anything to Heart: An Old Lady's Advice

Jigten Sumgon was an erudite and enlightened pandit, renowned as the "second Nagarjuna." In the twelfth century, Jigten Sumgon founded the Drigung Kagyu lineage within the Kagyu Mahamudra school. Various practicing lineages sprung from the enlightened disciples of Gampopa, who founded the Kagyu school in the twelfth century.

Mahamudra, literally meaning the Great Symbol or Great Seal, refers to the absolute quintessence of one's true nature, the ultimate view of reality, in which everything is "sealed," or revealed, by emptiness. The Great Stance or Great Symbol of the non-dual Mahamudra teachings unveils the inherent sacredness of all things by directly introducing innate awakened awareness, rather than by merely striving to develop its potential over many decades and lifetimes.

Samsara and Nirvana represent—to our habitual dualistic way of thinking—this world as we know it and the dimension that is totally transcendental.

ONCE JIGTEN SUMGON WAS IN his family's home at Den in eastern Tibet when a neighbor died. The bereaved widow came to him for solace.

Entering the house of the master, the wailing woman first encountered the master's aged mother. The old lady told her grief-stricken neighbor, "I am sorry, dear sister, but this is the way of all composite things. Don't take it to heart; rather, meditate on the inevitability of death and impermanence, and from your present misfortune happiness will come."

The widow, however, continued to weep and tear her hair. The old lady then said, "Listen, it's no use to dwell on your husband's death. Don't keep thinking about it; let your tears fall like rain now, but remember that this experience will soon pass, just like everything else. If you dwell on it, you will continue to suffer. I am rich with years, and my advice is don't take anything to heart!" Thus the wise old woman consoled her friend.

The widow immediately experienced consolation and peace. She forgot about Jigten Sumgon and went home; she completed her mourning period in the traditional way, yet without excessive misery and despair. By reflecting upon the themes that her neighbor had suggested at the critical moment when her anguish was most intense, she vastly developed in both virtue and insight, and her spiritual practice progressed enormously.

Months later, Jigten Sumgon, the second Nagarjuna, was giving a series of profound Mahamudra teachings in central Tibet. He spontaneously sang:

"I am the carefree yogi who has realized
the inseparable unity of the Buddha, the guru,
and my own heart and mind—
Happy am I!
There is no need for artificial devotion.
As the Hevajra Tantra says:
'Samsara and Nirvana, good and evil,
have no real, concrete existence.
Everything is relative.
To realize the true nature of samsara
is to attain Nirvana.'"

The next day he cheerfully recounted the story of his aged mother's intercession, stating that to his way of thinking there was no non-dual Mahamudra teaching superior to that bit of motherly advice: to recognize the impermanence and unreality of all things and to take nothing to heart.

The Sage, the Lady, and the Fish

In the fifth century B.C. *lived an enlightened monk, venerable in wisdom and years, named Katyayana. He was an arhat, a fully liberated being, free from the vicious cycle of birth and death known as samsara. Renowned among Buddha's disciples for his prescience, he rarely displayed it except as an aid to his teachings.*

Katyayana, through his miraculous powers and abilities, could have produced whatever he wished or needed. However, like Lord Buddha himself, he chose to join the other monks of the order in collecting their daily alms.

ONE DAY KATYAYANA, WHILE PURSUING his daily round for alms, encountered a woman seated in front of her house, dandling a small child on her lap. She was eating a fish, whose bones she threw to the barking dog hovering nearby. When the dog became too insistent, the woman gave him a kick.

Confronting the scene, the kindly old arhat—much to the woman's surprise—suddenly burst into laughter. Then he chanted:

"Devouring the flesh of one's father,
kicking one's mother;
chewing the bones of one's father
while nursing one's enemy upon one's breast
—What a gigantic melodrama, what a spectacle
is this magical illusory wheel of samsara!"

The clairvoyant monk clearly perceived that the baby in the woman's arms was the reincarnation of her recently deceased enemy, the fish between her teeth was the rebirth of her late father, the dog her own recently deceased, oft-mourned mother reborn. . . . Unconsciously, she was eating the flesh of her own father, tossing his bones to her mother, and kicking the latter's recently assumed canine form, while unknowingly succoring her former enemy at her breast.

Opined the sagacious old arhat, "Thus it is that the wondrous wheel of cyclic existence, like a waterwheel, endlessly turns—refilling its buckets again and again, ceaselessly emptying and replenishing itself."

Who knows from whom the meat on our table has been butchered, whose bones we chew upon?

Wisdom Can Be Contagious

Until recently, Kham in eastern Tibet was a pristine, sparsely inhabited wilderness, not entirely unlike the American Wild West of a century ago. It was not uncommon for clans there to war against one another. Lawlessness was rife, and feudal rule prevailed.

Paradoxically, because people were few, life was simple, and solitude was easily achieved, Kham also was for centuries one of Tibet's foremost centers of meditation and yogic practice.

Bodhichitta (awakened mind) is synonymous with true greatness of heart. It refers to the impartial, altruistic enlightened mind of a bodhisattva, a spiritual hero.

PATRUL RINPOCHE WAS ONCE WANDERING alone in the rugged mountains near Markhog, camping in the wilderness. He meditated on Shantideva's Bodhichitta teachings regarding the altruistic aspiration for enlightenment. It was Patrul's aspiration to be sufficiently unbiased to treat others as himself.

A rough dirt track cut through the range and connected the valleys of two warring clans. The solitary meditation master's sensitivity to the violence surrounding him served to inspire his compassionate prayers and devotions.

One day the warring parties became aware of the vagabond by the roadside; they wondered who he was and what he was pretending to be. They found Patrul lying across a narrow bend in the mountain track, where every traveler was obliged to step over him. In this unusual position, Patrul could pray for each traveler individually, hoping to pacify their violent emotions.

After a time, three young armed riders came upon the weathered old mendicant next to his cold campfire. Forced to halt their horses abruptly and dismount, they demanded, "Are you sick, deranged—a leper, perhaps? What is wrong with you, lying across the path like this?"

The insouciant master replied, "Don't worry, young fellows, you won't catch my disease. It's called Bodhichitta, and it is hardly contagious for healthy young warriors like you!" Somewhat confused, the three remounted and trotted off.

Later Dza Patrul said, "Perhaps it *is* contagious, this impartial Bodhichitta, for you *can* catch it from the greatest spiritual practitioners. But these days, although so many claim to have it, so few seem really to develop its symptoms of unconditional love and selfless compassion."

Then he prayed, "May all beings without exception be infected by precious Bodhichitta."

Miraculously, the ongoing blood feud in Markhog soon came to an end. The local folk claimed that the young warriors must have caught the infectious disease of peace from that anonymous enlightened vagabond blocking the mountain pass, whom they never saw again.

A Haunted Fortress

Patrul Rinpoche taught Shantideva's lengthy Sanskrit classic Bodhicharya-avatara *in detail, from memory, over one hundred times. His own written commentary, elucidating the essence of Bodhichitta and the Six Perfections, is a Tibetan classic.*

During the last half of his productive life, this master kept his vow never to sleep indoors and lived as a mendicant yogi. Patrul was a vegetarian, never rode horses or exploited beasts of burden, accumulated no possessions or retinue, and truly embodied Great Compassion, Avalokitesvara. Patrul was Shantide-va's reincarnation.

AT NYARONG THERE STOOD A haunted fortress where spirits were heard crying out, even in daylight. No one ever dared to go near it.

Once, upon the conclusion of some teachings, Patrul Rinpoche said that if someone would go into the fortress and recite the *Bodhicharya-avatara* one hundred times, the spirits would be freed. A close disciple, Tsanyak Sherab, immediately volunteered. All the villagers shook their heads, fearing that they would never see that popular young lama again—what a pity!

Upon arriving at the haunted fortress, the intrepid Tsanyak Sherab laid his mat on the floor of an empty room. Then he generated intense compassion and altruistic Bodhichitta, meditated on emptiness, and began reciting aloud the ten chapters of Shantideva's *Bodhicharya-avatara*.

Day after day, he continued. When the villagers spied smoke rising from the fire that Sherab kindled to boil tea, they exclaimed, "After all, he is not dead!" One of the boldest villagers plucked up his courage and went to see what had transpired in the haunted fortress.

To his surprise, he found Sherab peacefully teaching the scripture aloud to his invisible audience. After the man returned and related the news, day after day more villagers journeyed to the stronghold to listen. By the time Tsanyak Sherab had reached his one hundredth repetition of the lengthy book, the entire village sat enraptured before him.

Mysteriously, from that time on, no spirits cried out. Instead, people often went there to pray and meditate and to be inspired by recalling Patrul's presence.

A Donkey Leads the Chanting

ONCE THE RIBALD ICONOCLASTIC YOGI Drukpa Kunley stumbled upon a congregation of monks in a temple in the countryside. The monks were dressed in rich burgundy and gold robes and held gilded ritual instruments, while they were comfortably ensconced amid colorful carpets and brocade cushions.

The irascible Drukpa entered the temple, neglecting to offer the three customary prostrations. He simply took a seat in the middle of the floor. There he sat while the rites and rituals proceeded, listening intently, his head cocked to one side. Those who knew him could foresee nothing but trouble!

The chant master was not at his musical best that day. However, he wore a high yellow hat with a crest.

"What a gay feathered headdress!" thought Kunley. "What sort of tropical bird could he be?"

Drukpa Kunley took in the entire scene. He listened to the chanting and then rose to stomp off in disgust. He had concluded that the elegantly attired monks were without much sense of the genuine significance of their elaborate rituals.

Soon, Kunley returned, leading an old donkey. On the creature's head sat a crested yellow hat similar to the lama's. Leading the donkey over to the chant master, he had the beast kneel down. Then he prodded the donkey into braying in a rhythmic fashion, in imitation of the haughty old chant master.

The monks were scandalized, but Drukpa Kunley simply laughed. One arm slung over the donkey's neck, the divine madman and his ass departed, continuing merrily on his carefree way.

Two Sages Debate

In India and Tibet, logic and debate have long been utilized as tools to clarify the mind and sharpen the spiritual faculty. By custom, the vanquished debater would convert to the viewpoint of the victor once the superior philosophy had been clearly ascertained. Nagarjuna's Middle Way dialectic, called Madhyamika, is preeminent among Buddhist philosophical schools.

Debate continues to be one of the principal means of training geshés (doctors of divinity) in Tibetan Buddhist monasteries and colleges.

ARYADEVA WAS A GREAT BUDDHIST pandit and logician and the foremost disciple of the peerless enlightened sage Nagarjuna. Ashvagosha was an equally great contemporary Hindu master and debater. When Ashvagosha challenged Nagarjuna to a debate, Aryadeva was sent in his stead.

In order to prepare Aryadeva, Nagarjuna trained him through practice debates, himself propounding the Hindu point of view while Aryadeva defended the Buddhist outlook. Nagarjuna argued so passionately in favor of theistic philosophy and practice that his student became uneasy, wondering if his master was not actually a Hindu!

The day came when Aryadeva was ready. He could uphold either side of the argument. Nagarjuna sent him forth to meet the challenge.

Ashvagosha was purifying his sins in accordance with Hindu custom through his daily ritual bath in the Ganges. Unheralded, Aryadeva descended the riverbank. Within sight of Ashvagosha, Aryadeva filled a gold pot with feces and urine. Reverently, he proceeded to scrub and scour its outer surface.

Amazed, the Hindu pandit inquired, "What possible purpose is served by cleaning the exterior of a pot filled with uncleanliness?"

The anonymous Buddhist replied, "Dear sir, your sins are within your mind; how can you purify them by washing your body in this river?"

Aryadeva had confounded his challenger's Hindu philosophy: Ashvagosha had no answer. Aryadeva disappeared among the countless riverside temples and shrines.

On another occasion, Ashvagosha was performing a ceremonial rite for his deceased parents. The provocative Geshé Aryadeva again appeared. Now Ashvagosha began to be suspicious about who this anonymous character might be.

Aryadeva gathered a great armful of dry grass and sprinkled it with water as if expecting something to happen.

Ashvagosha, curious, could not refrain from asking what Aryadeva was doing and who he was. Aryadeva simply told the Hindu that there was a withered tree on Mount Parvata; he was watering it to make it grow.

Ashvagosha snorted, "How can you water a dead tree on that mountain by sprinkling water here? What sort of charlatan are you?!"

Aryadeva quietly replied, "Likewise, your ancestors died long ago and have gone far away. Why make offerings to them now?"

Then Ashvagosha knew that he had met his debate opponent, the renowned Aryadeva. Preparations for an extensive debate began under royal auspices.

The widely publicized formal debate was held in front of the king and his ministers. After numerous discussions, debates, and a multitude of different dialogues over a period of weeks, the king and his sages declared the Buddhist Aryadeva victorious. Ashvagosha, who had foreseen this outcome, swiftly flew up into the sky in order to escape the necessity of converting, as custom demanded.

Aryadeva flew after him. He bound Ashvagosha through superior psychic force and delivered him back to earth. There the Hindu scholar was locked in a temple filled with Buddhist scriptures.

With nothing better to do, Ashvagosha after many months began to read the Buddhist books. With Aryadeva's well-reasoned arguments etched upon his mind, eventually his own studies convinced him that the Buddhist path was ideal as a means to perfection. When he told his captors about his conversion, he was released.

Ashvagosha became an erudite and realized Buddhist master, the finest Buddhist poet of India. His inspired long poem, *Fifty Verses of Guru Devotion*, is his most famous extant work.

Shantideva's Teaching

Shantideva lived twelve hundred years ago in northern India. He is the author of the Sanskrit classic elucidating the bodhisattva's way of life, known as the Bodhicharya-avatara, *or "Engaging in the Bodhisattva's Way."*

Shantideva was by birth a prince, and when he was still a boy, the goddess Tara warned him in a dream about the miseries of worldly existence. On the very eve of Shantideva's royal enthronement, the wisdom deity Manjusri likewise admonished him, so Shantideva forsook his throne and went into the forest to practice yoga and meditation. Later he became a monk at Nalanda University.

This story shows how deceptive appearances can be, especially in the spiritual realm. Isn't it difficult to recognize the hidden saints among us?

At Nalanda University, Shantideva kept to himself, ate rice five times a day, and stayed in his room. His brother monks nicknamed him "Busuku," meaning "he who only eats, sleeps, and shits." No one knew that he was illumined. Instead, he was generally called "that fat rice bag."

Some monks wished to have the indolent shirker expelled from the prestigious monastery, but a strong pretext was required in order to do so. Therefore, a plan was contrived in which each monk would be obliged to recite, before the entire assembly, a complete scripture from memory. Everyone assumed that the lazy Shantideva would be unable to do so and would be so embarrassed that he would leave the learned community of Nalanda of his own accord.

Initially, Shantideva resisted the idea. But when his brethren insisted, he finally agreed—on the single condition that they would provide a high teacher's throne for him if he was to recite a sacred scripture. The monks were astonished. Nonetheless, they agreed to comply with this bizarre request, since it would obviously further contribute to their eccentric brother's disgrace.

On the day chosen for his humiliation, Shantideva ascended the grand throne with a gait like a lion's. Sitting on the throne with regal assurance, he asked the assembled monks whether they wished him to recite a scripture that had previously been taught or something never before heard in this world. The nonplussed gossips who had plotted Shantideva's ruin shouted in unison for something never heard before, feeling certain that this would prove their victim's total ignorance.

Shantideva proceeded to invoke the Buddhas and bodhisattvas of the past, present, and future, spontaneously chanting the lovely verse that begins his great extemporaneous work called *Bodhicharya-avatara*. Then he extemporaneously chanted that masterpiece in its entirety.

When Shantideva, the Peace Master, reached the ninth chapter, which concerns transcendental wisdom and the nature of emptiness, he levitated above the throne and disappeared into the heavens. Only his stentorian voice could be heard, proclaiming the final chapters.

Now everyone present recognized that an enlightened master had lived unknown in their very midst. Shantideva, however, was nowhere to be found.

His enemies had achieved their object, although they now regretted it. When some monks went to clean Shantideva's cell, they found the two other literary masterpieces for which he is known hidden on a tiny shelf above the lintel.

Glorious Shantideva is venerated even now as one of the greatest enlightened authors of Buddhist India. Today his lengthy Sanskrit classic, the *Bodhicharya-avatara*, is still widely studied and memorized.

Midway Founds Kashmir

Ananda was Buddha's faithful companion for several decades. He became an arhat (a liberated sage) after Buddha's demise.

In India when a king or revered leader converted, his entire following did so as well. To cut one's hair is traditionally symbolic of renouncing the world and entering the Buddhist order.

Even today saffron remains one of the most precious and sought-after spices of the Orient. Kashmiri saffron is considered to be the finest.

It was to the nagas (semidivine, serpentlike creatures who thrive in water) that the Buddha secretly entrusted the Wisdom Scriptures known as the Prajna

Paramita Sutras, in order that later generations might benefit from them. Centuries later, the philosopher-sage Nagarjuna (Lord of the Nagas, also called the Serpent Master) retrieved the Wisdom Sutras and promulgated them in our thorny, rosebush-like world.

BY POPULAR ACCLAIM, BUDDHA'S COUSIN Ananda became the patriarch of the Buddhist order after the demise of Buddha's designated successor, Kasyapa. One day, while crossing the Ganges on a raft, Ananda met in midstream a great *rishi*, or seer, accompanied by five hundred followers.

Perceiving Ananda's extraordinary sanctity, the rishi requested monastic ordination. Ananda instantly materialized an island in midstream. Then, in one miraculous motion, he cut the rishi's long, flowing hair, along with the tangled dreadlocks of his followers, and taught the entire entourage the Buddhist precepts.

The rishi, whose spiritual practice had already vastly matured through many lifetimes, immediately became a fully liberated arhat. He became renowned as Madhyantika, or Midway.

Having completed his karma and been emancipated from the tides of birth and death, Madhyantika requested permission to precede his beloved preceptor, the venerable Ananda, into ultimate Nirvana, so as not to have to bear witness to his gracious teacher's inevitable demise.

Ananda had heard and remembered every word spoken by his master, Lord Buddha. He reminisced that Sakyamuni Buddha himself had predicted that an arhat named Midway would attain liberation from the boiling rapids of birth and death in the middle of a great river and would subsequently spread the Dharma throughout mountainous, uninhabited Kashmir. Therefore, Ananda commanded, Madhyantika must do just that.

Arhat Madhyantika agreed to fulfill his destiny. Soon afterward, having achieved the ultimate purpose of being by reaching enlightenment, the beatific Ananda displayed miraculous signs and omens and passed into the ultimate peace of Nirvana.

Twenty years later, the venerable Midway fulfilled the prediction and reached remote Kashmir. Sitting cross-legged in meditation, Midway magically covered nine valleys, all of which converged in a single lake.

The nagas were enraged. They created crackling lightning, awesome thunderstorms, and earthquakes. However, through the power of one-pointed concentration, not even the yellow cotton robe of the meditation master was disturbed. The huge spears, boulders, and tree trunks that the nagas hurled at him simply transformed into a fragrant shower of flowers.

Somewhat subdued, the nagas approached Madhyantika. "Why have you come to our country?" they demanded, grimacing and contorting their serpentine members.

"In fulfillment of a prophecy by the Enlightened One, Gautama Buddha," Midway replied. Then he requested the nagas and local earth guardians to offer their land for the use of the Enlightened One's followers and to relinquish into his care the Prajna Paramita Sutras for the benefit of the world.

"We shall act as the good stewards of this lovely vale," the arhat promised. "We cherish all forms of life as we do our own."

The nagas asked, "How many followers do you have? We will offer the land covered by your seat. As for the Wisdom Sutras, it is not yet time for their revelation; we, too, follow the Buddha's command."

Madhyantika replied, "Five hundred venerable arhats are with me."

The proud naga chief proclaimed, "So be it. One less than that number, and your claim is forfeit."

Arhat Midway rejoiced; the Buddha's prophecy had been fulfilled. In order that the noble community be supported there and the Dharma be spread throughout that region, he commanded a sorcerer to construct a magical city, called Srinigar, and he consecrated it to remain imperishable.

In the course of time, many people came to Kashmir to follow the wise and compassionate Madhyantika. He transplanted the saffron flower from the Gandharmala Mountain. Through the power of prayer and benediction he blessed the valuable spice to flourish in that land, thus bestowing bounty upon his followers.

Thus was founded the delightful Himalayan kingdom of Kashmir, where the saffron-colored robes of the Buddhist order were long in abundance.

Raksha-Bead Nose

A rudraksha bead is the pockmarked, blood-red seed of an Indian tree, often used in rosaries, particularly for the recitation of wrathful mantras. It is a bead sacred to Lord Shiva, the Lord of Ascetics.

The Teaching of Three Words is a secret Dzochen teaching on the immutable essence of being. Hung Benzar Phet! is a mantric exclamation, unrelated to the Dzogchen Teaching of Three Words. This forceful exclamation is used by lamas to dispel evil forces, exorcise demons, and dissolve apparitions.

ONCE THERE WAS A HERDSMAN living in the hinterlands, who tended the cattle and slept in the barn of his employers. Sometimes the family would go to receive teachings from a lama of the region, but the herdsman always remained behind, tending the herd. This simple fellow was nicknamed "Raksha-Bead Nose." Due to a violent childhood bout of smallpox, his nose was blood-red and pockmarked like a rudraksha bead.

Although his employers considered him a moron, he was wise enough to inquire of them each time when they returned, "What teachings did he give you today? What did he do and say?"

The family members didn't take his interest seriously; what could he know about Dharma? They shrugged him off, claiming that they failed to remember or that the teachings were secret, for themselves alone, and they could not tell anyone about it.

Then the simpleton would inevitably ask, "How many teachings did you receive today?"

They would reply, "We only received three words, a three-word teaching—but everything is included in that!" And they would say no more.

The poor man fervently implored them to share with him the lama's wisdom. They told him, "Such teachings are not to be spread in the marketplace; they must be practiced in the depths of the heart." They would say no more.

Needless to say, this only served to pique the humble herdsman's curiosity. One day he realized that he could run away and seek the famous Three-Word Teaching on his own, since no one there would let him in on it. Every day from then on, he saved up a portion of his daily ration of roasted barley flour. After one year, he had an entire sack of provisions; then he escaped in the middle of the night, telling his plans to no one.

Raksha-Bead Nose had no idea where to find the lama he was seeking; he did not even know the lama's name. But he innocently imagined that he could receive the three words of Buddhist teaching from almost any master, so he wasn't fazed.

Wandering from village to village, eventually he found a group of yogis' huts in a solitary mountain meadow. Every day, the head lama taught that group of hermits. The herdsman would attend, although everything he heard sounded terribly complicated to one who only sought three incisive, all-inclusive words. He concluded that this lama must be an impostor, talking so much about all kinds of different teachings and esoteric practices when even a simple herdsman knew perfectly well that all the essential teachings could be transmitted in three simple words.

Raksha-Bead Nose decided he might as well seek elsewhere for an authentic lama who could give him the panacean Three-Word Teaching. He began making preparations to leave.

It so happened that on that day the head lama's servant noticed that Raksha-Bead Nose was not attending the teachings, and the monk went to inquire after his health. The simpleton explained himself to the servant; then the servant invited him to have tea with the teacher the next morning before leaving, for he took pity on the poor herdsman and thought that a few words of friendly advice from his master might be helpful.

On the following day, Raksha-Bead Nose was brought into the august lama's presence. He unhesitatingly requested the secret, all-inclusive Three-Word Teaching he had heard so much about. When the lama told him that he did not know about such a teaching, the simpleton insisted, frustrated to be turned away once again. The kindly teacher wondered what the peasant was irate about and how he might help, but Raksha-Bead Nose flew off the handle, accusing him of being a charlatan, a walking dictionary swaddled in priestly robes. . . . And he got up to leave.

Then the lama himself became angry. Reaching for the large bodhi-seed rosary he habitually wore around his neck, he shouted, "Hey, Raksha-Bead Nose! What to do with you? *Hung Benzar phet!*" Swinging his rosary overhead, he hit the bemused simpleton with it; then he left the room in a huff.

Raksha-Bead Nose seemed to be in a world of his own; the hapless servants could hardly get rid of him. The herdsman was wondering, "What happened? I asked for a teaching, and he hit me with his rosary, intoning a mysterious mantra. Maybe that was the teaching. . . . What did he say? 'Raksha-Bead Nose, what to do with you? *Hung Benzar Phet!*'

"Aha!" he exclaimed joyfully. "That is the Three-Word Teaching I have long been after!" Then he rejoiced greatly.

From then on, the satisfied simpleton thought of little else but the arcane three-word "teaching" that he had, after such a long search, so fortuitously acquired. Again and again he repeated to himself the mystic formula ending with *Hung Benzar Phet*, mulling it over in his mind. Soon afterward, having nowhere else to go—and reciting his secret mantra to himself at every step of the way—he returned to his native hamlet.

When Raksha-Bead Nose appeared, the whole family wanted to know where he had been. "Had you forgotten us?" they demanded.

He told them that he had been to see the lama and received all he needed in order to fulfill this life's purpose and meaning. They asked what variety of instructions he had received, but he only told them it was a little three-word teaching, something to be practiced deeply and taken to heart—not something to talk about. . . .

At home again in his barn, Raksha-Bead Nose made a small meditation seat for himself amid the straw and began putting into practice the secret teaching he had received. During the day, he would tend the cattle, repeating his new mantra to himself. At night, alone in the hay, he would recite that unique three-word mantra tirelessly: Raksha-Bead Nose, what to do with you? *Hung Benzar Phet!*

The dim-witted practitioner had inexhaustible faith in this three-word teaching—which was, in fact, the only teaching he had ever received from a lama. With utter devotion, with all the one-pointedness of the feebleminded at his command, he unwaveringly concentrated upon this simple formula.

Years later, an aristocrat in the next valley became crazy, as if possessed; none of the local doctors could cure her. A member of her household arrived unexpectedly at the home of the herdsman's employers, looking for the anonymous yogi rumored to have been meditating alone in a barn for the last several years. It was the family's last hope that a yogi's powerful mantras and prayers could cure the noblewoman of her mysterious malady.

Raksha-Bead Nose was surprised to hear such a request. Finally he said, "I have a secret, all-inclusive three-word teaching that I have never told anyone but have practiced for many years. Let us see what can be done." Then he rose from his dingy pile of hay and set off.

When the mismatched pair of travelers arrived, the yogi was ushered directly into the madwoman's chamber. There she lay on her high, carpeted bed, feverishly tossing and turning. Raksha-Bead Nose never hesitated; he acted exactly as his gracious master had done long ago. Removing his bodhi-seed rosary from about his grimy neck, he swung it overhead and down upon the madwoman's head, while shouting "Raksha-Bead Nose, what to do with you? *Hung Benzar Phet!*"

Miraculously, the tormented woman seemed to awaken from a nightmare. She was cured!

Raksha-Bead Nose gained a great reputation as a wonder-working adept. His eccentric, feebleminded ways lent an added dimension to his mystique. Numerous were the faithful who benefited from his unique three-word ministrations.

One day, inevitably enough, the aged master from whom Raksha-Bead Nose had received the marvelous three-word teaching fell ill, apparently beyond recovery. He was afflicted with what Tibetans call "white blood," a scab in the throat that continuously reproduces itself.

No one could cure the malady. The wonder-working crazy yogi renowned for his ugly nose was sent for. Servants carrying banners came to escort the famous miracle worker back to their camp.

Raksha-Bead Nose, hearing of his beloved guru's illness, immediately began to run. . . . And since he was empty-handed, he arrived long before his encumbered escorts.

When the Nose Yogi arrived, the old teacher was informed that one of his former disciples who had become an enlightened wonder worker was there to try to cure him. The lama disclaimed any knowledge of the man. He had taught so many during his long and productive life; how was he to remember them all?

The eccentric yogi was ushered into the tent where the sick lama lay. He immediately took off his rosary, waved it overhead, and hit his master with it, shouting the magic formula for which he had become renowned: "Raksha-Bead Nose, what to do with you? *Hung Benzar Phet!*"

Choking, the lama stirred from his sickbed and demanded to know what the madman was doing. The irrepressible Nose Yogi said, "I am practicing the holy teaching you gave me."

"What kind of teaching was that? I don't know what you are talking about," he said. Raksha-Bead Nose reminded him about the secret, all-inclusive three-word teaching—Raksha-Bead Nose, what to do with you? *Hung Benzar Phet!*—which he had faithfully practiced, alone in a barn, all these years . . . and through which marvelous results had been achieved.

Then the sick lama suddenly remembered the crazy yogi standing before him. Understanding everything, he burst into uncontrollable peals of laughter. And sure enough, marvel upon marvel—because he laughed so hard, the scab obstructing his throat broke up and came out of his mouth, and he was cured of his disease!

He could only shake his head with wonder and thank the powers that be. He thought, "This insane herdsman is quite a special disciple after all. In a bizarre, convoluted way, he has seemingly arrived at an unusual state. . . . Perhaps he is, after all, a suitable receptacle for the snow lion's milk of secret Dzogchen teachings."

The lama said to Raksha-Bead Nose, "In return for curing me, I have something special to give you: the most extraordinary of secret teachings."

The Nose Yogi, however, seemed to take umbrage at the elderly lama's gentle suggestion. "What?! Something not already included within the precious Three-Word Teaching? That is impossible!"

The experienced teacher, however, was adroit in handling all kinds of disciples. He explained to the Nose Yogi that what he actually intended to impart to him was only a *commentary* on the profound Three-Word Teaching he had already mastered through reciting the recondite formula "Raksha-Bead Nose, what to do with you? *Hung Benzar Phet!*"

Then the sage lama taught the Nose Yogi the peerless view, sublime meditation, and natural action of the innate Great Perfection according to the authentic Three-Word Teaching of Dzogpa Chenpo. During the ensuing years, Raksha-Bead Nose assimilated and understood those profound teachings concerning the effortless nature of primordial being and became a realized Dzogchen master himself.

A Lama's Mother

The enlightened vagabond Patrul and his disciple Lungtok lived in the wilderness near the Gémang Monastery in eastern Tibet, subsisting on minimal provisions and meditating on Dzogpa Chenpo, the innate Great Perfection. Yak butter was a valuable commodity among the nomadic herders of Kham and was often used as a means of exchange.

ONCE PATRUL RINPOCHE AND NYOSHUL Lungtok were in retreat at a secluded mountain hermitage in Dzachuka. Lungtok's far-off mother sent him a big lump of fine yak butter, which she had painstakingly churned from fresh milk day after day with her own aged hands. He immediately offered the fresh butter to his teacher.

Patrul exclaimed, "Ah-zi! See how tenderly your old mother cherishes you! I cannot accept this gift."

Some days afterward, Patrul asked Lungtok, "Do you often remember your mother in your prayers?"

"I think of her, but not that much," Lungtok confessed.

"Shame on you!" cried Patrul. "She brought you into this world and did everything for you when you were a helpless tot. For seven days you must meditate only on your mother's incomparable kindness."

Within a week, the obedient disciple gained a clear understanding of his mother's kindness and consequently of the kindness of all beings, since everyone has been one's mother at one time or another through the endless rounds of rebirth. Gratitude blossomed in Lungtok's heart, and a deep experience of altruistic Bodhichitta dawned like sunlight in his mind; his former bodhisattva aspiration to emancipate all living creatures without exception was immensely enhanced.

Nyoshul reported this to Patrul, who commented, "As Shantideva said, 'There is nothing that does not become possible through meditating upon it; everything becomes easy through familiarization.' It's too bad most folk don't meditate; if they did, they could easily progress toward enlightenment."

Then Patrul prayed aloud:

"May all beings have happiness
and the cause of happiness;
May all beings be free from sorrow
and the cause of sorrow.

May all beings be inseparable from
everlasting fulfillment and harmony;
May all beings find rest in impartial equanimity
and inner peace."

Through his prescient powers, Patrul knew that Lungtok's mother was not long for this world. He told his student, "Although formerly I instructed you not to accept offerings, now you should accept offerings and take them as presents to your mother."

Nyoshul Lungtok journeyed through the wilderness to see his mother before she died. He presented her with everything the faithful people of Dzachuka had offered him and brought joy to her during her last moments. When she was on her deathbed, he guided her to superior rebirths.

Lungtok felt extremely grateful to his teacher on his mother's behalf and was satisfied to have fulfilled his teacher's wishes. After that time, he did not accumulate possessions. Returning to the mountain retreat, he soon attained enlightenment.

Silver Is Poison

ONCE PATRUL STAYED IN A valley where people were exceedingly devoted to him. One day a few learned khenpos (abbots), along with the treasure master Chögyur Lingpa's son Tsewang Norbu, came to his solitary retreat in order to receive teaching; all sat around Patrul in a meadow bedecked with wildflowers.

In the valley there was an old man who fervently desired to offer Patrul a hoof-shaped piece of silver the size of a stone. But he knew that Patrul rarely accepted offerings.

The old man arrived suddenly on horseback, dismounted, prostrated himself three times, and placed the silver at Patrul's feet. He cried, "Here is an offering. Please save me from being reborn in the infernal realms!" Then he jumped on his horse and galloped off, aware that if he stayed, Patrul would reject his offering.

Tsewang Norbu thought to himself, "Patrul will probably use this offering for some meritorious purpose." Patrul, however, never picked up the silver ingot. When he had completed his teaching, he simply stood up and left. One by one the disciples returned to their homes and monasteries, and the ingot was left, round and bright, lying like a full moon in the grass. Tsewang Norbu could not help thinking that it would have been better to use it for some virtuous deed, rather than just abandon it there, but he kept these thoughts to himself.

As he walked away, he looked back again and again: the silver was still there, a sparkling dot in the green meadow. This image stayed with him as he descended the hill, and a tremendously powerful feeling of world-weariness and genuine renunciation arose within him.

Tsewang Norbu thought to himself, "When I think of my gracious guru and those around him who have totally renounced the illusory attachments of this fleeting life, it makes me think that it must have been just the same during the life of the Buddha and the liberated arhats."

Then he recalled a story:

Once Lord Buddha and his disciples—including Ananda, Kasyapa, and others—were walking along when they came across a large piece of gold lying on the ground. As they passed it, one after the other would exclaim, "Poison!"

A little girl who was collecting firewood nearby heard this. After they had gone, she saw the nugget of gold, without knowing exactly what it was. She thought, "How strange—here is a beautiful, bright yellow piece of stone, and all the esteemed arhats stepped aside and avoided touching it, exclaiming, 'Poison!' That must be something I also should not touch."

The child rushed home to tell her mother. "Today I saw a curious kind of poison," she began, relating what had transpired. Her mother went immediately to see for herself. She found the gold, brought it home, and used it to sponsor religious offerings.

The news spread like wildfire that the Buddha and his renounced followers had intentionally bypassed a piece of gold, leaving it in the grass, and had called it poison.

Tsewang Norbu was greatly edified, inspired to see how—even in modern times—his teacher Patrul Rinpoche naturally followed in their footsteps.

Naked Tara

Chandrakirti was a monk at Nalanda University in Bihar; he was the foremost proponent of Nagarjuna's Middle Way philosophy. Chandragomi, a lay master, upheld a slightly different Mahayana point of view, the Mind-Only system propounded by Asanga. During the seventh century, Chandrakirti and Chandragomi once debated for seven years; neither emerged victorious.

There are twenty-one principal forms of the goddess known as Mother Tara, the Swift Savioress, who appears in this story. Tara literally means "star."

UPON READING A BRILLIANT EXPOSITION by Chandrakirti, Chandragomi threw his own work into a well. Instantly the deity Tara told him, in a lucid vision, "Faithful sage, your text was composed with more compassion and less scholarly pride than Chandrakirti's, even if it is inferior in literary style. Therefore, yours will be of greater benefit to future generations."

This actually came to pass. Generations of students at Nalanda claimed that drinking water from the well (where Tara had blessed the pandit's original commentary) brought remarkable increases in their intelligence.

One day a beggar approached Chandrakirti, the Moon Master, at Nalanda, requesting alms for her daughter's dowry. The monk told her he had no possessions to offer. He sent her to the lay master Chandragomi's hut, but all the lay pandit possessed were the Prajna Paramita wisdom scripture and the clothes on his back.

Chandragomi felt such pity for the woman's plight that he was moved to tears. He prayed to a picture of jewel-bedecked Tara on the wall, which served as his altar, requesting her gracious assistance.

Tara, universally revered for her alacrity in answering supplications, instantly came to life. She gave her silken clothes and precious ornaments to Chandragomi to be passed on to the incredulous beggar for her daughter's dowry.

After the miracle, the Tara image remained without silks or jewels. She became greatly revered as Naked Tara, Bestower of Gifts.

Chandragomi said, "Holy Tara instantly answers all unselfish prayers. The other type of prayers may take longer."

A Great Dharma Lady

NINE HUNDRED YEARS AGO IN Shoto, near Drigung, lived a husband and wife who could not conceive a child. The attempts of local soothsayers having proved unproductive, the childless couple were advised to make a pilgrimage to the great self-arisen stupa (monument) of Swayambhu in the Kathmandu Valley in Nepal, to pray to Lord Buddha for a boon.

Months later, still in Nepal, the pair shared a marvelous dream: the sun and moon radiated crystal light rays upon them. When they woke in the morning, both knew they would be blessed with a wonderful child. They made grateful offerings at the stupa before the huge Buddha images; they lit hundreds of lamps, fed all the beggars, and eventually set off on the long trek home.

During the following year, a radiant girl-child was born to them, amid many auspicious signs. Rainbows arched over the house at her painless birth, water turned to milk, and divine fragrances filled the air.

Everyone agreed that the girl must be special. They wondered if she was the prophesied karma-dakini, an incarnation of the Dakini Queen Vajra Yogini, for it had been foretold that the karma-dakini would be born near Padma Sambhava's Tidro Cave in Shoto. When the tiny tot began reciting Tara's mantra and teaching it to other children at the age of three, everyone was overwhelmed. They named her Drolma, which is Tibetan for Tara. Drolma means "Liberatrice."

The girl's parents died when she was very young. Later, when her uncle, who raised her, wished to give the teenager away in marriage, Drolma objected.

"I am destined to go to Kham and marry a noble yogi of the Kyura clan," she insisted. "Our offspring will be practitioners who spread the Dharma and benefit innumerable beings." Disregarding the importunate pleas of her uncle and relatives, Drolma remained adamant.

One day the stalwart girl joined a merchant's caravan leaving for Kham. Her unhappy uncle could do nothing to restrain her. Youthful Drolma told him, "We shall always be together, although all mortal gatherings inevitably end in parting. In future aeons, we will reach enlightenment together in Tara's Buddhafield of Beautiful Lotuses. Constantly pray to Mother Tara for protection, blessings, and guidance." With these words, she departed.

When the caravan arrived at Dento Tsongur, Drolma quit the party. As if armed with foreknowledge, she went directly to the hut of the great yogi Tsultrim Gyamtso. Presenting herself to him, she declared, "Dharma lord, as in the days of old when Queen Yeshé Tsogyal served Guru Padma Sambhava, now I shall serve you. Free from worldly attachment, we shall unite so that our enlightened descendants may benefit the world."

Tsultrim Gyamtso had been forewarned of her visit in a dream, in which an emerald green karma-dakini had told him that she would bless his lineage for centuries to come. Now he understood the actual significance of that premonition.

The renounced yogi had no wealth to provide for a wedding ceremony. But Drolma, his bride-to-be, told him she would take care of everything.

"I have been born intentionally in this world in order to serve and liberate others impartially. All my followers will achieve spiritual realization," Drolma proclaimed. Miraculously producing a dakini's hand drum and skullcup from her traveling robe, she played the drum while gazing up into the firmament with a fixed, mystic stare.

Within minutes, the humble shelter overflowed with festive garments, celestial decorations, and divine food and drink. "Look, these square sheep bones," Drolma prognosticated, "augur that we will have four illumined sons."

All the yogi's followers and friends spontaneously gathered and the wedding ensued, to everyone's delight.

This unusual couple produced four sons, as Drolma had predicted; each became a learned and realized practitioner. When they were grown, Drolma led them—along with her other disciples—to a sacred cave near where Guru Rinpoche Padma Sambava had taught one hundred thousand dakinis in the Tidro Cave.

This large Shoto Tidro cave held rocks naturally shaped like deities, as well as scattered bone ornaments, semiprecious stones inscribed with mantras, and other arcane relics symbolic of great sanctity. Drolma produced an illusory corpse, which she transformed into all that was necessary for a grand vajra-feast offering; then the tantric rite proceeded.

All who partook of this feast attained miraculous powers and achieved enlightenment. Announcing that her Buddha-activities in this world were completed, Drolma solemnly vowed to protect practitioners of the Buddha's teachings.

She placed a small handwritten meditation text on the rock altar before her. Then she mounted her blue horse and soared away into the dakini Buddha-fields, singing to the accompaniment of heavenly musicians.

Drolma's grandson was the Drigung Kagyu patriarch Jigten Sumgon. Drolma became revered as Achi Chökyi Drolma, Grandmother Tara, the Dharma protectress of the Drigung Kagyu lineage. To this day, whoever prays to Achi Chökyi Drolma and practices the instructions left as her legacy is swiftly delivered to freedom, fulfillment, and enlightenment.

Trulshik Rinpoche's Dream

Trulshik Rinpoche is the august abbot of one of the world's loftiest monasteries, Thubten Chöling, which is located not far from the Mount Everest base camp eighteen thousand feet above sea level. For years this Nyingmapa master rarely left his Himalayan retreat. In 1991, he taught at Madison Square Garden in New York, along with the Dalai Lama.

DECADES AGO, TRULSHIK RINPOCHE ASPIRED to receive the esoteric Mahakala empowerment from His Holiness the sixteenth Gyalwa Karmapa, the hierarch of the Kagyu lineage. However, no matter how often Trulshik tried to meet the living Buddha Karmapa, his plans were always thwarted.

When he tried to travel to the Karmapa's monastery in Sikkim, it was impossible. Whenever he tried to meet His Holiness in India, unexpected events intervened.

The abbot wondered, "Is there a negative force or inner obstacle hindering me?" Therefore, Trulshik performed the appropriate rites and offerings in an effort to dispel karmic obstacles, accumulate favorable conditions, and purify himself.

Above all, he prayed. How disappointed he was, then, when His Holiness Karmapa passed away in 1981 without conferring upon him the desired empowerment.

One night, however—as if in answer to his wholehearted prayers—the late great Buddha Karmapa himself appeared in the clear light of Trulshik's dreams. Karmapa, the Action Master, bestowed the complete Mahakala Guardian of the Dharma empowerment upon him.

"What is real?" the abbot asked.

"Everything is equally real and unreal," Karmapa replied. "Nothing is real. In the absolute, everything is equally empty; in the relative, each act counts."

Trulshik Rinpoche later acknowledged His Holiness's unique power and benediction. "Innate wisdom is the ultimate protector of the holy Dharma," he said.

For him there was no difference between dream experience and the daydream of everyday reality, life and death.

Consciousness Transference

It was customary in Tibet to summon a lama when a family member passed away, which usually took place at home. Priestly rites would then be performed, and—if possible—the consciousness of the recently deceased would be transferred to one of the Buddhafields, or transcendent paradises.

A powerful practitioner can instantaneously deliver his own consciousness or that of the deceased to a Buddhafield through the secret yogic practice known as Phowa (consciousness transference).

ONE DAY THE HEAD OF a nomadic household in desolate, windswept northern Tibet passed away. In such a sparsely inhabited region, it was rare to find monasteries and lamas, so the family members wondered what to do. They happened to spot a ragged individual traveling on foot, whose appearance bespoke that of either an itinerant yogi or a beggar. They approached him to find out if he could help.

The mendicant turned out to be, in fact, a lama. The grieving family requested his ministrations for the deceased, and he complied. When he reached the man's deathbed and began his incantations, the family respectfully requested the lama to perform Phowa in order to deliver the deceased to a superior rebirth in the western Buddhafield of Dewachen, the sphere of Sublime Delight.

The lama, however, said, "I am just a poor, unlettered practitioner of the Buddha's teachings; I have not mastered that esoteric practice. But I do have one positive quality: infinite faith in the living Buddha named Lama Karmapa. He is like the great gate to Dewachen." Then he began reciting again and again the famous name of the Karmapa as a mantra: "Karmapa Khyenno!" ("Karmapa, heed me!")

"Karmapa Khyenno, Karmapa Khyenno . . . " After each and every one hundred fervent recitations on his rosary, he would hit the corpse with his prayer beads, commanding that in the name of the Buddha Karmapa the consciousness principle of the deceased be reborn in Dewachen, the paradise beyond the setting sun.

After some time, everyone noticed that the signs of successful consciousness transference began to appear. Hair fell from the top of the corpse's head, there was a pleasant fragrance in the air, and a large bump appeared at the crown aperture where the stream of consciousness of the deceased had departed for the other world.

Everyone present rejoiced and showered gratitude on the mendicant lama. Moreover, all began to practice faithfully the mantra of the Karmapa, praying to realize the great freedom and bliss of Dewachen in this very lifetime.

The traveling lama soon continued on his journey. One day he heard that the omniscient Karmapa was visiting southern Tibet; he traveled there to meet him.

The first thing the clairvoyant Karmapa said to him was "That was a difficult Phowa we performed up there in the north, wasn't it?" Karmapa laughed, hitting the other lama with his rosary.

Then the mendicant knew with unshakable certainty that the Karmapa is an omniscient living Buddha, who always keeps his disciples, wherever they are, in his heart and mind.

An Auspicious Incense Offering

To offer food and other forms of support to an Enlightened One and his realized followers has always been considered a great honor and an excellent way to gain meritorious karma and good fortune.

Vipasyi Buddha was an Enlightened One of remote antiquity. According to Buddhist cosmology, there are one thousand Buddhas who will appear during the present aeon; Sakyamuni, the historical Buddha, was the fourth. Maitreya Buddha, the fifth, is now awaited.

Arhat Angaja is one of the sixteen arhats, or enlightened elders, who preserved and spread Sakyamuni Buddha's teachings after his demise in 483 B.C.

AGES AGO, A WEALTHY PATRON named Nyemay offered to feed the Buddha Vipasyi for three months. The local king then made the same offer.

The Buddha thanked the king but reported that his needs were already cared for. "The king can make offerings to other worthy ones," Vipasyi said.

His Majesty was agitated. The king told his advisers that he could not match even a commoner in making offerings to the Enlightened One; therefore his royal dominion was diminished.

After hearing the story in detail, one wily old minister devised a plan. "Your Majesty," he said, "simply prohibit the sale of firewood in your kingdom. The arrogant householder who has outmatched you will be thwarted, unable to cook food. Meanwhile, with the royal woodpiles we will have no trouble in providing for the Buddha and his followers for months."

The king was pleased. Everything was arranged. However, the indomitable Nyemay contrived to cook the Buddha's meals on fires stoked by bundles of incense—thus perfuming the entire town while accumulating merit by feeding an Awakened One the most fragrant of meals. Moreover, every day Nyemay made the following aspiration: "As I am allowed to serve you now, Enlightened Lord, may I later be able to serve the liberating teachings and provide all beings with whatever they want and need."

The arrogant king was thwarted. The righteous householder achieved his heart's desire, providing the Buddha with his meals for three months.

By virtue of this merit, the layperson Nyemay was reborn as the arhat Angaja, the Incense Master. He is always portrayed holding a smoking incense burner in one hand. Whoever sees, touches, smells, or even merely *hears* about that sweet-smelling censer will be blessed with the perfume of self-discipline, full of piety and charm, and free from illness and disease, and he or she will effortlessly embark on the noble path leading beyond confusion and bondage.

Yahden Tulku Meets Manjusri

Manjusri is the Buddhist wisdom deity, who personifies innate gnosis. The flaming, golden sword held aloft in his right hand cuts through the veils of illusion, dispelling the darkness of ignorance. His mystic abode is said to be the legendary mountain in western China known as Wu Tai Shan.

ONE DAY YAHDEN TULKU WAS climbing the one hundred and eight stone steps leading to the Lamaist temple on the crown of Manjusri's fabled residence, the Five-Peaked Mountain known as Wu Tai Shan. The Tibetan monk had trekked for six long months in order to reach this holiest of mountains, chanting the scripture "One Thousand Names of Manjusri" with every footstep.

He knew that every sincere pilgrim to Manju's mountain was guaranteed a meeting with the wisdom deity—for the sacred scriptures say so. His own handwritten guidebook, composed of notes inherited from his own master, asserted that Manjusri himself appeared once a day on those blessed stairs, although in disguise. Only those with pure vision can recognize him.

Some magpies resting atop the great white bell-shaped stupa enshrining Manjusri's hair relics pierced the air with song. Otherwise, all was silent. In all directions, peaks adorned the horizon as the solemn lama slowly climbed. No one else was in sight, neither human nor deity; only one bedraggled mongrel dogged his steps, awaiting a morsel.

The golden roof of the Lamaist temple gleamed brilliantly in the sun. Above, a great gong boomed three times, as three prostrations were offered by some unseen disciple inside the sacred shrine. Inspired, the weary lama continued his ascent.

Near the uppermost steps, a legless beggar suddenly appeared. Hauling himself along with his powerful arms, he dragged his truncated torso along the ground like a horse-drawn sled.

"Homage to one and all!" the cripple cried, seemingly seeking alms. But when the lama tried to offer a pittance, the brilliant smile he received in return bathed him in a warmth unlike anything he had experienced since departing from his master's monastery several seasons ago.

"Homage to one and all! Alms I need not," the beaming beggar exclaimed. "I accept devotion."

In a flash, Yahden Tulku knew who sat before him. But by then, wisdom's mysterious incarnation was gone.

Soon after, the gong boomed one hundred and eight times in succession, while the lama offered that many prostrations before Manjusri's hilltop shrine and the magpies perched atop the stupa continued to sing.

An Enlightened Nun

Khenpo Yonga was a famous abbot-professor at the Gémang Monastery in Kham during the last century. He was a close disciple of Patrul Rinpoche and of Dzogchen Wangpo Tenga.

A HUMBLE NUN NAMED TURSI was extremely devoted to the erudite abbot Khenpo Yonga and the reincarnate lama Tulku Mura. She was always attentive to their teachings, served them, and practiced meditation continuously.

Tursi was rather shy. If the monks teased her, she would cry. One day, while listening to the teachings, she broke wind. Everyone laughed, and she started crying. Later Tursi felt compelled to apologize to Khenpo Yonga; he assured her that there was nothing to worry about.

Tursi never lived in a monastery. Whenever Khenpo Yonga taught, she pitched a small tent somewhere nearby, subsisting on whatever provisions she

happened to come by. After the teachings were concluded, she would quietly disappear to pursue her solitary practice.

Her parents were wealthy, and Tursi was their only child. They were willing to support her, and she could have stayed quite comfortably at home with them if she chose. But although they often sent her provisions, she never kept them. Even when she visited the family, Tursi pitched a tent outside; she would not even enter the house.

Once when she went to visit her family, Tursi pitched her tent, went down to the river, shed her clothes, and washed. Everyone was shocked. Her mother said to her husband, "Tursi has become completely crazy; something is very wrong with her."

When Tursi returned from the river, her mother chided her, saying, "What do you think you are doing?"

Tursi replied, "I'm coming for my final visit in this house."

Her mother said, "What's happened to you? Are you crazy? You never enter my house; today, suddenly, you want to come in. Are you all right?"

However, Tursi's father said, "There must be a reason; let her come in. You always wanted her to come in before."

Her mother said, "You are shameless. You took a bath, naked, in the river; now you want to come home. What is all this?"

Tursi entered the house and stayed all day. Then she picked up a volume of the celebrated *Seven Treasures* by the omniscient Longchenpa and said, "This is the most precious *Seven Treasures*. This tome has been blessed by Khenpo Yonga and Mura Tulku."

Then Tursi went away to meditate in the wilderness. After several days, she returned. By then she intuitively knew that her teacher Mura Tulku had just passed away.

Actually, her parents had known before but had refrained from telling her because she was very sensitive and was already acting in an unusual manner. Tursi said, "You knew Mura Tulku had passed away, but you didn't want to tell me."

They replied, "We were worried about you. We were afraid that if we told you, you would be overwhelmed."

"There's nothing to worry about," the nun replied. "It makes absolutely no difference; my teacher is in my heart."

Tursi again explained that the volume of the *Seven Treasures* had been blessed by Khenpo Yonga and Mura Tulku. "There is nothing more precious than this in the world; you don't need anything else. You should put it on your altar and bow down to it. One cannot imagine holy relics more precious than this sacred book.

Before I leave, each of you must please place it upon your head and make a sincere prayer; then there is nothing that cannot be accomplished."

The father was entirely willing to receive this blessing, but his wife said, "I've already received empowerments and transmissions from Khenpo Yonga and Mura Tulku myself. I don't need to put your old book on my head!"

But her husband told her, "Don't talk like that. She's our only daughter and a nun as well. This is a blessed text; it can't hurt. Just do what she wants."

Afterward, Tursi reverently placed the *Seven Treasures* on the household altar; then she returned to her tent.

Snow fell that night. The next morning, Tursi was gone.

Her mother wailed, "Now she's really gone crazy! She's lost herself in the snowstorm. We must look for her."

Tursi's father discovered footprints in the snow. He followed them up the hill behind his house and found a nun's robe and shirt. Finally he found his daughter on a windswept knoll in a remote charnel ground, completely naked, seated erect in meditation, her hands in the gesture of the female Buddha Tara. She was dead.

He was impressed rather than dismayed. His own daughter had consciously transcended the vicious cycle of life and death! Here she was, displaying the behavior of the enlightened yogi adepts of old.

Upon further investigation, the faithful old man found that, although deceased, the area around her heart was still warm, exactly as described in Tibetan yoga and medical texts. She was obviously absorbed in profound clearlight meditation, which continues into the intermediate state beyond death, prior to rebirth. He did not dare to move the body but left Tursi sitting undisturbed.

By chance, Khenpo Yonga was passing nearby with his retinue on his way to the Dzogchen Monastery. Tursi's father intercepted the party and related what had happened.

Khenpo Yonga went to investigate. For three days Tursi remained in her extraordinary meditative state, sitting in the snow like a lovely, unadorned icon of Tara, her skin imbued with a rosy translucence as if she were in suspended animation. Khenpo Yonga and his students camped nearby.

After three days, the body slumped, and all vestiges of heat and life disappeared. Khenpo Yonga told the monks to prepare a small cremation stupa of the type made for lamas and to venerate Tursi's remains.

A fire offering was prepared, and Khenpo Yonga performed the ritual in a very elaborate ceremonial fashion. Moreover, he declared that Tursi was a special incarnation, an enlightened nun. In her ashes was found a perfectly clear, naturally formed image of White Tara, formed from one of her vertebrae. This talisman was kept as a relic in the Gémang Monastery.

Khenpo Yonga directed that a small bell-shaped stupa be fashioned from the remaining bones. This sacred object was also carefully preserved as a spiritual treasure.

The Sheep, the Ox, the Goat, and the Great Vegetarian Debate

In Tibet, innumerable yarns, fairy tales, and fables claim that animals are endowed with faith in the Buddha Dharma. Since much of Tibet is barren, certain monasteries found it necessary to keep herds of animals to help provide their daily sustenance, although the oppression and slaughter of any living thing is known to be inimical to the teachings of the compassionate Buddha. Needless to say, not all lamas and monks are saints.

IN AN INFORMAL DEBATE ONE day, a vegetarian lama accosted a meat-eating opponent on certain points relating to the karma involved in partaking of butchered products as food. The other lama replied jokingly, "The Buddha said that we should never kill animals; he never said we should not *eat* them!" In this way the lama tacitly accepted his opponent's point.

"But what about those leather boots you're wearing—not to mention the silk brocade adorning your altar, woven from the tears of ten thousand boiled silkworms?" another lama demanded of the vegetarian. "And have you ever considered the great elephants killed for the ivory beads of your shiny rosary?"

The onlooking lamas all acknowledged these points, too. Another added, "Consider the countless insects killed in the furrowing, flooding, and harvesting of the fields to provide us with a few grains of rice or barley and with our fruit and vegetables. Might it not be better conscientiously to offer the life of one large beast, which can nourish multitudes, than to be compelled to destroy countless small creatures in order to provide a few pinches of flour?

"What is the propriety of wealthy patrons slaughtering the finest of the flock in order to offer a sumptuous feast to visiting lamas, all of whom have dedicated themselves to selfless altruism and impartial compassion for one and all, high and low, great and small? Doesn't it seem hypocritical for us to accept such feast offerings? I feel that blood on my conscience."

Another member of the august company spoke up. "Wouldn't it be less immoral for those devoted to the evolution of consciousness to nourish ourselves on creatures of less evolved intelligence, rather than on those higher on the evolutionary scale?" . . . And so the discussion proceeded.

How was this debate concluded? The single overarching conclusion until now has been only that one must refrain from taking life, and one must cherish it in all its forms. Lord Buddha himself stated that these matters are difficult to judge, for only an omniscient Enlightened One can fully fathom the depths and intricacies of karmic concatenation.

Karma is beyond the reach of our limited intellect, and the sufferings of beings are vast and unimaginable. Therefore, what is essential, if human beings are to be impeccable stewards and guardians of this world, is a heartfelt moral sense of universal responsibility.

A fine sheep, a goat, and an ox, who with other animals were feeding in the courtyard of this monastery, happened to hear about the great vegetarian debate, and their faith in the Dharma was greatly renewed. Free from excessive ambition, the three companions were content with their karmically ordained place in the cosmic mandala, the interconnected web that is the inviolable oneness of being.

"We take refuge in the Triple Gem," they thought, "in the wise and compassionate Buddha, in his meaningful message—the Dharma—and in the Sangha—those who follow his non-violent creed. Wonderful are the monks who protect the well-being of us poor, helpless, destitute domestic animals— who live only to serve!" Such thoughts slowly reverberated in the dreamlike consciousness inside their thick skulls, as they contentedly munched their fodder.

The vegetarian debate taking place inside the lama's house must have concluded, for the assembly dispersed. Suddenly one of the lamas appeared in the midst of the animals, holding an old and well-polished bodhi-seed rosary and muttering to himself, *"Om Mani Padmé Hung,"* the mantra of Great Compassion. Meanwhile, he was eyeing the herd. A beefy peasant accompanied him.

"Kind and venerable sir," thought the large sheep to himself, "how fondly you gaze my way, praying to compassionate Chenrayzig for me. I take refuge in the sangha of the Buddha!"

The lama suddenly pointed at the sheep. The servant rushed forward with a large knife in one hand and a rope in the other and led the bemused sheep away to be slaughtered.

The faithful ox and devoted goat observed these proceedings, not without alarm. Sudden dismay about their own possible fate and doubt about that particular lama's compassion brought the Dharma itself into question.

"Anyway," the ox mused philosophically, "our Mr. Sheep was just a little bit too proud of his fine fleece and overfed paunch; no wonder the poor hungry monk took him to the table. Nothing of the kind will happen to a hardworking draft animal like myself, who has been dragging the monks' heavy plow through the rocky soil day after day in the hot sun for such a long time. Surely their appreciation will protect me. The Dharma is our refuge!"

All too quickly, the monk with his prayer beads and the knife-wielding servant returned, as if they had nothing else to do. The lama eyed Mr. Big Ox with favor; then he, too, was hustled away.

Casting a wry eye on all these proceedings, the horny old goat still remained undaunted, his faith unshaken. "Who would want a useless old crock like me? Even my skin is scarred, not to mention my tough flesh!" And kicking up his heels, the goat gloated, "All praises to uselessness! I take refuge in the compassionate Buddha, who impartially protects all beings!"

Just then the lama and his servant returned, the knife wet with blood. The befuddled old goat was likewise taken away.

The rest of the herd, feeding contentedly, observed what had transpired. "How lucky our friends are, to be invited for dinner by the lamas!" they thought. Their faith in their masters was renewed.

However, one of the bats hanging upside down in the eaves, who was shaken out of a fitful, daylong sleep by the pitiful cries coming from the slaughterhouse, thought to himself in a fleeting moment of lucidity, "The enlightened Buddha-mind is my sole refuge. The power of a monk's mantras and prayers is only as great as his heart."

Then he dozed off again.

A Bard's Cure

There were countless tantric practitioners, male and female, in the Indian subcontinent during the heyday of Buddhism between one and two thousand years ago. Some followed what was prescribed in the tantras, the mystic scriptures, while others pursued more unorthodox paths.

Manjusri is the meditational deity personifying transcendental knowledge and wisdom. Avalokitesvara is the deity who personifies unconditional loving-kindness and compassion.

LONG AGO, A POPULAR BARD named Vajradeva perceived the ultimate nature of reality through meditating on the deity Manjusri. On a solitary pilgrimage to the mountains of Nepal, he encountered a female yogi, a yogini whose tantric practices seemed to Vajradeva to be degenerate, riddled with perversities inimical both to truth and morality. Therefore Vajradeva composed a song deriding her.

The irate yogini cursed the yogi poet, performing black magic rituals aimed at harming him. Soon after, he contracted leprosy.

Vajradeva then prayed to his tutelary deity, Manjusri, for a solution. Manjusri appeared and told him that if he would compose a particular type of traditional metric verse in praise of Avalokitesvara each day for one hundred and eight days (as many days as there were beads on his rosary), the Buddha of Compassion would cure him.

Composing metric verses in praise of the great Compassionate One became an important part of Vajradeva's daily spiritual practice. After three months he had a vision of Avalokitesvara: thousands of brilliant light rays from the transcendent deity's ethereal body instantaneously purged his own corporeal form of all impurities and afflictions.

Thus the great bard was cured of leprosy, as well as of all other infirmities. For the rest of his long life, he never again fell ill, and his "One Hundred and Eight Verses Praising Avalokita" became a model of poetic excellence.

Atisha's Awakening

Atisha was the greatest Indian Buddhist pandit of the eleventh century and the leading light of Vikramashila University, the last great center of Buddhist learning. He was invited to Tibet by an imprisoned king in the western part of that country; this king offered to give up his own life so that his ransom money could be used to bring the Dharma to his people. Atisha spent the last twelve years of his life teaching in Tibet, establishing the Kadampa school.

Atisha's classic Mahayana treatise "Lamp on the Enlightenment Path" and his teachings regarding the seven-point thought transformation elucidate how to develop and train in Bodhichitta, the altruistic aspiration for enlightenment. Atisha's pithy epithets and practical advice are widely taught and practiced today among Tibetan Buddhists of all schools. Taking refuge vows is the formal manner of entering the gate of the Buddha's teachings.

ATISHA WAS A PRINCE IN eastern Bengal; he was born in 980 A.D. Green Tara appeared to him in a dream when he was a youth, advising him not to become enmeshed in the barbed snares of worldliness, for he had already been an ordained monk and learned pandit for five hundred fifty-two life-times, and his destiny was to liberate beings from the miseries of conditioned existence.

Recognizing the necessity of assuming his karmic responsibility, Atisha renounced the world and was ordained a monk. Tirelessly seeking enlightened masters under whom to serve an apprenticeship, he eventually became an erudite and accomplished *acharya*, or Buddhist teacher, under the tutelage of the tantric master Rahula. Atisha studied all the texts in the *Tripitaka* (Three Baskets) of the Buddhist canon as well as the Sanskrit Mahayana sutras, committing many of them to memory, along with related commentaries, as was customary in that era. He became renowned as a great teacher.

One day Atisha wondered aloud to himself, "Which path is swiftest in leading directly to the attainment of enlightenment?" For he doubted that he would ever reach enlightenment if he undertook the strenuous Mahayana path of the bodhisattva, who strives for the deliverance of others for endless aeons before he or she can enter Nirvana.

"How will I ever reach Nirvana, the other shore?" the young scholar lamented. "Will there be no end to samsaric existence for me?"

Just at that moment, the clairvoyant guru Rahula suddenly summoned Atisha, as if he was privy to his student's thoughts. Rahula informed Atisha that all forms of self-concern are inimical to perfect awakening and that visions, psychic powers, meditative absorptions, learning, skill in debate, and even the experience of Nirvana itself would prove of little use in the end. It would be far better if he would assiduously cultivate Bodhichitta and develop universal loving-kindness and compassion. Guru Rahula then predicted that his pupil, through identifying with the meditational deity Chenrayzig, Great Compassion, would ultimately achieve the supreme good for both himself and others.

"Forget your own interests, and take up the welfare of others," Rahula admonished. "Consider others more important than yourself. Clinging to oneself is the source of dissatisfaction and suffering; subjugate the great two-faced demon, egotism! The separate self is just another illusion.

"Therefore, *who* escapes from samsara and reaches Nirvana? It will be difficult to achieve absolute freedom if you foolishly strive to avoid samsara and obtain Nirvana—far better to transcend such dualistic concepts and bring everything to perfection through realizing non-duality. Great peace is always accessible; don't overlook it!"

One day soon afterward, Atisha was performing ritual circumambulations of the Great Enlightenment Stupa at Bodh Gaya, where Buddha was enlightened. Two divine young women, who seemed far too beautiful to be ordinary mortals, were standing by the south side of the stupa near a lotus pond. One asked the other, "What is the best practice for achieving perfect enlightenment?"

The second goddess replied, "Selfless Bodhichitta is the Buddhas' great highway. How can one turn one's back on others?"

The next day, Atisha was again circumambulating the stupa and the Bodhi Tree beside it, beneath which Sakyamuni Buddha himself had actually sat in meditation, when he heard an ugly old beggar woman telling another aged leper that impartial compassion and Bodhichitta were the best way to transcend the sufferings of existence and attain perfection. "Put yourself in the place of others. Relinquish egotism," she explained.

Atisha thought, "Everyone here, from the most divine to the most despised, seems to know the best way to enlightenment, in perfect conformity with what my guru said. How is it that I alone remain unsure?"

The next day, Atisha was slowly circling the sacred shrine, prayer beads in hand, when he saw a little bird perched upon the knee of a statue of Chenrayzig that was carved into one of the many stone niches on the side of the stupa. He heard the statue tell the bird, "Altruistic Bodhichitta is the best way to perfect enlightenment. Put others first: give the victory and profit to others, accept the losses upon yourself." At this moment, inexplicably enough, Atisha himself found that all his doubts were cleared.

While Atisha stood lost in thought, contemplating the serene visage of the golden Buddha beneath the Bodhi Tree, he suddenly realized that the guru Serlingpa on the island of Sumatra was the master who truly upheld the precious Bodhichitta. Atisha resolved to seek Serlingpa in order to achieve his goal. After twelve years of studying and practicing under this guru, Atisha became heir to his spiritual legacy.

In his later years, whenever Lord Atisha, now an acclaimed master himself, uttered the name of his gracious teacher Serlingpa, he would close his eyes and bow slightly, with palms joined in front of his heart. From this compassionate master, Atisha learned the unique Mahayana practice of Tonglen, or "exchanging"—putting oneself in the place of others and taking the burden of others upon oneself—an extraordinary method at the core of the Kadampa attitude-training.

Atisha became a great teacher in his native India and took up residence at the Vikramashila monastic university. After many years, he was invited by royal Tibetan messengers loaded with offerings of gold to teach in their benighted country. Questioning whether or not it would prove truly beneficial, Atisha prayed to Chenrayzig and Tara for guidance.

Tara told Atisha that it would be very beneficial to the Land of Snows if he would go. However, she added that if he journeyed to Tibet, he would die there at the age of seventy-two, while if he remained in India, he would live to the ripe old age of ninety-two. Atisha, exemplifying the selfless bodhisattva vow, then began the long trek to Tibet.

Atisha reformed Tibetan Buddhism and society, restoring ethics to its rightful position as the fundamental basis of the Dharma. In Tibet he became known as the Refuge Pandit because he gave Buddhist refuge vows to so many. At the age of seventy-two, as prophesied, the Dharma-lord Atisha passed away.

A Forest of Taras

Tara embodies the female principle of liberation. She is the protectress of Tibet, venerated for her swift compassion.

Ages ago, an intrepid female bodhisattva named Wisdom Moon, when advised by some monks to pray for fortunate rebirth as a male, empowered the entire intuitive universe by vowing to reincarnate again and again in female form until the ocean of samsaric existence is dry and all beings liberated from suffering.

"There is no such thing as man or woman, 'I' or 'me' or 'mine'; how can you talk like that?" she replied to the monks' indecent suggestion. Eventually, after many aeons on the enlightenment path, she became Tara, the liberator.

It is recorded that on one occasion at the outset of this very aeon, Avalokitesvara, in the midst of a multitudinous gathering of exalted beings on the summit of his own Potala Mountain paradise, intoned Tara's tantra and mantra ten million times for the benefit of all beings.

Tara is renowned as "she who protects from the eight great fears and dangers." Once a Tara statue carried beneath a traveling merchant's coat saved him from being gored by the sharp horn of a wild yak. Another time, a small Tara image in a monk's breast pocket stopped a Chinese bullet, thus saving his life.

AT ONE TIME A DEMONIC sprite lived in a forest near Mathura. Five hundred monks and nuns meditated nearby. Through supernatural powers, the sprite assumed multifarious forms in order to distract and beguile the spiritual practitioners—seducing some by appearing as a celestial maiden, frightening others into madness through infernal apparitions.

One monk lost his memory; another seemed possessed; a third became a drunken reveler. Others began singing and dancing wildly in the middle of the meditation periods, for no apparent reason. In this way, evil prospered and virtue declined.

One elderly monk remembered a bit of advice a teacher had once bequeathed to him, regarding the panacean activity of Arya Tara, the savioress. He prayed to Tara, protector of the endangered; in a dreamlike vision, Tara revealed her numinous form and told him what to do.

The monk attached twenty-one images (one for each form of the deity Tara) to trees all over the haunted forest. From then on, whatever phantasmagorical apparitions the mischievous sprite contrived, the monks and nuns spontaneously perceived them as nothing other than the various forms of Tara. Thus they were protected from fear and harm.

Needless to say, their faith and devotion flourished. The lovely medieval hymn called "Twenty-One Praises to Tara" resounded everywhere throughout that country to the delight of one and all. It is still chanted today in all Tibetan monasteries and nunneries.

Ashoka's Son Opens His Wisdom Eye

King Ashoka united and ruled India two centuries after the Enlightened One's demise. He built many roads, wells, infirmaries, and resthouses, as well as Buddhist temples, stone monuments, and shrines, many of which remain today. Originally a warrior, he was converted to the Buddha's non-violent way when he saw a Buddhist monk walking along the dusty road, radiant with inner serenity. Tisya Raksha was King Ashoka's last queen.

QUEEN TISYA RAKSHA WAS UNHAPPY. Would her devout husband never cease his visits to the Bodhi tree in Bodh Gaya? King Ashoka seemed more taken with the Buddha's teachings than with her!

The queen became so obsessed that she began to record how much time the king spent at the temple at Bodh Gaya with how much time he spent with her. At last she conspired with her royal guards to destroy the sacred tree. The tree, however, miraculously regenerated itself.

Tisya Rakya was infatuated with the crown prince Kunala, her stepson and heir to Ashoka's throne. When he rejected her amorous advances, she sought revenge and had him blinded, using a forged decree with her husband's seal.

As his eyes were being mercilessly plucked out, Prince Kunala recalled the teachings on impermanence and egolessness that a kindly old arhat had once imparted to him. "One day, in your moment of need, you will remember what I have taught you," the elder sage had predicted. "Your loss will become great gain."

In fulfillment of that prophesy, Kunala achieved sudden insight into the true nature of reality. Soon after, a clairvoyant arhat unveiled the queen's duplicity, and she was punished. Blind Kunala's son eventually inherited the throne.

Kunala himself, the former crown prince, retired in northeastern India to meditate in the forest, where he became a liberated sage. Selflessly meditating on forgiveness and compassion, he purified his misdeeds and exhausted his karmic residue. Eventually he even blessed and thanked his evil stepmother, who had deprived him of both his sight and his throne, while facilitating his great awakening.

Through the miraculous power of purification and forgiveness, Kunala's sight was restored. He then became a teacher of multitudes.

Karmapa's Blue Sheep

The late sixteenth Karmapa, head of the Kagyu order, was an avid collector of exotic birds and an animal lover. Wherever he went, he was always accompanied by various pets, including parrots that he had trained to recite "Karmapa Khyenno," his own name mantra.

AS A YOUNGSTER IN THE Tsurphu Monastery, His Holiness Karmapa, Rangjyung Rigpai Dorje, had a pet Himalayan blue sheep that followed him around. Everyone said the sheep was the reincarnation of a former servant who had suddenly abandoned the Karmapa's employ.

The servant's name was Yonga. He left mysteriously in the middle of the night and never returned. The Buddha Karmapa divined that no harm had befallen Yonga and simply let the matter rest.

Several years later, news of Yonga's death reached Karmapa's retinue. Appropriate prayers and benedictions were made in his memory.

Time passed. The young Karmapa hierarch was traveling with his followers in the sparsely inhabited northern plains of eastern Tibet. When the party dismounted to rest, His Holiness wandered off, and an elderly attendant followed him.

Suddenly the Karmapa called, "Yonga, Yonga," as he used to do when hailing his late servant. The elderly attendant monk wondered what was going on but kept his own counsel.

"After all," he thought, "what harm can possibly come to His Holiness here? The enlightened guardians and Dharma protectors are always watching over the Action Master, a living Buddha."

For a time the Karmapa wandered through that lonely, deserted grassland, gently calling his former servant's name: "Yonga, Yonga . . . " Suddenly there appeared, mewling, a little blue sheep. Fearlessly, the sheep approached and licked the kneeling Karmapa's outstretched hand.

The Karmapa turned to his faithful old attendant, smiling sweetly. "Now Yonga has come back to me," he said.

From that time on, they were inseparable. Even today old lamas from the Tsurphu Monastery say that near where Karmapa left hand- and footprints embedded in a boulder, the sheep's hoofprints can also be seen in the rock.

Manjusrimitra Meets a King on an Elephant

Manjusrimitra was the spiritual successor of the first Dzogchen siddha (tantric adept), Garab Dorje, the Diamond Laughter Master, who flourished in the century following the historical Buddha. Manjusrimitra was an orthodox Buddhist pandit.

At first Manjusrimitra was critical of the non-dual teachings beyond the law of cause and effect—those teachings that imply effortlessness. Manju was converted, along with five hundred learned followers, by the profundity and directness of Garab Dorje's oral instructions. Becoming an ardent Dzogchen practitioner through the swift and direct path, Manjusrimitra quickly realized perfect enlightenment.

Mudras, or ritual hand gestures, have as much power as the mind that is behind them and can often work miracles. Combined with mantras and yantras (visualized geometric mandalas), mudras augment the exercise of innate wakefulness.

ONCE MANJUSRIMITRA WAS WALKING ACROSS a bridge spanning a great river. At the midway point, he met a king who was renowned as an influential patron and supporter of several unorthodox spiritual teachers. The smug king sat on an ornate platform atop an immense war elephant.

Neither Manjusrimitra and his followers nor the resplendent, arrogant king and his martial entourage was going to be the first to make way for the other to pass. The king, from his towering perch, raised his regal, jewel-encrusted war fan in a gesture of intimidation, commanding obeisance from the party on foot before him. The Dzogchen master, however, was unperturbed.

Raising the index finger of his right hand menacingly in the mudra known as "dispelling obstacles and hindrances on the path," Manjusrimitra instantly split the king and his royal mount asunder. As if struck by lightning, their bodies fell in two pieces on either side of the bridge.

The terrified members of the royal retinue were aghast. Their leaders, two hoary old ministers, swiftly came forward and begged Manjusrimitra's forgiveness and compassion, beseeching him to further exert his marvelous magic powers in order to restore the lives of their erstwhile sovereign and his elephant. They hastily added that, of course, the Buddhist master would naturally have the right to proceed across the bridge, having unilaterally asserted the Buddha's spiritual sovereignty.

Manjusrimitra smiled, instantaneously revived the riven king as well as his elephant, and restored them to wholeness. Then he said:

"I revere not mundane, worldly lords,
nor step aside even if an army of war elephants confronts me.
Intoning the king of profound, secret mantras,
my winged feet pass unhindered through rocky mountains
and ascend the firmament."

The king dismounted, bowed reverently to the Buddhist siddha, and requested that Manju accept him and his followers into Buddha's fold.

Manjusrimitra told them, "Karma, the law of cause and effect, is unerring. What else could produce anything in the vast, immaculate expanse of emptiness? You are already accepted.

"Hold not to 'I' and 'mine.' Relinquish clinging to the concepts of inner and outer, subject and object, good and evil; then everything will be perfectly clear."

A Rainbow Body in Manikengo

The Rainbow Light Body is a unique achievement resulting from the efficacious practice of Vajrayana Buddhism. Om Mani Padmé Hung *is the popular mantra of the Buddha Avalokitesvara, Great Compassion; its simple literal meaning, "Hail to the jewel in the lotus," belies its profound mystical import.*

A stupa is a bell-shaped Buddhist monument, often of immense proportions.

AT A VILLAGE CALLED MANIKENGO in Kham, near the Dzongsar Monastery, an extraordinary event occurred in 1955. An old codger, a servant and carver of mani (prayer) stones, manifested after death the signs of having attained the exalted Rainbow Light Body of supreme enlightenment—much to everyone's surprise.

No one knew that the old man had been an accomplished practitioner of Dzogpa Chenpo, Buddhism's consummate teaching. He had been a servant for a wealthy family; in middle age, he left that position to receive meditation instruction at a Nyingma (Ancient School) monastery. After that period, he eked out a meager living by carving the mantra *Om Mani Padmé Hung* on rocks, later erecting a great pile of them into the form of a rough stupa.

Though he worked all day, he spent his nights in contemplation, sleeping only two or three hours. Poor and simple, he had a small family. He helped everyone in need, and his humble abode was at all times open to pilgrims and beggars.

While carrying out his daily work, the old man continued his spiritual practice, integrating meditation with activity through continuous mindfulness. His son, a monk, often advised him to perform more formal spiritual practices: to sit in meditation, do yoga, and so on. However, this did not alter his father's habits.

"Intrinsic wakefulness is the main point, my son," he told the earnest monk. "Simply try to maintain lucid awareness of intrinsic awareness itself, the natural state of being. There is no other Buddha."

Three years before his death, the old man fell ill. Though the family fretted, he himself appeared increasingly happy. Rather than chanting the traditional Buddhist liturgies, he sang original songs of spiritual praise. Performing no rites or rituals, reciting no mantras, repeating no sutras or prayers, he seemed to have entirely abandoned all forms of ceremonial observance.

When his son, the monk, again exhorted him to devote himself to religious practices, the old man replied, "There is no external Buddha worth worshiping. The innate wakefulness of intrinsic awareness is one's primordial nature."

As his illness became increasingly serious, lamas and doctors were called for. His son reminded him that this was the most important time to recall all the Dharma teachings he had received. The old man simply smiled and said, "Son, I have forgotten religion. Anyway, there is nothing to remember! All is illusory, yet I am happy—everything is perfect!"

Just before departing from this world, the beatific old man made one request: "When I die, do not move my body for one week. This is all I desire."

After his death, the corpse was wrapped in his own old clothes. The lamas chanted and prayed for him, and the body was placed in a tiny room. While this was going on, people noticed that although the old man had been tall, the body now seemed to have become smaller; at the same time a rainbow was observed above the house.

Six days later, the family looked into the small room. Inexplicably, the body had continued to shrink! A cremation was arranged for the morning of the eighth day. On that day, when the shroud was undone, they found nothing inside except fingernails and hair.

Everyone was astounded. No one could have entered the room and removed the body, for the room was kept locked. When the old man's son asked Dzongsar Khyentse Rinpoche, the abbot of the local monastery, about this matter, he said that such things had happened before to Dzogchen masters. The corporeal form of the saintly old man had been transformed into radiant luminosity, the clear light of Dharmakaya, an enlightened state of essential being: this was the true significance of the remarkable occurrence.

Dzongsar Khyentse added that there could be no doubt about it; the old man had actually achieved, in a single lifetime, the legendary Rainbow Light Body. Chögyam Trungpa Rinpoche as a teenager visited the place, heard the story, and viewed the remaining relics.

Thus, even today, enlightened masters live discreetly among us, having perfectly mingled profound spirituality with their daily lives, their inner accomplishments rarely perceived.

A Feast Offering

Chakra Samvara is a blue, many-headed, multiarmed tantric meditational deity. Symbolic of universal wholeness, a mandala is a symmetrical configuration of elemental forms, primary colors, and deities, all imbued with various levels of mystic significance. Each major tantric deity is envisioned (by those with eyes to see) as attended by a complete entourage of subdeities. A siddha is a tantric adept in the Vajrayana practice lineage, often known as a "crazy yogi" or "divine madman."

KING CHANAKA BUILT A CHAKRA Samvara temple in Shantapuri and requested the powerful yogi Vagisvara Kirti to consecrate it for the benefit of the populace. The king sent a royal messenger to seek the master at his hermitage in the forest, where he was known to remain in deep meditation all year round.

When the courtier reached the humble hut, he was met at the door by a young voluptuous dancing girl and a swarthy, bellicose woman, who together blocked the entrance.

The two consorts refused admittance to the courtier, saying that the master was in meditation. But they agreed to convey the king's message to Vagisvara Kirti. Eventually, much to the impatient courtier's consternation, the master replied that he would come and bless the new temple when he was ready.

The royal messenger hurried back to the king's court. How well he knew what might lie in store for the bearer of unwelcome tidings! But upon arriving, he was relieved to find that the tantric adept and his two consorts had already arrived.

The king ordered that elaborate preparations be made for a sumptuous vajra-feast offering rite to be held in the new temple; Vagisvara Kirti would perform the rites of blessing and consecration. The eccentric siddha, however, surprised everyone by stipulating that no one but his own retinue of sixty-five was to be admitted.

The bemused king and his entourage, who saw before them only the be-draggled tantric yogi and his women, had no alternative but to agree. "What kind of vajra-feast to bless and empower our temple will this turn out to be, with only that tattered trio in attendance?" they laughed among themselves. "What sort of madcap is this Vagisvara Kirti, anyway?... Who does he think he is, inviting no one but his own followers?" Many tongues wagged that day at King Chanaka's court.

Meanwhile, Vagisvara Kirti and his consorts had other business at hand. They remained for hours within the new temple, while everyone, including the king and his ministers, waited expectantly outside.

After the rite was complete, King Chanaka was astounded to find that the mountains of fine delicacies were gone; only the remnants of the vajra-feast remained. He also noticed that the entire atmosphere of the place felt as if it had been totally transformed and that the new temple was now indeed a sacred sanctuary.

"What did you do in there?" the king asked Vagisvara Kirti, as the adept began to make an unceremonious departure. "Where did all the other yogis and yoginis come from, and where are they now—the ones who obviously enjoyed the feast offering with such tantric relish? I only saw two followers in your entourage when you entered the temple and locked the door behind you."

Vagisvara Kirti said nothing; he just pointed to the sky. There King Chanaka saw the sixty-two attendant deities and subdeities of Chakra Samvara's mandala enshrined as his entourage, enjoying the lavish offerings that had been set out on the altar earlier. The temple had been consecrated by the actual presence of its own deity.

When the king turned to pay homage to Vagisvara Kirti, the yogi was gone.

The Musket Master

Doe Khyentse Rinpoche was a siddha of the last century, a carefree yogi in wild eastern Tibet. A layperson, he hunted, drank firewater, ate meat, and beat recalcitrant disciples into awakening.

Doe Khyentse would offer on his altar the meat and blood of the wild animals he shot. On many occasions, he purportedly would then snap his fingers and bring his prey back to life, sending them back to the wilderness; Doe Khyentse had achieved total mastery over life and death.

Why did Doe Khyentse live like a gun-toting hunter in the mountains and forests? Who can encompass the full meaning of the life-style that a truly enlightened vajra master (tantric guru) chooses to display in this fleeting, phantasmagorical world?

ONE DAY A GRAND RITE was being celebrated by an august assembly of monks and yogis when the siddha Doe Khyentse and his followers emerged from the forest, weapons in hand. The awesome master himself wielded an ancient musket.

One of the lamas, who was acting as master of ceremonies, respectfully approached the great siddha. He requested Khyentse (the recognized emanation of wisdom and love) to put aside his weapons—which seemed out of place at a monastic ritual—and bestow his blessings in a traditional manner. Doe Khyentse, instead, lifted his muzzle-loading rifle, took aim, and with a resounding blast, shot at a passing cloud.

The master of ceremonies and several others instantly recognized the true nature of reality and experienced great awakening.

Before they could express their gratitude and pay obeisance, the intrepid hunters had disappeared among the trees, following the Musket Master.

A Long-Life Empowerment

Jo Rigdzin was one of the great hidden yogis of the last century. He spent decades in solitary retreat and received personal guidance from countless masters. In his later years he retired from teaching and making pilgrimages to pursue his meditations unknown and undisturbed. During his youth, he lived as a solitary practitioner in the mountains; much later he married and became a divine madman, a crazy yogi nicknamed "Old Demon."

At one point, he was the teacher of the king of Dergé. Infirm, the king was carried everywhere by royal palanquin. One day his bearers were forced to halt, for the River Dza was in spate. Jo Rigdzin asked for a fistful of sand from the riverbank and blew mantras upon it. Then he threw the sand into the raging current; a path opened, and the king was carried to the far shore before the waters closed behind him.

Jigmé Özer was the first Dodrup Chen Rinpoche. He was one of the two main disciples of the eighteenth-century Dzogchen master omniscient Jigmé Lingpa.

Jigmé Lingpa, the Fearless Master, used to tell Jigmé Özer, "You will attain great realization but won't have a long life." This he repeated on three different occasions.

On the first two occasions, Jigmé Özer listened without inquiring further. "Anyway," he thought to himself, "I seek only realization, not longevity."

The third time, however, the disciple felt compelled to inquire further. "Can you advise me of anything that would help me remove the obstacle to my long life?" he respectfully asked his master.

Jigmé Lingpa said, "There is nothing I can do, but there is a yogi in Kham named Jo Rigdzin who can do something for you. Find him, and ask him to dispel your obstacle." Therefore Jigmé Özer set out for the region where the miracle-working master was known to be.

Eventually he reached a place in Sechuga not very far from Dzogchen, just slightly east of where Lama Mipham and Patrul Rinpoche later lived. There he found a small nomad encampment of about ten tents.

One tent was crowned with a flag. Jigmé Özer asked everyone at the camp the whereabouts of Jo Rigdzin, the great siddha. Everyone said, "We don't know anyone by that name. There is no Jo Rigdzin here among us simple herders. There is, however, one Grandfather Jo, who lives in that tent with the banner. Maybe he knows something."

Jigmé Özer went to the tent and asked the woman who met him at the door if there was anybody named Jo Rigdzin living there. The lady told him, "Only old Grandfather Jo lives here."

The seeker was disappointed. Then he happened to remember that his teacher Rigdzen (Vidyadhara) Jigmé Lingpa had made a point of telling him, "You go and ask Jo Rigdzin. He is the one who can help you. Whatever he says or does, he is a genuine tantric adept, so don't have any doubt. Just do whatever he says."

Therefore he entered the dim interior of the tent. He saw a grizzled old man sitting on the floor in a low wooden box, not unlike the meditation boxes favored by hermit lamas. He was wrapped in shabby lambskin, adorned by untidy long white locks and a tangled beard.

Jigmé Özer, who was no mere neophyte himself, knew immediately that this must be the Great Yogi of Jo whom he was seeking. Therefore he reverently offered three full-length ceremonial prostrations on the hard earth.

The old man asked, "Where do you come from?"

Jigmé answered, "From central Tibet."

"What did you come for?"

"My teacher, the omniscient Jigmé Lingpa, sent me to you because he can't dispel the imminent interruption of my life span. He said you can," the visitor explained.

"Phooey!" scoffed Grandfather Jo. "What do you mean, 'omniscient' Jigmé Lingpa? He's called omniscient, but he can't even remove such an obstacle? He's just a loudmouth, unworthy of his own highfalutin' name."

Jigmé Özer was greatly upset to hear his beloved teacher lambasted; he himself thought of Jigmé Lingpa as a living Buddha who could do no wrong.

The churlish old man noticed Jigmé Özer's obvious discomfort. "All right, all right!" he exclaimed grudgingly. "Just give me my chamber pot. It's right over there." Then he pointed into the dim recesses of the tent.

Jigmé Özer did as he was asked. He brought the beat-up corroded copper pot and respectfully placed it in front of Grandfather Jo.

Grandfather Jo said nothing. He seemed to be inwardly absorbed, as if in a meditative trance. After a while, he looked up and inquired, "What was it that Jigmé Lingpa said?"

Jigmé Özer repeated what had been said before. "He sent me to you to remove the obstacle to my longevity."

Again the old man scoffed. "What is this about omniscience, if he can't even remove an obstacle in your life? Such grand titles makes no sense at all!"

Jo picked up the chamber pot and shook it upside down to see if there was anything inside; it seemed to be empty. He placed it on the low prayer table in front of him.

Once more he asked, "What did Jigmé Lingpa say?"

Again Jigmé Özer told him, "He sent me to you to remove the obstacle in my life; perhaps he intended that you bestow upon me a long-life empowerment."

Yet again the old man scoffed. "Nonsense! *He* knows how to give longevity initiations; what do you need me for? What kind of omniscient one is he if he can't remove paltry obstacles?"

The old man remained silent for a while, as if in meditation; then he again shook the copper chamber pot. This time, amazingly enough, something sloshed around inside.

Grandfather Jo exclaimed, "Oh! Hey! Come here!" He reached over and placed the piss pot like a ritual initiatory vessel on the crown of Jigmé Özer's head. Then he offered him a thick, nectarlike, amber-colored drink from its corroded copper mouth, as if the battered pot were a jeweled chalice.

Jigmé Özer was by then in an extraordinary state; he drank without thinking. Never before had he tasted anything like it, even from the hands of his own guru during rites of empowerment! He intuitively understood that through the aged yogi's miraculous powers, something special had transpired.

The old man ordered him to drink again, pouring the thick amber elixir from his repulsive copper chamber pot straight into Jigmé Özer's wooden teacup. Jigmé Lingpa himself had instructed Jigmé Özer to do whatever Jo Rigdzin ordered; he drank again.

Then the old man said, "Hmph! . . . Take more! More!" So he did.

Again and again he drank, until the old copper pot was completely drained. Jigmé Özer was euphoric, but because of the copper taste and all the filth that had been in the pot, he also became nauseated.

"I feel like vomiting," Jigmé said.

Grandfather Jo said, "Why not? Go right ahead!" Jigmé Özer did.

The lady of the house ordered him to clean it up. He did. "This is a nice way for a guest to act," she exclaimed. "Why don't you leave Grandfather Jo in peace?"

The wizened yogi took a few pinches of musty, dried barley flour from an old hide sack, spit into his hands, and casually proceeded to roll up two or three red pills, in appearance identical to ritual long-life pills. "Hmph!" he said. "Eat these."

Then Old Man Jo told him, "Now you can live for two hundred years, for all I care."

As Jigmé Özer prepared to leave, Jo Rigdzin picked up a stick from beneath the shabby jumble of bedclothes beside him and whacked Jigmé Özer's head very hard three times, in a gross imitation of the rites of initiation.

"All right, that's done," the crazy old yogi exclaimed. "Yah! Get out!"

The next day, Jigmé Özer came again to visit. "Should I leave now or stay nearby for a while?" he reverently inquired.

"Just go away. No need to stay any longer. Just carry on with your obstacle."

Jigmé Özer left and went immediately to see his guru, Jigmé Lingpa. "What happened? What did the old man tell you?" Jigmé Lingpa, the Fearless Master, demanded.

Jigmé Özer did not dare to inform him about what Jo Rigdzin had said about Jigmé Lingpa himself, so he remained silent.

Jigmé Lingpa asked him, "Did you get the long-life initiation?"

"Yes, I got it," he replied.

"What did he say?" Jigmé Lingpa demanded.

"He said it's all right, that I can have a long life."

"But did you get the genuine longevity empowerment?" the omniscient master insisted.

"Yes, yes," the disciple replied.

"That enlightened lunatic didn't say anything else?"

In the face of his teacher's insistence, Jigmé Özer had no choice but to explain everything in detail, including how Jo Rigdzin had insulted Jigmé Lingpa.

After listening intently to the entire tale, Jigmé Lingpa laughed and said, "That's great! Your vital energy is now perfectly balanced. The current of your life force is realigned and will maintain its continuous flow. That obstacle is now dispelled.

"That old yogi is truly like Guru Rinpoche in human form; you are very lucky. Jo is far beyond the confines of good and evil, clean and unclean; to him, gold and shit are equal."

Jigmé Lingpa continued: "As for what he said about me, an insult from him is better than others' blessings and praise!"

Bride-to-Be

Many Nyingma (Ancient School) visionaries have received prophecies from their gurus or deities concerning where to find their predestined wisdom consort. The right companion in tantric practice is known to help a lama fulfill his altruistic aspirations, extend his life span, and attain realization. Such authentic incarnate dakinis facilitate mystic revelations and increase enlightened activity.

In the Vajrayana tradition, women are considered to embody the fertile wisdom of emptiness; men, compassion and the dynamism of skillful means. At the same time, each is complete and perfect in and of themselves.

ONCE A GREAT LAMA RECEIVED a prophecy from the terrific one-eyed, single-breasted Dharma protectress Ekajati that he would take as consort a woman in a neighboring valley. Once he did so, he would discover a cache of Dzogchen teachings of inestimable value to subsequent generations.

Sending three disciples to seek the woman, the lama prayed and meditated, keeping a vigil in his shrine room. But after one week, the three monks returned without fulfilling their mission.

"Where is she?" their master demanded.

"We found no one answering to your description," they replied, "only one ragged woodcutter, blind in one eye and covered with vines and creepers, her skirt tattered, carrying gnarled branches of firewood on her back, an old rusty sickle in her hand. . . . She was truly terrifying, impossible even to approach. We did not find anyone who seemed a suitable consort for Your Reverence."

"That must have been her!" exclaimed the master. "The woman you describe as a harpy is the unique Dzogchen Protectress Ekajati in human guise. Bring her to me immediately!"

The disciples hurried out. Eventually they brought in the shabby woodcutter. Their master greeted her with respect and delight, for unlike them, he knew a true dakini when he saw one!

The master accepted her as consort and flourished magnificently. She inspired everyone who dared to enter her intense presence.

The lama became a great teacher, and his numerous revelations spread widely. He became renowned as a remarkable terton, a finder of spiritual treasures. And the awesome lady regally ruled his household and entourage.

The Master Known as "Every Form"

It is said that the siddha Lilavajra was born in the country of Samsara, was ordained in the dakini-land known as Uddiyana, and became an expert in the sutras and tantras.

Practicing the non-dual tantric way, Lilavajra lived on a small, uninhabited island in the middle of a noxious lake in northern India. There he became the guru of the renowned master Buddhaguhya.

ONCE A HERETICAL YOGI WAS in search of a Buddhist scholar's sense organs, to be used as sacramental substances for unorthodox magical practices. When he sought to kill Lilavajra, the prescient Dzogchen master was instantly aware of the sorcerer's malicious intent and playfully confounded his would-be murderer.

With bewildering rapidity, transforming himself into an astonishing variety of forms—including elephants, horses, buffalo, peacocks, and snakes—Lilavajra reveled in the uninhibited freedom of total mastery over appearances, and he thoroughly confused his antagonist. Faced with such phantasmagoria, the perplexed evil yogi left the island, having failed to find the dwelling of the Buddhist scholar named Lilavajra whose organs he perversely desired.

In celebration, Lilavajra sang a wondrous song of delight, full of outer and inner significance:

> "No one seems to know
> who is using one's own sense organs today.
> Illusory forms are innumerable,
> yet one's true identity,
> like quicksilver amid dust,
> is unique and unmistakable."

From that time on, the master Lilavajra was also renowned as Vishvarupa, or "Every Form." His songs were many, and his teachings profound and effective, for he had the gift, like any true master, of becoming whatever spiritual seekers might want or need.

The Lepers' Stupa

Lodrak Drubchen, also known as Namkhai Gyaltsen (the Heavenly Victory Banner), was a Nyingma siddha of the fourteenth century. One of Tsong Khapa's gurus, he met regularly with the Buddha Vajrapani, the Master of Secrets, in visions so vivid that it was as if the deity was present in person. The Gelugpa patriarch Tsong Khapa himself was wont to meet with Manjusri in the same manner. Transcripts of the spiritual questions posed by the Onion Master Tsong Khapa to Lodrak Drubchen—who received answers to them from Vajrapani himself—compose an exquisite tome of gnostic lore.

The embalmed body of this great siddha from the Lodrak region was kept in eastern Tibet after his demise, at Benpa Thichi Gompa, a place well known to pilgrims as Benpa Chador. Lepers used to flock there in droves for relief from their affliction, which Tibetans believe to be caused, like smallpox, by nagas, or serpent deities. The Nyingma saint's reliquary stupa was widely regarded as possessing miraculous healing qualities. Some lepers claimed that the disease reappeared if they left the immediate precincts of the stupa; others claimed permanent cures.

It was the custom for lepers to circumambulate the monument and to paint gold directly on the face of the embalmed body. When the gold would begin to crack, buckle, and pustulate, the leper who had offered a fresh, smooth skin of gold to the stupa would be cured.

ONCE A PILGRIM WHO SUFFERED terribly from leprosy came to Benpa Chador from afar. He had heard of the remarkable cures effected through the power of the late saint Lodrak Drubchen's prayers to take on the sufferings of all faithful followers, and was determined to avail himself of that miraculous promise—although previously he himself had been without much faith in the Buddha's teachings.

The pilgrim hobbled around the stupa, reciting the requisite prayers and mantras, praying that Lodrak Drubchen would deign to look kindly even upon him, giving him faith as well as alleviating the leprosy that so painfully afflicted him. . . . For he had heard that, even if one didn't completely understand the words of the unique prayers and mantras that had been passed down, the results were inevitable because of the late saint's own compassionate prayers and aspirations.

And lo and behold, as the fresh coat of gold on the stupa began to crack and buckle in the sun—not unlike the suppurating skin covering his own body—the pilgrim's faith increased by leaps and bounds, while the sores on his hands began to dry up and heal before his very eyes. . . . And his faith—long buried by the mist of doubt—was confirmed.

Slowly but surely, like so many before him, he was healed. Speechless with gratitude, he spent his remaining years in worship near that shrine.

The Guru Is Supreme Among All

Pandit Naropa was a siddha who flourished one thousand years ago in northern India. For a time he was the abbot of one of the main monastic colleges of Nalanda University.

Marpa the Translator was Naropa's principal Tibetan disciple. Marpa made three lengthy journeys to India in order to receive and practice Vajrayana teachings under tantric adepts. He brought the Mahamudra (Great Symbol) lineage teachings to Tibet, became Milarepa's guru, and fathered the Kagyu lineage.

ONE DAY NAROPA APPEARED IN the sky in the form of the multiarmed meditational deity Hevajra, surrounded by eight ecstatic goddesses. He asked his disciple Marpa the Translator, "Spiritual son, do you bow first to me, the guru, or to the deity? Who is preeminent?"

Marpa, who was no fool, thought, "I meet my guru every day and receive teachings from him, but today I am extraordinarily fortunate in being blessed with a vision of my tutelary deity. Therefore, he is more important."

"I bow and make obeisance to the glorious deity," said Marpa.

To Marpa's dismay, the marvelous divine display suddenly disappeared, dissolving back into Naropa's heart. Then Guru Naropa proclaimed:

"Son, without the guru one would not even have *heard*
of the Buddha, not to mention your personal deity—
So who comes first, the guru or the deity?
Obviously, guru devotion is most important for your development.
All deities are merely the guru's manifestations.
Don't be deceived by mere magical displays!"

Marpa, greatly chastened, from then on worshiped his guru above all other forms and images; through guru yoga, mingling one's own mind with the master's wisdom mind, he initiated the devotion lineage of the Kagyu school.

It is universally taught that one's principal spiritual guide is more kind than even the Buddha, for the teacher has accepted one as his or her personal responsibility, carrying one along the direct path to freedom and enlightenment. The tantras state that you should meticulously examine a teacher before accepting him or her as your spiritual master, for afterward, your teacher's word is law.

A Rat's Corpse and a Ring

Tsangpa Gyaré was a patriarch of the Drukpa Kagyu school; he lived in the twelfth century. Chakra Samvara is one of the principal Kagyu meditational deities.

In order to perform a vajra-feast offering, a ganachakra *rite, one usually needs sumptuous foodstuffs and other beautiful altar offerings—flowers, candles, and so on.*

ONE SUMMER THE DRUKPA KAGYU patriarch Tsangpa Gyaré and his followers were camped at Tsari, a holy place considered to be the residence of the deity Chakra Samvara. The master wished to offer a vajra-feast offering at that auspicious site, but the band of yogis wandering in the wilderness had nothing to offer in the way of food, drink, flowers, or any other desirable substance.

The master noticed a dead rat under a rock. It was hot and humid; a cloud of flying insects and a veritable army of crawling bugs swarmed around the rotting rodent. However, Tsangpa Gyaré, through the power of pure perception, envisioned the entire mandala of Chakra Samvara and his sixty-two attendant deities right there in the form of that maggot-infested corpse. The master ordered his disciples to offer the dead rat on a stone altar as a feast offering, in honor of the residence of the awesome deity.

This they proceeded to do, although no one except the master possessed the visionary purity necessary to perceive the rat's corpse in this transcendental way. The master himself, in sonorous, majestic verses, then invoked the presence of the deity and requested all the dakas and dakinis of the three worlds to convene for the feast. Innumerable enlightened ones deigned to display themselves, partaking of the splendid sense offerings in the transcendental light of such a powerful sacred outlook.

After the rite was successfully completed and the sacraments enjoyed to the utmost, the entire company, mortal and immortal, dispersed. Soon afterward, Tsangpa Gyaré realized he was missing his gold ring, but search where they would, his followers could not find it.

Tsangpa Gyaré laughed. "Maybe the dakinis were so delighted with that rat, they took my ring, too!"

Several months later, the master and his followers happened upon a solitary house in the wilderness. The daughter of the house appeared, and the yogis requested shelter. When the girl asked her mother, the mother was delighted to welcome the traveling yogis. "Today is the day of the deity. I wish to offer a dakini feast offering; now you can do it for me," she declared.

Tsangpa Gyaré replied, "Dear faithful lady, we would be glad to offer the vajra-feast you request. However, we ourselves have no provisions or delightful substances to offer."

The girl objected, speaking boldly, "But before you were able to offer a vajra-feast to Chakra Samvara with nothing but a rat's carcass!"

Tsangpa Gyaré was amazed. He asked the women how they knew about that. The girl reached into the voluminous folds of her dress, pulled out his gold ring, and handed it to him. "Shall we sell this in order to provide for the feast offering?" she inquired.

Then Tsangpa Gyaré recognized the pair as incarnate dakinis. The entire company—master and disciples—made manifold vajra-feast offerings and were immensely edified.

Just as the master was chanting the invocation, Chakra Samvara manifested in a colorful swirl of lights over the altar. Everyone present received empowerment directly from him, culminating in the attainment of enlightenment.

The young girl and her mother, momentarily appearing as one, danced in an ecstatic embrace with the radiant deity. Tsangpa Gyaré fingered his ring and smiled.

The Vulture Man

It was the funeral custom in Tibet to expose corpses to the elements, rather than to bury or cremate them. Firewood was often scarce in that frozen land. By dismembering and scattering the remains, hungry wild animals would also derive some benefit.

No action is too insignificant to be accomplished impeccably. It is as if the Buddha is always watching, for according to the unfailing law of karma, one cannot avoid reaping the fruit of whatever seed one sows.

It is said that the dakas and dakinis, as well as the Buddhas and bodhisattvas, receive offerings in an infinite variety of ways and are capable of assuming an infinite variety of forms.

ONCE A WANDERING YOGI WAS meditating in a lonely charnel ground, where the gory remains of human corpses were being devoured by huge black vultures. To scare off the voracious birds of prey, the yogi threw a stone; it struck one of the gigantic birds on the upper part of one wing.

At that, all the birds suddenly startled into flight and scattered. Then, in that forlorn solitude, the mendicant proceeded with his austerities. Sitting upright day and night, he filled the vale of the dead with his rhythmic, dolorous chants, offering himself, body and soul, and inviting the restless, tortured spirits to feed and be satisfied.

Months later, that same yogi was wandering in search of alms. He came upon a tiny hamlet of rough stone huts at the foot of some hills on an arid, windswept plateau. By begging for alms from the nomadic herders and scattered settlers, such a spiritual practitioner could survive on a subsistence diet of roasted barley flour, fresh curds, dried yak meat, and hard cheese—preferring the sweet joys of contemplation and spiritual solitude to the sensuous delights of a more settled existence.

The yogi approached the door of the first house he came to; he was playing his bell and hand drum and singing the Chöd offering song—a liturgy in which one offers one's own flesh and blood; this is a tantric practice that effectively cuts through self-centered attachments. Thus he solicited alms in the traditional manner of the wandering mendicants of Tibet's many religious orders.

Suddenly, a large, dark man with a long neck, prominent jaw, and protruding teeth, dressed in an old and ragged black coat, threw open the door, picked up a stone, and exclaimed, "Hey, begging minstrel, my shoulder still smarts from that stone you threw! Seek your food elsewhere, or I will eat *you!*"

Momentarily hunching up his large shoulders in a vulturelike manner, he made a frightening gesture, gave a toothy grin, and slammed the rough-hewn door with a bang. The mendicant went hungry that day.

Chögyur Lingpa and the Wolves

Chögyur Lingpa, the Treasure Master, was an enlightened visionary who flour-ished during the nineteenth century. His numerous revelations, which now are rediscovered treasures, are practiced widely in the Kagyu and Nyingma schools.

Dharmapalas are ferocious guardians, higher energies dedicated to protect-ing practitioners and the teachings. Thighbone trumpets and black banners are ritual implements used in propitiating such deities and invoking the powerful forces associated with them.

Nup Sangyay Yeshé was a disciple of Padma Sambhava and was known for his magical powers.

ONCE CHÖGYUR LINGPA AND HIS group of lamas and monks were slowly traveling through wild eastern Tibet. Some bandits imagined that the travelers were wealthy ecclesiasts and decided to rob the party. They followed the group at a discreet distance until nightfall.

Each night the robbers considered attacking the monks, but after sundown unexpected circumstances unfailingly prevented them: one night the weather was terrible, another night there was lightning, another night an earthquake. Their superstitions aroused, the thieves began to think the head lama must have placed a powerful spell around his camp as protection.

In total darkness, the boldest brigands finally approached the camp after midnight. Chögyur Lingpa's *katvanga*, his ritual trident, was planted upright in the earth behind the grand lama's tent. The iron trident was glowing and shoot-ing out sparks like fireworks. The robbers dared not attack and thus wasted another night.

The bandits swore, "No matter what happens—whatever illusory magical apparitions the lamas conjure up to thwart us—tonight we will attack! These lamas are completely harmless, a helpless bunch of unarmed, pious nobodies. They must have gilded ritual vessels, if not bags of gold dust. Let's get them!" They vowed to attack that very night and make off with the loot.

The clairvoyant Chögyur Lingpa told his attendants, "Tonight we might have a little danger. Let's offer a special rite for the Dharma protectors."

He told the monks who blew the thighbone trumpets, "Nup Sangyay Yeshé had a special way of blowing them. You should blow for the guardians like this tonight . . . " And he taught them how to do so. He told the master of ceremonies to shake the Dharmapalas' black silks menacingly to the four directions, as a protection.

The robbers stole up under the cover of darkness. Suddenly they found themselves face to face with a pack of howling wolves that surrounded the tents, their eyes livid and phosphorescent. The brigands turned and fled, never to return.

Even nowadays, Tibetans who camp in dangerous places follow this tradition, since it worked so well for the Treasure Master Chögyur Lingpa.

Karma Pakshi's Troubles

The second Gyalwa Karmapa, Karma Pakshi, was the guru of Genghis Khan's grandson, the thirteenth-century Chinese emperor Monga Khan. After Monga Khan's demise, Karma Pakshi fell into disfavor with Kublai Khan, Monga's successor.

Marco Polo mentions the powerful Tibetan lamas, called bakshis, *at Kublai's imperial court. These were presumably Karma Pakshi's followers, if not the second Karmapa himself.*

KUBLAI KHAN ORDERED HIS SOLDIERS to do away with the famous Tibetan hierarch, Karma Pakshi. On several occasions they attempted to poison, burn, smother, drown, or slay him with swords, but Karma Pakshi's magic protected him, and he overawed his assailants through forgiveness and compassion. Then the Khan ordered Karmapa incarcerated in a dank dungeon for seven days without food and water; there he was unceremoniously hung from the ceiling by his flowing black beard.

Through prayer, Karma Pakshi invoked the assistance of his personal Dharma protector, wrathful Mahakala. However, great Black Mahakala took so long to arrive that when he did, Karmapa slapped him in the face; to this day, Mahakala has a red welt on his cheek. Moreover, the irate Karmapa vowed never again to be reborn with hair on his chin!

Karma Pakshi's jailers reported that lovely celestial maidens daily served the imprisoned lama food and drink, which they could do nothing to prevent. The Karmapa seemed imperturbable, peacefully meditating and chanting in solitary confinement.

Vexed, Kublai Khan sent the Action Master Karmapa into exile on a desolate island, where, his advisers assured him, the uncowed lama's health and spirit would swiftly deteriorate. Carefree Karma Pakshi, however, seemed content simply to spend his time meditating and writing.

The arrogant Khan eventually relented. He offered the former imperial guru free passage back to Tibet. At the last minute, Kublai requested the living Buddha's forgiveness and blessing.

Karma Pakshi began the long overland trek back to his Himalayan homeland. Along the way, on a desolate windswept plain, he found a huge golden temple roof lying in the sand where the returning Mongol hordes had abandoned it after plundering India. In an incredible feat of psychokinesis, he threw the entire roof into a nearby spring, entrusting it to the care of his protectors. When Karmapa arrived in Tibet, the golden roof was miraculously waiting for him, at the edge of a lake near his monastery.

Long before, Karma Pakshi had received inspiration in a vision to construct a huge Buddha statue for the peace and welfare of the world. At home in Tsurphu, Karma Pakshi found nearing completion—as he himself had ordered—the largest cast-bronze statue of that era, a sixty-foot-high image of the Buddha. To bless and empower it, he filled the towering statue with authentic relics from Sakyamuni and his disciples.

When Karmapa sat facing the statue, it was obvious that the gargantuan image was tilted to one side. No one had dared to mention this flaw for fear of displeasing the mercurial master.

Karma Pakshi went into meditation. He leaned over slightly to one side, in imitation of the colossal image before him . . . and as he slowly straightened his own torso, the great metal Buddha statue did likewise—to everyone's utter amazement. That magnificent statue remained the most venerated relic in Tsurphu until the Red Guards dynamited it in the early sixties.

Karma Pakshi's writings were among the most voluminous of any Tibetan master; unfortunately, few of them have survived. A few small remnants from that massive bronze Buddha statue are with us today as relics.

Rain of Flowers

ONCE PATRUL RINPOCHE TAUGHT THE Secret Essence Tantra near his cave in Upper Doe. Among the disciples was an elderly nomad. Crossing the river on his yak every morning, he returned home each night.

One day a downpour of rain swelled the river. Nonetheless, the devout old man attempted the crossing. Carried away by the raging current, he drowned. A couple of villagers carried his body up the hill to Patrul.

"Ah-zi! Poor old man!" Patrul exclaimed. "He died because of his desire to receive teachings. We must pray and make profound aspirations for his further evolution."

The corpse rested on the ground before the compassionate master. The wife and relatives of the old man were wailing loudly. In eastern Tibet, death by drowning is considered especially ominous, since the nomads believe that one who dies in this way will take rebirth in inferior realms of existence.

"Please protect him through your unfailing compassion!" the bereaved widow begged Patrul again and again, lamenting and crying. "Deliver him from the torments of hell."

Accompanied by his assembled disciples, Patrul started to chant the Phowa practice, which transfers the consciousness of the deceased to higher realms and on toward freedom and enlightenment.

A gentle drizzle, which Tibetans whimsically call a "rain of flowers," had begun to fall, and delicate rainbow-hued clouds began to appear. Gazing up at the sky and then down at the corpse, Patrul suddenly laughed aloud, leaving his recitation unfinished. The assembled monks and lamas completed the ritual on their own, but no one dared to question Patrul.

A few days later, a disciple respectfully inquired, "Rinpoche, everyone knows that loving-kindness and compassion are the principal focus of your meditation. Why did you laugh when that old nomad died?"

Patrul replied, "That old man surely was worthy of compassion. But something funny happened just then."

"What happened?" the disciple asked.

"Feeling great pity, I prayed that he would take rebirth in a delightful realm; suddenly I saw him reborn as a celestial being in the Paradise of the Thirty-Three Gods. Out of gratitude for my teaching of the 'Secret Essence Tantra,' he smiled and showered a rain of divine flowers upon us.

"I looked at that wizened, gray-haired corpse before me and at all the relatives sobbing in fear of hell—and I cracked up. I thought to myself, 'This is truly samsara's delusion!' Then I thought, 'Seeing me laughing, these people think I am strange; seeing them crying, when the old man is already a celestial being, I think they are strange. This, too, is samsara's delusion!'"

Dodrup Chen Shows How to Die

The first Dodrup Chen Rinpoche, Jigmé Thrinley Özer, died in 1821. A disciple of Jigmé Lingpa, the Fearless Master, he was the principal lineage holder and transmitter of the Longchen Nyinthig (Heart Essence) tradition. An exemplary monk as well as a Dzogchen master, his enlightened disciples included the siddha Doe Khyentse.

Mahayana Buddhists often strive to take upon themselves the sufferings and burdens of others. Accomplished bodhisattvas can actually do so, thus curing disease and other forms of disorder.

THE SECOND DODRUP CHEN FOUNDED the Dodrup Chen Monastery in Golok. Choosing not to keep monastic vows, the youthful incarnation wore lay clothes and became renowned for his handsome features and youthful panache.

When he openly took up with a consort, he was forced to leave the monastery by his scandalized followers, although the young lama had already gained fame for his miraculous powers and psychic abilities. No one was like Dodrup Chen for transferring the dead to the transcendent Buddhafields!

Dodrup Chen II left for Dartsay-Doe. There, on the Chinese border, he became the guru of a local king. When a fearsome smallpox epidemic attacked the citizens of the area, Dodrup Chen made efforts to pacify the serpentlike nagas who spread the disease, but to no avail. Then, through the magical power of Tonglen and Bodhichitta—putting himself in the place of others—he took the disease upon himself in an effort to quell the epidemic.

As he was approaching death, some of his former disciples from the Dodrup Chen Monastery arrived. They requested him not to display miraculous signs when he died so as not to besmirch the reputation of the monastery that had cast him out for unorthodox behavior.

"If everyone marvels at your spiritual attainments after you are gone, how will it look for the illustrious Dodrup Chen Monastery that spurned you?" they remonstrated.

The young Dodrup Chen seemed agreeable. He gave them his blessings, and they began to leave. However, some people of Dartsay-Doe prevailed upon them to stay a short time longer in order to attend the death of their preeminent master and see that all the proprieties were maintained.

Only a few days later, Dodrup Chen II succumbed to the ravages of small-pox. Feverish, he writhed on the hard-packed dirt floor of his room, gouging out four little pits where his frenzied hands and feet clawed the ground in his death agony. Then he died.

The hardhearted monks from the Dodrup Chen Monastery were saddened. Yet they were cheered to think that at least the young tulku had not displayed miracles while passing away, which would have exposed their own foolish narrow-mindedness. Their mission had been accomplished.

That very day the siddha Doe Khyentse, a teacher of the second Dodrup Chen, appeared on the scene, dressed, as always, like a hunter. Aware of Dodrup Chen's death, the Musket Master stormed into the lama's room. Finding Dodrup Chen's corpse on the floor, Khyentse berated him. "Don't you know anything? How can a Dzogchen master die like this? Get up, sit up! Reveal your proud heritage."

Hearing the uproar, everyone came running. Dodrup Chen's former monks were there as witnesses.

Doe Khyentse shouted again at the dead lama. Dodrup Chen's corpse suddenly sprang unassisted from the floor, leapt into the cross-legged, full-lotus posture, and sat unsupported in the air, a few feet above the ground. Rainbows arched overhead, flowers fell from the sky, heavenly music thrilled the air, and everyone rejoiced. Doe Khyentse clapped his hands, loud as gunshots.

The monks from the Dodrup Chen Monastery returned to their brethren with the bittersweet news. Everyone marveled about their late master, whose unconventional behavior they had been unable to appreciate during his brief lifetime.

Dodrup Chen Gets Enlightened

THE PRESENT DODRUP CHEN RINPOCHE was born in 1927. At an early age, he was enthroned as the fourth grand incarnation, or tulku, of Dodrup Chen at the Dodrup Chen Monastery in Golok.

When he was twelve, his aged master Yutok Chadrel handed him a large skullcup full of wine and bade him drink. The boy protested that alcoholic beverages were proscribed by the vows of ordination. His teacher, however, commanded him to drink.

Dodrup Chen Tulku thought to himself, "It is against my monastic vows, yet if my teacher—the Buddha incarnate—bids me to do so, I will. His word is my command."

The moment he drank the wine, Dodrup Chen experienced a great awakening. Everything was suddenly transformed. This extraordinary state had nothing to do with ordinary intoxication.

He sang a little song:

"Today the Buddha in person turned this monk
  inside out and upside down,
  and I have understood the essence of Dzogpa Chenpo,
  the innate Great Perfection."

Transubstantiation

A NEPALI BRAHMIN WHO LIVED near Tsurphu had a beautiful wife who was in the habit of disappearing from time to time. He suspected that she was meeting another man.

On one occasion, just as she was leaving, her husband asked if he could accompany her. To his displeasure, she denied his request. The next time his wife was leaving, he insisted upon joining her.

Laughing aloud, she agreed. "Don't be surprised, whatever happens," the lady said. "Trust me, as I trust you." What could the hapless husband do but agree?

The lovely lady, an incarnate dakini, readied herself as if for an evening out. Then she exclaimed, "Let's go. Climb on my back." And she flew into the sky, with him aboard.

Eventually they reached a sacred site where everything seemed to be made of vermilion; it was the fabled dakini land called Urgyen Khandro Ling. The couple landed. Innumerable nubile women of all ages with reddish skin, naked and adorned with flashing jewels and ornaments made of bone, were on their way to an imposing palace, inside of which, on a grand throne, sat a dignified lady who was obviously their sovereign. It was the enlightened dakini queen, Vajra Yogini!

Everyone was seated as if about to perform the rite of a vajra-feast offering. The Brahmin's wife, whom he now recognized as a dakini, told him to sit in one corner.

The majestic queen of the dakinis called his wife over and said, "Today it is your turn to perform the feast offering." The wife then disappeared momentarily. When she reappeared, she was bearing the severed upper half of the skull of a recently deceased leper.

"This is today's feast offering," she proclaimed grandly. "Enjoy!" Then the tantric rite was performed, during which the awestruck Brahmin and his liberated wife were mystically united.

When the transubstantiated substances were distributed as blessings, the leper's brains were ladled in tiny portions from the consecrated upturned skull-cup, to be imbibed by the enchanted company. The Brahmin was filled with unspeakable revulsion due to his orthodox concerns about ritual purity and uncleanliness. What normal Nepali would willingly touch a leprous corpse, not to mention eat brains?

He refused the tiny portion of blessed brains, offered to him from the very hand of the deity Vajra Yogini. She laughed and insisted, "Here, take this. It's good for you!" But still he refused.

Quickly placing something in his hand, Vajra Yogini told him, "Go now, and do not open your fist until you get home. If you had accepted my feast offering, you could have remained forever here in this dakini paradise of Urgyen Khandro Ling. However, now you must go and be reborn into ordinary existence. Yet today you sowed the seed of benefiting others, so rejoice!" Then the dakini queen dismissed the Brahmin with a wave of her bejeweled hand.

Riding on his wife's back, he returned home. Although so many extraordinary events had transpired since their departure, only one hour seemed to have elapsed in human time. He respectfully asked his wife, "May I look now?" She gave her consent.

Opening his hand, the Brahmin saw seven grains. His wife said, "Lord, if you had imbibed as blessings that drop of transubstantiated brain, you could have stayed there forever. Because you hesitated, you will have to be reborn once more. The seven grains mean that you will die in seven days. Immediately afterward, you will be reborn in the dakini paradise, from there swiftly to attain perfect awakening. This is my gift to you."

When seven days passed, he died and was reborn in the celestial dakini paradise called Dumatala. His wife later gave birth to twin girls with auspicious dakini marks upon their bodies; their birth was surrounded by marvelous signs and promising omens. Absorbing dakini lore from their liberated mother, the twins grew up to become spiritual teachers.

A Monk's Golden Elephant

A bhikkhu is an ordained Buddhist monk. Kasyapa Buddha was the Buddha prior to our historical Buddha Gautama, or Sakyamuni. Magadha was the kingdom in northern India, east of Benares, where the enlightened Buddha was active after his great awakening under the Bodhi Tree at Bodh Gaya.

ONE DAY DURING SAKYAMUNI BUDDHA's lifetime, a beautiful boy was born to a well-to-do family in Magadha. The boy was named Gopala. At the very same moment that he was born, a golden baby elephant emerged from the large family storeroom.

A soothsayer consulted the stars and informed the proud parents that the boy had a great destiny awaiting for him. Moreover, he said, the golden elephant signified that great riches and success lay ahead for Gopala. Everyone rejoiced.

The boy and his pet elephant grew up together and became inseparable. Wherever Gopala went, the golden calf accompanied him, leaving small piles of golden droppings and golden pools of urine, much to everyone's amazement. Many wondered whether or not the elephant's glittering excretions were genuine gold, but few could ascertain this with certainty, for most of the curious lacked authentic expertise in the matter. . . . And so the years passed.

News of the boy and his miraculous pet eventually reached the ears of the jealous young Prince Ajatasatru. He resolved to obtain the golden elephant, no matter the cost, for he coveted its riches.

When Ajatasatru became king, he ordered Gopala to present the remarkable elephant to him as an offering, contriving a royal decree: "All regal possessions—such as golden elephants—belong to the keepers of the kingdom, the royal household. They are not to be misused as pets by commoners."

Youthful Gopala asked his father, "How can anyone take my elephant from me? We took birth simultaneously, like twins; he is like a brother to me."

His father replied, "The king is jealous and arrogant; he will stop at nothing to get what he wants. Let us go to see him, as he commands. Perhaps righteousness will triumph."

Gopala and his father mounted the golden elephant and rode to the palace. Their lumbering mount carried them straight into the courtyard. When they were presented to King Ajatasatru, in unison they uttered, "Lord and master, may you be happy, healthy, and wise."

The greedy king fed them royally. Then he dismissed them, commanding them to leave the golden elephant in his care for the benefit of the kingdom and the entire populace.

Gopala turned to his father in silent dismay. His father calmly took the boy's arm, bidding the king good-bye for both of them. Then the pair strode off.

Miraculously, Gopala's golden elephant greeted them at the edge of the forest. Gopala cried with joy.

His father told him, "Son, I dreamed last night that your elephant sank into the ground beneath the king's weight when he first tried to mount him, and then your elephant appeared in our own courtyard. This was an excellent omen. Therefore, I doubted not when we faced the king today. Now, by the power of propriety, our marvelous elephant has returned to us. Let us rejoice in the virtues of humility and righteousness!"

Not long afterward, Gopala grew disillusioned with worldly life in a kingdom where even the king had to steal from his subjects. With his parents' permission and blessing, the teenager mounted his enchanted elephant and sought ordination from the Buddha in the Jeta Grove near Anathapindaka's Park.

The Omniscient One knew what had transpired, without hearing a word from Gopala. As the boy approached reverently on foot, the Buddha spoke the decisive words, "Come, bhikkhu, into a life of purity."

With those fateful words, which the Buddha used to ordain monks, youthful Gopala was instantly transformed into an upright young bhikkhu, with shaved pate and yellow robes—as if he had always been one. His beautiful, well-oiled, long jet-black hair was gone, his layperson's dress nowhere to be seen. A begging bowl lay in his folded hands.

In that instant, his mind was still, his attention absolute. Thus Bhikkhu Kanakavatsa was born.

The golden elephant awaited the young monk when he walked slowly and mindfully into the forest for his evening meditations. Once again, the two were inseparable.

Kanakavatsa eventually realized the empty, dissatisfactory nature of all worldly pursuits and the transitoriness of all possessions and experiences. He was freed from the last vestiges of attachment, even to his beloved pet elephant. The elephant, however, remained attached to him and would not be left behind.

Meditating deeply, the young monk eventually intuited absolute truth and became an arhat. People began to follow him and gratefully attend his quiet discourses.

One day some traders became enthralled by the golden elephant and his miraculous droppings; they began to create a disturbance wherever the arhat and his marvelous elephant went. Word of these events soon came to the attention of Lord Buddha.

The Buddha sent for Kanakavatsa. "There is much commotion caused by the confused emotions of the worldly, quarreling over illusory nuggets of golden elephant dung. It has begun to encroach upon the harmonious atmosphere of the sangha's peaceful sanctuary," the Enlightened One declared. Therefore, although the good monk was blameless, the pet elephant had to go.

Kanakavatsa informed the Buddha that he had already, on several occasions, attempted to divest himself of this, his last worldly connection, but that the faithful pet proved impossible to discard. Moreover, Kanakavatsa said, "I feel sorry for him, who has been faithful to me for so long. How can I free my poor brother from bondage?"

The Buddha replied, "All beings are equally like brothers, young monk. All equally wish freedom from bondage. Do not stray into partiality."

The Enlightened One told his disciple, "Your golden elephant has been a boon to you. This good karma is due to your generous offerings in a previous life to a statue of the white elephant that Kasyapa Buddha rode when he descended from the formless sphere and entered his mother's womb in order to benefit the world. Now say this to him: 'I no longer need you, dear friend. By attaining liberation, I have fulfilled the purpose of life; now you, too, must be freed.'

"Tell him that three times, with your benediction and sincere best wishes, and send him on his way. Then he, too, will be free. There is nothing better we can do for our loved ones than free them from ignorance and attachment." Thus spoke Buddha.

The kindly Kanakavatsa spoke to his beloved friend just as the compassionate Buddha had advised. The golden elephant instantly dissolved before his eyes and was reborn in the heavenly sphere, eventually to attain liberation.

Kanakavatsa became renowned as one of the sixteen great arhats. He effectively propagated the Buddha's teachings in the lovely land of Kashmir.

A Lama Meets Manjusri

Manjusri's upraised right hand brandishes a flaming wisdom sword, which cuts through the veils of illusion and illumines all forms of darkness. This gnostic deity dwells atop the fabled Five-Peaked Mountain, called Wu Tai Shan, in western China.

ONE OF MANJUSRI'S TIBETAN DISCIPLES prayed for many years for a vision of his tutelary deity, the Gentle Lord who is the color of the rising sun. He longed to meet Manju in person, but to no avail.

The middle-aged lama decided to make a pilgrimage to the sacred Five-Peaked Mountain to seek Manjusri. He resolved to accomplish the pilgrimage by prostrating, step by step, all the way to the mountain and back—even if he died on the way.

Through countless difficulties—bad weather, rough terrain, wild beasts, highway robbers—the pilgrim persevered. Prostration by painstaking prostration, step by step, month by month for years, he crossed the arid, windswept plains of central Tibet and the predator-infested forests of eastern Tibet, where bandits dwelt in abundance.

The name of his chosen deity remained always on his lips; for him it had a savor sweeter than wine. Faith and diligence never faltered, nor did his steps, his prostrations, his prayers . . . until eventually he found himself at the foot of the Five-Peaked Mountain. Exhausted, he prostrated reverently, prayed, and fell asleep bent over his prayer books.

Waking suddenly, he could think only of Manjusri. With renewed energy, he began the steep ascent. Snow began to fall; the snowflakes seemed to him to be white lotus flowers, which he took as a sign of blessing from the deity. But when darkness descended, the weary pilgrim could find no shelter from the storm.

On and on he went, picking his way through the growing darkness from one almost indiscernible mountain path to another. Stumbling again and again, he finally came to a staggering halt and conceded that he had lost his way. In the midst of the snowstorm, wallowing in a drift, he almost panicked—but then he remembered the clear, calm face of his meditation deity, Manjusri, whose seven-syllable mantra *Om A Ra Pa Tsa Na Dhi* had continuously sprung to his chapped lips throughout the long journey, and he found the strength to continue, staggering blindly uphill in the blizzard.

Suddenly, from out of the darkness, a young mendicant dressed in white appeared. With a simple gesture, he led the lama to a cave that was little more than a cleft between two massive, impenetrable rocks. Here there were firewood and shelter sufficient for two. But before the lama could regain his senses and make inquiries to his mysterious companion, the other was gone. He had disappeared into the swirling storm from which he had miraculously manifested, without leaving a single trace behind.

Then Manjusri's disciple knew for the first time the joy of meeting his tutelary deity face to face, for it was Manjusri himself who had saved him from a frozen fate. To this day that cave is remembered by the cognoscenti as the secret overnight resting place of gentle Manjusri.

The graying lama never descended the holy mountain. For many years he was seen prostrating and praying before the hoary old stupa containing the relics of Manjusri's hair.

Eventually the lama dissolved into the deity's heart, leaving before the golden image of Manjusri his well-worn bodhi-seed rosary and rosewood walking staff, which remain today in a carved case on the shrine.

A Guru Stones His Disciple

ONCE THE MANJUSRI MASTER, JAMYANG Khyentse Wangpo, and his disciples were camped near a lake in eastern Tibet. Although ill, the erudite abbot Garmé Khenpo accompanied them.

One day, as Garmé Khenpo spoke, Jamyang Khyentse suddenly picked up a handful of rocks and flung them at him. The dignified khenpo (abbot-professor) ran toward the lake, with Jamyang Khyentse in pursuit, still pelting him with stones.

When the khenpo reached the shore, he unhesitatingly plunged into the crystal clear, icy water. Khyentse Rinpoche hit him with a few more rocks and then stopped.

Everybody laughed. Although distraught, Garmé Khenpo knew that Khyentse Rinpoche was, in a playful way, blessing him. The other disciples were touched by the unique relationship between them. Jamyang Khyentse, the Manjusri Master, was never frivolous; everyone present perceived the outrageous incident as a baptism.

Soon after this unforgettable affair, Garmé Khenpo's chronic illness miraculously disappeared. Khyentse Rinpoche had purified him! Garmé Khenpo outlived his teacher, Jamyang Khyentse, by decades, surviving into the twentieth century.

At the age of one hundred and twelve, Garmé Khenpo was blind. He explained to the lama who recounted this story, "It is due to the unique blessings of Jamyang Khyentse Wangpo that I have lived so long in good health. Until one hundred years of age I had my sight, as well as good health, thanks to being stoned by Khyentse Rinpoche that day long ago. A rock from the master is superior to gold from an ordinary mortal."

A Poor Student Becomes a Great Master

NÉTEN CHÖLING WAS THE TULKU, or incarnation, of the nineteenth-century Treasure Master Chögyur Lingpa. From an early age he was taken to his illustrious predecessor's monastery and enthroned, where he displayed psychic powers and an unruly temperament. He would not obey his teachers, who had been his disciples in his previous incarnation, nor would he follow monastic regimens. Once, before the eyes of his astonished elders, he unthinkably hung his clothes on the rays of the sun to dry.

When his elderly tutor tried to teach him to read, Néten Chöling would neither learn nor study; he would only play. Regardless of the well-intentioned tutor's beatings, the carefree tulku remained unintimidated. When the stern tutor locked his young pupil in his room as punishment, the tulku was soon seen playing outside—much to the devoted tutor's amazement and dismay. . . . What to do with such an adept?

One day little Néten Chöling was playing on the roof of his house. His tutor scolded him, threatening to spank him. At that, Chöling leapt three stories down from the roof, landing safely on the ground. Just as his concerned tutor rushed over, the boy leapt up onto the roof again. How tongues wagged about that!

Chöling failed to learn to read, and his aged tutor continued to punish him. One day the guru Wangchuk Dorje told the white-haired lama, "You must not beat Chöling Tulku. It is impossible in our family that anyone should not know how to read. This must be his karma; who can understand such things?"

Wangchuk Dorje was proved correct. When Néten Chöling grew up, he certainly seemed to know how to read without ever having learned. In fact, he could read both sides of a page of scripture at once!

As a grown man, Néten Chöling spent long periods of time meditating in solitary retreat. He also drank wine and took snuff, shocking disciples into questioning their own preconceptions. Through impeccable unconditioned awareness, he acted like the illumined siddhas (tantric adepts) of medieval India. He enjoyed many consorts without producing a single child, and whoever he touched intimately was liberated.

When venerable ecclesiasts deigned to visit him in search of teachings and benedictions, he would immediately call for women, wine, and music. Through his higher perceptions, he always knew what his visitors were thinking; relentlessly he would expose their foibles and point out their sensitive spots. When great lamas and dignitaries came to visit, Néten Chöling liked to order the boys who were his servants to serve tea naked and to belch loudly, fart, and compete in making grotesque faces.

Néten Chöling perfected all the practices of Maha Ati Tantra, Dzogchen itself; his body barely cast a shadow. The Dzogchen Khenpo Ngakchung said, "On this side of the River Ganges there is no practitioner with greater realization."

Néten Chöling was the teacher of Dzongsar Khyentse Rinpoche, Chökyi Lodrö (who died in Sikkim in 1959), who in turn was Dilgo Khyentse's last master. One day Khyentse Chökyi Lodrö said to Néten Chöling, "People say that you are able to read very fast. I would like a demonstration of that." Khyentse brought the Kalachakra Tantra and asked Néten Chöling to read it.

Néten Chöling said, "I cannot see very well. I can't read."

Khyentse Rinpoche said, "You must read a little, just for me." Painstakingly, Chöling began slowly to spell his way through the huge book, one letter at a time—not unlike a child learning to read.

Khyentse exhorted him, "Come on now, read it properly!"

Chöling Rinpoche replied, "If I cannot be allowed just to sit here in peace, then I guess I have to read; but first I need some snuff."

He opened his snuffbox and withdrew a heap, cleaning his fingers on the lovely silk cloth that wrapped the precious text—an unimaginable transgression. Then he started to read the Kalachakra Tantra text at a previously unheard-of speed.

Dzongsar Khyentse was amazed. Chöling Rinpoche said, "All right, you wanted to see something remarkable. Actually, I can see both sides of the page at the same time, but my tongue can only recite what is written on one!"

Those who knew him were ceaselessly amazed by Chöling's powers. Once, while performing before a gathering one of the tantric dances (of which he was the acknowledged master), lightning struck his head. He did not flinch or interrupt the ritual, although several of the flagstones on the paved courtyard beneath his feet were shattered, blackened by the charge.

Another time he was carried away by a raging river. Praying to the Dharmapalas, he touched the river with his hand; a giant serpentlike naga carried his small boat back upstream and safely to shore. In the rock where he stepped ashore that day, a deep imprint of Chöling's boot remained.

Tibetan Dentistry

One of the world's largest monasteries until 1959, the renowned Sera Monastery near Lhasa housed four thousand monks. Many contemporary Tibetan lamas and geshés (doctors of divinity) studied and meditated there. The late Gelugpa sect teacher, Lama Thubten Yeshé, recently reborn in Spain, was trained at Sera. He was the first Tibetan lama to teach Buddhism widely to Westerners.

There is little modern surgery or health care in Tibet. However, Tibetan medicine and herbal cures, combined with the healing powers of mantras, often have remarkable results.

WHEN LAMA THUBTEN YESHÉ WAS a fourteen-year-old monk at the Sera Monastery, he developed a terrible toothache. His jaw was swollen with infection, and he could not eat or speak. He did not know what to do.

While there were no dentists nearby, Lama Yeshé's uncle, who looked after him, was a wise old monk. He offered prayers, then sent the boy to a monk renowned for his healing powers.

The grizzled healer dwelt in a dark corner of the sprawling monastic establishment. He seemed so filthy that the boy felt a great aversion to him, and he wanted to run away. Still, his jaw felt as if it was ablaze, so he felt compelled to remain.

The ragged old monk seemed kind. He welcomed the boy, offered him thick, salty, buttered tea, and muttered a few unintelligible mantras. Suddenly he leaned over and blew his fetid breath directly onto Yeshé's swollen jaw.

Yeshé was disgusted but held his tongue. He was instructed to return the next day for another treatment. For a week the gentle old monk treated the boy's abscess in this way, blowing his blessed breath upon it.

One day the old healer blew three great gusts on the infection, and the painful protrusion suddenly opened. Pus erupted in a thick stream. The swelling disappeared, and the infection was gone. Lama Yeshé was cured.

Over the years, people marveled over the scar, rejoicing in the miraculous power of prayer and mantra. Finally one day Lama Yeshé pointed out that the scar, too, had disappeared.

The Black Yogi and the Dog Master

The Dog Master Kukkuripa, an Indian yogi, had a following of five hundred bitches. All of the dogs were actually incarnate dakinis, with whom he reveled deliriously. This ugly siddha lived on a small, deserted island in the middle of a poisonous lake, where Marpa the Translator sought esoteric teaching and spiritual transmission from him.

Later Lord Marpa praised the Dog Master to the limit, saying, "My glorious Dog Master made me realize that even one's base sensual nature is more precious than gold, since it is, like all things, innately pure, free, and untarnished. Everything is a manifestation of the absolute unborn Mahamudra, the innate clear light of reality; even shadows are nothing but light!"

THE BLACK YOGI, NAGPO CHÖPA, wandered naked in ancient India, adorned only by ornaments made of bone. In graveyards and charnel grounds,

he performed various austere tantric rites, striving to transcend habitual clinging to the duality of good and evil and thus reach perfect freedom.

One day he happened to meet a weaver, who was actually an incarnate
dakini. She tested him, "O Black Yogi, what powers have you gained through
your stringent austerities? A yogi without powers is like a tree without fruit or
shade! Has your practice borne fruit?"

Then Nagpo Chöpa gazed intently at a large tree, and all its leaves fell
suddenly to the ground. "Externally, my body has dropped all ordinary ap-
parel; internally my mind has been divested of all attachments," proclaimed
the Black Yogi, not without hubris.

The dakini was unimpressed. "If you can destroy, you should also be able
to restore," she exclaimed. Dropping her weaving, she pointed to the leaves
strewn everywhere about them. Suddenly all the leaves were in place on the tree
again!

Nagpo Chöpa bowed reverently before her and went on his way.

On an auspicious day, the Black Yogi was preparing elaborate ritual offerings and oblations in order to provide a great vajra-feast for the dakas and
dakinis. When he invoked them from their mystic realm, inviting them to partake of the offering, a wisdom dakini appeared. She informed him that their
enlightened assembly had no time to attend his sacramental rite, for they were
obliged to participate in the vajra-feast being offered by the hairy Dog Master,
Kukkuripa.

Nagpo Chöpa was astonished. "What does that dog offer that I don't?" he
exclaimed. "I follow all the rites and rituals, as prescribed in the esoteric tantric
manuals."

The wisdom dakini, again assuming the familiar form of the weaver, replied, "You, naked yogi, do everything according to the book; even your ec-
centricities are regulated. Kukkuripa, however, is free from concepts, sleeps
in an outhouse, consorts with bitches, is without material offerings, plays no
ritual instruments, and parrots no scriptures. Since he relies on no higher authority than the innate wisdom of intrinsic awareness, we are bound to sport
with him!"

In a flash, she was gone.

The Scripture of Transcendental Wisdom Is Transmitted

In the Buddhist tradition, the oral whispered lineage is one of the principal means of preserving the continuous transmission of the unborn and undying flame of enlightenment. The Prajna Paramita Sutra, the Scripture of Transcendental Wisdom, is one of the most essential Mahayana texts.

The venerable Kangyur Rinpoche was a Dzogchen master born in Riwoché in eastern Tibet just before the turn of the century. He received complete transmission of the sutras and tantras from many of the greatest teachers of his time, and spent many years meditating in retreat. An author and spiritual treasure finder, he taught widely, passing away in 1975 at the monastery he built in Darjeeling.

ONCE THE YOUNG KANGYUR RINPOCHE and a friend heard from the turn-of-the-century master Mipham Rinpoche about an immortal siddha, or adept, who had totally transcended this world and roamed in the mountains like a wild animal. It was reported that this master of crazy wisdom had received the unique, intact, lineal transmission of the lengthy Prajna Paramita Sutra directly from the Tibetan Queen Yeshé Tsogyal, who in turn had received it from Guru Padma Sambhava himself. No living person could say how old the siddha was; as far as anyone could remember, he had always been old!

The two carefree young yogis were determined to receive that precious oral transmission directly from the siddha himself, no matter what they had to do to find him. So into the mountains they went, carrying basic provisions and singing happily.

For weeks the young men wandered through the remote wilderness, seeking the siddha. One day they caught sight of him, galloping along on all fours among a herd of Himalayan antelope. He was the shaggiest human being they had ever seen!

They were ready for anything—still, this sight amazed the youthful pair. Following the herd, they tracked the immortal adept. He tried to escape, disappearing into the half-hidden mouth of a cave.

Undaunted, the yogis stood before the entrance to the cave, respectfully requesting teachings and inviting him to emerge. The siddha, however, did not reappear. The lamas made numerous entreaties, offered prostrations and prayers, sang delightful songs of invitation and praise, and invoked the deity Prajna Paramita, the personification of emptiness itself, the infinite openness of absolute reality.

Then Kangyur Lama and his friend proceeded to offer a vajra-feast. When the enlightened ones, lineage holders, dakas, and dakinis were invoked and invited to partake of the offering, the divine madman—as if he was one of them—was compelled to come forth.

"What is your name?" they asked.

"What is your name?" he echoed, blinking his eyes.

"How old are you?" the lamas wanted to know.

"How old are you?" the siddha replied.

He would only echo their remarks. Otherwise, the naked, bright-eyed siddha kept silent. The lamas offered him the elixir of gnosis, utilizing a skullcup brimming with barley beer, and they sang spontaneous songs of realization. Finally the exalted siddha himself began to sing.

First he sang that he had not spoken in human language for over a decade; there were no teachings within him nor any teachings without, he sang. Suddenly the two lamas thrilled with joy and their hair stood on end, for they recognized the opening verses of the glorious Prajna Paramita Sutra pouring like a waterfall from the mad yogi's lips. It went on uninterrupted for hours, until he reached the end of the lengthy text.

As if awakening from a trance, the siddha blinked his eyes. Astonished, he sprang up and galloped off into the mountains, rejoining the herd. The two lamas returned to the human world and spread the transmission.

The name of that siddha, Samma Drubchen, even now awakens the heart to song. They say he is still alive in Tibet.

Resurrection

Mantrayana is the path of esoteric mantra practice. Generally synonymous with Tantrayana, or Vajrayana, it was brought to Tibet in the eighth century by the Indian siddhas Padma Sambhava and Vimalamitra.

Vajra Kilaya (or Dorje Phurba in Tibetan) is a wrathful, dark blue meditation deity known for his energetic Buddha-activity and unique ability to dispel obstacles. A magic dagger in the shape of a spike with a wrathful head as its hilt is his symbol; this ritual implement is called a kilaya, or phurba. Vajra Kilaya is the principal meditational deity of the Nyingma (Ancient Translation) school.

THE TRANSLATOR NYAK JÑANAKUMARA, PADMA Sambhava's disciple, had prodigious powers. Once he was reviled as a sorcerer and charlatan by unbelievers, although both his life-style and pith-instructions (oral guidance from master to disciple) revealed him to be an authentic Mantrayana adept.

One critic who particularly persecuted Nyak was named Chim Carok (the Crow of Chim). He destroyed Nyak's hermitage and attacked the master himself, pursuing him with a blacksmith's iron hammer.

Once Vimalamitra and Nyak were propitiating Vajra Kilaya together in a cave in Lhodrak. The twenty-one magic daggers arranged in a mandala on the altar started knocking against each other and emitting sparks. Meanwhile, Nyak was absorbed in meditative concentration.

Suddenly he thrust his own ritual dagger before him at chest level, then pointed it menacingly at the sky, shouting, "This is for that crow from Chim!"

A pair of passing crows, who happened to hail from Chim, approached the yawning mouth of the cave. Nyak wrathfully brandished his magic dagger in their direction, and one crow fell dead at his feet. The other crow sped away alone.

The Dzogchen patriarch Vimalamitra said, "Yes, you can kill through sorcery, but can you bring the dead back to life? If so, little hero, do it now; if not, cease and desist!"

Nyak Jñanakumara failed to revive the dead crow. Pandit Vimalamitra sprinkled sand over it, gently blowing whispered mantras and prayers upon the carcass. The bird sprang to life, shook its feathers, cawed, and flew away.

Vimalamitra commanded, "Until you have realized the unborn and undying nature of reality, do not transgress the moral precepts. Until you are totally beyond duality, be meticulous regarding actions; act conscientiously and with compassion. To undertake wrathful activity prematurely and act like a siddha without having realized how to liberate oneself and others is a crime against Buddha's non-violent teachings. When you know how to deliver the dead directly to the blessed Buddhafields, then you are free to do as you will."

Nyak took the master's advice to heart; later, he became unimaginably compassionate. Wherever he went, his compelling personality, wisdom, skillful means, and loving-kindness attracted followers. His realization eventually outstripped even his remarkable psychic powers; then he was a true master indeed.

Nyak had eight illustrious disciples, masters of the Vajra Kilaya practice. Ultimately, Nyak attained the Rainbow Light Body of perfect enlightenment.

The Kingly Treasure Master

In the Nyingma, or Ancient Translation, school, tantric Dharma teachings called terma *(rediscovered treasures) are often brought to light by visionary masters, even today. These spiritual treasures were hidden for posterity by Padma Sambhava, the Lotus-Born Guru, Yeshé Tsogyal, and other siddhas.*

Guru Chowang was one of the five kingly tertons, or treasure finders. As a boy, he was blessed by visions of Tara, Manjusri, and Vajrasattva. When he was thirty, a yellow parchment scroll fell into his hands, containing a list of nineteen termas that Guru Rinpoche had predicted Chowang would rediscover.

In a vision of the paradise called the Copper-Colored Mountain, Guru Rinpoche told Chowang:

> *"The supreme path is service to others.*
> *Whoever grows weary of selfless service*
> *lengthens the path to enlightenment.*
> *Bodhichitta is the ultimate boon for beings;*
> *Propagate the liberating teachings.*
> *Do not be attached to staying here in Zangdok Palri with me;*
> *I am ever-present."*

THE TREASURE FINDER GURU CHOWANG had a fine Nepali disciple from the Kathmandu Valley called Baro. Baro actually perceived his guru, Chökyi Wangchuk, as the Buddha incarnate, Padma Sambhava himself.

Guru yoga was his practice, and Baro sought no other deity. Mingling with his enlightened master's Buddha-mind, he attained awakening.

As it is said:

> If one perceives the guru as Buddha,
> one will attain Buddhahood.
> If one perceives the guru as a bodhisattva,
> one will become a bodhisattva.
> Perceiving the guru as an ordinary mortal,
> one will remain an ordinary mortal.

One day, Guru Chowang poked Baro in the chest with his finger, exclaiming, "Recognize this so-called I." At that instant, Baro's clinging and dualistic fixations evaporated, and Buddha-mind dawned—infinite, open, and luminous, like the sky.

Then Guru Chowang instructed, "Do not deviate from this crystal-clear recognition of the empty, illusory nature of the so-called I. In that spacious lucidity—without a single thing to meditate upon, nor anyone to meditate, neither subject nor object—that is true meditation!"

Then and there the Nepali disciple realized the absolute, unconditioned essence of the innate Great Perfection, Dzogpa Chenpo—beyond activity, free from fixation or bias, untainted by habitual tendencies of any kind.

Baro sang:

"Even if the Buddhas of the past, present, and future appeared,
I would have nothing to ask them.
Should I still go on pilgrimage to India, as planned?"

Guru Chowang replied, "If a Buddha in this world did not give the semblance of wandering in samsaric existence, he would be guilty of attachment to the peaceful quietude of Nirvana. Go to holy India, my son, by all means!"

Chowang continued:

"If you find an enlightened guru, serve the guru, fulfilling his wishes in
    every way.
To serve the guru is the swiftest way to attain enlightenment equal to his.
If you find disciples, serve them by educating them, liberating their innate
    enlightened potential.
In such a way, through serving both those above and those below,
Impartially serve the sublime Dharma and all beings."

Baro later fulfilled his lordly treasure master's command. However, before taking leave, the Nepali offered Guru Chowang sixty measures of powdered gold, well aware that Chowang was totally free of materialism.

Chowang mixed the gold dust with flour and threw it into the fireplace as a burned offering for the starving spirits. Soon afterward, Baro offered his guru his last three remaining measures of gold. Chowang offered them to the dakinis, casting them into the nearby river accompanied by the appropriate prayers and mantras.

Then Guru Chowing sang a little ditty by the fireside:

"If someone harms what is sacred,
  even if he is your own son, throw him out.
  If an anonymous beggar does a service for the temple, honor him;
  To me, everyone is equal."

Kumaradza Passes Away

Rigdzin Kumaradza was an enlightened Dzogchen master of the fourteenth century, successor of Mélong Dorje, the Diamond Mirror Master. Kumaradza became the Dzogchen teacher of both Longchenpa and the third Karmapa.

Regarding Kumaradza's two omniscient students, Dudjom Rinpoche said, "Longchenpa elucidated the profound essential doctrine in all its glory; Rangjung Dorje spread it throughout the universe."

Kumaradza was reputed to be an emanation of the immortal Indian Dzogchen master Vimalamitra, who had taught in Tibet during the eighth century, attained the deathless Rainbow Light Body, and taken up permanent residence in a hidden cave on the Five-Peaked Mountain, Wu Tai Shan, in China.

KUMARADZA, AFTER TEACHING FOR DECADES, died in his late seventies. Innumerable miraculous signs and portentous omens surrounded his demise, including rainbows, divine music, showers of flowers, and earthquakes.

His disciples were overawed, both grief-stricken and rapturous with devotion. Then Kumaradza rose from his bier.

Sitting cross-legged, he told them not to grieve. "How can unborn illusion come to an end?" he said. Prolonging his mortal existence for thirteen days by yogic means, Kumaradza continuously imparted oral instructions and personal guidance.

One day his disciples asked if they should request further teachings and instructions from the omniscient Longchenpa after Kumaradza himself had finally departed.

Kumaradza replied, "Why bother him? Do not indulge in endless idle chatter and searching. I have given you all the teachings you need for enlightenment in this lifetime; what else could you possibly need? For those of you who have not yet resolved your doubt and uncertainty, more practice is required, not more discussions!" He would say no more.

Soon afterward, Kumaradza passed away. When the master's body was cremated, his entire skull remained, unburned, in the ashes. Inside it, as if painted on its white surface, was vividly displayed the intricate mandala of the five Buddha families.

Innumerable tiny, translucent white pills and other relics—similar to those left by Sakyamuni Buddha—were also found in the ashes. These were distributed as talismans and cherished by the faithful through the ensuing centuries.

The Cuckoo's Cry of Awareness

Vairotsana was an eminent eighth-century Tibetan meditation master. Along with the Indian Buddhist masters Padma Sambhava and Vimalamitra, he brought the Dzogchen teachings from India, to where he had traveled in order to receive them from Manjusrimitra's disciple, the Lion Master Sri Simha.

Vairotsana was a child prodigy, ordained at an early age under royal auspices as one of Tibet's first monks. At Padma Sambhava's bidding, he was brought to the first Tibetan monastery, Samyé, and trained as a translator. He later made the arduous trek to India at the command of King Trisong Deutsen, who wished him to spread the Dharma in Tibet; there he received the Dzogchen teachings.

IN INDIA, AFTER CROSSING THE Himalayas on foot, the young Vairotsana proceeded to Bodh Gaya; there he was able to receive all the Dzogchen root tantras of the mind and space categories. He then traveled to the great Nine-Story Pagoda miraculously created by the Dzogchen siddha Sri Simha, the Glorious Lion—the acclaimed guru of both Padma Sambhava and Vimalamitra.

In the cool and shady sandalwood forest where a magnificent, towering pagoda stood, the young Tibetan monk met a lithe yogini carrying water in a clay jug on her head. He respectfully introduced himself and made discreet inquiries as to the whereabouts of the lordly master renowned as the Glorious Lion, but the female tantrika pretended not to notice Vairo and simply continued on her way.

Using his powerful psychokinetic gaze, Vairotsana made her water jug sink to the ground as if it weighed a ton; she was unable to lift it. The yogini suddenly bared her breasts, in a flash revealing in her heart the majestic diamond space mandala, Vajradhatu—a marvelous multidimensional, kaleidoscopic vision of deities, mystic symbols, and celestial paradises amid swirling geometrical forms. . . . It was a psychedelic light show of overwhelming proportions, replete with profound significance for the initiate.

After an eternal instant, she led the silent Vairotsana to Sri Simha. The Lion Master sat alone in the forest beneath a tree, wearing only a lion-skin loincloth.

The humbled Tibetan monk prostrated himself three times with exceptional deference. He offered a mandala of pure gold and reverently requested from the Glorious Lion the teaching of the effortless path, Maha Ati Tantra, the Peak Vehicle.

Sri Simha said that he would have to consider the Tibetan's request carefully. For one thing, he elaborated, not everyone was a suitable receptacle for such sublime, non-dual teachings. Wouldn't it be worse than useless to pour snow lion's milk into a chamber pot? And moreover, the master continued, the local king had prohibited anyone, on pain of death, from teaching the secret doctrine that is beyond karmic cause and effect, for he feared that such a non-dual doctrine would undermine his authority and lead to chaos.

The Tibetan translator again and again implored Sri Simha for the Ati Yoga teachings, for which he had come so far and endured so much. Finally the Lion Master consented, stipulating that the utmost secrecy must be preserved if the esoteric transmission was actually to take place. Furthermore, he instructed Vairotsana to study the common Buddhist teachings regarding karmic cause and effect with other scholars during the day and then come to him, the Glorious Lion, only under the cover of darkness, when the secret Dzogchen pith-instructions would be imparted. Vairotsana agreed to comply with all these conditions.

At midnight, Sri Simha for the first time committed to writing the incomparable eighteen secret pith-instructions of the mind class of Ati Yoga Tantra, writing on white silk with the milk of a white goat. He demonstrated to Vairo how the written characters appeared, as if by magic, when the silken cloth was fumigated by warm smoke. He made Vairotsana swear before the Dharma protectors to maintain total secrecy regarding these proceedings; then Sri Simha initiated Vairotsana into the ultimate mystery of being.

Within these teachings was the first Dzogchen text Vairotsana would translate into Tibetan, the "Cuckoo's Cry of Awareness," which affirms:

The many never stray from oneness;
all things are beyond concepts regarding them.
All created things are beyond the mind-made duality
of good and evil.

Since everything is perfect and complete in itself,
beyond the disease of effortful striving,
one remains effortlessly absorbed in primordial presence.

Vairotsana remained as long as possible with Sri Simha in the sandalwood forest, secretly receiving all the Dzogchen empowerments, explanations, and whispered instructions. Sri Simha pointed at the sky and sang:

"The expanse of reality is infinite,
But if you realize what is *as-it-is,*
Everything is inherently perfect and present therein,
lacking nothing.
What power or accomplishment goes beyond that?"

Soon afterward, Vairotsana left the Lion Master and sojourned in the Smoky Cremation Ground, meditating on the wondrous non-dual teachings he had received. There he had a vision of Garab Dorje, the first Dzogchen teacher, and received from him the sixty-four hundred thousand verses of Maha Ati.
The Diamond Laughter Master, Garab Dorje, sang:

"The pure nature of intrinsic awareness, innate wakefulness,
    is Buddhahood from the very beginning.
Mind is like space: open, unobstructed, insubstantial, unborn,
    and undying.

Having grasped the single true nature of diverse phenomena,
    and remaining thus,
In true meditation one settles naturally, without striving, into that.

Eventually, Vairotsana returned to his native Tibet in record time by means of the yogic power known as "swift feet," controlling his breath to augment his psychic energies while all but flying over the ground. Later, under the cover of darkness—just as he himself had received it—Vairo secretly taught Dzogchen to King Trisong Deutsen, while during the day he appeared as an impeccable Buddhist monk and pandit and publicly taught the fundamental doctrine of karmic cause and effect common to all Buddhist traditions.
During his long and fruitful life, Vairotsana had many accomplished and realized disciples. He eventually attained the Rainbow Light Body of perfect enlightenment in the wild forests of Nepal.

Yogi Dzeng and the Vajra Bridge

Lama Dzeng was a member of the Maha Ati lineage succession, following in the footsteps of Vairotsana's aged disciple Mipham Gonpo, who had begun to meditate at the age of eighty-two and eventually attained enlightenment. This line of masters was particularly renowned for attaining the Rainbow Light Body through practicing the Dzogchen pith-instructions called the Vajra Bridge, which Vairotsana had disseminated in Tibet a few centuries earlier.

DZENG WAS THE SON OF a nun and a prince from Thang-chung. In his middle age, he became the Dharma heir and spiritual successor of the enlightened tantrika (lay lama) Bagom. The latter received the whispered Vajra Bridge instructions from Nyang Sherab Jungnay, an old monk and remarkable Dzogchen master. Sherab Jungnay left this world at an advanced age in a great blaze of light on top of Mount Lhari in Phukpochay—hanging his robe, hat, skullcup, and large bodhi-seed rosary on a juniper tree and leaving no other remnant of his mortal body . . . thus signifying achievement of the Rainbow Light Body of perfect enlightenment.

When Dzeng was sixteen years of age, he encountered the extraordinary Indian adept Padampa Sangyay; he attended Padampa as a servant and acolyte for fourteen months. Then Padampa gave him a blanket and sent him home with a caravan of traders. As they parted, the dark-skinned Indian master embraced the teenager and said:

> "That which is nothing at all,
>   transforms into myriad forms.
> When one recognizes the single essential nature
>   through all its manifestations,
>   non-duality is grasped."

When the master and disciple touched foreheads (in the traditional manner of greeting equals—an unprecedented honor for the boy), Dzeng suddenly awoke to a vivid and profound insight into the nature of reality. Padampa Sangyay predicted that Dzeng would ultimately traverse the Vajra Bridge and attain the Rainbow Light Body.

Dzeng had already understood, at an early age, that—other than the Dharma—nothing is of any use in this ephemeral world. As a farewell gift, Padampa gave him other, more advanced teachings. He predicted where Dzeng would meet his root guru and enter into the practice of the marvelous Vajra Bridge. Then the affectionate pair separated.

After praying and meditating for many years, Dzeng met the acclaimed Dzogchen master Bagom, who accepted him as a servant and disciple. Dzeng begged for alms among the local villagers, wishing to present offerings to his new teacher before requesting the priceless teachings. Bagom, however, refused to accept the huge sack of roasted barley flour that Dzeng offered him, insisting that the newly arrived disciple use it for his own provision over the coming months—because during that time he would be intensively engaged in full-time meditation practice. The disciple was delighted.

Bagom confided what he had never before divulged—that he, Tantrika Bagom, was the sole holder of Vairotsana's Vajra Bridge transmission, through which one could attain Buddhahood in a single lifetime, actualizing the death-less Rainbow Light Body and leaving behind not a single trace of one's mortal body when departing from this world at death. He moreover confirmed what Dzeng had already heard—that each lineage holder of the Vajra Bridge had actually accomplished it.

Now Dzeng knew he had found his predestined master, as well as the teaching through which he would reach Buddhahood. All he had to do was to put that precious teaching into practice.

Dzeng served Tantrika Bagom faithfully, pleasing him by his sincerity. Again and again Dzeng requested the Dzogchen teachings of the Vajra Bridge leading to the Rainbow Light Body. Finally Lama Bagom imparted that unique esoteric doctrine to Dzeng, along with many other related teachings and trans-missions. When Dzeng actually practiced those teachings, he accomplished their true import and achieved perfect enlightenment.

After that, Yogi Dzeng wandered naked for five years in the province of Tsang, impervious to both heat and cold. He practiced various austerities, sim-ilar to those endured by the Indian adepts of old: bathing in ice floes, leaping from towering precipices, subsisting only on mineral pills and water, entering fire, halting his heartbeat and respiration for days. . . . Then he became re-nowned as Pawo Dzengchung—Little Dzeng, the Heroic Yogi.

Meanwhile, Lama Bagom passed away in a blaze of rainbow light at the ripe old age of ninety-eight. Yogi Dzeng began to spread Bagom's teachings.

Once when Dzeng taught several other yogis about mystic heat, their inner incandescence instantaneously blazed, illumining everyone present. Other dis-ciples of Lama Dzeng had visions, encountered deities, experienced ecstasy, and achieved sudden awakenings. When Dzeng taught Mahamudra (the Ultimate Symbol), one ripe disciple realized that delusion is, at heart, the same as pristine gnosis and was freed from duality. In that moment, he intuitively actualized the inherent freedom of being.

On the first occasion that Dzeng expounded the mystic Vajra Bridge, a nun and a man from Kham both realized its profound essence and achieved the Rainbow Light Body, disappearing in bursts of light without leaving a single trace behind. Dzeng recognized this as an extremely auspicious sign, and he assured his followers that whoever would assiduously practice those instructions for five or six years would attain the same, regardless of their previous karmic disposition. Dzeng conscientiously passed on to his disciples all that he himself had received, practiced, and realized, along with other Vajrayana instructions and teachings.

Dzeng developed inconceivable supernatural powers and psychic abilities over the years, although he attached little significance to them. At various times it was obvious to everyone present that he was immune to contagious disease, since he never fell ill. He read minds, made accurate prophecies and detailed predictions, and appeared instantaneously in distant places. Dzeng made the local gods and demons obey him and help him spread the Buddhist teachings everywhere. Thus the Heroic Yogi attained immense popularity and recognition, yet he still displayed humility and loving-kindness, for which he was venerated wherever he went.

Once Dzeng leapt onto a frozen lake. The ice cracked beneath his weight, and he plunged into the icy water. Great hissing clouds of steam rose around him, partially obscuring the clear sky—astonishing everyone, who saw that the yogi's body was like a red-hot iron ablaze with mystical inner heat. However, humble Dzeng himself claimed afterward that he felt frozen!

On another occasion, Lama Dzeng—carrying a great armful of firewood—perceived all phenomena in its dreamlike, unreal nature and inexplicably leapt from a cliff.

The Heroic Yogi floated down like a bird. His consort, who was also collecting wood, simply stared down from above. Then she exclaimed:

"Marvelous master, are you human or not? You remind me of the legendary Padampa Sangyay, whom I lacked the good fortune to meet!"

Laughing aloud, Dzeng remembered his first mentor. He said, "Lucky you met Dzeng; *he* met Padampa!"

When Guru Dzeng was one hundred and two years old, he seemed ill, and his countless followers feared for his life. Dzeng allayed their anxiety by reporting a very auspicious and significant dream. "The dakinis commanded me to come after four years," he explained. "I have four more years here."

Later, the disciples requested him to do whatever was necessary, through yogic means, to prolong his life, for they could not bear to go on without him. They had heard Dzeng say that—through the power of virtuous deeds and meritorious actions, rites, and rituals, combined with spiritual alchemy—one's longevity could be extended. Innumerable siddhas had thus lived for far more than one hundred years; they fervently requested the Heroic Yogi to do likewise.

Dzeng agreed to prolong his life for another decade through alchemical transformation. "But I prefer to rely on the deathless state of the unborn and undying, rather than cling to mortal existence," he said. "As my followers, I hope that you will do the same."

Lama Dzeng finally passed away at the age of one hundred and seventeen.

It is recorded that, for the benefit of his followers, Dzeng left his remains rather than fully actualizing the Rainbow Light Body. When he was cremated, innumerable numinous relics and tiny stupas remained among the ashes, many marked by mantric seed-syllables (mantras inscribed on his bones) and eight auspicious signs connected with Buddha-nature.

These mementos have been cherished and handed down to us through the centuries by faithful generations of followers.

Jomo Manmo, the Sleeping Dakini

The thirteenth-century treasure finder Jomo Manmo was the authentic incarnation of the Tibetan queen Yeshé Tsogyal, Padma Sambhava's mystic consort and chief disciple. Jomo Manmo became the consort of another treasure finder, the kingly terton Guru Chowang.

As A YOUNG GIRL, JOMO Manmo cared for her father's herds. She also worked hard trying to please her unsympathetic stepmother by performing the most unpalatable household chores.

One fine spring day, when young Jomo was thirteen, she was grazing the cattle, as usual, when she accidentally dozed off, falling into a deep slumber on a slope near a cave, where the Lotus-Born Guru Padma Sambhava had meditated centuries before.

Suddenly a sweet, lilting song awoke the sleeping girl. The cave's hidden entrance, overgrown for years, inexplicably revealed itself. Everything around her seemed marvelously transformed.

"Is this paradise? Have I died?" she wondered.

Entering the cave in an enraptured state, Jomo Manmo saw a group of dakinis in a charnel ground, surrounded by decaying, dismembered corpses and carnivorous animals, their jaws dripping with gore. There the girl, who was not frightened by this awesome spectacle, beheld Vajra Yogini, the Diamond Sow, presiding over a tantric rite.

The dakini queen Vajra Yogini stepped forth and invited Jomo to join the ranks to which she, by birth, belonged.

"You are of the dakini race, child, like all women," the ruby-red, sow-crowned deity proclaimed. "Are you unaware of your own pristine Buddha-nature?

"You are perfectly free, liberated since the beginningless beginning," she told the girl. "Dare to actualize that inherent freedom, beyond doubt and hesitation. The entire universe is your body, all beings your mind."

Vajra Yogini took a book with faded yellow pages from inside a rock and touched it to the crown of Jomo Manmo's head. In that instant, Jomo was enlightened. Thus the wisdom dakini empowered her, directly introducing that transcendental reality from which she remained inseparable.

She handed the book to the girl, prophesying that through practicing what was contained within, Jomo Manmo would attain inconceivable enlightenment and benefit generations to come. The text was written in the mystic script of the dakinis.

After that experience, Jomo Manmo began to act in an eccentric manner that was reminiscent of the siddhas of India. Free of dualistic concepts and clinging—perceiving everything as inherently pure and sacred—the youthful dakini felt neither attachment nor aversion to good and bad, acted without inhibition, and enjoyed perfect peace and ease.

Because she had fallen asleep on the mountainside by Padma Sambhava's long-hidden cave, about which there are many legends and fairytales full of both gods and demons, she gained the nickname Jomo Manmo, meaning "she who was possessed by a demoness."

The tome given to her by the dakini queen later became renowned as Jomo Manmo's revelation, the terma called "The Gathered Secrets of the Dakinis"; it had originally been taught centuries before by Padma Sambhava and then hidden in that rock by Yeshé Tsogyal. Based on it, Jomo later taught the esoteric Dzogchen pith-instructions elucidating the innate freedom of the natural Great Perfection to many practitioners.

On the tenth day of the lunar month, a day sacred to Guru Rinpoche, Jomo Manmo, at the age of thirty-six, and two other yoginis performed a vajra-feast offering atop a windswept mountain in central Tibet. Then they soared like birds into the sky and entered the dakini paradise.

Some shepherds witnessed the miracle. Amazed, they gathered the scraps of that tantric feast and ate them, entering immediately into profound meditative absorptions.

The oral transmission from Jomo Manmo regarding the dakini practice still flourishes today.

Inside Out

Zurchungpa was one of the patriarchs of the Zur clan of Dzogchen practitioners, the lineage holders who for generations inhabited Owl Valley. He is famous for his "Eighty Oral Epigrams."

Remarkably persevering, Zurchungpa once spent fourteen years in a strictly solitary meditation retreat. Bringing supplies, his disciples found him in such an extended contemplative absorption that his entire face was covered with cobwebs and birds nested in the tangled hair on his head.

Dzogchen teachings regard as ever-present one's inalienable Buddha-mind, which consists of the wisdom of innate wakefulness. However, in most cases this intrinsic awareness seems to function in an inverted manner. Due to the veils of deluded perception, the ignorant misconstrue what is primordially pure and perfect to be imperfect, defiled, separate, and incoherent—and thus they are deluded. Zur's reversed wolf-skin coat symbolically exposes, through proper interpretation, this paradoxical situation.

ONCE A LAMA NAMED KYUNGPO Trasay sent his four exceptionally erudite disciples to challenge Zurchungpa, the Little Yogi of Zur. They accused him of supporting unorthodox doctrines, including the Maha Ati teaching on effortlessness, which goes beyond cause and effect.

When the four scholars approached, Zurchungpa was wearing a furry coat, a tanned wolf skin displaying its fur—in contravention of the Tibetan custom of keeping the warm fur near one's own skin. To them the perverse Owl Master was wearing his coat inside out.

The eminent emissaries wasted no time in challenging the master of the prestigious Zur clan.

"What sort of pseudo-spiritual tradition includes customs such as wearing an animal hide inside out, Little Zur?" the first scholar asked. "Have you neither deference for social custom nor compassion for wild animals?"

Zur retorted, "The wolf skin is just as it has always been; the hair naturally grew out, not in! It is your fabricated concepts that are inverted."

One of the other visiting scholars said, "Let us discuss the essentials of the Buddha's doctrine."

Zur replied, "The essence of the Buddha's teachings is inexpressible, inconceivable, and inexhaustible. How can fireflies measure the sun?"

The third dialectician interjected, "Even according to your Great Perfection, in which the perfect freedom of being exists effortlessly from the outset, isn't meditation important?"

Zur replied, "Enjoying innate freedom and natural ease, upon what possible object would my attention be fixated? If one does not meditate, what is lost?" ·

"All right, then!" cried the fourth, in exasperation. "Is non-meditation the principal thing?"

"What could distract me, and from what would I be distracted?" Zur replied.

The four visitors were stymied. Here was a master who had obviously achieved the peace and freedom of Nirvana.

Filled with faith, they resolved to become Zur's followers. Returning to their own master, they respectfully took leave of him and returned to blessed Owl Valley.

Zurchungpa's final instructions to his disciples, when he left this world, became renowned as the "Eighty Oral Epigrams." This work begins:

Be a child of the mountains.
Live amid cloud-girded peaks.
Wear ragged, cast-off clothes.
Eat plain and simple food.
Ignore both friends and enemies.
Leave worldly work undone.
Do not hanker after quick results.
Be content with inner peace.
Decide conclusively regarding the truth of Dharma,
and practice accordingly
throughout your life.

Non-Meditation, Non-Distraction

ONCE A YOGI SPENT TWENTY years meditating in a cave in Golok. He had many deep insights and realizations, including experiences of profound bliss, clarity, and non-thought. Eventually he concluded that his practice was complete, and enlightenment won. He decided to go to Jamgon Kongtrul Rinpoche, Lodro Thayé, to offer his realizations.

Several weeks later he arrived on foot at Kongtrul's monastery and sought an audience with the renowned master. Kongtrul welcomed him graciously.

Not without hubris, the yogi told the meditation master about his twenty-year retreat, reporting his deepest experiences and his present state.

Kongtrul Rinpoche exclaimed, "Oh, too bad! Dreadful! That's nothing. Drop it right now. Just as mountain cascades become more aerated by falling from rock to rock, so does meditation improve by being broken up again and again.

"Go back to Golok," Kongtrul advised. "For three years stay alone in your cave without meditating, without the slightest explicit spiritual practice. Simply sustain the innate natural state, however it presents itself, without distraction. By carefree freedom from both action and inaction, the Dharma is accomplished.

"Unless you give up everything, even Dharma activities, you'll never reach enlightenment in this lifetime. Forget about your twenty-year-long career as a professional hermit. Stop meditating!"

Then he shooed the yogi out.

The hermit trekked back to his mountain retreat in Golok. At first it was not easy putting into practice the illumined master's instructions about non-doing, but gradually he got used to effortlessness and naturalness as a way of life. Non-dual awareness, Buddha-mind, blazed within him like the sun illuminating infinite space.

At the end of three years he returned to Kongtrul Rinpoche, as instructed. Bowing before the master, he said nothing.

Kongtrul gave him the thumbs-up sign. He later became one of the most simple and direct Dzogchen masters of eastern Tibet, and liberated many disciples.

Offerings to Jigmé Lingpa

The vidyadhara (knowledge holder) Jigmé Lingpa, the Fearless Master, lived in the mountains at Tsering Jong, in a hut surrounded by the makeshift dwellings of the yogis who had gathered to meditate under his tutelage. Many among that carefree band of Dzogchen practitioners actualized the Rainbow Light Body, the ultimate fruit of Maha Ati, the luminous Great Perfection.

ONCE A PAIR OF FAITHFUL monks in eastern Tibet set out from their monastery intent upon making offerings to Jigmé Lingpa. They also hoped to receive Dzogchen meditation instructions and personal transmission from the Fearless Master.

As the two monks were on their way to Tsering Jong to meet the master, they came upon a monk who offered to change their currency for them. The pair intended to use one portion of this money to procure the traditional offerings and then to set aside the remainder as a gift.

In order to effect the transaction, the so-called monk went into his house with their large, old-fashioned Tibetan bank notes in hand, while the pilgrims waited outside. When he failed to return, they went looking for him, but he was nowhere to be seen. He must have escaped out a back door or window, for no one was inside the house.

The pilgrims were nonplussed. What else could they do but shake their heads sadly, mutter a few prayers, and continue on their way, eking out a meager subsistence by collecting alms as they traveled? Eventually, after several weeks, the pair reached Tsering Jong, where they were made welcome. The next day they were presented to the master himself.

The two monks prostrated themselves again and again to the omniscient yogi, whose splendid presence was indescribable. Simply to *be* with Rigdzin Jigmé Lingpa reportedly allayed all thought of past and future, all plans, doubts, and hesitations, and effectively terminated all worldly preoccupations.

The monks told the Fearless Master how their offerings had been purloined—and by a person wearing the red Dharma robes, no less! The buoyant yogi, whose white hair was piled in a topknot on his head and who sported a snowy flowing beard, simply laughed. Then Jigmé Lingpa spontaneously sang a melodious, moving song of profound, unconditional acceptance.

In the song, the master accepted their offering, made—albeit unwittingly—to the scoundrel who had taken advantage of them, for it is the intention that counts, not the material offering itself. And he gave them his benediction.

Then Jigmé reminded the entire assembly to let go of all attachments—whether to material objects, comfort and pleasure, status, or to the more seductive snares of spiritual materialism. He exhorted his followers to rest effortlessly, actionlessly, in the primordial presence of inherent awakened awareness, rather than manipulating the mind in a misguided effort to exploit ephemeral states of consciousness.

Thus Jigmé Lingpa delighted everyone with his extemporaneous song and its non-dualistic theme of complete acceptance, freedom, and ease—the resonance of the innate Great Perfection. The two humble monks received the teachings, fulfilled their hearts' desire, and became his followers. They, too, became realized yogis.

Gampopa's Great Void

Gampopa founded the Kagyu order in the eleventh century. A doctor, he renounced the world and took monastic ordination after the premature death of his wife and children. Under Milarepa's guidance, Gampopa meditated unstintingly until achieving his goal, enlightenment.

Gampopa combined the Kadampa precepts of Atisha, the Refuge Pandit, with the Mahamudra teachings, thus establishing the basis of the Kagyu school.

GAMPOPA, THE DOCTOR FROM DAKPO, habitually sat in his cave all day, braced by a woven meditation belt. Once Milarepa asked him how long his meditation periods lasted; Gampopa replied that he usually sat for six hours at a time.

Milarepa, the singing yogi, inquired, "What do you experience during that time?"

Gampopa replied, "Nothing at all—a great void."

Milarepa exclaimed, "That is hardly the great void! How can you practice meditation for six hours at a stretch without anything occurring? Fool, you are suppressing yourself, resting in an indifferent, neutral state—pleasant as it may seem. Give up this so-called practice, and begin anew according to my instructions." Then Milarepa sang a song about genuine meditation practice:

The ultimate view is to observe one's mind,
   steadfastly and with determination.

Buddhahood cannot be found outside,
so contemplate your own mind.
Behold and watch unborn awareness;
how can common meditation match it?

The ultimate guru is Buddha-mind within;
do not seek elsewhere.
All forms are nothing but mind.
Recognizing one's true nature as Dharmakaya,
swiftly actualize immanent Buddhahood.

Humbled, Gampopa announced his intention to discard his maroon monastic robes and adopt the white cotton dress of Milarepa.

Again Milarepa chastised him. "Don't copy others! Each one of you must follow your own spiritual path." Then Milarepa sang a song, explaining the original monastic state—detachment, surrender, simplicity, solitude . . . recognition of the truth of egolessness.

Milarepa concluded, "Heal yourself, good physician-monk; then you will naturally heal others. My teaching is mine; yours must be yours. Do whatever is necessary in order to evoke it from within."

Gotsangpa's Vajra Feast

Gotsangpa Gonpo Dorje was a Drukpa Kagyu yogi who lived eight centuries ago. His master, Tsangpa Gyaré, founded the Drukpa Kagyu (Dragon Lineage) school. Gotsangpa was a dedicated meditator who lived for many years in a bare cave, a burlap sack serving as his bed, blanket, and meditation mat.

The swiftest way to accumulate merit and good fortune in the Vajrayana tradition is through the practice of offering tsok (ganachakra), a vajra-feast offered to a myriad of enlightened guests—dakas, dakinis, and others. Gotsangpa was renowned for his practice of such offerings. Once, alone with an attendant on an uninhabited island, Gotsangpa was moved to place all of his remaining food supplies on the altar as tsok offerings. Because of this generosity, during his remaining years, Gotsangpa never experienced hunger or want.

ONE DAY GOTSANGPA ASKED HIS master's leave in order to attend a vajra-feast in the mystic dakini land of Uddiyana. His teacher, however, said that his karma was not exactly ripe for such a visit.

"On the other hand, if you wish, you may go to the mystic land of Jalandara," Tsangpa Gyaray added, "where the dakas and dakinis are secretly gathered at a temple near a mountain river in a deep valley."

Gotsangpa, accompanied by one young disciple, set off immediately.

The happy-go-lucky yogis eventually arrived in the remote Himalayan foothills embracing Jalandara. A delighted Gotsangpa saw bevies of dakinis carrying gilded ritual implements, altarpieces, and sumptuous offerings into a magnificent temple. His attendant, however, prey to doubt (due to his particular karma and lack of merit), saw nothing unusual. What he perceived was an abandoned mountain shrine, where women were working with rusty, broken tools. This monk did not bother to go further, preferring to idle in the sun along the verdant riverbank.

Gotsangpa left his attendant by the river and approached the shining portal. When he attempted to cross the threshold, two wrathful dakinis blocked his entrance, telepathically demanding his credentials. "No ordinary mortal passes here!" they cried.

The Mahamudra master instantaneously recollected his inherent enlightened nature, and in a flash, the ferocious doorkeepers transformed into a pair of beautiful goddesses, inviting him in.

That brief moment of Mahamudra recognition manifested in him the transcendental pride of a deity. Therefore, Gotsangpa was immediately ushered to the throne at the head of the assembly and invited to preside over the vajra-feast offering rite. Spiritual experiences blossomed; spontaneous songs of realization were chanted aloud, in the haunting melody of the dakinis' secret language. Infinite blessings ensued, pervading the universe.

The young monk waiting by the river never knew what had transpired. Gotsangpa silently smiled.

When they traveled back to their master, the attendant confessed that their mountain sojourn had seemed like a waste of time. Had they either reached fabled Jalandara or enjoyed the mystical fruits of a tsok offering?

Gotsangpa, concerned for the skeptical boy's spiritual development, assured him, "Today you have served the Dharma. We have together accomplished more than you can now understand, for the benefit of beings now and in future generations. Never doubt that those who have the karmic fortune and faith to see will one day be able to see."

Later the boy, under Gotsangpa's guidance, became a realized master.

A Yogi Outfoxes Kublai Khan

Many Mongol and Chinese leaders enjoyed deep, long-standing relationships with leading Tibetan lamas, whose spiritual prowess and supernatural powers they recognized. Important Tibetan masters often assumed the role of imperial guru.

Dotokpa was a Dzogchen master in the lineage of the legendary Zur clan. Once he was so moved by pity that when no one else would undertake the chore, he volunteered to carry a leprous corpse to the charnel ground. When he cremated the corpse, gold nuggets appeared near the remnants—a sign from Jambhala, the god of wealth, signifying Dotokpa's wealth of spiritual accomplishment.

DOTOKPA HAD A REALIZED DISCIPLE named Chökyi Sengay, the Lion of Dharma, who was adept in the magic dagger practice called Vajra Kilaya. After Karma Pakshi's departure from China, Chökyi Sengay met Kublai Khan.

At the instigation of imperial advisers jealous of the foreign lama's influence over their emperor, Kublai decided to test Chökyi Sengay's spiritual powers. How would this lama compare with Karma Pakshi? everyone wondered.

The arrogant Khan ordered the Tibetan yogi sealed up inside a stone stupa and left without food, drink, or ventilation. Then, through various distractions, his wily advisers helped Kublai to forget the entire matter.

After one year, the Khan happened to be reminded of Karma Pakshi; only then did he remember the incarcerated yogi.

The stupa was immediately opened. Chökyi Sengay had transformed into a magnificent, life-size, jewel-encrusted statue of the wrathful deity of enlightened activity named Vajra Kilaya.

As it is said:

On the island of jewels,
there is nothing that is not valuable.
In the realm of divinity,

there is nothing that is not divine.
In the realm of the unreal,
there is nothing real.
In the realm of the absolute,
there is nothing other than the absolute.

Kublai Khan was astonished and impressed by the lama's extraordinary manifestation. He sent many precious offerings to the distant master Dotokpa, inviting him to visit and teach at his court. Some say that the arrogant Khan even begged Dotokpa's forgiveness.

The Blanket Master and the Witches

King Indrabhuti received Vajrayana transmission and empowerment directly from Vajrapani, the Diamond Wielder. This historical king was a personal disciple of the celebrated householder Vimalakirti, protagonist of the Vimalakirti Nirdesa Sutra. The masters in this lineage are noted for attaining enlightenment without abandoning their positions in society.

Practitioners in the Orient often retired to lonely caves in order to pursue their spiritual exercises intensively in peaceful solitude. In such a situation, one's swiftly unfolding spirituality is occasionally challenged by negative forces, either outer or inner.

King Indrabhuti's son and spiritual heir, Crown Prince Sakraputra, was known as Indrabhuti the Younger. He later became renowned as Kambalapada, the Blanket Master. His meditation cave in the dakini land of Uddiyana—the Swat Valley in northwestern Pakistan—still shows signs of his supernatural powers, including handprints and footprints embedded in rock.

ONCE THE CROWN PRINCE WENT to sleep beneath the main gate of his palace. All those who silently tiptoed past their recumbent lord, entering the palace without prostrating themselves to him as custom required, soon after became paralyzed from the waist down. From then on, each and every visitor had to bow down to the master, even when he slept.

No ordinary sleep it was. For twelve years on that very spot he slumbered without waking, quietly commanding obeisance from all who would enter. Later he said that the entire period, one complete astrological cycle, seemed to him—absorbed in meditation—one brief, incandescent moment of inner radiance. Afterward, Kambalapada returned to his forest hermitage.

Once five hundred witches sought him out. They conspired to hinder his flourishing tantric practice and thus obstruct the legendary spiritual development of the kingdom. In his place, however, they found only a tattered blanket.

Being well versed in the black art, they were convinced that the powerful yogi-prince had momentarily transformed himself into a blanket in order to deceive them. With unimaginable ferocity, they tore the blanket to shreds, divided it into five hundred bits and pieces, and proceeded to gobble them all up—one shred for each malevolent spirit present.

Suddenly, thunderous peals of raucous laughter echoed throughout the sky. Then the Blanket Master Kambalapada appeared. He cursed the sorceresses, who were immediately transformed into five hundred sheep-headed demonesses.

Panic-stricken, the demonesses trotted to Indrabhuti's palace and sought audience with the king. Accusing his son of a lack of princely virtue and compassion, they begged forgiveness for their past misdeeds and asked to be restored to their former form.

When the kindly old king forgave them and did as they requested, the impenitent witches mischievously skulked away.

King Indrabhuti the Elder then summoned his son from his hermitage. The crown prince appeared at court naked and boldly announced, "Your Majesty's favorite witches have eaten this yogi's only clothing!"

He requested his father, the king, to summon the witches at once.

The crowd of sorceresses soon appeared before King Indrabhuti. The naked Kambalapada pointed menacingly at each of them in turn, transforming them into various creatures with bestial heads. Then each creature vomited forth one fragment of the yogi's old blanket.

A courtier swiftly sewed all the fragments together. However, three pieces remained unaccounted for. "Three more pieces will complete the puzzle," he said.

"Three witches are missing!" roared the irate Blanket Master.

"Summon them forth!" ordered the king, snapping his ring-covered fingers.

Then the three sorceresses, who happened to be members of Indrabhuti's harem, were brought forth. They were summarily transformed and forced to regurgitate their bizarre booty.

Thus the yogi's blanket was restored, and the evil witches thwarted. Kambalapada covered his nakedness and returned to the forest, until such time as he would be called to ascend the throne.

The two royal Indrabhutis, father and son, taught and transmitted the Vajrayana tantras until the entire kingdom of Uddiyana was enlightened.

A Dove and Tara of the Beans

Vasubandhu was a fourth-century master of the Chittamatra, or Mind-Only, school of Buddhist philosophy. Asanga, that school's peerless patriarch—who received directly from Maitreya Buddha the classic texts known as the "Five Ornaments"—was his brother. Both were at different times the abbot of Nalanda University.

Abhidharma is the seminal collection of Buddhist psychology, much commented upon and developed by this pair of pandits.

ONCE VASUBANDHU WAS SITTING IN a tub of oil while reciting the long Wisdom Scripture, the Prajna Paramita Sutra. A dove who inhabited the beams of the pandit's humble shelter spontaneously felt reverence and bowed low—although he could not understand the words. Soon thereafter, the little bird died.

The dove was reborn in the human realm as a merchant's son. This infant immediately asked his parents, "Where is the Buddhist master Vasubandhu of Magadha? I must meet him again."

The parents were astonished: how could their infant son Sthiramati speak, let alone know about a Buddhist master named Vasubandhu? They made the necessary inquiries, and after some years the couple contacted Vasubandhu himself, offering the seven-year-old boy as his servant and pupil.

The karmically predestined neophyte was an extremely gifted student. He pleased the master with his humble service as well as with his quick intelligence and wit. One day the boy was given a handful of beans, which he began eating inside a temple dedicated to the savioress Tara.

The devout young novice suddenly thought to himself, "I must offer some to exalted Tara, too; otherwise, it is improper for me to eat them here." But when he tried to offer some beans to the statue of Tara, no matter where he placed them, they kept rolling onto the floor behind the large image.

The boy thought, "If she won't accept these beans as an offering, it would be unseemly for me to eat them." Again and again he tried to offer the beans, respectfully placing several at a time before the life-size, jeweled statue of the deity. . . . But the beans again and again rolled away into the dusty darkness behind the image, where the patter of tiny feet and the sound of squealing could be heard.

Regardless of Sthiramati's efforts, he could not get Tara to accept his offering. Finally the dejected novice's hands were completely empty and all the delicious beans gone, amid a flurry of movement on the floor in the shadows behind the altar.

Being a mere boy, be burst into tears. No beans, no offering—it was too much for him!

Then the loving protectress, Arya Tara herself, appeared before him in all her sovereign glory. "Do not weep, child," she said. "You will always have my blessings."

Sthiramati's intelligence immediately became as vast as Vasubandhu's. After this encounter with a deity, it was apparent to everyone that the boy was no longer a neophyte. As he grew older, he authored countless texts, especially regarding the psychological Abhidharma commentaries by his own teacher.

That Tara statue was known forever afterward as "Masa-Tara," meaning Tara of the Beans.

Dignaga's Cave

Dignaga was the foremost disciple of Vasubandhu. Invincible in debate, his logical analyses were unmatched in his time. The father of Buddhist logic, he gained the epithet Elephant Master, signifying the majesty of his genuine knowledge.

DIGNAGA MASTERED THE ENTIRE BUDDHIST canon, the Tripitaka. Then he received from the abbot Nagadatta the "Special Instructions on Discovering the Self."

He assiduously practiced this teaching, searching everywhere—inside and out—for the elusive "I." Eventually, the Elephant Master Dignaga came to great inner certainty concerning the non-existence of independent selfhood, and he was emancipated.

After many years, Dignaga grew weary of epistemological dialectic. His written treatises on valid reasoning scattered far and wide, he retired to a cave deep in the jungle on Botasela Mountain. There the Elephant Master—king of the jungle of philosophy—meditated.

After several years, the hermit began composing a commentary synthesizing all the subtle points he had elucidated during his long career as teacher, debater, and author—enhanced by his recent inner realizations. The new work would be called "The Synthesis of All Reasoning," Pramana-Samuccaya.

He composed his text with chalk on a slate, seated outside his cave. When he had completed the first verse, the earth quaked, thunder roared, and light shone down from the heavens. The pandit understood this as an auspicious omen and gave thanks to the Buddhas past, present, and future. Then Dignaga went to collect alms.

Meanwhile, a clairvoyant non-Buddhist seer named Krishna Rishi divined the source of the cosmic disturbance and became jealous. He had sought the gods' approbation for many years, without such success.

Thinking on this, he sought out Dignaga's cave. There he erased the verse from the slate before disappearing back into the jungle. When the Buddhist master returned, the slate was blank, and he wondered what had happened in his absence.

The next day, Dignaga again composed the first verse of his well-planned composition, but when he went for alms and returned, the same thing had occurred. On the following day, it was the same. The next day, he wrote on the slate, "Whoever you are, this writing is no joke but has lofty import and significance. If you do not accept the Buddha's teachings, come and debate with me; the loser shall be convinced and converted."

When he returned that night, Dignaga found the learned Rishi seated before his cave. Dignaga proceeded to defeat him in debate. But instead of abiding by their agreement, Krishna Rishi blew a torrent of flame from his mouth—burning everything Dignaga owned, including his robe, before disappearing into the jungle.

Discouraged, Dignaga felt it was hopeless to continue to work for universal salvation. "Most people seem so uninterested in achieving freedom!" he lamented.

In a moment of frustration, the Elephant Master threw a charred bit of his writing slate up into the air, telling himself that when it hit the ground he would relinquish his bodhisattva aspiration and seek personal salvation.

The slate went up but failed to come down. Surprised, Dignaga gazed upward—and saw Manjusri, wisdom deity and patron of reason, holding the slate in his hands in midair.

"Despair not," Manjusri said. "Your writings are beyond the scope of non-believers; I have inspired them. I shall be your guardian until you reach perfect Buddhahood. This 'Synthesis of All Reasoning' you are about to commit to writing will illumine the way for future generations; my flaming wisdom sword will guide your hand."

When Dignaga actually completed his lengthy and profound composition, the gods rained heavenly flowers upon him, the trees bent in his direction, and even wild animals bowed in reverence. At Manjusri's bidding, the local king and his ministers came to pay homage to the eminent Elephant Master.

Accepting neither servants nor offerings, Dignaga maintained his life-style of renunciation. His treatises spread throughout India. Dignaga later taught widely in Kashmir.

Atisha Meets Rinchen Zangpo

When the Indian pandit Atisha came to Tibet, he was welcomed by that country's foremost translator, the aged monk Rinchen Zangpo, who was twenty-four years his senior. Atisha was invited to bless the Tibetan translator's pride and joy, a three-story temple where Rinchen Zangpo meditated daily at twilight, midnight, and dawn on the mystic mandalas of his three principal meditational deities.

AT THEIR INITIAL ENCOUNTER, ATISHA courteously addressed the senior Tibetan master, "Meeting you, I see that there was actually no reason for me to come to Tibet, for as a national teacher, you are certainly sufficient." Then the pair retired to the master's inner sanctum where they discussed the Buddha Dharma in exhaustive detail.

The Tibetan translator seemed realized as well as erudite. Atisha asked, "In your experience, should the various tantras be practiced separately or together?"

"Separately, one by one," was the reply. But Atisha was not satisfied with Rinchen Zangpo's opinion.

"All the tantras should be practiced together and realized in one sitting!" opined the Indian master, whose word was law. "All deities are of a single savor; sufficient it is to experience them all in one moment, on one spot." For as Dudjom Rinpoche says in his "Dharma History," "What is the use of knowing many things, without knowing the single point that frees and liberates all?"

Atisha continued, "Now I see that it was indeed necessary for me to come to Tibet for the benefit of the Buddha's doctrine and of all beings."

Chastened, Rinchen Zangpo bowed his white head; he offered Atisha all his worldly possessions. Atisha asked Rinchen Zangpo to act as his interpreter.

The elderly Tibetan bowed low again, displaying his white hair. He begged Atisha to instruct him in tantric theory and practice and then seal him in a solitary meditation retreat.

Atisha complied with the aged translator's humble, heartfelt request. Rinchen Zangpo meditated on Atisha's personal instructions for ten years and realized awakening.

Rinchen Zangpo later said, "I studied until old age. When I met my Indian teacher, Atisha, I began to truly meditate."

Buddhaguhya's Meditation

Buddhaguhya was a yogic adept, a disciple of the Dog Master, siddha (tantric adept) Kukkuripa.

Puja is a Sanskrit term referring to a ritual ceremony. Clarified butter (ghee), flowers, and other beautiful shrine offerings please the gods and deities, while inculcating gratitude and generosity in the donor. When withered offerings are restored, when ghee boils spontaneously, and when pictures come to life—these miraculous events signify mystic power.

Buddhists consider that the ultimate miracle is the accomplishment of perfect awakened enlightenment, Buddhahood, rather than the development of mundane supernatural powers. This non-theistic approach views the principal demons (negative forces) at work in the world as one's own delusions and internal defilements, and egotism as the chief demon.

ONCE BUDDHAGUHYA PROPITIATED MANJUSRI CONTINUOUSLY for several weeks in Benares, without moving from his meditation mat. The painting of Manjusri on the altar before him smiled; the offering bowl containing ghee spontaneously began to boil; and withered flowers, strewn about the altar from past pujas, miraculously blossomed and became again both fragrant and colorful.

Recognizing these signs as an omen of approaching spiritual accomplishment, Buddhaguhya redoubled his efforts. At the same time, he wondered whether first to imbibe as elixir the clarified butter or to offer up the miraculous flowers. . . .

Just at that moment, a haughty demoness slapped his face in an effort to prevent his imminent awakening; for wherever the light is rising, the shadows also darken. Buddhaguhya fell unconscious.

When he awoke, unaware of how much time had passed, the master found the picture of Manjusri covered with dust, the butter spilled, and the flowers withered. He was momentarily disappointed.

Then Buddhaguhya remembered the Dog Master's pointed words: "All appearances are merely productions of the conceptual mind. Do not be deceived!"

He rejoiced, amused at his own folly. He saw that he had been deceived by negative forces—preeminent among them, ignorance itself.

"That obstacle maker almost shook my immutable realization," he thought. "I need no external signs or miracles to transcend duality."

Shouting "Ho!" Buddhaguhya leapt off his seat. Licking up the hardened butter, he tossed the dead flowers into the air, wiped the dusty picture clean with his flowing beard, and strode off, shaking the earth with each stride—free as the wind.

Thus the masters rule the earth.

The King Barks Like a Dog

ONCE TWO RIVAL MINISTERS OF the king of Nétang vied for control of the kingdom. As the New Year celebration approached, one minister boasted to the other, "I bet I can make the king bark like a dog on New Year's morning."

His rival instantly retorted, "It's a bet! How will you do that—by black magic?"

On New Year's Day, his majesty was seated cross-legged on his throne, surrounded by ministers and officials. Each came forward, according to rank, to offer his lord and master the traditional white silk scarf and wishes for health and longevity. Recalling their wager, the rivals leaned over to speak into the king's ear.

The protagonist said to the king, "Your Highness, outside the walls this very morning I saw a nomad selling a huge, magnificent mastiff. Would Your Majesty be pleased to receive it as a New Year's offering?"

The king replied, "You know I love fine dogs, but they must be perfect in every way. How are his teeth? What sort of bark does he have?"

The cagey minister continued. "His teeth are fine, Your Majesty, but his bark . . . " Disdainfully, he uttered small meowing sounds.

"Sounds like a cat to me!" barked the king.

"What sort of bark should a royal mastiff have?" the minister inquired, all innocence.

The king placed his ringed fists on the elaborately carved wooden table before him, reared up on all fours in front of his astonished audience, and barked loudly.

Thus was the wager resolved.

Shabkar's Female Yak

A dzomo is a crossbreed female yak. It is valued highly as a beast of burden as well as for its milk, from which the nomads make butter, cheese, and yogurt.

Shabkar Rinpoche was a singing yogi and Dzogchen master of the nineteenth century. His "Life and Collected Songs" have been compared with Milarepa's.

ONE DAY SHABKAR RINPOCHE'S GURU, Jamyang Gyatso, passed away. Shabkar and his mother decided to offer a yak, their sole material asset, for use during the funeral ceremonies. When their other family members heard the news, they were aghast.

One relative came immediately to visit. "Is it true that you intend to offer that splendid dzomo of yours for the funeral rites?" he inquired. When they answered affirmatively, he remonstrated with them, "But the entire congregation of yogis, the deceased lama's closest disciples, are only offering a few sacks of flour; it would be quite sufficient for you to offer only a fraction of that. After all, this isn't your parents' funeral. . . . Why not keep the dzomo? How will you survive without it?"

Shabkar answered, "I have a slightly different way of looking at things. The kindness of the guru is totally unrepayable, for he offers the possibility of perfect liberation and enlightenment. Therefore, his kindness is greater than my father's and mother's, loving as they have always been."

Then he sang:

"Even if without this dzomo our household is ruined,
  I have no regrets.
  With one voice, all the Buddhas have said
  That to offer anything to one's guru
  Surpasses making offerings to a thousand Buddhas,
  For the gracious master is the Buddha incarnate,
  whom we meet face to face."

The funeral rites for the deceased guru were truly splendid. Countless miraculous signs and omens were perceived, inspiring the faithful followers to pray and give offerings, request teachings, and engage in service to others. Shabkar perceived his guru's smiling face in the sky above the funeral pyre.

Afterward, many poor folk remarked, "Isn't it truly remarkable how that carefree bard Shabkar offered his only dzomo? Did you notice his exalted state of mind during Jamyang Gyatso's cremation? . . . Wasn't it wondrous to behold!"

Lo and behold, in perfect accordance with the workings of karma, Shabkar soon afterward received a dzomo as payment for copying by hand a sacred scripture for a wealthy patron. Not long after that, he received two more dzomos as offerings on different auspicious occasions: for one can receive only as much as one gives.

Shabkar knew in his heart of hearts that his abundant good fortune could only be due to the blessings of his late guru, whose presence always remained within him, an intimate reminder of the profound import of generosity and non-attachment.

The Equality of All That Lives

IN 1982 HIS HOLINESS THE Dalai Lama of Tibet was dining in France with Pawo Rinpoche X. The pair were recounting stories of the past and anticipating the rebirth of the recently deceased Gyalwa Karmapa.

Just then the elderly Pawo Rinpoche spied an ant struggling across the polished floor, wending its way toward the sun.

The aged Pawo Rinpoche no longer had the use of his legs. He requested the Dalai Lama to be so kind as to rescue the little creature and help it on its way.

His Holiness did so with alacrity, blessing the insect with a whispered benediction. Gently, he carried the insect across the regal chamber and set it down safely in the warm sun. Chuckling with delight, he rejoined his venerable colleague.

"Now I have done a service for you, Rinpoche. Your old eyes are better than mine! People talk about emptiness and high Mahayana philosophy, but loving regard for the equality of all that lives is the true sign of a bodhisattva."

His Holiness himself later recounted the story, during a teaching in France about the necessity of compassion, selfless service, and universal responsibility. "My religion is loving-kindness," he stated.

Tantric Travels

Chöying Rangdrol was an enlightened master who possessed no earthly goods. Day and night, he sat in meditation on a floor mat, wearing only a loose sheepskin coat. Without formal education, he had traversed the path to awakening.

"Yogis want and need nothing other than the immutable nature of authentic being," he sang.

ONE DAY, PATRUL RINPOCHE—WHO RECEIVED extensive teachings from Chöying Rangdrol—was sitting with the meditation master, when the latter inquired, "By the way, what is Mingyur Dorje of the Dzogchen Monastery doing these days?"

Patrul Rinpoche gave him some news. Chöying Rangdrol remarked, "Those Dzogchen folks don't treat Mingyur Dorje the way they should. If they knew his true identity, it would be different. A genuine siddha rarely reveals all his inner qualities."

Later, for no apparent reason, Chöying Rangdrol said, "During the great gatherings at the Dzogchen Monastery, Mingyur Dorje sits on a high throne, not far from the door, facing inward; that's rather unusual, isn't it? The teacher's throne used to be near the altar." Then he proceeded to recall various customs and personages at Dzogchen.

Throughout the conversation, Patrul Rinpoche—who had studied at Dzogchen—nodded in agreement, apparently sharing the meditation master's reminiscences. A young neophyte, Pema Dorje, who happened to be present (and who later became the head khenpo [abbot] at the Dzogchen Monastery) thought, "How does this unlettered lama know so much about our monastery? He must have gone there in his youth."

Finally the curious boy asked the meditation master, "Venerable lama, have you been to the Dzogchen Monastery?"

"You might say so," the master replied.

"When?"

"Every year, you perform the ceremony of the Great Gathering. When, on the throne, Mingyur Dorje plays a small ivory hand drum and sings the invocation: 'Vidyadharas, awareness holders, dakas, and dakinis, come with your retinue—come and enjoy the vajra-feast,' then all the deities of the universal mandala, as well as all the old-lineage patriarchs, *must* respond to this auspicious invitation. So it was that I visited Dzogchen. Otherwise, I have never physically visited your monastery."

Young Pema Dorje realized that Chöying Rangdrol was a clairvoyant siddha, with extraordinary inner qualities, and that he could transcend time and space. Filled with faith, the boy bowed low before the master and received his blessing.

Pema Dorje ultimately followed Chöying Rangdrol and Patrul to Buddhahood.

The Dakinis' Rainbow Bridge

Gotsangpa lived eight hundred years ago. A Drukpa Kagyu (Dragon) lineage holder, he was renowned for diligence in meditation and generosity in making offerings.

For many years Gotsangpa lived in a cave, with only a burlap sack. When a wild thornbush grew over the mouth of the cave, the hermit could not spare the time to trim it back, although it tore at his robe whenever he passed in and out. "I might be dead before I come out of the cave again," he thought. "What is the use of cutting it down before I go in?"

ONCE GOTSANGPA AND A DISCIPLE went discreetly to a deserted island in the middle of a lake to practice meditation in total solitude. No one knew their whereabouts.

In early winter, they crossed the frozen lake on foot and reached the island. They meditated there throughout the year.

Gotsangpa had nothing to eat except *tsampa*—roasted barley flour, a Tibetan staple. He and his student subsisted on tsampa and tea, supplemented by whatever herbs they could find on the island.

Gotsangpa had nothing to eat except *tsampa*—roasted barley flour, a Tibetan staple. He and his student subsisted on tsampa and tea, supplemented by whatever herbs they could find on the island.

Gotsangpa had vowed to offer one hundred thousand tsok tormas (ritual offering cakes) to the dakas, dakinis, and Dharma protectors. Therefore, with most of their stock of tsampa the yogis handcrafted the cone-shaped tormas daily and offered them on their modest shrine, until the vow was fulfilled. By then their supply of tsampa was depleted.

After about nine months, they were without food. The disciple asked, "What should we do, master?"

The master replied, "We have offered all those tormas to the deities on behalf of the well-being and enlightenment of the world. Never fear; they will take care of us."

The lake prevented them from leaving the island. Surviving on broth and infusions concocted from the various medicinal herbs they managed to forage, they were weakened by austerity. Winter, which would freeze the water separating them from the mainland and provide them with a bridge to civilization, was long in coming.

Then Gotsangpa said to his disciple, "Our meditation practice and offerings are auspiciously completed. Let's go!"

Gotsangpa proceeded to the shore, followed by his astonished attendant; then he started to walk across the surface of the water as if there were a transparent bridge of ice connecting the island to land. His amazed disciple followed him, not daring to look beneath his feet, fearing a fall into the freezing waters. "Don't look back!" the master commanded.

When they finally reached the far shore and peered back into the mist, there was no ice spanning the gulf. Instead, the yogis saw a bridge of rainbow light woven by the joined hands of the one hundred thousand adoring dakinis who had partaken of their oblations.

"Not a Damned Thing"

Konchog Paldron was the daughter and spiritual successor of the Treasure Master, Chögyur Lingpa. Recognized as Green Tara incarnate, she was a remarkable teacher and the mother of several tulkus, reincarnate lamas.

KONCHOG PALDRON RECEIVED EXTENSIVE TEACHINGS from many enlightened masters, including the Manjusri Master Jamyang Khyentse and the first Jamgon Kongtrul. However, it was Patrul Rinpoche's oral pith-instructions that awakened her inherent Buddha-mind. She later transmitted Dza Patrul's pithy Dzogchen teachings to many practitioners.

One day, speaking in verse, Patrul told her:

"Don't prolong the past,
Don't invite the future,
Don't alter your innate wakefulness—
Don't fear appearances.
There is nothing more than that!"

Hearing these words, Konchog Paldron suddenly experienced great enlightenment.

Patrul had spoken in an earthy nomadic dialect. The final phrase sounded like "Apart from that, there is not a damned thing!"

This became renowned as the "Not-A-Damned-Thing Instruction." It has been passed down, from master to disciple, to this day.

The King of Ghosts

Chögyur Lingpa and Dza Patrul were younger contemporaries of Jamgon Kongtrul and Jamyang Khyentse Wangpo, who sparked a Buddhist renaissance during the nineteenth century in eastern Tibet. Each of these enlightened masters studied in a non-sectarian manner under the guidance of many of the greatest teachers of their time, receiving transmission of all the extant teachings and oral lineages.

Wicked monks are said to be reborn, in certain cases, as kinglike ghosts or spirits. Samaya refers to tantric vows and commitments.

ONCE CHÖGYUR LINGPA TOLD THE abbot Khenpo Rinchen Dargyé, one of his principal disciples, "You should go to Dzachuka and receive teachings from Patrul Rinpoche, especially Shantideva's *Bodhicharya-avatara*, which he knows by heart. He is a remarkable teacher, overflowing with wisdom and blessings."

The Treasure Master graciously provided his erudite disciple with a personal letter of introduction, addressed to Patrul, saying, "Please give clothes, food, and Dharma to this proud disciple of mine."

Khenpo Rinchen Dargyé was a fully ordained monk, an exemplary upholder of the three vehicles of the Buddhist tradition: Theravada, Mahayana, and Vajrayana. His outward appearance showed him to be a perfectly renounced, unattached, homeless wayfarer and monk, while his internal attitude was that of a compassionate bodhisattva whose altruistic vow unfailingly places the concerns of others before his own. Secretly, he was an uninhibited practitioner of the non-dual Vajrayana teachings of Buddhist tantra.

Carrying his immaculate monastic robes on one shoulder, his large begging bowl on his back, and his mendicant's staff in his hand, eventually the khenpo, after many days on foot, arrived in the presence of Patrul. As the venerable abbot began to prostrate before him, Patrul exclaimed, "Ah-yii! Here comes the king of ghosts!"

He stood up abruptly, affording Khenpo Rinchen Dargyé no chance to offer three formal prostrations. Rinchen Dargyé barely managed to present his letter of introduction, which Patrul summarily tossed in a dark corner, before being ushered out of the lama's spartan cell.

The next day, mustering his courage, the khenpo again presented himself before Patrul, the enlightened vagabond. He requested spiritual instruction and guidance, especially teachings on "Engaging in the Bodhisattva Path," the *Bodhicharya-avatara*, as his teacher Chögyur Lingpa had urged him to do.

Patrul retorted, "I can't give those teachings. I am not a teacher; there is nothing I can do for an important person like you. What do you want from an old fool like me?" And the khenpo was again ushered from the room.

On the following morning, Rinchen Dargyé renewed his petition. Patrul told him, "Well, stick around a while; then we'll see."

For one month, the implacable Patrul did not utter a single word of instruction in the khenpo's presence. Rinchen Dargyé would appear daily, prostrate to the master, sit nursing his hopes and drinking weak tea—and finally take his leave.

One of the highest regions of Kham, Dzachuka was cold and buffeted by winds. The unaccustomed rigors of Patrul's rugged mountain retreat proved uncomfortable for the elegant abbot. Eventually Rinchen Dargyé sadly confessed to the master, "Treasure Master Chögyur Lingpa sent me to receive teachings from you. But if you are not going to impart a single word of advice or instruction, I shall have to return to him empty-handed. However, if, out of your compassionate concern, you would kindly consent to teach me, please be advised that I have fervent faith and devotion in both yourself and the impeccable lineage you represent and embody. I truly wish to practice your teachings to the utmost. I have no broken monastic vows, nor impaired Vajrayana samaya, and have purified all inverted thoughts. Please teach your humble servant!" The renowned abbot and scholar continued to beseech the sheepskin-clad master.

Without taking much notice of this elaborate speech, the laconic Patrul offhandedly replied, "OK, come back tomorrow."

The next morning, when Rinchen Dargyé appeared, Patrul gave him first a monastic robe, saying, "Here is clothing." Then he presented the abbot with a leg of dried mutton. "Here is food," he said. Third, Patrul presented the khenpo with a volume of the *Bodhicharya-avatara*, saying, "Here is Dharma."

Then the provocative master concluded, "So, now you have received clothing, food, and Dharma, as the Treasure Master intended. Tomorrow you may go."

Utterly dismayed, Rinchen Dargyé prostrated himself before Patrul on the earthen floor, bowing again and again, fervently crying out, "Please give me teachings!"

Patrul was adamant. "Chögyur Lingpa said to give you clothing, food, and Dharma. You got them; that's it."

However, Rinchen Dargyé persisted, begging Patrul to free him from delusion by imparting the precious teachings for the benefit of one and all.

Finally, when he intuited that Rinchen Dargyé was ripe, the uncompromising master began to teach. He continued for several months. Khenpo Dargyé swiftly progressed, eventually becoming one of the greatest teachers of his time.

The khenpo remained forever grateful to Patrul for the personal lessons he received—not only for the formal teachings but also for the gruff manner and toughness the master continued to display in order to vanquish Rinchen Dargyé's pride and pretense.

The khenpo often recounted that Patrul had called him "king of ghosts" at their initial encounter and purified him by making him wait so long, because he saw that Rinchen Dargyé was burdened with a hidden residue of self-esteem for being an exemplary monk and scholar.

Holy Hair Relics

Patrul Rinpoche never appreciated flatterers. If this straight-shooting, outspoken, down-to-earth impartial master had a pet peeve, it was what he called "crooked minds."

Lamas often tie red cords around the necks of their followers, as a protection and blessing. A lama's hair, fingernails, clothes, and so on are considered to be imbued with blessings communicable to the faithful and are therefore often preserved and cherished.

ONE DAY, A LAMA NAMED Longna Tulku came to visit Patrul Rinpoche. While Longna Tulku was prostrating himself at the door, Patrul Rinpoche observed facetiously, "It seems that someone is doing prostrations here—what for?"

Longna (which means water reed) introduced himself. "Ah-zi!" exclaimed the master. "What strange times we are living in; nowadays even reeds have tulkus!"

Laughing aloud, Longna retorted, "Well, if there can be 'log' tulkus, why not 'water-reed' tulkus—at least it's green, living wood!" This was a clever pun on the name of Patrul's guru's reincarnation, Dza Trama Tulku—for "trama" can mean small cut logs of dry wood, as well as a place in eastern Tibet.

Patrul Rinpoche said nothing. He was obviously pleased with the lama's answer. And he knew that his visitor had boundless veneration for the Dzogchen practitioners.

Longna Tulku sat at Patrul's feet. While they conversed, he discreetly picked up some human hairs from the carpet to keep as a relic. Realizing what his visitor was doing, Patrul roared, "What are you up to?"

Knowing that Patrul Rinpoche wouldn't approve of his stray hairs being kept as relics, Longna Tulku glibly replied, "My disciples' cattle are plagued by epidemics, and wolves often attack them. If I tie these hairs around their necks, it will protect them."

Patrul Rinpoche was not duped. However, aware of his visitor's sincerity, not only did he let him collect the hair but he also tore away a piece of the clothes he was wearing and presented it to Longna—a unique courtesy indeed.

"Here is a protection for your flock," he gently jested. "With a devious herder like yourself to care for them, they need all the protection they can get!"

Name and Fame

IN MIDDLE AGE, JAMYANG KHYENTSE Wangpo resolved never again to quit his room. He would spend his forty remaining years meditating and praying in retreat. "I will never again cross the threshold of this house," said he.

After taking that vow, Khyentse gave his shoes to his servants. They were discarded in the nearby river.

One morning some years later, the clairvoyant Manjusri Master unexpectedly instructed his servants to welcome whoever might wish to visit him.

Later in the day, an anonymous tramp arrived. He went directly to Khyentse Rinpoche's personal quarters and rested his battered homemade knapsack on the kitchen counter. "I have come to see Ngédon. Where is Ngédon?" he demanded.

The servants instantly took offense. They completely forgot their master's instructions. Who was this shabby vagabond to insult their glorious master by using his intimate childhood name, Ngédon?

They ordered the beggar to leave. "The master is in deep meditation," the beggar was told. "Maybe another time!"

The beggar spoke bluntly, "He has really become so very important now! When we were young I shared my cheese with him, and now I can't even get past his servants! I have no time to waste." He began to leave.

Suddenly the servants remembered Khyentse Rinpoche's unusual instructions. Hastily, they asked the tramp's name. The irascible Patrul, already on his way, shouted, "Orgyen"—Padma Sambhava's name (as well as his own)—over his shoulder and disappeared into the hills.

That night, Khyentse Rinpoche inquired if anyone had come to see him. One servant answered, "Only one obnoxious old beggar, who insulted your name. He grandly called himself Orgyen and would not wait."

"What?!" exclaimed Khyentse Rinpoche. "You didn't let him in? That was my Dharma brother Patrul Rinpoche, Orgyen Chökyi Wangpo. Find him, and bring him to me."

The humiliated servants finally, after a long and wearying search, found Patrul camped in the forest far up the valley. Prostrating themselves, they apologized profusely and invited him to be their venerable master's honored guest. Laughing, Patrul replied that he was too busy meditating to pay social calls.

That was the last direct contact between the legendary pair. However, each was aware of the other's activities, and they often regaled their disciples with stories and anecdotes about each other.

Grains of Rice

It is a custom in Tibet to carve mantras on stones. These are then piled in specially chosen places—which might be considered the earth's acupressure points—to encourage world peace as well as to serve as a benediction and protection for whoever, human or animal, might encounter them. These are known as mani stones, since the most commonly used mantra is that of Great Compassion, Om Mani Padmé Hung.

To bless and consecrate, lamas often whisper prayers and blow their hallowed breath upon saffron- or rainbow-colored uncooked rice, which is then tossed over the object of benediction, whether animate or inanimate. Through the master's efficacious visualization of each grain transforming into whatever the sentient beings want or need, great benefits ensue.

The late Nyingmapa (Ancient Translation School) leader, His Holiness Dudjom Rinpoche, once blessed a new monastery in Mysore, southern India, from his sickbed in Kalimpong. At the prearranged moment, when the long-awaited public consecration was to take place, His Holiness tossed up rainbow-colored rice in Kalimpong, and rainbow-colored grains of rice fell on the newly constructed site in far-off Mysore—a miraculous blessing indeed.

PATRUL RINPOCHE USUALLY TRAVELED IN anonymity. When they recognized his exalted spirituality, people would spontaneously request teachings and blessings from him. Granting whatever was needed, he would then simply continue alone, leaving behind whatever offerings he had received.

This detached behavior came to the attention of Jamyang Khyentse. He sent a message to Patrul: "Why do you discard what your disciples and patrons offer? Wouldn't it be better to use that wealth for virtuous projects?"

Patrul had the highest respect for the Manjusri Master, whom he recognized as a living Buddha. Therefore, from that time on, Patrul offered to beggars whatever he accumulated. He also used such gifts to sponsor carvings of the mantra *Om Mani Padmé Hung* on rocks.

It came about that eventually there existed a long wall composed of thousands of such mani stones. Delighted, Patrul sent a message to Khyentse Rinpoche: Would the latter deign to consecrate the mani wall? A message returned: Jamyang Khyentse would bless the great wall on an auspicious date soon to come.

Everyone rejoiced. The Manjusri Master was coming! A religious festival was planned for that day.

On the appointed day, everyone gathered in anticipation of Khyentse Rinpoche's arrival. Patrul warned them not to be disappointed if the great master did not appear in person, since he was in retreat ten days' journey away. Moreover he explained, "Jamyang Khyentse can just as effectively consecrate the mani stones at a distance through the great power of his prayers and blessings. Whatever happens, don't be surprised."

Immediately, rain began to fall. It pounded triumphantly upon the huge pile of rocks, streaming across the innumerable inscriptions. Brilliant rainbows embroidered the sky. Divine flowers and saffron-colored rice fell upon the stones as well as on the assembled company as, at the appointed hour, the extraordinary consecration took place, although the Manjusri Master Khyentse was nowhere to be seen.

Patrul Rinpoche clapped his hands with delight. He bowed in the direction of Khyentse Rinpoche's distant residence and then—without a word—continued on his humble, solitary way.

Everyone who ate a grain of that miraculous rice or one of those succulent flowers was later reborn in the celestial sphere, ultimately to reach deliverance.

Two Masters and a Crystal

To meet the guru in a dream, vision, or after death in the intermediate (bardo) state can be as meaningful as to meet the master in our day-to-day waking reality. A powerful enlightened master can, through symbolic if not verbal means, inexplicably initiate sudden awakening.

A crystal is often used in rites of tantric empowerment to represent the absolute spiritual essence, the fundamental nature of being. How often it has been said that everything is created by the mind, that everything is energy—or, in a visionary sense, that all is light.

Deity yoga (yidam practice) is an essential form of Vajrayana meditation, in which one totally identifies oneself with a meditational deity, who—like one's own spiritual master—mirrors one's most perfectly enlightened pure nature. In the creative phase of such meditation practice, one generates and develops this experience of identification through visualizations, contemplative absorptions, mantras, invocations, and gestures.

To mingle with the guru implies truly transcending one's ego-centered self; it means that one realizes that one has never really been separate or apart from absolute being, for there is actually no "one" to be mingled, just as there is nothing outside to mingle with. Kuntuzangpo (Samantabhadra in Sanskrit) is the primordial Buddha; his kingdom is one's own innate perfection and wholeness, Buddha-mind.

ONCE THE FIRST JAMGON KONGTRUL had a vision at dawn. In a magnificent, translucent temple of splendid radiance sat his teacher and colleague, the Manjusri Master Jamyang Khyentse Wangpo, whose corporeal form seemed composed of nothing but a scintillating swirl of rainbow light.

Thrilled with devotion, Kongtrul bowed again and again while reciting refuge prayers, generating Bodhichitta, making imagined offerings, and requesting teachings. The entire universal mandala seemed to be arranged about the still point at the center of Khyentse's heart, where on a radiant lotus throne dwelt Padma Sambhava, the Lotus-Born Guru.

Khyentse Rinpoche performed the creative-phase practice of deity yoga, becoming apotheosized; then he bestowed tantric empowerment. When he placed a blazing chalice brimming with the elixir of gnosis upon Kongtrul's head, indescribable ecstasy filled the latter's heart and mind.

From Khyentse Wangpo's heart instantaneously appeared a perfect crystal—sparkling, luminous, brilliant, flawlessly pure and clear. Khyentse Rinpoche showed the transparent crystal to Kongtrul, displaying its multicolored radiance with stunning effect.

Then he said:

"All things are primordially pure and perfect,
  clear and transparent,
  like this crystal.
  Like the radiant light of a crystal,
  whatever forms appear to manifest before us
  arise as the uninhibited creative expression
  of sheer luminosity,
  which is always spontaneously present—
  the light by which we see
  and are seen.

Within this illusory, phantasmagorical self-display,
  where is the difference between inner and outer,
  oneself and others?

This centerless primordial presence is open, free, immaculate,
void and untrammeled;
its nature is sheer lucency.

See through everything, conceptualize nothing,
and remain undeceived—forever
free and at ease."

Jamgon Kongtrul's hair stood on end, as he vividly perceived the brilliant, scintillating magic dance of the uncreated absolute nature, the immanence of Buddha-mind. Meanwhile, Khyentse Rinpoche's illusory form dissolved, disappearing into radiant light like a rainbow fading in the infinite sky. When Jamgon Kongtrul returned to his senses, it was daybreak.

The two masters were never again prey to the illusion of separation. Actualizing innate Buddha-mind, they together ascended the throne of Kuntuzangpo's kingdom.

Gampopa's Business Advice

ONCE A BUSINESSPERSON BECAME A follower of Gampopa, Milarepa's successor. The trader confessed to Gampopa that for many years, he had earned his livelihood by trading in religious statues, scroll paintings, sacred texts, and ritual implements.

He was well aware that this type of commerce was not what the Buddha had in mind when he exhorted laypeople to practice "right livelihood." Therefore, the trader asked his teacher how to purify the bad karma associated with such unwholesome activities, which could only hinder him on the path to freedom and enlightenment.

Gampopa advised him to earn by another means as much as he had gained by his previous business and then use the profits to build a temple.

The businessman followed his teacher's instructions and eventually established a beautiful shrine. However, the substantial undertaking allowed him little time to pray or sit in meditation.

After fulfilling this task, he approached Gampopa. "Venerable Dharma master, now I have purified my karma. Still, it is necessary to acquire countless books, statues, and paintings to decorate the temple so that it will be an authentic sanctuary where people can worship. With so much to do, how can I find time to meditate? And without meditating, how can I progress on the path?"

Gampopa replied, "There is no need to decorate the temple further; the faithful shall see to that. If you can sustain for even an instant a clear recognition of emptiness, through the clear light of Mahamudra (Ultimate Reality), all karma and emotionality will instantly be purified. There is no need to strive further in worldly good works nor to seek for illusory signs of spiritual progress.

"Regarding the path of Mahamudra, simply rest in naturalness and simplicity, recognizing your innate Buddha-nature. Buddha is in the palm of your hand. Abide carefree, beyond the dichotomy of action and inaction. Don't try to accomplish or manipulate anything; let it go as it goes. Enjoy everything as a display of Buddha-mind; just leave it as it is."

The trader suddenly saw that Buddha-mind had always been his, and he achieved awakening. No longer would he value graven images.

Beyond Discipline

Khenpo Gangshar was one of the principal gurus of the late Chögyam Trungpa Rinpoche. From a family of tantric yogis, this awesome crazy-wisdom master appears in one rare photo with a fierce expression on his face and wielding a large phurba, a ritual dagger used to subjugate demons and sever the aorta of duality—only in this case, Khenpo Gangshar is holding the phurba pointed at his own heart!

GANGSHAR WAS A MISCHIEVOUS, HIGH-SPIRITED young boy. In order to learn self-discipline, he was sent at an early age to a monastery in Kham where his uncle, a learned khenpo (abbot-professor), personally guided him. However, even the venerable khenpo, used to teaching peasant boys, could not tame this remarkable youngster.

One winter a few birds settled on a small patch of earth left uncovered by snow, to eat seeds that had been scattered there as an offering. The little five-year-old picked up a large, flat stone and dropped it on the oblivious birds.

"Why did you kill those poor, helpless creatures?" his uncle shouted. "Didn't I teach you never to kill? Would you like a giant to drop a mountain on top of you?"

The boy protested, insisting that he had not killed anything. "The hungry little birds were cold," he said. "I protected them with that stone, like a roof."

The uncle boxed his ears and dragged him over to see the result of his mischief.

When the dignified old khenpo bent to lift the stone, the birds, chattering gaily, flew up into the sky. All the seeds were gone.

From that time on, it was apparent to everyone that Gangshar was truly remarkable. His uncle let him do as he pleased: the boy was truly beyond earthly discipline.

A Dying Monk's Bird

GELONG SANGYÉ DIED IN BHUTAN a few years ago. During this monk's final illness, a large black bird followed him wherever he went. When he was finally transported to a hospital, the bird perched on the windowsill of the sickroom.

Some said the bird was a vulture; others, an eagle; yet others saw a large crow. The benevolent old monk and his friends daily offered the creature scraps.

When his demise seemed imminent, Gelong Sangyé asked to be dressed in his maroon monk's robes and helped to sit in the full-lotus posture. The spectral bird held a silent vigil as the yogi passed away, keeping him company for three days after his death, during which time Sangyé sat in deep meditation. Then the bird faithfully hovered above the funeral procession as the corpse was carried to the cremation ground.

Many Bhutanese felt a renewal of faith due to the masterful, transcendent manner in which the spiritually accomplished Sangyé spent his final days, facing death with perfect equanimity. The rainbows and other portentous signs manifested at his cremation served to confirm his greatness.

After the lama's body was cremated, the mysterious bird was seen no more. Thus it is said that the guardians and sky-dancing dakinis appear in various guises to welcome accomplished practitioners to the celestial sphere.

A Frog Enters the Stream of Reality

The Tibetan oral tradition includes countless stories that tell how, through no personal effort of one's own but through the agency of a powerful enlightened one, great blessings ensue. This in no way contradicts the traditional Buddhist doctrine that each must work out his or her own salvation.

ONCE A FROG WAS SQUATTING contentedly in a muddy pool near Lord Buddha's grassy seat. A bent-over old farmer, intent on paying his respects to the Enlightened One, accidentally impaled the poor little creature with the tip of his rosewood staff.

Through having heard the Buddha expound his teachings, the fortunate frog had accumulated sufficient good karma to be reborn in a heavenly state. Not only did he encounter the Buddha there but he also received direct spiritual guidance.

With his keen divine faculties, through meditation he soon perceived the true nature of reality and became a stream enterer, the first of four stages of enlightenment. After seven rebirths, he was fully liberated.

The frog begot merit through hearing the teachings, and the unwitting old farmer did, too. For his part in the drama, he was later reborn in a noble family and became an erudite abbot.

Anyone Can Get There

It is possible to reach enlightenment without exhaustive training. Simple, wholehearted practice is often sufficient. One of the most popular forms of Buddhism is the Pure Land school, in which faith in Amitabha Buddha is enough to deliver one after death to his western paradise, Dewachen.

The Lotus-Born Guru Padma Sambhava is the tulku (living embodiment) of Amitabha. The So clan was a family lineage of Dzogchen practitioners descended from Yeshé Tsogyal's disciple, an illumined yogi named So Yeshé Wangchuk.

The seventeen Dzogchen tantras are a rare transmission of the Maha Ati (Dzogchen) lineage, brought from India and disseminated in Tibet by Padma Sambhava and Vairotsana. The late Nyingmapa (Ancient Translation School) leader Dilgo Khyentse Rinpoche aurally received this precious transmission from Kangyur Rinpoche of Riwoché.

KANGYUR RINPOCHE'S MOTHER HAD THE habit of faithfully reciting the Dewachen aspiration prayer every day, praying to be reborn in that Buddha-field. An ordinary householder, she never engaged in solitary retreats or esoteric meditation practices; prayer, morality, and devotion were her path.

When death approached, mother and son retired to a blessed cave in Nyémo Drébso Lung.

There she was often visited by visions of Amitabha, although she did not recognize him. "What is this radiant red monk doing here every day?" she asked her lama son. Kangyur Rinpoche said nothing but smiled knowingly.

One day she told him, "The splendid red monk must be a deity; he is becoming more clear and vivid daily."

Then her son said, "That is Amitabha Buddha, dear Mother. He has come in answer to your prayers, to welcome you to Dewachen, in accordance with his vow."

Immensely gratified, the old lady burst into tears. "He even comes for someone like me!" she cried joyously.

In that instant she experienced sudden awakening. "Now Amitabha is no longer outside of me!" she exclaimed.

"He never was, dear Mother," Kangyur Rinpoche said.

One day, she called Kangyur Lama, "Aphu (Sonny)—who is that mustached yogi who visits here every day?"

"I didn't notice," the lama replied.

"But he comes here often," she protested.

"All right, let me know next time he comes," he said.

The next day, the old lady called from her bed in the cave, "Aphu, Aphu—look!" Kangyur Lama spied a stately yogi in a white robe standing there; a small prayer book was tied up in the topknot on his head, while half of his long hair tumbled down.

"Welcome," Kangyur Rinpoche said. "Who are you?"

"I am Yeshé Tsogyal's disciple So Yeshé Wangchuk," the unexpected visitor replied.

"Where do you live?" Kangyur asked.

"Up there in the celestial Buddhafield," he answered, pointing up the mountain slope. "I had three sons and a daughter. The oldest is serving the people of eastern Tibet; the youngest is with Guru Rinpoche in Zangdok Palri. The middle son attends me. My daughter is reborn as a shade in Nyémo."

"What practice do you do?" Kangyur inquired.

"The seventeen Dzogchen tantras. I received them directly from the Lotus-Born Guru and his queenly dakini, Yeshé Tsogyal."

Kangyur Lama fervently requested this transmission from him, bowing low three times. So Yeshé Wangchuk recited the seventeen Dzogchen tantras by heart, while the enraptured pair—mother and son—listened.

"My old books are up there. You may keep them," the yogi said. He again pointed up the mountain. Then he disappeared.

Kangyur Rinpoche climbed the rocky mountainside. Eventually he found an abandoned cave; it was obvious that yogis had once lived there. Inside he discovered So Yeshé Wangchuk's priceless handwritten rice-paper manuscript of the seventeen Dzogchen tantras, which had been consecrated eleven centuries ago by Yeshé Tsogyal herself.

Kangyur Rinpoche and his elderly mother remained in their cave until she passed from this world. Inseparable from Amitabha, she spent her last moments sitting peacefully in meditation, a beatific expression on her face. Thus true practitioners pass peacefully from this dreamlike world.

Yeshé Tsogyal Liberates a Consort

ONCE YESHÉ TSOGYAL WAS ON pilgrimage at the Bodhanath Stupa in Kathmandu Valley. She offered a handful of gold dust before the sacred shrine and prayed for guidance and inspiration. "The sufferings of beings seems endless; I lack the energy necessary for liberating them. How to free one and all from the slavery of rebirth in cyclic existence?" she mused.

Light rays radiated from the golden crown of the monumental stupa. The Lotus-Born Master, her own beloved guru, appeared in their midst, riding the rays of the sun. He proclaimed, "Blessed daughter, in the bustling marketplace today acquire the predestined consort you need to fulfill certain stages of the path, and enhance your energies through ecstatic awareness. Return with him immediately to the Land of Snows. There I will further instruct you in the tantric mysteries."

Yeshé Tsogyal walked to Kathmandu and entered the bazaar, letting the inner guru, her own intuition, guide her. Where, amid all these exotic goods, might be the unmistakable object of her search?

Failing to find anything of interest, near the southern gate of Bhaktapur a teenage lad wearing only a loincloth approached her. Handsome and bright, he was adorned with a radiant red mole in the center of his chest and had webbed fingers—mystic signs that the incarnate dakini immediately recognized.

The youth accosted her. "Where are you from, spiritual lady? Have you come to set me free?" Tsogyal knew that here was the answer to her prayers.

"Charming boy, predicted consort," sang Tsogyal. "What is your name, where is your homeland, and what are you doing here in samsara's busy marketplace? I require you as an ally in the Lotus-Born Guru's service."

He told her that his name was Arya Salé. Kidnapped from his Indian parents as a youngster, he had been brought to Nepal and sold into slavery, living in Bhaktapur for seven years as a servant.

Yeshé Tsogyal accompanied Salé to his master's house, where she parted from him. She remained on the doorstep, chanting prayers and singing songs of mystic experience and realization.

Eventually the master of the house appeared. He demanded to know her identity and intent. Tsogyal informed him that Guru Rinpoche Padma Sambhava had sent her to ransom the servant Arya Salé.

The merchant was taken aback. Salé had become like a son to him, he explained; moreover, much gold had been spent in acquiring him. He suggested that Tsogyal would be welcome to stay with Salé in the household, if she so desired.

Tsogyal was invited in. The lady of the house heard her tale and was sympathetic. "You have come so far, faithfully following your guru's command. Give us five hundred gold coins, which is what we paid for him, and although he is worth infinitely more, he shall be yours. You are a mature, respectable woman; will you marry him? Or will he be your servant?"

"I will liberate him," Tsogyal declared.

Tsogyal had offered everything she had at the Bodhanath shrine. Therefore she went in search of good fortune, although she knew not where she would find it.

In the bazaar, she heard that a wealthy merchant had just lost a son in a border war. The corpse was in his parents' home.

Tsogyal offered thanks to her guru for his continuous guidance. Then she sought the bereaved household.

Meeting the grieving parents, Tsogyal's heart was filled with compassion. In song, she explained her quest for Arya Salé. "A true hero is rare in this world," sang Tsogyal. "Equally rare is an authentic spiritual consort."

Before her on a woven mat was the corpse of the twenty-year-old warrior. His parents told Tsogyal, "You are a singing yogini, a tantric practitioner. If you can bring our son back to life, we will ransom even a prince for you. . . . But is it possible?"

Tsogyal bowed in acquiescence. Again she gave thanks to the wish-fulfilling jewel, Guru Padma, for his teachings and guidance; what else could one possibly need?

Then she sang:

"Homage and obeisance to the immortal Lotus-Born Guru,
   the perfect embodiment of deathless reality.

"The fundamental ground of being is primordially pure and unborn
      Buddha-mind,
   giving rise to the appearance of infinite forms.
   Within the inseparability of emptiness and energy,
   Positive and negative actions inevitably produce their respective karmic
      results.

"I am a master of non-dual tantra;
   neither life nor death hold the slightest fear for me!
   Therefore I have the power to alleviate afflictions:
   May all blessings flow!"

Tsogyal pointed her right forefinger at the corpse's heart and leaned over to drop a tiny bit of her own saliva directly into his mouth. She chanted a mantra in his ear and with her hands caressed his deep stab wounds. His eyes fluttered open; then he sat up.

The resurrected warrior's parents and the household servants all prostrated to Tsogyal, overwhelmed with joy and gratitude. "This is only the power of the Buddha's benediction," she told them. "Give thanks to Lord Buddha and Guru Padma Sambhava. One can do nothing without the lineage transmission of their blessings." Then, in humble gratitude, she offered a vajra-feast.

The merchant handed Tsogyal a sack of gold coins. For one thousand coins, Arya Salé was ransomed. Then Tsogyal enjoyed his favors, as prophesied.

Bringing him to Tibet, she returned to the Lotus-Born Guru. After receiving his personal teachings and guidance, the well-matched pair practiced yoga and meditation for months in a mountain cave near the snow line, where blissful experiences and great awakening eventually ensued.

The dakini queen Yeshé Tsogyal lived to the age of one hundred and six. As Padma Sambhava's spiritual heir and successor, she taught and liberated innumerable disciples. At his bidding, Tsogyal hid for posterity many of his teachings; these were later discovered as terma by the treasure masters, who were reincarnations of his original disciples.

No Mustard Seeds for Buddha

DURING THE BUDDHA'S LIFETIME, FIVE centuries before Christ, a grief-stricken mother came to Buddha. She was wailing and lamenting over the death of her baby, whose corpse she carried in her arms. All the compassionate monks reached out to her with their prayers, and she requested an audience with the Buddha himself, that well-known wonder worker.

The compassionate Buddha received her with peaceful, smiling eyes, gazing upon the infant's corpse. The Buddha's indescribable kindness and warmth instantly enveloped her, for no grief is greater than that of losing one's own child.

The woman said to the Buddha, "Lord, my son has died, and I am inconsolable. Can you bring him back to life for me? He was the light of our entire household. We waited many years for his birth, and now he has been stolen away by a sudden incurable illness. You who know all things, who have transcended life and death—please restore life to his little eyes. It is not fair that he should be taken from us so soon!" Thus, in her grief, she beseeched him.

The Buddha did not answer quickly. Gazing upon the infant, he gently touched his cold brow. Then he said, "Faithful woman, go from house to house in this town and collect a mustard seed from each household in which no one has died. When you have those seeds, bring them to me—we shall see what can be done."

The woman was overjoyed. She prostrated to the Buddha and reverently touched his feet. The Buddha placed his hands on her head as a benediction. Then she went on her way, carrying the dead baby in her arms.

All day long she went from door to door, from house to house, seeking mustard seeds from those who had not lost a household member. However, as she proceeded—telling her woeful tale wherever she went—she failed to find even one home that death had not visited. Undaunted, she persisted in her quest, hoping that those magic mustard seeds would, through the Buddha's unfathomable blessings, bring her baby back to life.

As the day waned, still she had not collected even a single mustard seed . . . for death is indeed ubiquitous. People were willing to give mustard seeds, whether or not they had lost relatives, but the woman was adamant. Only those from a house that death had not entered would do!

When at dusk she was still without a single mustard seed to reward her efforts, understanding finally began to dawn in her weary mind. "Is this not the way of all living things?" she thought to herself. "All things that are born must eventually die. This is the basic fact of life, the truth of Dharma, that Lord Buddha has introduced to me." Then she bowed reverently in the direction of his abode.

At nightfall, with the baby still in her arms, she returned to the Buddha's temporary dwelling place. Although the woman had no mustard seeds, she did not return empty-handed; she carried her understanding like a blazing torch within her.

As she approached the Buddha, bowing each step of the way, she laid her dead son before him and said, "O enlightened Compassionate One, I see now that there is no bringing the dead back to life. You asked me to bring a mustard seed from each household where death has never visited, and I could not find even one. Now I understand, and the light of truth has awakened within me.

"Please cremate this poor child, and pray for him. You have given me a gift as great as life. I trust your prayers will deliver this little one's stream of being into higher rebirths and ultimately to freedom and enlightenment."

The omniscient Buddha simply smiled his acceptance.

Patrul's Past Lives

In the practice lineage, where theory is less important than actual spiritual practice, diligence is more important than intellect, and meditation is emphasized, rather than mere learning. Patrul Rinpoche was among the most erudite of enlightened sages, yet it is his earthy lifestyle, outspokenness, simplicity, humor, and warmth that have endeared him to successive generations.

ONCE PATRUL MEDITATED IN THE lower Yamantaka Cave near the Dzogchen Monastery. In the upper cave resided a simpleminded practitioner from Gyalmo Rong; almost illiterate, he likewise exerted himself in solitary meditation.

One day, Patrul playfully provoked him. "If one practices in a place like this, far from all distractions, intrinsic awareness becomes naturally clear. Then it is easy to perceive deities, recall past lives, and so on. . . . Do you have such experiences?"

"Never!" replied the innocent recluse. "Do you?"

"As a matter of fact," Patrul mused, "I occasionally recollect over one hundred of my past lives."

"Tell me about your previous existences," pleaded the hermit. "Surely my meditation practice will profit from it."

"In one life, I was a prostitute in India, in the village where the great black sage Krishnacharya lived," said Patrul. "Moved by faith, I offered him a bracelet of pure gold. After that I was never again born as a simpleton but have had the good fortune to become a pandit."

"Unfortunately I don't have any gold to offer you," said the recluse, who may not have been as dim as he seemed. "Anyway, I aspire only to spiritual awakening, not to learning."

"And I'm not a sage like Krishnacharya!" chortled Patrul. "Too bad!"

A Saint Cannibalizes Padampa Sangyay's Relics

Padampa Sangyay was an Indian siddha of the eleventh century who reached southern Tibet in his later years. There Padampa enjoyed a friendly yogic competition with Jetsun Milarepa, Tibet's supreme hermit-saint, in which both displayed their supernatural powers. Truth was named the victor.

Padampa led to liberation the Tibetan yogini named Machig Labdron, who was Padampa's foremost disciple and (after Yeshé Tsogyal) the first true Tibetan matriarch, holder of the Chöd lineage.

In Machig's songs of wondrous praise, the dark Padampa, the Holy Patriarch, is still vividly called to mind, with his chocolate-colored skin, hawk's eyes, beaklike nose, knees like plowshares, legs like walking sticks, long fingernails and toenails, and his incisively sharp awakened mind—indeed, a legendary, hawklike enlightened guru.

Padampa taught many people in the border region between Tibet and Nepal at a village called Tingri, near Mount Everest; there, after his passing, his corpse was interred. Until recent years, continuous memorial rites were maintained at that sacred tomb for the blessed body of the master, which remained preserved by traditional Tibetan Buddhist embalming methods. Also extant was an original manuscript of a wonderful collection of oral teachings and epigrams called "Advice to the People of Tingri," spoken by Padampa Sangyay himself.

AFTER THE CHINESE TOOK OVER Tibet in 1959, some soldiers were about to destroy Padampa's reliquary shrine and scatter the sacred relics. A devout old Tibetan monk took a piece of the saint's embalmed body before all was lost.

This monk's "crime" came to the attention of the Chinese authorities; they had the old monk brought in chains to face a large public interrogation, a "struggle session" (*damzing*), where he was accused. The military officers demanded to know what the lama's real intentions were.

Why had the superstitious old monk perpetrated against the people such a counterrevolutionary crime? Did he intend to use the desiccated relic to perform illicit magic rites and rituals?

The old monk simply replied that he was brought up from an early age to venerate the holy remains of his village's greatest saint, Padampa Sangyay, the Buddha of Tingri. These relics were believed to confer liberation simply by sight or touch. He therefore wished only to preserve in some small way a precious memento of his centuries-old family faith, for the benefit of future generations. "Does everything from our past have to go?" he asked his implacable captors.

The Chinese interrogators said that if the flesh of a dead saint was so holy, perhaps the old monk ought to eat it. To their surprise, the monk gave his consent.

The relics of flesh seven centuries old were brought forth, amid many a murmur from the gathered Tibetans. In front of the crowd and the military officers, without the slightest hesitation, the old monk ate the age-old remains.

The people were visibly thrilled by this remarkable vindication of their faith. The relics had been permanently enshrined inside the venerable monk!

The bemused Chinese only shook their heads. They placed the old monk under arrest, charging him with cannibalism. "Superstitious Lamas Eat Corpses" reported the Chinese propaganda sheets. "Now the old monk is a walking shrine," murmured the Tibetans.

A Great Feast

PATRUL RINPOCHE AND HIS DISCIPLE Nyoshul Lungtok were in Doyul, meditating at a lonely mountain retreat. From time to time, other disciples joined them.

Hearing that his mercurial master Doe Khyentse was in a neighboring valley, Patrul told Lungtok, "Let's go for a walk."

Soon they came to a vast plateau. In the distance, near a big lake, they spied an encampment of white tents. Countless sheep grazed nearby. Here was Doe Khyentse, accompanied by the second Dodrup Chen; they were herding sheep toward Datsedo as they did every year. Facing their direction, Patrul raised his hands with palms joined in reverence.

Arriving at the tents, they found a lively scene. An attendant led them directly to Doe Khyentse Yeshé Dorje, who sat, dressed in white lambskin, his rifle at his side and his hunting dogs at his feet. Alongside was Dodrup Chen Rinpoche, also dressed in white.

With a huge hunting knife, Doe Khyentse simultaneously carved and ate huge chunks of meat. Delighted to see Patrul, he invited the newcomers to sit on a gorgeous handwoven carpet. He summoned an attendant and ordered a sheep slaughtered immediately for the newcomers.

Patrul was renowned for his non-violence. He would never harm a living creature, not even the tiniest insect. Moreover, he strenuously objected to the nomadic custom of killing livestock in order to make a feast for Buddhist luminaries, and he prohibited the slaughter of animals upon his visits. Unlike most Tibetans, Patrul was a vegetarian.

The attendant did as instructed. When he returned, he offered the choice cut to Patrul, who accepted it with relish. Nyoshul Lungtok, however, moved by compassion for the sheep, had to force himself to eat in order to avoid offending their exalted host.

Reading Lungtok's mind, Doe Khyentse tossed a hunk of meat into his lap. "Here—this is for you!" he exclaimed. Patrul silently continued eating.

When the meal was over, Patrul requested the Longchen Nyingthig dakini empowerment called the "Queen of Great Bliss." Doe Khyentse said, "I have been keeping these teachings secret, but now the time has come; today I shall give them to you. You will live eighty years and will help everyone you meet. Even to hear your name will close the doors to rebirth in the infernal realms."

Eventually Patrul and Lungtok took their leave. Gazing back from a mountain pass, they saw a white spot on the vast open grassland, which was the great herd of sheep.

Patrul Rinpoche said, "Those two, Doe Khyentse and Dodrup Chen, are living Buddhas. If you had pure vision, you would see them as the authentic incarnations of Rigdzin Jigmé Lingpa and his disciple, the first Dodrup Chen Rinpoche.

"I have been teaching the Dharma to you for a long time, but I cannot guarantee that you will go to Padma Sambhava's paradise of the Copper-Colored Mountain when you die. Yet all of those sheep, without a single exception, through the incredible blessing of those two enlightened sages, will go directly to Zangdok Palri the moment they expire. Wouldn't we be fortunate to be among their flock?"

The iconoclastic tantric masters' outrageous behavior was thus explained.

A Tibetan Tea Ceremony

PATRUL RINPOCHE WAS CAMPING NEAR the site of the famous mani-stone wall, which his previous incarnation, Palgyé Tulku, had begun and he himself had completed. It was the dead of winter when, early one morning, a young girl wearing a tattered coat of marmot skin entered his tent.

Patrul asked why she was out so early in such harsh weather. The little girl, chilled to the bone, replied that she was searching for her female yak.

The kindly old sage told her, "Come, have some hot tea and porridge."

Tibetan nomads usually carry their wooden tea bowl in the folds of their robes. As Sötsé, Patrul's attendant, was about to pour the tea, he realized that the child did not have her cup with her. Patrul immediately took his own bowl from the table before him, filled it with hot buttered tea and roasted barley flour, and handed it to the girl.

The shy child hesitated; Patrul's attendant was also surprised. . . . It is unthinkable that an ordinary person should drink from the bowl of a grand lama. But with the master's encouragement, she finally put the bowl to her lips and drank, instinctively thawing her cupped hands on the warm polished wood while doing so.

Patrul Rinpoche was pleased to see the child relax. After imbibing the hot food and tea, she thoroughly wiped the bowl with the filthy fur of her marmot coat. Then, with both little hands outstretched, she respectfully handed the bowl back to Patrul.

"Maybe my cup is too dirty for you, little one, since you wanted to clean it!" teased Patrul. Without washing it, he poured himself some tea.

He sent his disciple Sötsé to help the child find her family's missing yak. "And keep her hands warm!" Patrul commanded.

A Yogi Meets a Yeti

The Abominable Snowman, or Yeti, is—along with the Dalai Lama—the most celebrated denizen of the high Himalayas. The fabulous yeti was a protected species in Nepal until 1958. A purported yeti scalp is on display at a monastery in Tangboché Bazaar near the base camp on Mount Everest; photos of gigantic footprints and of burly gargantuans half-hidden among swirling snowflakes are also in evidence. Legerdemain concerning this subject is as common as the tall tales about the legendary Bigfoot, called Sasquatch by Native Americans. Recent sightings of a yeti have been reported by the peerless mountaineer Rheinholdt Messner.

Pema Kö is a region in southern Tibet where the late Nyingmapa hierarch Dudjom Rinpoche was born. This area is considered a mystic paradise on earth, like the Five-Peaked Mountain Wu Tai Shan in China. Ordinary people cannot easily enter that paradise, but highly realized yogis and masters can sometimes transport themselves there. Even the animals who live there are said to be delivered directly to the blessed Buddhafields upon death, often vanishing without leaving a trace amid rainbows and other wondrous signs.

ONCE THERE WERE TWO SPIRITUALLY evolved yogis from the Shechen Monastery who journeyed southeast, near the Assam border, to the sacred hidden land of Pema Kö. When the pair reached this paradise, the elder yogi was spiritually ready to experience the most secret power place there, the Yang Sang.

When he was ready to enter that secret land renowned as Yang Sang, his friend told him, "Take as provisions some of our silver; you might need it."

The elder yogi, for his part, wanted nothing. But since his young companion insisted, he finally accepted the silver. Then he threw it into the sky, making an offering of it to the Three Jewels—Buddha, Dharma, and Sangha. With no provisions or belongings, he passed through the diaphanous portal leading to the hidden land, ringing his vajra-bell and rattling his skullbone hand drum; he was instantly enveloped in clouds of rainbow light, never to be seen again.

The remaining yogi went on his way. One day he became crippled by an attack of gout and was unable to walk. He established himself in a pleasant place at the edge of the forest where he found some goats, who eventually followed him everywhere like pets. There he remained.

On the other side of the hill were some abandoned shacks. Every day he would see a huge dark man coming and going between the shacks and the river. Apart from this, there was no other sign of life.

One week he no longer noticed his strange neighbor on his daily walk. Having become intrigued by that mysterious man and feeling a bit better, the yogi decided to investigate the man's dilapidated dwelling.

Inside, the yogi was startled to come suddenly face to face with a *migö*, or wild man, as Tibetans call the yeti. The hirsute behemoth was lying out-stretched on the floor, eyes closed and fangs apart, seemingly unaware of the intrusion. He was feverish and obviously ill.

One of the yeti's feet was grossly swollen and full of pus. The yogi imme-diately noticed, protruding from the infected area of that vast foot, a sharp splinter of wood that could easily be removed. He thought, "I know he can jump up and devour me at any moment, but now that I have come this far I might as well try to help the poor creature."

While he gently extracted the long splinter, the yeti—aware that the lama was helping him—lay as still as a patient etherized upon an operating table. The kindly yogi cautiously cleaned away the pus. He washed the wound, using his own saliva as salve; then he bandaged the bizarre foot with a rag torn from his own clothing.

On tiptoe he left the yeti, returning to his goats, which were tied to a tree in the forest. Days afterward, he saw the yeti limping down to the river, presum-ably for water, and then slowly returning to his house. Eventually the creature's gait improved to the point where he could walk without difficulty. Miracu-lously enough, at the same time the yogi's crippling gout also began to subside so that his painful stride began to return to normal, until he, too, was com-pletely cured. After that, he no longer saw the yeti.

One day the ferocious yeti suddenly leapt down like a giant gorilla from the trees, grimaced at the yogi, then sprang back into the trees and was gone. A few days later the same thing happened—but this time the yeti was carrying a dead tiger on his shoulder. Placing the magnificent carcass in front of the lama as if in token of his gratitude, he again bounded off into the dense jungle.

The yogi did not wish to eat the meat, but he skinned the beautiful beast with meticulous care. Eventually, upon his return to the Shechen Monastery, he offered the splendid tiger skin to the monastery for use during tantric rites, and there it remained until recently.

Perfect Generosity

For many years, Patrul Rinpoche used whatever was offered to him in order to sponsor the carving of mantras upon stones, which were then piled up to form a prayer wall. In this way he supported many paupers and indigent artisans, inspiring them to engage in service.

Patrul once sang:

> "Be kind to the destitute,
> be patient and loving toward the wicked,
> Be kind to the afflicted,
> be gentle with the fool,
> Empathize with the weak and oppressed,
> be especially compassionate to those who cling
> to concrete reality."

INEVITABLY, AFTER GIVING CHARITY TO beggars, Patrul seemed even more happy than they. He preferred the sound of someone begging over the sound of music or chatter.

Once a poor stonecutter called Phukhop begged him for money. "Poor friend," said Patrul, "just say, 'I don't need money,' and I will give you some."

"What sort of trick is this?" Phukhop wondered, saying nothing.

After Patrul Rinpoche had repeated his command three times, the tongue-tied Phukhop finally stuttered, "I don't need money." The master then presented him with a large handful of coins.

Since Patrul never missed an opportunity to give charity under any circumstances, a disciple afterward requested an explanation of the master's behavior.

Patrul related this story: "Once, during the lifetime of our spiritual guide, Buddha Sakyamuni, a poor man offered him a piece of candy. A greedy Brahmin immediately asked for it, knowing that the Buddha never said no.

"The Buddha answered, 'Just say, "Gautama, I don't need this milk-sweet," and I shall give it to you.' So it was done.

"Later, Ananda requested Buddha to explain. The Buddha elaborated, 'Through five hundred lifetimes, this Brahmin has never pronounced even once the words, "I don't need." I helped him to utter these few simple words in order to instill in him the feeling of needing nothing. Undermining greed, these words will plant in him the seeds of generosity.'"

Thereafter, for several days, no needy stonecutters approached Patrul. Offerings from faithful devotees piled up, since there was no one to distribute them to. Suddenly, Patrul's weathered visage brightened. "They are coming!" he cried, gathering up all his money.

Four or five stonecutters soon arrived. Just as the beggars entered his presence, before they could utter a word, Patrul exclaimed, "Here it is!" and handed them fistfuls of currency and coins. "Carve mani stones!" he added. "Cultivate virtue."

After the carvers had departed, Patrul commented, "At last I got rid of that old stuff, useless as a corpse rotting on the floor!"

A Young Woman's Offering

ONCE PATRUL RINPOCHE GAVE EXTENSIVE teachings at the Katok Monastery. When the teachings were completed, the grand lama Katok Situ invited Patrul for lunch in his own residence within the monastery.

After being seated in the master's suite, Patrul exclaimed, "How luxurious it is here! The Katok Monastery is widely known to be rich and prosperous, but you seem to be the wealthiest of all. Look at all these tiger-skin and panther-skin carpets, inlaid boxes, gold and silver ritual implements, brocade dresses, antique porcelain cups, land and cattle everywhere—it looks like a celestial realm. There is certainly nothing like this on earth. How admirable!"

Then he casually added, "By the way, I have nothing but a clay pot for boiling tea. I heard you were going on a trip soon. Would you pack it along with all your things and bring it for me? I prefer to travel light."

Situ Chökyi Lodrö told Patrul, "Indeed, I shall take your clay pot. It is nothing in the midst of all my baggage."

After Patrul Rinpoche left Katok, Situ—who had understood the reprimand implicit in Patrul's request—renounced his monastery as well as all his possessions and retinue in order to live alone in a cave. After leaving Katok secretly, he reached the White Glacier of Dokham, a sacred place where he spent the rest of his life in solitude and simplicity—wearing ragged clothes, exchanging his fine porcelain cups for a single wooden bowl, and subsisting on minimal provisions.

One day he sent a letter to Patrul, saying, "Uncle, hooray for me. Following your advice I have left everything behind and gone to meditate."

When he received that message, Patrul commented approvingly, "Here is someone who listens to what I say."

One day a pilgrim came to Katok Situ's cave, accompanied by a girl who was a niece of the Manjusri Master, Jamyang Khyentse Wangpo. She received Situ's benediction and then offered him a small bag of barley flour.

The hermit said, "I have nothing to put it in. Just heap it up on this flat stone here."

"Please accept it, along with the sack," she insisted.

In front of Situ sat a precious stone, a rare kind of banded agate highly treasured in Tibet; someone had recently placed it there as an offering, along with a request for the saintly hermit's prayers. Situ handed the stone to the young lady, telling her to wear it around her neck for protection and blessings.

She was reluctant to accept such a precious present from an impoverished monk, but the lama was adamant. "You must take it," said he, "there is a great significance in this." She complied.

After the girl had completed her pilgrimage and returned home, she heard that Katok Situ had passed away. Not too long afterward, it was as her own son that he chose to take rebirth.

Self-Sacrifice

Dola Jigmé Kelsang was a great Dzogchen master in the Nyingthig (Heart Essence) tradition. A disciple of the first Dodrup Chen Rinpoche, Dola himself had many disciples and traveled widely, teaching Maha Ati in northeastern Tibet and Mongolia until his untimely demise.

DOLA AND TWO DISCIPLES WERE walking through a town in western China when they came upon a huge crowd. A thief was about to be executed. He sat astride an iron saddle on a metal statue of a horse, which was being heated up by a fire within its belly. The horse was a stove designed for torturing a victim!

The terrified criminal screamed for help and begged for mercy. The crowd taunted him, reminding him of his crimes. Moved by unbearable compassion, Dola stood forth and "confessed" to the crowd that he himself was actually the thief, and the prisoner should be freed.

The bloodthirsty crowd immediately cut the bonds of the convicted thief and seized Dola, strapping him in the saddle. Then they gleefully lit the fire.

The cast-iron horse became red hot: the transcendent yogi sat erect, his gaze fixed on the infinite, leaving this world without a murmur.

Dola's two companions were awestruck witnesses to this drama. From their firsthand account, practitioners everywhere learned how the master had sacrificed himself to relieve the suffering of another being—just as the Buddha himself had done, in a previous lifetime, when in Nepal, at Namo Buddha, he offered his body to a starving tigress and her cubs.

A Going-Away Party

KHENPO MUNSEL WAS A DISCIPLE of the incomparable Khenpo Ngakchung. He studied the Theravada and Mahayana, including all the sutras and tantras, in their entirety for over twenty years at the Katok Monastery; then he extensively practiced the tantric Vajrayana. He taught for three years while receiving the entire oral transmission from his master, then practiced the secret oral instructions in mountain solitude for ten years. As he progressed, stage by stage, through every step of the Dzogchen practice path, he attained the signs of accomplishment, exactly as described in the scriptures.

Khenpo Munsel was imprisoned by the Chinese in 1959 for failing to renounce his religious practice. After several years of incarceration in a work camp, he began teaching secretly at night to five hundred prisoners, who became devoted to him. He taught from memory all that he had studied, including dozens of lengthy sutras and commentaries that he had memorized in his youth.

During the fifteen years that these faithful people were imprisoned together, they practiced discreetly, in ways that the military guards could not recognize. Many of those five hundred disciples displayed the signs of genuine spiritual accomplishment, according to the swift inner path of Ati Yoga.

When the strict discipline eased up after the first few years, the Chinese guards stopped harassing the prisoners. The latter made rosaries out of threads from their clothes and strings with knots tied in them, which they kept hidden in their hats while working on the road gangs. Although some of the prisoner-disciples of Khenpo Munsel are still alive today, most of those indomitable practitioners died in prison.

Their daily food ration consisted of half a cup of barley flour per inmate. Toward the end of Khenpo's life, he did not eat all his half-cup of tsampa but saved some every day from his meager portion. On the day he "left" the prison, he presented his hoard to all the prisoners for what he heralded as a "happy party"; each inmate received an extra handful of tsampa that day! Then he told them to rely on nothing but the Buddha, Dharma, and Sangha, and he retired to his room.

Through the door, everyone heard a loud exclamation of the mantric seed-syllable *Phet*. Opening the door, they found the khenpo's corpse seated upright in meditation. Thus he chose to leave this thorny rose garden, showing no signs of illness. It was obvious to everyone that he had consciously returned to the Dharmakaya, the fundamental essence of unborn, absolute being.

Khenpo Munsel himself had told Nyoshul Khenpo how he saw the entire landscape as pure light, rainbows, Buddhafields, and deities whenever he sat to meditate, having reached the fourth stage of the visionary Dzogchen Tögyal practice. In relating this story, Nyoshul Khenpo said that many recent Dzogchen masters in this lineage had evidenced such remarkable signs of spiritual accomplishment, just like the Buddhas and enlightened yogis of the past.

"They don't think like human beings," he emphasized. "They just *look* like humans. Actually they are living Buddhas."

The khenpo's body remained sitting in meditation for almost two weeks, maintaining heat around the heart while his skin displayed a radiant, translucent luster. When his clear-light postdeath meditation was over, he slumped in his seat. Then his disciples cremated him. Many relics remained in the ashes.

Saraha's Radish Curry

Saraha was an Indian mahasiddha (enlightened yogic adept), a third-century patriarch of the Mahamudra (Ultimate Reality) lineage. Author of the oft-sung vajra-verses known as "The Royal Songs of Saraha," he was Nagarjuna's guru. It was often the custom in ancient India for a transcendent yogi to take up with an outcast woman to help break the rigid caste barriers and to demonstate the possibility of freedom from concepts. Many of the tantric practices involve sexual union, and to take as consort (and common-law bride) a fully matured young virgin is said to enhance and mature a yogi's spiritual development.

HOARY HEADS WAGGED AND VILLAGE tongues clucked when the crazy yogi Saraha took up with a low-caste fifteen-year-old servant girl and went off into the jungle with her. There he enjoyed mystic contemplation in solitude as well as the ecstatic delights of tantric yoga.

The girl was devoted to the crazy-wise master who had so suddenly, by spiriting her away, cracked open the claustrophobic vault of her life. She told Saraha that he could persevere in his yogic practices day and night while she took care of their basic necessities. In this way she served her lord and master.

One day Saraha uncharacteristically exclaimed, "Bring me radish curry!" although he usually ate whatever was placed before him without showing the slightest sign of interest.

The servant prepared the curry. Upon a plate of woven leaves she placed before Saraha a portion of curry and some yogurt made of buffalo milk. Then she noticed that he was in deep meditation, lost in mystic transport, impervious to outer intrusions. So she left him in peace.

Twelve years passed. Saraha did not stir from meditation.

Suddenly he stood up. "Woman, where is that radish curry?!" he exclaimed.

The girl was amazed. "Crazy master, the radish season is long over. For twelve years you've sat absorbed in mediation like a radish stuck in the earth. Now you still want curry! What kind of meditation was that?

"Sitting crosslegged in the lotus position: that's not genuine meditation," she continued. "Living alone, isolated in the mountains: that's not true solitude. Authentic solitude means parting from discursive thoughts and dualistic concepts. But you've spent twelve years sitting, mentally holding an illusory radish! What kind of a yogi are you, anyway?"

Saraha was awakened by the young dakini's wrathful exhortations. Later the pair realized the absolute nature of reality, the innate clear light of Mahamudra. Without undergoing death, they were able to leave this evanescent world and attain spiritual exaltation in the enlightened dakini's paradise.

A Singing Yogi Achieves Flight

ONE DAY IN THE LAST century, the singing yogi Shabkar Rinpoche, accompanied by two disciples, was leading a horse laden with provisions over a mountain pass. There he encountered an old hag lying in the road, unable to move.

Moved by compassion, Shabkar tried to help her to stand, but she could not budge. In a cracked voice, she begged for food and water.

Shabkar readily gave her tea, butter, and roasted barley flour sufficient for many meals. Then she requested clothing, which he also gave with alacrity.

Then the old crone eyed his packhorse and said, "You are able to walk, unlike me. It would be most worthy of you, kind sir, to give me your horse as well." The disciples were nonplussed, but Shabkar unhesitatingly began unloading the horse in order to help her mount it.

"Come along with us, Grandmother," he said. "I shall look after you."

Then the bedraggled beggar seemed to revive; she was suddenly full of vitality. "You, Shabkar," she exclaimed, "are said to be the most compassionate lama of all; now I have confirmed this for myself. I have no need of a horse to travel—nor anything else, for that matter. Don't you know who I am?"

Shabkar was bewildered. She continued, "If you don't know, just look and listen! I am no other than Vajra Varahi, the Queen of Great Bliss. I shall bestow spiritual success upon you, and always look after you. . . . Watch this!"

In the twinkling of an eye, she changed herself into the radiant form of the deity Vajra Varahi, blazing brilliantly red, with her wrathfully grimacing principal head surmounted by the grunting, smaller head of a black sow. Naked, adorned only with bones, jewels, and a garland of freshly severed skulls, she wielded a sharp flaying knife in one upraised hand and held a skullcup brimming with blood in the other. . . . Emitting rainbow light, embracing a trident in the crook of her left arm, she uninhibitedly danced and pranced about.

Handing Shabkar a multicolored medicine pouch containing various sacred relics, alchemical powders, and enlightenment pills, she suddenly soared up from the roof of the world into the azure Himalayan sky. Then, with the medicine bag tucked under the folds of his robe, a beatific Shabkar soared effortlessly up after her, as his electrified disciples watched.

Going to Paradise

ONCE THERE WAS AN ILLITERATE old carpenter, a widower who lived alone with his devoted daughter. All the other members of their family had left this world.

One day the young woman met a band of traveling lamas. She was inspired by the head lama's teachings about being reborn after death in the western Buddhafield known as Dewachen, the paradise of Exalted Bliss. From that day on, she never stopped praying to be delivered there; ceaselessly she recited the mantra of Amitabha, the Buddha of Infinite Light.

Her aged father, however, simply continued to work in his usual desultory fashion, ignoring her devotions. The girl's newfound contentment and peace of mind went totally unnoticed. Eventually the old craftsman became infirm and could no longer work.

The girl told her father, "Dear Papa, please pray to be reborn in the realm of great delight called Dewachen, where suffering and unhappiness are un-known—so that when the Lord of Death summons you forth from this life you may reach everlasting joy and peace. This is my prayer to you!" But her heartfelt pleas were all to no avail.

One day the young woman thought to herself, "Amitabha Buddha vowed to deliver anyone who recalls him. I am assured a place in that Buddhafield after death, but how shall I help Papa direct his thoughts thither?" After pon-dering and praying to Amitabha, she concocted a plan.

She told her father, "Papa, a great lama named Amitabha lives beyond the sunset. He has requested you to draw up some plans for a magnificent palace for him and then to come and personally supervise its construction. Can you fulfill his request?"

The old man replied, not without a touch of hubris, "Dear girl, tell me—has your old papa ever turned away from a building task, no matter how great or small? Of course I shall design the work and then go to see it done. What did you say that lama's name was?"

She was gratified, knowing that from that moment on the headstrong old builder would think of little else but Amitabha's palace. She told him what was necessary to keep his mind fixed on Amitabha and his palace in Dewachen, for in such a way he would unfailingly reach that paradise.

And so it actually came to pass, just as all the scriptures say: "As one thinks, thus one becomes."

Later the devout woman followed her beloved father there. Thus, one should never forget the delightful realm of Dewachen, beyond the setting sun.

He Died Singing

When the Chinese Communists destroyed the Dzogchen Monastery in Kham in 1959, the leading lamas and administrators were imprisoned and tortured. They were charged with exploiting the masses, living off the labor of others, and various and sundry other alleged crimes.

The Communists had little or no appreciation for the sort of work that bodhisattva lamas perform, selflessly dedicating their lives to spiritual service, nor did the invading soldiers understand the unique flavor of the Buddhist teachings, which seemed totally foreign to their own materialistic outlook and upbringing.

ONE ILLUSTRIOUS AND LEARNED KHENPO from the Sri Simha Institute, the Dzogchen Monastery's renowned college of philosophy, was unusually outspoken and totally unintimidated by the threats and violence of his captors. There was nothing the Chinese could do to make him recant his religious views.

Moreover, he continued to teach, advise, and counsel his fellow prisoners, just as he had done for years at the monastery.

The Chinese tried to force him to cease and desist, but even their ferocious accusation sessions, public interrogations, beatings, and cruel tortures did nothing to break the khenpo's resolve.

Exasperated, his tormentors finally shouted, "You're always telling everyone that pleasure and pain, samsara and Nirvana, are totally inseparable, identical in nature, and this world is unreal, like a dream. Now we'll see whether or not that is actually true!" Everyone feared what might be in store for the kindly old khenpo.

The Chinese inquisitors beat the khenpo mercilessly, with all the skill at their command, but taking pains not to end his life prematurely: they broke bones, ruptured internal organs, burned his members with red-hot branding irons. . . . Then they lashed him on horseback, where each and every movement of man or beast would be certain to provoke excruciating agony, and trotted the horse around the prison courtyard. Meanwhile they taunted the battered, bleeding lama, ordering him to sing and dance his Buddhist tune, while the entire company of prisoners watched, aghast.

Eyewitnesses report that Khenpo Rinpoche, a true Khampa (eastern Tibetan) horseman and warrior, sang spontaneous songs of realization, replete with pithy wisdom, while blood poured from his broken teeth and his mount pranced lightly about.

Finally his horse slowed, and his joyful singing abated. He shot his gaze upward to heaven, like an arrow, shouted "Hick!" and then suddenly slumped, lifeless, in the saddle. His knotted bonds prevented his body from falling.

The Chinese were stymied. The khenpo had traveled beyond their domain.

A Scowl Turns into a Smile

The Kadampa school was founded in Tibet one thousand years ago by the Indian pandit Atisha. Its principal tenets emphasize selfless service, altruism, and compassion.

THE RENOWNED KADAMPA GESHÉ LANGRI Thangpa lived eight hundred years ago. His was a peaceful soul, yet there was always a cloud over his countenance. Most of his time was spent in retreat in solitary caves, where he prayed, fasted, and wept. The more he observed the torments endured by all beings in samsara, the less cheerful he felt.

"It is like a dream," his colleagues would remind him, being well versed in Buddhist doctrine. "Why take it so seriously?"

"Then it is all the more tragic that all should be suffering so interminably at the hands of their own nightmarish delusions!" he cried in answer. Then Langri returned to his prayers and gloomy reflections on the absurdity of the samsaric situation.

On one occasion the morose master appeared even more blue than usual. The stern old geshé had his head tied up in an old cloth, as if in mourning. "Who died?" queried his monks.

"Who doesn't?!" Langri Thangpa replied with alacrity. Then he returned to his saturnine contemplations.

One day Geshé Langri was offering mandalas in order to accumulate merits and cultivate generosity. Huge mounds of saffron-colored rice, mixed with various gems, were heaped on the low wooden table before him. Suddenly a mouse appeared and tried to steal one of the turquoises from the pile of rice. But try as he might, he couldn't move it, for it was far too big for him.

"Little friend," muttered the old geshé, "that blue morsel is not cheese. Your senseless exertions remind me of the futile struggles of the worldly in this benighted world. You can't eat it or sell it, so of what use can a turquoise be to you?"

The mouse disappeared, only to return with an equally diminutive accomplice. Together, with one pushing and the other pulling, slowly but surely they moved the jewel from the pile of rice and disappeared with it beneath the table.

Then and only then—for the first time in years—Geshé Langri Thangpa's face lit up with a spontaneous smile.

Then he prayed, "May all beings have whatever they truly want and need."

Where All Prayers Are Granted

ONCE KHENPO TASHI ÖZER WAS returning from central Tibet, accompanied by a group of pilgrims. Among them was a young nun who was the reincarnation of the famous Dorje Pagmo of Yardrok. The company proceeded to a valley in the mountains above the Dzagyal Monastery, where Patrul Rinpoche, nearing the end of his life, was living alone in a yak-hair tent. The travelers doubted that they would be able to meet Patrul, who generally avoided casual encounters.

"Life is short," Patrul would say, "and death is imminent. Don't procrastinate."

Several of the pilgrims said they would rather continue on their way than take a chance on visiting the famous hermit. "Don't worry; we shall meet him," affirmed Khenpo Tashi.

When they approached the tent, Patrul's voice came from within: "Here comes the great Khenpo Tashi, showing off his aristocratic young nun from central Tibet. People never leave me alone! Ah-yii! They are going to be my death!"

Khenpo and his followers pleaded with the sequestered master, requesting an audience. From inside the tent came the answer: "You can't come in! You people will never listen to anything I say!"

"Yes, yes—we will, we will!" they all chorused in reply.

Patrul retorted, "Then go down to the Dzagyal Monastery where the embalmed body of my guru, Jigmé Gyalway Nyugu, is enshrined. He was the deity Chenrayzig, Great Compassion, in person; to face his remains is just like meeting the compassionate Buddha. If you make offerings to that sacred relic, you will encounter no obstacles in this life and will certainly progress toward liberation through all your future lives, eventually attaining the great peace of Nirvana. Any prayer made in front of that reliquary will unfailingly be granted."

In accordance with his command, all went down to the Dzagyal Monastery. For three days they offered prayers, butter lamps, prostrations, circumambulations, and sacramental feasts. Only then did they dare to return to Patrul's campsite.

The pilgrims, still skeptical about their chances of meeting Patrul, were again assured by Khenpo Tashi Özer, "Don't worry, this time you will definitely meet him."

As soon as they neared the tent, Patrul Rinpoche lamented, "These busybodies are going to be my end! Can't they leave an old man in peace?"

Tashi Özer then addressed him, "You said we wouldn't listen to you, but we did. We prayed and made oblations before the relics of Jigmé Gyalway Nyugu. However, you also said that any prayer we made would come true; unfortunately, this does not seem to be the case."

"What?!" a grouchy Patrul exclaimed. "That's impossible! What prayer did you make that did not come true? I have never heard of such a thing."

"We prayed, 'May we meet Patrul Rinpoche,'" the clever khenpo replied.

After a moment of silence, Patrul spoke again. Now he had dropped his gruff tone. "All right, all right," he acquiesced, "come in."

He slit open the curtain covering the door of his tent. Then he launched immediately into teaching, beginning with the four thoughts that transform the mind and continuing on through refuge, Bodhichitta, and other topics. Everyone present became Patrul's faithful follower.

Whenever Patrul went to pay homage to Gyalway Nyugu's remains, he fervently prayed:

"In all my future lives,
   May I never fall under the influence of evil companions;
   May I never harm even a single hair of any living being;
   May I never be deprived of the sublime light of Dharma.

"May whoever has been connected with me in any possible way
   Be purified of even the most serious sins;
   May he or she close the doors to lower rebirth,
   And be reborn in Chenrayzig's blissful Buddhafield, Dewachen."

From then until now, it is said that all his prayers have been fulfilled. Even to read about Patrul is to have the great good fortune that inevitably comes from such an auspicious connection.

EPILOGUE

Tibet is a land where beauty, grandeur, solitude, and the elemental forces of nature elicit a human being's most sublime aspirations, for it has a splendor that dwarfs petty, self-centered concerns. The human response to the challenges of surviving in the magnificent yet bleak and inhospitable wilderness of much of the Tibetan plateau, with its awesome citadel of the snowy Himalayas, its dense forests, and its deserted, arid northern plains—coupled with the crazy wisdom of the tantric siddha lineages from India and enhanced by the vivid Tibetan imagination—combined to produce the colorful chiaroscuro that is Tibetan Buddhism today: a veritable mine rich with the arts of self-transformation.

Zen and Tibetan Buddhism

The dazzling, eternally snow-covered peaks of the Himalayas seem charged with silence, emptiness, and infinitude. In contrast, a Tibetan Buddhist temple is a sumptuous, vibrant, almost psychedelic, visionary realm populated by an infinite variety of sacred images, scroll paintings and statues, silk brocade cushions and impressive thrones, framed photos, ritual implements, musical instruments, sights, sounds, and scents.

It is interesting to note, by way of comparison, that a Japanese Zen temple creates, instead, an atmosphere of unadorned, elegant simplicity. Perhaps these differences reflect the different external environments of the two countries as well as the differing temperaments of their peoples. In the Japanese archipelago, with its four distinct seasons and great variety of gentle natural beauty, people have turned to bare simplicity for an experience that would transcend their daily existence. In wild, remote Tibet, on the other hand—a country whose desolate northern steppes and mountainous natural defenses even the Mongols, Marco Polo, the Islamic hordes, and British imperialists failed to penetrate—people turned to a religious tradition full of color, pageantry, wealth, and beauty as well as transcendental experiences, for these are things that their simple, everyday lives lacked. They integrated their indigenous Bonpo religion into the Buddhism they imported from India and they supported this tradition with all their hearts.

Still, Zen and the Tibetan Vajrayana (Diamond Vehicle or tantric path) have more in common than meets the eye; both Buddhist schools emphasize the absolute immediacy and unwavering presence of immutable Buddha-mind, far more than is commonly taught in other schools of Buddhism. These two Mahayana schools both use the so-called "fruit" of spiritual practice (immanent Buddha-mind, Dharmakaya, ultimate reality) as the *path*, unlike other schools, which cultivate the potential seed of enlightenment for many lifetimes until the fruit is achieved.

However, preliminary Tibetan spiritual practices are more complicated and rich than basic Zen practice, which mainly consists of sitting in a lucid state of meditation. The Tibetan devotee energetically expresses his or her enthusiastic faith and aspiration through any number of outer manifestations of virtue. All of these activities are forms of meditation in action: they include performing hundreds of thousands of full-length bodily prostrations; reciting altruistic prayers; chanting millions of mantras; visualizing infinite meditational deities; performing elaborate physical yogas combined with bioenergetic breathing techniques; using prayer wheels, rosaries, and other devotional devices; erecting prayer flags; carving mantras on stones; circumambulating sacred sites; lighting candles; memorizing and copying scriptures; and feeding beggars. Tibetans engage in these practices with the expressed purpose of purifying the mindstream, achieving enlightenment, and liberating all beings without exception from the illusory sufferings of conditioned existence, or samsara.

Names, Lineages, and Rebirth

Unlike most Western names today, in Buddhist countries one's name has a clear, spiritual meaning, recognizable by all. For both mystical and practical reasons, names have always been considered important. When we know who we are, we know where we fit in the cosmic pageant. Each of us is like a link in a chain; by knowing what we are, we know what we are a part of, and our individual existence assumes greater meaning.

Reincarnation is an ancient and respected doctrine common to Buddhism, Hinduism, Taoism, Jainism—and not unknown to early Jews and Christians. One unique aspect of the Tibetan tradition is its recognition of continuously reincarnated teachers and sages, such as the Dalai Lamas and the Karmapas (also called tulkus, incarnate lamas, or bodhisattvas). By consciously controlling their rebirth, these tulkus intentionally return to this world and continue working selflessly for the welfare of all beings, lifetime after lifetime. In fact, such incarnate lamas often retain the name of their predecessors—that is, the name by which they were known in their previous lifetime. The nineteenth-century Dzogchen master Patrul Rinpoche, of whom anecdotes abound, is an example; his predecessor was Palgyé Trulku, abbreviated as Pa-trul. In other cases, tulkus may be known by the place or monastery from which their predecessors came. Such incarnate lamas inherit not only the name of their predecessor but also—at a very tender age—his entire monastic estate, entourage, position, and responsibilities, since they are considered in every way identical to their former illustrious personage. Women are also recognized as awakened incarnations, such as Samdring Dorje Phagmo, the famous incarnation of the deity Vajra Yogini, who served as abbess of the Samdring Monastery.

New names endowed with deep significance are often received during monastic ordination ceremonies or tantric rites of initiation, and they signify spiritual rebirth. In Tibet, where women often give birth at home, legal birth records are not generally kept, and family names are secondary. Everyone celebrates their birthdays en masse at New Year (which usually falls around February, according to the lunar calendar used in Tibet). Important personages can claim several names and epithets, even within the same tale. One individual, especially a high lama, can claim as many as a score of grandiloquent names—a fact that often adds to the difficulty of the historian's task.

A master can be known by a host of honorific titles as well as by personal names, clan nomenclature, nicknames, pen names, and other pseudonyms. Prolific authors like Patrul and Longchenpa enjoy sprinkling the colophons to their works with a variety of different signatures; often these are self-effacing diminutives. Traditionally, the author's name does not appear on the cover or title page of a Tibetan text but only at the end. Extemporaneous songs of spiritual realization (like Milarepa's) are sometimes signed within the final stanza by including in the composition itself the singer's current sobriquet; this was common practice in the oral tradition. Various deities, major and minor, are also endowed with an abundance of diverse and, for the most part, salutary names and epithets, which can vary from region to region.

Fact and Fiction in Teaching Tales

One person's mythology or magic is another's religion, science, or philosophy. Within the Tibetan teaching tale, where levitation, mind reading, clairvoyance, and clairaudience are not at all unknown, it can become difficult to distinguish fact from fancy. Legend has it, for example, that the Dalai Lamas traveled from monastery to monastery on the backs of the greatly revered black-necked cranes—a rare species known by zoologists to breed exclusively in Tibet. On the other hand, the preliterate Tibetans knew that they had an ape in their family tree fifteen hundred years before Darwin espoused the theory: their native creation myth includes the inception of their race through the lusty coupling of a divine monkey and a red-faced rock-dwelling ogress who happened to be in heat, producing six red-faced offspring. Thus, mythology plays an indispensable role in transmitting tribal knowledge.

Geographical considerations and historical accuracy often pose little hindrance to the inspired bearer of a tale, who is intent upon achieving the desired effect at all costs. Occasionally the same tale is recounted starring different protagonists—as in the well-known story of the meditating hermit who had no time to emerge and trim the overgrown thornbush blocking the entrance to his cave. Some say it was the Drukpa Kagyu master Gotsangpa, while others are sure it was Longchenpa. Moreover, historians in Tibet, whose national history dates from 127 B.C., can ascribe dates to historical events and personages that differ by as much as sixty years.

The vast and marvelous pantheon of Buddhist meditation deities has never ceased to play a role in the day-to-day existence of the average Tibetan. For things are not exactly what they seem to be—nor are they otherwise. Even if we may feel far from any sort of divine reality, we can rest assured that the ultimate or absolute is never far from us. This is what the grand masters of Tibet would have us believe and, moreover, would have us see for ourselves.

Psychic powers and spiritual alchemy were not uncommon in ancient Tibet and endure even today. Fakirs and yogis with paranormal abilities are still almost commonplace. In the Himalayan foothills, advanced Tibetan meditator-monks still manage to flourish on a diet of nothing but mineral powders and water; other lamas have apparently demonstrated to scientists their ability to halt both respiration and heartbeat for thirty to forty minutes through yogic mind-control techniques—a seemingly impossible feat. (Some living lamas claim to be capable of holding their breath for twenty-four hours through yogic accomplishment.) Tibetan doctors, with documented accuracy, diagnose almost entirely by palpating a patient's pulse. Traditional medicines are concocted by doctor-lamas from formulas that include powdered jewels as well as rare plants, some of which are found only in Tibet. Other arcane recipes produce longevity pills, the pill of third-eye vision, and an eye salve purportedly facilitating omniscience. Pressure-point massage, moxibustion (the application of burning herbs to acupuncture points), and herbal treatments combined with precise astrological calculations and shamanistic rites produce, in many cases, remarkable cures.

There are respectable, not uncommon, spiritual and yogic practices to stave off disease and untimely death, prolong life, transfer consciousness into other forms of existence, cause rainfall and hail, inhibit or enhance fertility, and transmute poison. Resurrection is not unknown. As one lama told a disciple, "Until you can resurrect the dead, you shall not kill."

Women in Tibetan Buddhism

All Tibetan monks are men, but not all Buddhist masters are. Examples are numerous: Pajapati, Buddha's aunt, walked barefoot one hundred fifty miles in order to request the Buddha's permission and blessing to found an order of Buddhist nuns. She was ordained, became liberated, attained the level of arhat, and reached Nirvana, as did many other nuns. The eighth-century Tibetan queen Yeshé Tsogyal was Padma Sambhava's chief disciple, successor, and lineage holder. Naropa's consort Niguma, along with the dakini Sukkhasiddhi, is the source of the Shangpa Kagyu lineage. The young Tibetan shepherdess Jomo Manmo was a terton (treasure master). Grandmother Chökyi Drolma is the original matriarch of the Drigung Kagyu order. The yogini Machig Labdron was Padampa Sangyay's immediate successor, matriarch of the Tibetan Chöd lineage. The fifth Dalai Lama's Dzogchen teacher, Terdak Lingpa, was the founder of the Mindroling Monastery near Lhasa, and his daughter succeeded him in transmitting the teachings and empowerments of the Mindroling lineage.

In 1953, A-yu Khandro (one of Namkhai Norbu's teachers), then one hundred fourteen years old, attained the Rainbow Light Body in her stone hermitage in eastern Tibet. The contemporary Dzogchen master Chatral Rinpoche claims a woman, Drigung Khandro, as one of his two root gurus. The Sakyapa master Jetsun Kushog teaches today in Vancouver. An American woman in Washington, D.C. was recognized in the 1980s as a tulku, an incarnate lama, and has been empowered as a teacher in the Tibetan tradition.

Mother Tara is one of the most popular deities in Tibet, like Kuan Yin in China. The classic Wisdom Scripture called Prajna Paramita Sutra exhorts the veneration of women as embodiments of gnosis. Prajna Paramita is envisioned as a deity in female form, the very personification of *sunyata* (infinite emptiness or openness). The brilliant and fertile void of sunyata is the cosmic womb, the fundamental ground of being, the unborn and undying mother of all the Buddhas. The late Tibetan meditation master Kalu Rinpoche remarked that female practitioners often progress more quickly in the Vajrayana path than do men, because of women's greater intuitive openness and receptivity; in the higher tantras, goal orientation and forceful striving—those archetypal male attributes—can hinder the actualization of innate perfection. Namkhai Norbu Rinpoche says that women are more likely than men to attain, through Dzogchen practice, the Rainbow Light Body of perfect enlightenment; he claims to quote Garab Dorje, the first Dzogchen patriarch, in that vein.

Padma Sambhava, the second Buddha, said, "Male, female: no great difference. But when she develops the aspiration for enlightenment [Bodhichitta], to be a woman is greater." Thus spoke the eighth-century founder of Buddhism in Tibet.

Children and Teaching Tales

Mythology is generally acknowledged by educators as being no less essential than music, arts and crafts, peers, animals, and sports in developing in young children an intuitive comprehension of life—thus giving them greater courage, freedom, and confidence to face the unexpected challenges of an unknown, mysterious, and often paradoxical world. Very small children love to hear the same story retold again and again; this gives them increasing security and confidence in their growing grasp of the human comedy. At each stage of a child's development, the same tales assume different levels of meaning and are therefore imbued with renewed value. Myths explain the world and our place in it. Teaching tales always reward rereading.

Folktales naturally function like a magic mirror. Vividly reflecting in their phantasmagoria the workings of the subconscious mind, these tales unexpectedly reveal truths and possibilities beyond the limits of ordinary reason, freeing and supporting one's own imagination. At their best, they allow the impossible to become conceivable. How many breakthroughs might have remained undiscovered without such encouragement!

For children the world is wondrous and magical; this is part of the charm of childhood. Fundamentally animistic, children assume that everything is equally alive. Adults, on the other hand, are often less than pantheistic, yet their need for an animating principle that underlies all life remains remarkably undiminished, even if this need goes unacknowledged. Having faith in something greater than themselves enriches people in all walks of life. Hopes, dreams, fantasy, art, enchantment—what would life be without them? Faith is illogical. Everyone has his or her own religion; everyone believes in something. Young children believe in everything.

Concerning mythology, the wizards, sorcerers, witches, genies, ghosts and goblins, dybbuks, ogres, giants, dragons, elves, trolls, sprites, nature spirits, phoenixes, unicorns, cyclops, and fairies of the West correspond in Tibetan lore to omniscient yogis and wonder-working sages; powerful dakinis and yoginis; one-eyed single-breasted wrathful Dharma protectors and multiarmed, omnieyed, many-headed deities who have attained various levels of perfection; enormous nagas (serpentlike, semidivine creatures); ferocious Himalayan guardians; towering warlike demigods; mountain gods; animal-headed spirits with human bodies; snow lions and garudas (celestial hawks); hungry ghosts; and other forms of illusory beings, both seen and unseen . . . including the elusive yeti, the Abominable Snowman, whom many still believe in today. A storytelling rabbi once remarked, "If you take all my stories literally, you're a fool. If you don't believe them, you're wicked."

Crazy Wisdom

Technically known as the Vajrayana, or Diamond Vehicle, the gnostic tantric tradition in Tibet originated with the enlightened yogic adepts and "divine madmen" of ancient India. These inspired upholders of "crazy wisdom" were holy fools who disdained speculative metaphysics and institutionalized religious forms. Carefree iconoclastic yogis called siddhas, or great attainers (a coterie that included such illustrious personages as Saraha, Tilopa, Naropa, and the Tibetan Drukpa Kunley), expressed the unconditional freedom of enlightenment through divinely inspired foolishness. They vastly preferred to celebrate the inherent freedom and sacredness of authentic being than cling to external religious forms and moral systems. Through their playful eccentricity, these rambunctious spiritual tricksters served to free others from delusion, social inhibitions, specious morality, and complacence—in short, from all variety of mind-forged manacles.

Crazy wisdom is a heightened form of lucidity; it sees through everything. It is a delicious, higher form of sanity, based on trenchant insight into how things actually are (as well as how they appear); this exquisite irony is unveiled by a cosmic sense of humor. Crazy wisdom is what the Sufi author Idries Shah has dubbed "the wisdom of the idiots."

Non-dual tantricism is a potent, often ecstatic brand of transcendence, emphasizing the inherent sacredness and equality of all things. Crazy wisdom epitomizes the untrammeled essence of spirituality; flouting conventional dogma and self-righteous piety, it is the antithesis of puritanism. The ribald humor and outrageous behavior of these anarchic itinerant mystics, the siddhas, never strayed into mere frivolity or licentiousness but effectively functioned to break the spell of worldly illusion by shaking those who slumbered into wakefulness.

Why crazy? Why fools? Because what the religious functionaries of this world call wisdom, these fearless yogis and unconventional sages perceive as nothing but folly.

Irreverently flaunting their uncompromising freedom, they skillfully subverted all forms of social convention and superficial value systems. These enlightened lunatics had a genius for shaking up the religious establishment and keeping alive the inner meaning of spiritual truth during the time of Indian Buddhism's external decline. Presumably, this is why Saint Francis of Assisi once appeared stark naked in church and why he once referred to himself and his disciples as "the Lord's jesters." Milarepa sang, "My lineage is crazy: crazed by devotion, crazed by truth, crazy about Dharma!"

Oral Tradition in Tibet

A great deal of the learning that took place in theocratic Tibet was done by rote. Vast quantities of scriptures and prayers were committed to memory by every upstanding member of the Buddhist establishment, and many of them were often obliged to participate in elaborate daylong liturgical rites or lengthy classical debates, which relied on precise scriptural quotation, without so much as a single text or prayer book to refer to. Moreover, to be thoroughly conversant with the biographies of the enlightened masters and the rich lore of the oral tradition was a fundamental part of every lama's education.

Here, as in other traditional societies, the role of the raconteur or storytelling bard often included functions as diverse yet interrelated as educator, entertainer, priest, prophet, poet, troubadour, shaman, historian, and metaphorical keeper of the keys to the culture's treasure chest. Tibetan historians of old regarded the ancient, pre-Buddhist storytellers and singing bards as protectors of the kingdom; the correct recitation of legends regarding Tibet's origin was considered a religious act, necessary for upholding the order of the world and of society.

Outside of the educated clergy stood the peripatetic professional storytellers known as lama-manis, whose fire-and-brimstone moral tales provided an inexhaustible source of delight to their predominantly unlettered audiences. (Two aged representatives of this near-extinct breed of bard have recently committed their phenomenal wealth of lore to audiotape at the Library of Tibetan Works and Archives in Dharamsala, India, the Dalai Lama's capital-in-exile.)

Other Tibetan raconteurs specialized in lengthy verbatim renditions of "Gesar of Ling," Tibet's national epic.

Another class of bards is called *pawos* (heroes); they are mediums who enter into a trance, allowing a god or epic hero to tell his or her tale through them. Thus they enter the hero path and give themselves to something greater than they ordinarily are. The pioneering efforts of Elisabeth Kübler-Ross find precedent in a subgroup of Tibetan raconteurs, known as *daylok*, who claim to have returned from the dead; they are tireless in recounting their afterdeath, out-of-body experiences, often describing infernal netherworlds where people reap the karmic fruits of their evil actions. These tale bearers serve the function of raising moral standards in the general populace.

Several lamas with seemingly miraculous powers of memory have been known to retain by rote the entire Buddhist canon, the Tripitaka—difficult to believe as this may be. This is said to be a power that can be developed by, among other things, praying to Manjusri, the Buddha of Wisdom.

The Kangyur, the Tibetan Buddhist canon, consists of approximately eleven hundred texts. Under the patronage of the Ming emperor Yung Lo, it was first printed in Tibetan in 1410 in Peking in over one hundred volumes, utilizing incised wooden blocks known as xylographs; the canon had been re-produced in the original Pali and in Chinese centuries earlier.

The global, ecumenical value of preserving Buddhist culture may be symbolically suggested by the fact that the oldest extant printed book in our world is, in fact, an ancient Buddhist wisdom scripture—a Korean xylograph copy of a Chinese version of the very popular Diamond Sutra, one thousand years old. Moreover, it is due to the undisputed authenticity of detailed Buddhist and Jain scriptures that modern historians know more about Indian life and society in the centuries immediately preceding Christ—the era when those two Indian religions were founded—than about eras both before and after.

Indigenous oral and written traditions predate the advent of Buddhism in Tibet. However, the Tibetan literary language as we know it was purportedly created in the seventh century, under royal auspices, by a learned Tibetan official named Tonmi Sambhota (who based both written script and grammar on Sanskrit) for the explicit purpose of transmitting the authentic original Buddhist teachings from India, their land of origin. Nonetheless, until recently Tibet was largely an oral culture. In order to receive full transmission of the Buddhist tradition, lamas in Tibet are still required to receive oral transmission of Buddhist scriptures and teachings from a qualified lama in the oral lineage; this is called *lhung*, or oral authorization.

Even today, many of the ancient tunes for chanted liturgies, as well as songs and prayerful invocations, remain extant after centuries of being passed orally from teacher to student. Other oral traditions include Tibetan opera, known as *Achi Lhamo*, created by a lama in the Middle Ages. Now, as before, it remains among the most popular forms of entertainment at Tibetan festivals, along with the so-called lama dances (*cham*, in Tibetan) which are actually a disciplined form of spiritual practice. Moreover, spontaneous songs of enlightenment (*dohas*) continue to be sung extemporaneously today by the remaining members of this spiritual line. The oral wisdom tradition is like the cosmic serpent Ourobouros, forever feeding upon and replenishing itself.

Tibetan Teaching Tales

Tales from the heart enter the heart, instilling both wisdom and compassionate action. Easily recalled, short and to the point, yet variegated enough to perk up the interest of any kind of audience, teaching tales preserve and communicate Buddhist thought and values while achieving a life of their own. Benighted modern humans may have forgotten that reading, reciting, and aurally receiving spiritual lore are a devotional act, meaningful in itself. Yet an enduring fascination with traditional tales continues, for everyone loves a good story.

In truth, tales ought to be told, not read. The stories in this collection are part of this living oral tradition of Buddhist teaching. Each tale was told by the learned and accomplished lamas who are among the last remaining representatives of that endangered tradition; they are truly a boundless source of faith and inspiration in our turbulent times.

Due to their inherent value, tales often enjoy extraordinarily long lives, appearing in different guises in different times and places. The same story may take on different cultural trappings, but it still makes the same moral point when incorporated into the native literature of a different country. One example is the Tibetan tale of two monks encountering a leper on a riverbank, which appears in the guise of a Christian tale in France and a Zen tale in Japan, differing only in small details. For many centuries, Jewish folktales have helped maintain and enliven that people's cultural identity, wherever their travels have taken them; oral literature serves a similar purpose for the Tibetan in exile.

The purpose of Tibetan tales, through preserving and transmitting the sublime Buddhist teachings (with which even the most mundane are imbued), is to provoke, instruct, motivate, edify, and amuse—and eventually lead to spiritual awakening. They are therefore universal stories, transcending any particular culture or religious context. Why spend one's time merely looking at the bejeweled finger (culture) pointing to the full moon, when we might enjoy to its fullest the perfect, luminous, celestial sphere (true spirituality) itself?

In such an oral tradition, it is rare to find the same story retold in exactly the same way twice, which accounts for the multiplicity of versions to be found today among the various Tibetan schools and lineages. However, as the eminent Nyoshul Khenpo Rinpoche has said, although one cannot affirm with absolute certainty that every factual detail of the tales and stories in the living oral tradition is perfectly accurate, yet one can be certain that, unless preserved and transmitted, this wealth of vibrant spiritual lore will soon be lost.

There is a Tibetan saying:

"The purpose of meeting a teacher
    is to receive the Dharma teachings.
The only purpose of receiving spiritual teachings
    is to put them into practice.
The purpose of spiritual practice
    is to realize the ultimate nature of things.
The purpose of realization
    is to actualize perfect freedom, inner peace, and enlightenment."

I offer infinite prayers, praise and obeisance
To boundless Buddhas and bodhisattvas
So that countless beings everywhere
May realize limitless freedom and enlightenment.

May one and all have the extraordinary good fortune
To meet the wish-fulfilling teachings,
Which are the source of all true peace,
Well-being, and felicity.

May all beings awaken in the light of the innate Great Perfection!